THE BACK OF HIS HEAD

THE BACK OF HIS HEAD

Patrick Evans

Victoria University Press

TE WHARE WĀNANGA O TE ŪPOKO O TE IKA A MĀUI
VICTORIA
UNIVERSITY OF WELLINGTON

VICTORIA UNIVERSITY PRESS
Victoria University of Wellington
PO Box 600 Wellington
vup.victoria.ac.nz

First published 2015

National Library of New Zealand Cataloguing-in-Publication Data

Evans, Patrick, 1944-
The back of his head / Patrick Evans.
ISBN 978-1-77656-046-2
I. Title.
NZ823.2—dc 23

Published with the asistance of a grant from

creative nz
ARTS COUNCIL OF NEW ZEALAND *TOI AOTEAROA*

Printed by Printlink, Wellington

In memory of
Howard Douglas McNaughton
1945–2014

and for
Ferdinand Evans Ortiz
El Terremoto

A novelist is someone who confuses his own life
with that of his characters.

Alain Robbe-Grillet

. . . what we remember is probably fiction anyway.

Beryl Bainbridge

THE BACK OF HIS HEAD

July. No green left. The pines, the pistachio trees, the palmettos and the cork-oaks black against the rust of the earth, among the dying oleanders dried riverbeds that wounded the landscape and exposed the bones of rock beneath. Ahead, harvested fields, tinting the hills to a lion colour. Above, the colourless sky, slowly killing, killing.

He'd pulled a stick from a wild olive tree and now he held it bowed behind his neck as he walked. He could feel the press of it, and his chest thrust forward, and the heat of the stones on the track.

Somewhere across the bare plains was the dark spot where the bordj stood. He couldn't see it, but he knew it was there in its setting of eucalyptus trees. Something was there, something would be there when he came to it.

The land, burning under his feet. The stick, against his neck. To suck, a stone in his mouth.

Hamilton had been reluctant when the young sous-lieutenant first suggested it to him. Follow the little shit and get it back! the man said. Kabyles always travel on foot, you'll always be catching him up. Find him and slit his throat. At least we've taught you how to do that!

He was a Huguenot farm boy, Gost, from the Cévennes highlands, but the 25th Dragoons had taken all that out of him. The dragoons, and being here in the war. They were beginning to call it that now, the locals. Yes, they'd say when you went to the town or the market. Yes, it was a war now, all right. Not good, not good.

'You aren't meant to be here with us, anyway, Thomas,' the Frenchman told him. He said his name the usual way, the end melting into nothing. 'So just—fuck off and find him.'

Allez! Foutre le camp!

There was a train, which creaked all night as if it was falling apart around him. Early in the morning it stopped, and boys came aboard selling oranges. Hamilton watched them carefully, but they were younger than the Amazigh who'd taken his wallet. The Amazigh wasn't one of them. These were children.

He knew already how crazy it was to come out here, through the mountains and out to the Hodna, and all of it just for a wallet. Its cheap gilt-and-niello work was worth more than the money in it. Watching the little orange-sellers, though, before the train jerked to a start again and they hopped back into the darkness, he began to know something of what it was the wallet had come to mean to him since he'd found it gone. He had to get it back.

Tangerines, of course it'd been tangerines the boys were selling, not oranges. He'd bought one but hadn't eaten it. There it was, in his pocket, moving when he moved. A couple of times he found himself touching the thing, as if he was afraid that it, too, would be taken.

As the train came into the early morning the faint mist that still hung above the dark cedar ravines disappeared and the countryside came nearer. Huge, soft, serene, something more nearly imagined than ever. He was entering it.

In the square of the little town white forms stretched on the earth against walls, men escaping the overnight heat indoors and the scorpions. This was M'sila. Above its low roofs the silhouettes of young palm trees were just showing now against the greenish blue of the sky. In the sparkling, clear dawn Hamilton waited for the harki with the mule.

Not soon, a tall sunburned Arab came for him. Hamilton looked into his sombre eyes and knew that, to this man, he would always be the askari, the soldier. He knew that by coming here he was a kind of traitor, someone who'd left a self behind him. The truth was that he'd left two. How did you say *journalist* for a man like this? And how did you talk about a petty theft in a land of petty thefts? He showed the man the commission Gost had lent him, but to this Bedouin it obviously meant nothing. He tried to say something about the missing wallet, but the man's Arabic seemed even worse than his own. There was no way of telling whether he was really a harki, either, or of knowing what it meant if he wasn't, where the man might take him now and what might be done to him there when he did.

The Bedouin had a mule for him. Once up, he struggled to hold his seat. The man watched him without expression from astride a small, shaggy horse whose coat was pale, almost white. When Hamilton was steady he turned the mule's head away and set it off after the little pony and its playful, innocent jog. The Arab didn't look back at them as they moved away and out of M'sila and onto the flatland.

When they got to the countryside the smell of the air became sweet, delicious, and a vague, fresh scent began out of the ground like springwater. There were adobe houses, and, far apart, the saints' tombs with their strange, unexpected shapes. As the two men passed them the new light seemed to give the buildings form, to give them colour and even existence.

Hamilton knew it was wrong to think like this. He knew he was thinking like a white man. *Remember where you come from*, he told himself. Ahead, there was a deep-cut river he knew they had to cross. The mule would get him wet, and that would help. A baptism, he would have said once, before he came to this country. Already he was beginning to know better than that.

At Guerfala, though, the palm gardens really did astonish him. The animals drank in the vast artificial lake, carefully and at length, their ears cocked forward, their nostrils held above the water. Hamilton watched them and the way their steady lapping trembled the inverted image of the trees and buildings and the pale, golden reflection of the sky. He was sitting exactly between two worlds.

Eventually the man pulled his little horse away from the lake and turned it about. He looked back to Hamilton. 'This plain is called the Hodna,' he said, not clearly. He pointed ahead. 'And over there by those hills is Bou Saada.'

The plain, stretching before them, pink, empty, infinite. Far to the south, the mountains of the Ouled Naïl, pale blue, diaphanous, barely visible to him. The mountains and all that was around them, floating in air.

I

One of the Master's ashtrays is missing.

I've texted the other Trust members and told them to be early for tonight's meeting: they should be here at the Residence any minute now.

I can't tell you how angry I am. All thought of other problems falls away. It's not that the ashtray was worth anything in itself—it's just a paua shell Raymond picked up from the beach and stubbed his cigars in for twenty years and more, each day he wrote.

No, it's the *principle* involved. We go to the trouble of keeping his house exactly as it was when he was alive and writing in it, we open it for the public good, and what's our reward? Constant pilfering—*constant* pilfering. This week alone, a teaspoon, four books and a toilet roll—can you believe that? Someone would actually steal a *toilet roll?* Given the circumstances, it's hardly likely to have been used by the great man himself, is it?—but apparently that doesn't matter, that doesn't stop them: off it goes to the black market that seems to have developed for his memorabilia, along with much of the other *bric-a-brac* that helps us represent the life and work of Raymond Thomas Lawrence, our greatest living author: now, of course, lamentably and officially, deceased.

We'll start our search for today's culprit with the most recent names from the Visitor Book, of course, as we always do when a theft occurs. For small parties such as today's, one of the Trust members is usually enough to take them through and keep an eye on things, though when we get a large tour bus we all turn up to the Residence, and when a planeload of over-excited Danes booked in a couple of years ago we had to bring some of our gardening ladies inside to help restrain the visitors' Viking hands. Not that there was any sign of actual pilfering, as it happened, but their scrub-faced enthusiasm was almost as bad as they milled about, bumping into furniture, and one of them *actually lay full-length on Raymond's bed*, if you please, on the very spot where, the Visitors' Brochure assures us, the Master breathed his last.

Let me take you through the Raymond Lawrence Residence now, as I begin to close down and lock up before our monthly Trust meeting. The usual guided tour, but in reverse: for here I stand at its far point, in the Blue Room, an elegantly long addition to the south-eastern corner of the original hillside villa, the Pluto of the little solar system of which Raymond of course was the Sun.

Naturally, I can't render here the feeling this room always has for me, its sense of the past caught in the best of ways, not as in a museum or mausoleum but as if in a place of genuine transition, a place where time itself is annihilated or suspended—rendered irrelevant in whatever way: it hardly matters to explore or explain. I confess that sometimes when the day gets a little taxing I sustain myself through its desolations with the promise of an hour of solitude here in this timeless room, with a very dry sherry to help me remove the sour taste of the quotidian, and the familiar sound of one of the Master's vinyl records from fifty years ago—my favourite is a Geminiani Concerto Grosso that has a little Vivaldi piece for castrato on the far side of the third disc as a *bonne bouche*.

It is the colour of the walls here, though, that would truly take your breath away if you could but see them (which you may, of course, during the advertised visiting hours: donations always appreciated since the place doesn't maintain itself, as I'm sure you will understand).

We four Trustees simply wore ourselves out finding the right tone for the paint, and I imagine the city's paint-shops were glad to see the back of us the day we realised we'd done it at last, we'd finally persuaded them to mix us *exactly* the right blueness of blue!

And when we got back to the Residence it was as if each brushstroke we began to make was reviving the entire house—as if all the scuffs and abrasions of time were being cancelled out, and we were back there thirty years before and more, all of us, when Raymond arrived at this house a handsome young man and the entire the world was young. When we were done, none of us needed to say a thing. We simply stood there. We'd travelled through time together: it was as simple as that.

I'll tell you a little later about the trouble we had with the curtain material and how Semple got caught out when he had the fabric replaced on the rather lovely belvedere *fauteuil* over by the piano—we hadn't taken the work of the sun into account, and you can imagine what happened next!

Pause, now, instead, before the *pièces de résistance*, the *termini ad quem* of our tour: the Medal itself, and, below it, framed, the Citation from the Committee. Of course, they're not the *actual* medal or the *actual* citation, which are both in a bank vault, as you'd expect: but they're such perfect replicas that even I, who have seen and held the originals—who travelled with Raymond to Stockholm, in fact, and witnessed his investiture—even *I* find myself catching my breath now for the sheer *meaning* of them, for the sheer achievement they represent.

For Raymond was the first in our little country to win the greatest prize of all, in a time of overwhelming excitement each of us remembers and remembers and remembers, and in which we all seemed suddenly to loom a little larger in the world, each of us, all of us—yes, yes, I know, people say I've let it come to mean too much to me, and Robert Semple reminds me from time to time—unnecessarily—that I didn't actually win the prize myself. He also tells me to remember that, in a sense, the original medal and citation are themselves both replicas, too: all fashionable nonsense, of course, and really and typically irritating. Why he refuses to see the transformative, the *redemptive* nature of what Raymond achieved, the true, inner *meaning* of it, I simply cannot understand.

No matter: come away with me now, instead, through the little hallway and past the door of Raymond's bedroom, with its sea view through the arch of the trees beyond its window to the sea and peaks beyond—elderberry, native honeysuckle and, much further down the hill, a big burly rata, each helping to form an exquisite frame for the view. Then, past the kitchen door—not because the kitchen isn't interesting but precisely because it *is*, distractingly so, and would require a chapter to itself for justice to be done. Kitchens of all rooms in any house have the most potential for something that lies beyond nostalgia, Raymond used to teach us, and are places where one is most likely to find not just *the pastness of the past* at its most fully preserved, but that pastness at its most nearly available. I mean somewhere so close *we might actually enter it*. A portal, if you like. I'm talking Raymond-talk here, of course, as you'll know if you've read his books.

Now: the dining room. Here, the eye is first drawn to the Henri II buffet against the eastern wall, with the remarkable Italianate walnut panel carving on its doors—birds, fruit, landscape, even the effect of clouds: authentic, I'm all but certain, and—like the Louis Quatorze sofa in the Blue Room—one of many such pieces from the Lawrence family estate as distinct from the various items

Raymond picked up in his travels overseas. There's the hand-painted lacquer Shoji screen we've just left behind in the Blue Room, for example (which we were told by a recent Japanese visitor in fact represents a brothel scene rather than just four artless *geisha*).

For all its magnificence, however—its wood like molten toffee—the buffet is not what I seek in the dining room. I seek Raymond. Not the actual Master in the flesh, alas, since not even art can bring him fully back, not yet: I seek Raymond in the flesh of paint.

And here he is, framed over the extinct old front room fireplace at 56 inches by 64, courtesy of Phyllis Button at her best, before the visionary period that signalled the onset of her dementia. The painting hangs here and not on the long walls of the Blue Room as something to confront the public: they enter, pause, look at the buffet and (always) ask whether it is real or not (meaning, of course, whether it is authentic), then how much it is worth (I've no idea but I conjure up imaginary figures to make them gasp), and then turn right and—well, here he is, here he is in glorious Technicolor.

In truth, though, in far better: in Phyllis's sparkling, even shocking end-times style, with its splatters and scrapes of oil straight from the tube, oranges and reds and (of course) bright blue, his defining colour, smeared on the canvas as if she were trying to get straight from the medium or through it or even around it, to the man himself, to Raymond Thomas Lawrence—Nobel Laureate, Master, genius: martyr. It's an extraordinary work, full of life and all the evidence you need of the way a work of art can show its artifice while at the same time transcending the strokes and smears of which it is made, and (even if only for a moment, even if only to particular eyes) make that impossible leap into life itself, hot, quivering and *now*.

And the oddity is (I am reminded yet again as I stand here before him) that the more she flung the paint on the canvas, and scraped and smeared at it with her knife and hands (brushes all discarded at this late urgent hectic potty stage of her life), the more nearly she seemed to make that leap: so that here we have a work of art which, at first glance, looks very nearly abstract expressionist in its mode, yet at second or third becomes very nearly representational, its chaos almost capturing the very man himself. And from behind—from *behind!*

For that is what is so mad, and so utterly inspired, about this portrait: it shows no more than the back of Raymond's head, his veriest *occiput*, a smear *left* and a smear *right* giving a sense of the shoulders below, a wild plump dab of paint giving the nape, and then three or four greyish upward scrapes his back hair to the thinning crown, of which she takes care with a bluish flick of *green*, somehow: and, on either side of the big, gestural bonce thus confected, with cadmiums yellow-orange-red, a vegetal ear. Beyond and behind the right, the tiniest line of paint indicates something of his steel-framed spectacles. And it is *he*, Raymond, the Master, forever caught!

Like Michelangelo's David, I said to him when it was exhibited: turning away, I meant, always turning away from the viewer. *Michelangelo's David*? he said. *It's a bugger's-eye view!*

Vulgar, this last, alas, yes, yes, regrettably so: but it must be recorded because so very much *Raymond*, and Raymond it is whom I'm after in this account. My uncle, and in due course my adoptive father, too. I seek the very man himself.

Ah, Raymond, Raymond, Raymond—*where are you*? No idle question, this: it comes up every time I find myself alone at the Residence—which happens more and more often lately, I've found, given that the other Trust members increasingly make this or that last-minute excuse to avoid turning up for touring parties and for the board meetings we're supposed to have here on the first Tuesday of each month, not to mention the occasional working-bee that I call. More often than not it turns out I'm the only one prepared to attend the former, and end up spending a solitary evening at home after all. Sometimes there are no apologies whatever and I find myself coming down to the Residence to find it looming above me closed and dark, and with absolutely no idea whether the others will eventually turn up or not.

Whenever that happens, there is the eerie business of feeling my way up the steps, and to the front door and, after the work of finding the lock with the nose of the key, pushing inside, lighting the place room by room and then turning back through the bright house and sitting and waiting at the oak dining table—*Patience on a monument smiling at Grief*, as Raymond would have said—until it becomes obvious that no one has remembered: or that indeed they've remembered all right but simply can't be bothered.

Or worse, in the case of the appalling phrase Semple used when I made an acid phone call to him on one of these occasions and discovered him involved yet again with some silly little tart in his bed. Urgent Business Elsewhere, he said, with the woman's giggles in the background. Well, I told him what I thought of indulging in *that* kind of business when he ought to have been at the Trust meeting, and that's when he said the phrase in question. For *Raymond's* sake, I said to him—*come on!* Can't be arsed, he told me back. You can't be *what*—? I said, unable to believe my very ears.

Now, here I am yet again with a deserted building to confront and the prospect of yet another wasted evening to be spent inside it. And, always on these occasions, that question—*where are you, Raymond*?—and the strange sense, whenever I'm standing at the top of the front steps with the wind blowing in my hair and my key tapping blindly against the plate of the lock in the darkness, that Raymond is inside the house, that when the door finally opens and I click the stiff brass light switch just inside and to the right—lo!—he'll be sitting there like Jeremy Bentham in his stall at University College, staring back at me, waxen of head and *tissue preserved!*

Sometimes when this fancy takes me Raymond is as I first met him, barely forty and ruddy with health, his look sardonic, his purpose, as always, impossible to pin down. At other times, it's as if he's in his last months and crouched atop the elevator platform in his *fauteuil roulant*, as he used to call his wheelchair, his head and his hand going *tick-tick-tick* as was often the case in the final days. Once, as I fumbled the key at the front door lock, I was sure I could hear the buzz of the wheelchair elevator inside as it made its climb to the main floor, ready to greet me. With what?—would he be there at last on its platform, when I got the door open, would he be crouched there and waiting in his wheelchair?

And, of course, he wasn't, and hasn't been, and never is, and part of me knows he never will: but the *feel* of him is here, always, the feel of his colossal, overwhelming presence is everywhere as I push into the house and its darkness, banishing the world of enchantments with each click of successive brass light switches: till I reach the Art Moderne plastic switchplate of the Blue Room at last and expose for myself the final disappointment: that, once more, I have driven him before me and away.

He is nowhere. He is somewhere. He is *everywhere.*

I have paused, here, to take in again *the pastness of the past*, but now I turn back to the actuality of the dining room and the business of setting the papers before each place at the table. *Order, gentlemen, please:* ladies, too, Marjorie will always say indignantly, whenever she can be—well, whenever she can be *arsed* to be there, I suppose, to use Semple's hideous phrase. At which objection he, Semple, always laughs like a hebephrenic: if, that is, he can be *arsed* to be present as well. Then, at some point, he will call someone or other a *tit*, and Marjorie will bristle and say, *well, there's nothing wrong with hers*, and Semple will say once again that the word has nothing to do with breasts but comes from a Middle English word that means *small* and *insignificant*, and Julian will add, irrelevantly, that *birds* has derived by metathesis from *brids*—women, and hence *brides*—and Semple will say, There y'go, Marge, you're a bride not a broad! And another monthly meeting of thc Raymond Lawrence Literary Trust will have begun. *Order, order please, gentlemen; we have business to do*—ladies, too, of course, of course. Ladies a plate.

And indeed we *do* have business to do tonight, as you can see on the agenda that I place around the table. Item 1 involves money, an ongoing discussion past which, frequently, we fail to move in two or three hours. Item 2, related, involves the upkeep of the Residence and its surrounds, always a concern. Item 3, which I think I'll move up to Item 1 in view of my latest discovery, refers to theft by visitors and an update, which I think will impress my fellow members, of my attempts to track down recent thefts.

Now, though, it seems someone is actually turning up

at the Residence: a soft clump of a car door down on the drive and—yes, up the steps and through the door the first Trustee struggles, carrying her past around her in the clutch of bags and reticules that weigh her shoulders, wrists and hands: Marjorie Swindells, dabbing a hankie at what seems to be a perpetual slight cold (Semple assures me she's a secret Catholic, since, according to him, Catholics always have colds).

A loud parp at her nose, and then:

'Hello, Peter,' she says to me in her defeated, resigned, slightly creaky private-girls'-school voice, and down the bags go, one by one, slumped on floor and chair and tabletop, and away goes the hankie in a quick tuck at her wrist. She straightens: 'Well, what's the problem?' she asks.

'I'll tell you when the others get here.' I prefer all the Trust to be present when it's serious business. 'But it *is* important.'

Now her face comes into the not-unsubtle light I have arranged over the table and I can marvel once again at the workmanship of it, her phiz I mean, the craquelure of tiny lines that comb her brow and upper lip, the cockling of her cheeks. In *that* process, even her ear lobes have developed sudden, abrupt little folds, as if beginning to close in on themselves, as if starting the business of rolling her up like an ancient canvas that is to be put away once more to allow a real, a still-youthful Marjorie to go on living and sinning. Or, possibly, to reveal no one at all: one never knows.

All nonsense, of course: *here* she still is, after all, caught in the unforgiving present like the rest of us, just come from the ladies seminary at which she plies her trade as a teacher of art history, drama and creative writing. *Whatever that is*, Raymond always used to say whenever the topic came up. *Teach writing?* he'd say. *What d'you fucking mean, teach it? They don't teach you how to shit, do they?* Well, actually, they do, Raymond dear, Marjorie always used to tell him whenever he got to this point. They do but you'll have forgotten. You can't just let *fly*, you know, you've got to learn to aim at the pot. *Fuck the pot*, he'd always tell her. *The pot's the problem—*

Why is she here; I mean, why is Marjorie Swindells part of the Raymond Lawrence Literary Trust? (In fact she's *not* here at the moment, having just slipped off to *spend a penny*, as she puts it, tinkling distantly on his big old porcelain throne: whose craquelure, it must be said, rivals hers). You may take your choice of answers to the question of why she is a Trustee: (a) there was a long period many years ago when Raymond frequently took her to his bed—yes, *that* bed, the one in the front bedroom—and had sport with her: (b) she has a genuine literary achievement in her own right, a big, sad, first-and-only novel called *Unravel Me*, about (wait for it) a young woman who gets tangled up with a famous male artist. It is some years gone now, and nothing has come since—certainly nothing to rival the *éclat* of its Moment and the rather more than fifteen minutes of fame that followed.

I read it straight away, naturally—everyone did—and was dismayed, horrified, to see how good it was. I listened to the interviews that followed and marvelled—again, everyone did—at the disparity between the virtues of the novel and the cuckoo qualities of the person who had apparently written it. How did it happen, whence did it come, had it been written by someone else?—by Raymond himself, as part of some obligation about which we knew not, or as a joke whose punchline he would reveal in due course?

Time passed, though, and it became clear that there

was no such course: and Raymond insisted, all the while, that he had nothing to do with any of the book, neither its composition by sleight-of-hand nor as the original of its Magus-like antagonist, Begg (this despite the generosity with which Marjorie described certain parts of that character in certain parts of her text).

Now, though, the slam of a car door, a call from outside, *hulloo*—and it is Robert Semple's turn to arrive: gracious me! Here he is after all, swarming up the concrete steps to the front door, here's his ugly-handsome face beneath the curve of his silliest affectation, a wide-brimmed brown fedora he almost never removes: and here is his tender, stepping, haemorrhoidal gait.

He stops dramatically a pace or two into the room and spreads his palms, his eyebrows raised: what's up?

'The paua shell ashtray's gone. Stolen.'

'My *God*—!' His hand slaps his brow, his head goes back. 'Raymond's ashtray!' He holds the pose, eyes shut tight.

Exasperating, of course, infuriating—really, I sometimes wonder about his commitment to the Trust. But there's no changing things: his name is on the Trust document, Robert William Davidson Semple, along with those of Julian Howard Yuile and Ursula Marjorie Swindells. And, of course, along with mine, as Principal Trustee: Peter Edward Orr. I could easily do without any of them, to tell the truth (though perhaps Julian least, since he is harmless and has his uses), so that I might run the Trust myself. Semple in particular is a trial, in ways you've probably begun to pick up already. His poetry you'll have already judged for yourself, I imagine, if you're familiar with it. His other attributes—well, I'll let you judge those for yourself, too, as they unfold themselves.

His connection with the Master?—as in my own case,

from an early age, though not quite as early as mine: slightly post-pubescent rather than slightly pre-, and (I'm aware) with the same questions eventually raised as in mine: I mean questions to do with the price paid later in life for things gained earlier on. These are evident, one might say, in his behaviour, Semple's I mean, most obviously in his frenzied rutting, of course, and also—but here comes Julian now, our fourth Trustee, pushing in through the doorway as if conjured by my naming him a moment ago: and here is Semple, turning to him and seizing his shoulder:

'Come and see the missing ashtray!' He points wildly towards Raymond's bedroom.

Julian is mystified. He looks across at me.

'The paua ashtray is gone,' I tell him.

'Shit—really? That was authentic—'

'Authentic!' Semple, bursting into florid, contemptuous, simulated laughter.

'Well, it is,' Julian said. 'You could see his actual ash in it.'

'Excuse me, it's not *his* ash? It's just his *cigar* ash? Where he stubbed his *cigars* out?'

'No, but not everything in the Residence is, you know—' Julian looks around. He gestures at a bookcase. 'One or two of those books aren't his, some of them are second-hand—there's other bits and pieces we've replaced when things go missing.'

'Exactly, right, and the ashtray's the same, it's just a paua shell he picked up off some beach somewhere—'

'Yes, but I know what Peter's thinking.' Julian flicks a look at me and away. 'We should value everything—you know, everything he touched.'

'Christ!' Semple turns away dramatically. '"Is He present in the wafer?"' He really is getting angry now, and the theatrics are holding things in rather than the reverse. 'I thought they sorted this shit out five hundred years ago—'

'Hey, steady on.' Julian is a Christian, of the garden-God variety: Semple likes to goad him. Where's Marjorie got to?—we need her here, to play her customary role of scapegoat and victim: then the Raymond Thomas Lawrence Memorial Trust really will be in its full dysfunction. But Julian is on song tonight, it seems, and holds his own as the argument with Semple develops. It's an old issue, after all, the nature of the Residence and how properly to remember the Master, and during the last five years we've all heard one another's opinions on the matter.

By and large, on this issue, Julian and I are Catholics, if you see what I mean, and the other two are Protestants—in other words, two of the Trust feel that the old man is all around us, in everything, still alive, imperishable, and two of them feel—well, that he isn't, that everything we have accumulated in this hundred-year-old villa on a lower spur of Cashmere Hill simply *represents* the life of the great artist who lived here for forty years and wrote many volumes of fiction long and short. Which view (I hear Julian now, arguing once more against this) runs quite contrary, surely, to what the Master himself wrote about most often: I mean the power of art to take us beyond mere nostalgia, as I've said, to the very past itself—

And what has Semple to say, once Julian has finished his defence of the Master's presence in the ashtray?

He pauses. Then: '*Don't* call him the Master, Jules, old boy, it's bad enough Norman here calling him that.'

He means me, he is referring to Norman Bates, and I'll leave the rest to you—and, anyway, here comes Marjorie at last, back from her feminine *devoirs* in the bathroom, the strap of her principal handbag over her arm and her makeup evidently brighter.

Semple is upon her straight away, eyebrows up and brow glistening and furrowed. 'Have you heard the news?' he demands. 'The paua shell ashtray's gone! It's on the black market, selling for millions—'

She looks across at me. 'You've dragged us across town for *that?* I thought we'd at least had a fire somewhere.'

'Marjorie.' Semple takes her fingertips as if wanting to dance. 'Now you're here we can vote. "The Master" or just plain "Mister"—?'

'Oh, not that again.' She pulls away. 'You know I think it's pretentious. So does Jules.' She's into her bags again.

'Yes, but *he*'s started to use it. Julian here. He's caught it off Norman.'

'God, Peter, he was just a man. Raymond. Just a man.'

'A *great* man.'

'A great arsehole, come on, you know that—'

'I'm aware of your views and you're entitled to them.' I've long ago learned to keep my temper on this topic, but it isn't easy, it isn't easy. 'In my opinion and that of many others, he was a great man and a great writer. The proof is on the wall in there—' I'm pointing towards the Blue Room.

'God, if you knew him the way I knew him—that body!'

'I remind you who I am.'

'Yes, but you didn't bonk him—or did you? *Did* you—?'

'Yes, Marge, we all know you had in him in your *boodoyer!*' This is Semple, of course: he loves this sort of thing. Julian leans against the molten walnut of the buffet, arms folded, waiting as Semple and Marjorie begin to argue yet again ('*Don't* call me Marge', etc.). If only they were better writers. If only they were better people!

Was it Raymond's last great trick—I've often wondered this—to appoint three absolute nonentities to his literary trust to take care of his reputation after his death: was this his last great joke? Did he think *I* was a nonentity, too, was he saying that, we were *all* nonentities to him? I asked someone this, once, a theatrical friend of my uncle called Basil Bush, and the man gave me a very untheatrical answer. No, it wasn't because you're a nonentity, the man told me. It's because you're so bloody difficult. Like father like son. I'm not his actual son, I reminded him. No, but nearly, the man said. And it shows, because you're both complete and utter pricks. He doesn't want anyone getting near the truth about him, he said, and he knows you won't let them.

The old fellow looked at me hard when he said this. He knows you're as mad as he is, he said. Madder. He knows you've got his DNA.

And I wondered, how much of the story, the full story, did he know?

Now, at last, the September meeting of the Raymond Lawrence Memorial Trust, properly notified and quorate: Hon. Chairman Mr P. Orr, Hon. Secretary Ms M. Swindells, Hon. Treasurer Mr J. Yuile, *Order please—*

'Oh, shit, is there a meeting now?' Marjorie has just noticed the papers set out before each chair at the dining table. 'You just said it was an emergency.'

'*That's* the emergency, having a meeting!' Semple. 'Once a month, Marge, thought you'd remember once a month!'

For twenty seconds, the usual rattle of ill-tempered gunfire. *Order, order—*

We get through the prefatory nonsense—*is it your wish—those for—AYE* (Semple always very loud at this point, sometimes sustaining the note like a choirboy) *those against, CARRIED.*

There are no matters arising but under chairman's business I am able to report the ongoing sale of unauthorised Raymond Thomas Lawrence memorabilia online—cheap *bric-a-brac*, more a hangover from the time of the award of the Prize than a real and ongoing threat, but crass and irritating all the same: for example, a line in garden gnomes made to look like the Master—the Master sitting fishing, the Master as Rodin's Thinker, even (most lamentable of all) the Master as the Manneken-Pis. Appalling, upsetting, infuriating: but, according to our legal advisors, untouchable, since we'd lose more if we sued, apparently, than we might gain. And, as I said, this particular phenomenon does seem rather to be fading out.

'You've told us all this before,' Semple is slumped forward, his arms along the tabletop.

'True,' Marjorie works a moist refreshing tissue at a reddening septum. 'Next business please.'

'We haven't *got* to the business proper yet,' I tell her. 'I'm still doing chairman's business.'

'All right, do that,' she tells me. 'Come on, chop-chop.'

'Roof repairs,' I tell them.

'Isn't that Item 2 Upkeep?'

I remind Julian I'm still reporting from the last meeting. 'Eric the handyman's had a look at the roof,' I tell them, 'and he gives it a year.'

Pause.

'And then, what?' Marjorie demands. 'It all falls in on us?'

'And then it needs repairing,' Julian says.

'And then it needs *replacing*,' I tell them.

'Oh, shit. Let's forget about that, then, what's next?'

We move on to the agenda proper.

Proposed from the chair: That in light of today's theft, Item 3 Security be moved to Item 1: CARRIED nem. con.

Once it gets there, though, the perennial impasse returns.

'I can't believe we're discussing a fucking paua shell *ashtray*,' Semple groans. 'Who cares if some prick's nicked a paua shell?'

'It's not just a paua shell,' I remind him.

'We've discussed this before, aren't we rather thrashing it to death?' Marjorie asks. 'Next business *please*.'

But the next business is Financial, and there, the same issue threatens to come up again, melting—*order, order*—into Item 3 (as it is now), Upkeep.

Whichever item we deal with, of course, it's about the same thing, even I have to recognise that: the need to find money against the perennially rising cost of running the Residence and the fundamental, ineluctable fact that, even without our having spent a dollar of it, the Trust's endowment capital has become relatively smaller and smaller as each year has gone past. And against all this, the need to keep alive the authenticity, the integrity of the venture. Its *purity*, even: even its *spiritual* aspect.

Whenever we discuss these things, as I've said, Julian and I are always for the latter, and Semple and Marjorie are always (in effect) against: meaning that they want to start selling some of Raymond's *objets* to pay for upkeep, while Julian and I don't want to sell anything at all. They want to *represent* Raymond's life with bits and pieces from second-hand shops, imitation antiques or even rough approximations, used books by the carton-load from the back room of the university's bookshop, knives, forks and spoons from Bargain City out by the airport, and so forth. Julian and I have always held the line against these proposed atrocities, and for *authenticity*.

And here, at this evening's meeting, the perennial impasse, presenting itself yet again. Semple starts the show:

'Every single problem on this'—he taps his agenda—'would be solved if we cashed the place up.'

'There's no motion on the table.'

'If we cashed up, it wouldn't matter what they nicked, they'd be nicking crap anyway, we'd just replace the crap with more crap. If they gouge it we'd, you know, use wood-filler? If they keep on gouging it we'd replace the whole item from a junkshop. It'd all be crap.'

'I have only one thing to say about this.' A pause, as I look around the table. 'Mabel Carpenter.'

'Oh, *fucking* Mabel Carpenter. Not her again. *Christ*, she was dreary.'

'Yes.' Julian. 'Some of her stuff's unreadable.'

'*All* of it's unreadable.'

'She was a great writer, though,' Marjorie says.

'Oh—no doubt about that, she was a great writer all right.'

'No doubt about that at all.'

'Her Memorial Residence is a *disaster*,' I remind them. 'We all know that.'

And it's true, both that the Residence of the late Mabel Carpenter—she whose fiction brought Dargaville to the world—is a joke, and that we all *know* is so. When it was first opened we had a look at the place, Julian and I, driving north after a conference in Auckland at which the pair of us represented the Master late in his life, when he was too ill to travel. Naturally, given his condition then, we had thoughts of what might soon—and now, alas, has—come to pass: I mean how a writer's home might most properly be turned into a memorial residence once he has (as Raymond used to put it) *passed on to the great whisky decanter in the sky.*

Not like that! the pair of us chortled happily as we drove away from Mabel's Residence afterwards. It was her house all right, I mean it was one that she had lived in: but for years after her death it had been rented by civilians (as Raymond used to call the inartistic), and there was not a thing she'd actually owned in it once her memorial trust decided it was time to commemorate her, nor anything very much to guide them in their sad little reconstruction.

A desk very similar to one Mabel might have written on is a line I remember—with laughter—on a notice tacked to the wall above a very ordinary table that had been sanded down to nothing, no past in it, no life. *A bed typical of beds of the period* was another. The *pièce de résistance*—the nearest they could manage to the real thing, the nearest to achieving, for the literary tourist, the true and authentic moment—was a clothes-wringer in the outside laundry, certified to be authentic on a nearby placard, though described as a mangle all the same. *Mabel's mangle*, we came to call it, and we were quite clear that, when the time came, the Raymond Lawrence Memorial Residence would do better, far better, than that.

Naturally, I remind the meeting of all this. *We mustn't get caught in Mabel's Mangle* is my concluding line—rather a good one, I can't help thinking.

There is a pause, and then Marjorie continues as if I haven't even spoken!

'It'd have to be good-looking crap,' she's telling Semple. 'It'd have to look almost the same as the stuff we're talking about selling.'

'It's not stuff and we're not talking about selling it,' I remind her. 'There's no motion on the table.'

'You mean if there was, you'd discuss it—?'

'If it had a seconder.' I look across at Julian. 'Then I'd have no choice.'

'All right.' Semple. 'I move we sell the Steinway.'

'Oh, not the baby grand,' Marjorie says.

'I think'—this is me, feeling my way towards a deferral—'I think it'd be better if we addressed the principle first rather than the particulars.'

'My motion's on the *table*, fuck it—'

'No, it's not, there's no seconder.'

Semple looks at Marjorie. 'Come on, Marge,' he says.

'Ask somebody else. I don't want to sell the baby Steinway. And don't call me Marge.'

'It's worth more than all the rest. It's worth more than the entire house and garden. It's worth hundreds of thousands. It's a fucking *Steinway*, for God's sake, with art casing, I don't know how it got here in the first place—'

The Steinway is in the corner of the Blue Room, covered in framed photographs and with a large table lamp on it. It's one of several items in the Residence obviously with some monetary value, though (it has to be said) not necessarily as much as Semple and Marjorie would like to think. Though they don't realise it, I've had it valued, and found it would bring in about fifty thousand local dollars according to when and where it was sold and by whom. Overseas, of course, it would be a different matter, sold overseas it would fetch rather more. But then one would have to *get* the piano overseas in order to sell it, which would cost all we might realistically sell it for once it was there. Checkmate: and, in some ways, the history of our little country in a single proposition.

Marjorie, meanwhile, is casting around for alternatives. 'That thing.' She's pointing at the carved buffet behind me. 'Let's sell that.'

'The Henri II buffet?' Julian asks. 'You'd have a job replacing that, you'd have a job getting something cheap that looked like that.'

'You'd have a job getting it out of the house.'

'It'd have to be authenticated first,' I remind them.

'What about the berber rug, then?'

'No,' I tell them. 'The berber rug is off-limits.'

Mr Semple's motion that the Trust sell the Steinway baby grand piano lapsed for want of a seconder.

Ms Swindells' motion that the Trust sell the carved buffet lapsed for want of a seconder.

Ms Swindells observes that the answer is to increase visitor numbers. Mr Semple expresses reservations.

'You must be fucking dreaming,' he says. 'How are we going to get more of the bastards in?'

'How many did we used to get?' Marjorie asks me. 'You know, in the good old days?'

'Two or three hundred a month. More. Admittedly a while ago—'

'Admittedly ten years ago,' Semple says. 'When he was still famous. Christ, when he was still *alive*—'

'Yes, but—' Julian. 'We—'

'They used to come here to get a sight of him drooling in his fucking bath chair. Ray. That's the only reason they came, that's why we got so many people through, the old boy was still around to gob in front of them.'

'But—'

'Yes, but even so, show me the literary residence in the country that ever got—'

'How many literary homes *are* there—?'

'Show me the literary residence *anywhere*—'

'Yes, but—'

'—that has consistently made a profit—I mean a meaningful profit, not just pocket money.'

I sit back.

Marjorie squirms her mouth. 'Yes,' she creaks at me. 'That's all very well, Peter, but you're telling us yourself, dear. *You've* brought it up, *you're* telling *us* we've got a crisis. Item 2, Financial crisis.'

'A problem. A challenge.'

'Yes, but'—Julian at last—'it's not just visitors, they don't bring in that much, for God's sake, they never have, we didn't ask for anything at all for a long time and what do we ask for now? A voluntary contribution that hardly anyone actually makes.'

A pause.

'True,' says Marjorie. 'We'll have to start charging them to get in—'

'Then nobody'll come,' says Semple. 'End of story.'

'But we'd have to charge a hundred dollars a visit to get anywhere near what we need.' Julian turns to me. 'What needs doing?'

I look at my list. 'We pay quarterly rating, the phone, electricity—'

'Well, *fuck* the phone for a start.' Semple rocks from cheek to tender cheek. 'Who needs a fucking *phone* when there's no one here most of the time?'

'Robert, darls, don't tilt back like that.' Marjorie. 'These chairs just won't take it anymore.' Then (to me): 'Maybe *they* need replacing, too—the chairs?'

Proposed Mr Semple, that the telephone be disconnected forthwith, seconded by Mr Yuile: carried nem con., Mr Orr to action.

What else?

'The guttering needs replacing—'

'It needs *placing*, there isn't any at all round the side—'

I stick to my script. 'The garden. We're down to one gardening lady now. Val—'

'How many did we used to have—gardening ladies—?'

'Back then? Seven. But we didn't pay them. Deciding to pay them was a mad idea. We were paying four at one stage—when those Austrians came and made that documentary we had four gardening ladies on the payroll—'

'Yes, but doesn't it look spiffing, in the doco, I mean—the house and the garden—doesn't it look *spiffing*—? Summertime, and all that—?'

And now we sit for a moment, each of us, and think just how spiffing the Raymond Lawrence Memorial Residence really did look in the high summer of 2001–2, when an Austrian crew of astonishing seriousness came over and filmed Raymond pottering about among the lacecaps and the agapanthus. He refused to wear his partial upper denture for the actual interview and consequently looks like Klaus Kinski in *Nosferatu*, with just the two eyeteeth poking down on either side of his mouth. A section of this documentary opens the standard tour of the Raymond Lawrence Residence, which begins downstairs in the garden room with a closed-circuit showing after the signing of the Visitor Book, and then proceeds upstairs via the elevator: when the elevator is working, that is.

'Oh, and the elevator,' I remind them. 'Still not working.'

'It needs replacing,' Julian says. 'To tell the truth—doesn't it? Isn't that what's wrong? The whole bloody shooting-box? It's Apollo 11 technology, it's another age, it doesn't work anymore—'

A pause. They look at each other, Marjorie at Semple, Semple at Julian, Julian at Marjorie.

Suddenly Semple slams forward in his seat.

'Fuck it,' he says. 'Let's just close the place down.'

He holds the pose, looking around at us one by one,

then pushes back truculently and waits with his arms folded. Julian looks at me, and I look at Marjorie. This time Marjorie looks at Semple.

'We can't close it down,' Marjorie says. 'Can we—?'

'Got a better suggestion—?'

'Well, we just *can't*—'

'For Christ's sake!' Semple slumps forward, his palms on the tabletop again. 'It's like what Jules just said, it's another age—it's not *now* we need to think of, it's ten years' time—twenty.' He looks around. 'Kids don't read *books* anymore, they don't read *anything*—what's Raymond fucking Lawrence mean to them? The youngest people that come through the Residence are fifty-something. Readers are dying and illiterate cretins are being born—'

An awful silence in the room.

'I mean, let's stop kidding ourselves.' He looks around, but not at any one of us in particular. 'Let's stop *trying* so hard. It's the old, old story and it's caught up with us at last, so let's just face it.'

A slight pause: Marjorie looks at Julian, then at Semple. 'I'm afraid I'm not quite sure what exactly you're talking about, Robert, dear,' she creaks at him. She looks at me. 'Any idea?'

'He means we're past our use-by date.' Julian. 'That's what you mean, isn't it—?'

'We're irrelevant.' Semple's voice is so quiet it's disconcerting: I don't think I can handle him sincere. 'We've got the population of, I dunno, Boston?—a city, I mean, we're the size of a city—'

'We're a city-state—'

'No we're *not* a city-state, we're not even good enough for *that*—Athens was a city-state, Singapore's a city-state, *we're* not *anything.* For Christ's sake, *listen* to me, I'm trying to say something important—'

'*Listen* to you!—we've been doing nothing *but* listen to you all evening, for God's sake—'

'Order—order—'

'Oh, order yourself, Peter—'

'We're so fucking small, we're smeared across the country like Vegemite, we just haven't got the resources, we never have, and we tell ourselves it's not like that anymore, we tell ourselves Ray took us out into the world and we've come of age—it's not true, it's all bullshit, it's just pretending. This *place* is just pretending—' He taps the tabletop with a fingernail. 'If it wasn't, we wouldn't be talking about closing it down—'

'*You're* the one talking about closing it down—'

'We wouldn't have to grovel for support all the time, we wouldn't be talking about money all the time, we'd be lying around talking about art, we'd be endowed by some big corporation, we could have guttering with goldleaf on it and a helicopter pad out the back—we could even have writers in residence, the way we're actually supposed to but we don't, because—guess what, we've got no money to pay them—'

'Robert!' This is Marjorie: she's sitting back in her chair with her eyes fixed on him and a tiny smile. 'You're being sincere!—I quite like you like this, I can almost see what all those teenage trollops see in you—'

Suddenly, Julian leans into the discussion. He shifts about and begins to speak to the surface of the dining table.

'With great reluctance—'

'Here we go,' Semple sits up.

'Shut up, Robert.' Marjorie is looking straight at Julian.

'—I'm moving towards your position, Marjorie.'

'It was my position first—'

'Shut *up*, Robert—'

Julian flicks a look at me. 'Sorry, Peter,' he says. 'I've given it a lot of thought. We know some of the furniture's worth thousands, and the books.' He sits back and folds his arms. 'I move that the Trust affirm the principle of selling property items to fund upkeep.'

A stunned pause. I stare at him. I couldn't be more shocked, I really couldn't.

'Seconded.' Semple. 'Well done, Jules.' He slaps his palms together a couple of times.

'Come on, Peter, you have to hold a vote now—'

'Wait on.' My mind is racing. 'I don't think it's proper to the item.'

'Bullshit. You're making that up.'

'What item *are* we discussing, anyway?'

'Ah—one. Security. I don't think it relates to security.'

'No, we're on Item 2, aren't we? Upkeep?'

'That's no longer Item 2, it's Item 3, I think.'

'Then we're on Item 2, money—?'

'We're still on Item 1, security.'

'He's stalling.'

'I'd like us to discuss this,' Julian says solemnly. He's not looking at me. 'It's where we've been heading for years—well, at least five years. We should face up to it and sort it out.' Now he looks at me. 'I'm not particularly in favour of it, Peter, don't worry, I just think we ought to thrash it out.'

A pause. We all sit there, breathing hard at one other. I stare at him. How could he? How could he *do* this to me? *Julian*, of all people?

In due course, it comes to its end, this latest meeting of the Raymond Lawrence Memorial Trust, with its customary sense of dissipation, its bickering and repetition, its sheer inartistic *ennui*. Each meeting wears me out, each meeting leaves me with the sense of having been the only adult in the room. I watch the others descend the concrete steps and depart through the trees to their cars. They feel so far from me, so little a part of Raymond and what it was that he stood for: yet again I wonder just *what was he playing at* when he appointed them? And now they want to sell him up, to wrap up everything he was and everything he believed in and give it away.

Oh, don't be so melodramatic, Marjorie told me when I said as much just now, towards the end of the meeting. It's the only way to keep the old place going! So it is, I told her: but will it still be the old place once we've done it? And where will *he* be then, what will we have made of him?

That, of course, is the point. But do they understand that?

Outside, I wait at the foot of the ten concrete steps that reach down from the front door of the Residence, and listen to the other three of the Trust disperse in the night. Their cars are down by the garage: a car door slams. *Come on*, I can hear Semple calling. *Shake it up*. Then: *What's that*?

I'm spellbound, trying to catch what they're saying. Is it about me? There's a slight wind, off the sea, enough to stir the leaves. Hard to tell. Once, standing here in the dark after a meeting, I heard Marjorie say, *No, he sleeps in the Residence*, and the quack-rattle-and-bark of their laughter. Now, here it is again—has she said it again? No: Semple instead: *Well done*, he's saying. Then: *bang*, from another car door, and a moment later an engine starts up.

I creep forward, the smell of pine resin and eucalyptus gum in my nostrils, to look through the foliage as the Trust members reverse down the drive *en convoi*, the sweep of headlights creating a ripple of movement in the bushes and the trees around the driveway. I can see Julian waiting down there for the silly red MG or whatever it is that Semple affects: a pause, as he works his wheel this way and that, and then off he goes, blaring down Cannon Rise. Now Marjorie's Mazda Familia moves away behind it.

Well done—it stays with me, up the steps and through the doorway and as I close and bolt the door. The thought of what they want nags at me as I check the house and turn out its lights.

Marjorie's line about my staying the night here at the Residence has its own unintended irony since, unknown to them—to anyone—I frequently do just that, and intend to do so again tonight. Never on Raymond's bed, naturally, but (almost as great a desecration) on the long sofa in the Blue Room. I know I'm taking a liberty, but I do it simply for that moment when I wake into the room each morning as it slowly illumines. Especially at dawn in midsummer, the slow flush of daylight turns it into a *sanctum sanctorum* and an annunciation of *his* presence: a confirmation that, in some form at least, he is still here, still with us.

More than that, there is a moment, just once a year, when the first light strikes *exactly on the Medal itself*, and holds it, and seems to linger there: but, then, of course, it slowly moves away, having made its statement—having held me as well, having utterly held me in its moment. Just the two of us. The meaning of him, and of his life. And I, his child and servant: in truth, his creation.

Now, I turn the last light off. I know the house blindfold. Through the little hall—*there*, the tight floorboard creak that is always two steps in: I tread it and stand, reassured, in the doorway of the Room, looking for the familiar shapes in the dark, smelling that familiar blue smell.

Inviting him: is he here?

Raymond, I call to him.

Usually it scares me when I do this, as if I'm listening to someone else who's inside me and who shouldn't be there, who shouldn't be.

Raymond?

There've been moments when I've done this and really felt frightened but knew he was there somewhere and turning away from me, always turning away: once, I called his name in the dark and a moment later heard the floorboard creak behind me as he moved off, creeping from me, stealing off into darkness.

Raymond?

Raymond—

Tonight, though, nothing: I know there's nothing there. The Residence sits around me, inert, harmless, unthreateningly in the present tense, devoid of purpose, oblivious of danger.

II

II

I wake to Wednesday and the morning when, as the executor of Raymond's estate, I catch up with correspondence. As ever and yet once more, and so many years after the Master has left us: *still* people asking us for money!

As soon as he began to publish, he told me, they began to write: not often and not many of them, but enough to be rather more than simply irritating. Then, as he became known, then famous, then notorious, the number doubled, then doubled again, then doubled again after that. From once or twice a day the petitions became four and six and eight and then a dozen and sometimes more than a score. Once the Award was announced—well, after a week, we counted nearly seven hundred requests coming in, all of them grovelling for money, demanding money, *crying out* for money.

Often these petitioners rang instead of writing, and sometimes—the Lord help us—they even came to the door! I'd like to be able to say that when they did, they brought out my better side and I began to see in them the pity of the human condition—man's eternal struggle to survive the dust into which he is born. But in fact I thought them rubbish, trash, common folk on the make, people too stupid and uninteresting ever to transcend their inevitable immiseration—or, sometimes, simply too cunning for their own good. One of these idiots, I remember, expected us to invest in a revolutionary new engine of his own devising which, he claimed, ran on *honey*.

Cattle, all of them, but all of them convinced, nevertheless, it seemed, that other people's good fortune should by rights be theirs. I was struck by the simplicity of their assumption: *you have money, it should be mine, send it to me now.* As if the letter from the Nobel committee had somehow got itself misdirected from its proper destination: their own horrid, smelly little letterboxes.

For these people I devised a standard response as soon as I took over the Master's affairs, many years ago now:

> Dear Sir/Madam,
>
> The members of the Raymond Lawrence Trust were moved to read of the unfortunate situation in which you claim to spend your life, but not so much so that we feel obliged to do anything about it. If Raymond Lawrence's work does in fact mean something to you, we recommend that you return to it for further consolation and guidance, and particularly to what he has to say about charity. In other words, what Anir is told in *Flatland* is what we tell you, namely that you should regard your misfortune as your fortune, since to do so would free you to discover all the many possibilities the world offers to people who genuinely wish to transcend their heredity.
>
> Yours, etc.

It is important, you will note, never to use their actual name.

Those who rang (or climbed the ten hard steps to the Residence front door, or rattled the knocker here at the building we call the Chicken Coop, up behind and above the Residence) received a shorter shrift, no matter whether the person they met was me (abrupt, cold, contemptuous, brief), Raymond (who always affected to be the gardener) or (by far the most terrifying prospect) Edna Butt, our housekeeper, who would send these people on their way with a fierce bollocking and sound advice from the Book of Proverbs: *Go to the ant, O sluggard; consider her ways, and be wise! Whoever is slothful will not roast his game!* Of course, these terrible admonitions were no more than the words with which I'd overhear her berating her husband Eric from time to time, along with the occasional uplifting verse to set him on his way again once corrected to mow the Residence lawns and clean its windows, to hew its wood and draw its water.

I mention all this because, as I say, today is the day I always reserve to the business of dealing with the Trust's latest influx from the preterite. Aside from the rubbish just mentioned are the rather more reputable requests we receive regularly from academics across the world soliciting permission to quote from the Master's work or to have access to the various Lawrence collections that are around the country, in the United States and elsewhere—the Raymond Lawrence industry, as you might say. Do I wish to speak about Raymond at a literary conference to the north? Well, since they suggest a fee as well as travel and accommodation expenses, yes, I do. Have I remembered my appointment at 2:00 this afternoon to speak at the local university's creative writing school? Yes, indeed I have. Am I available for a symposium on Raymond Lawrence and music?—more ticklish, this one, and requiring further information. Might a certain young scholar, new to Lawrence studies, quote from certain passages of *Bisque* and *Kerr*? Well, yes, she may, as long as she uses not a word more than is prescribed.

Fair dealing, I like to remind the scholarly world, cuts both ways: *fair* means *fair*. We had our fingers burned early on—this was long ago, when Raymond was still with us—by someone who didn't understand this rule and simply went ahead with an unauthorised biography of sorts, something we first knew about only when it appeared, bristling with mistakes as it turned out to be. Her name? Geneva Trott—*Dr* Geneva Trott, I should say: a name still anathema to the Trust. An English academic in a university to the north who simply walked in and helped herself to the great man's life! Just like that!

Aside from infuriating matters such as these, there are those to do with finance—never-ending and insoluble, as you've already seen—as well as what one might call *safeguarding the Master's name in perpetuity*: the general housekeeping of a literary trust, the chores which, in truth and alas, draw my attention every day of the week in my ongoing role as Keeper of the Flame.

First, though, the business just mentioned, the standard letter to the money-grubbers. Each of them gets the same reply as the first, all those years ago, with the single alteration that it is my name that farewells them now and not Raymond's (although I long ago perfected his signature, three large capitals followed by a dismissive squiggle and a savage, Napoleonic underscore: thus, many people who treasure letters from him do not realise that in fact they treasure letters from me).

From time to time the others on the Trust wonder why I bother to answer these requests at all, given the recent diminution in their volume that I've mentioned. Predictably, Semple joshes me about it: *don't take away his greatest pleasure*, he tells the other two, *don't stop him shitting on people*. I'm happy to admit there's something to this: after all, the Master always said the parts of me he valued most were the parts others valued least and the same as those he liked most in himself. We're joined at the hip, he told me one day. Down in the dirt together! And there's something to that, I'm forced to admit, there's definitely something to that.

At the same time, as I've been saying, these importunities

from the great unwashed are diminishing in number, and, despite what I've just told you about them, there is a part of me that sees in that fading-away of attention exactly what I see in the sagging guttering and the exposed bargeboards down the side of the Residence, and which remembers those days (recently, *an entire fortnight*) when no one calls to tour the Residence, no one at all.

I'm talking about the passage of time, and—I can hardly bear even to think it—the slow decay of a culture's memory of its greatest writer and its finest moment. I mean the decay of the *things* in the old man's life, the evidences of his everyday existence, his *desiderata*. His books, for example—*his* books, I mean, the ones that he himself wrote—stacked in bookcases in every room of the Residence and stored elsewhere as well. The other day I found myself pulling one of them out of a shelf as I passed it and catching the undeniable, unanticipated whiff of *mildew* from the pages that I opened, and seeing the foxing near the gutter of each I turned, and the pale damp-stains gathering on them like liver marks on the backs of elderly hands. These are what appear as books begin to age. They're what happen when books remain unopened for a long time. They happen when books remain *unread*—

In other words, however distasteful they are to deal with, these grovelling emails and letters represent at least some kind of ongoing link with the world, some kind of attention, a sort of continuing belief. To tell the truth I've become aware that, on some days, they are almost my only reminder that Raymond ever existed in the first place, and as a result I have found myself (somewhat to my surprise) dwelling on one or two of them a little more than usual and wondering, for a moment, about the individuals who actually wrote them.

Here, for example, in today's intake of two: a woman who claims to have a child with *spina bifida*. I put from thought Semple's shocking joke on this topic, but find myself thinking of something that is, possibly, even worse: that terrible scene in *Frighten Me*, one of Raymond's early novels, where a sick child is abandoned and beaten to death: there is a strong implication that it is eaten as well—*she,* I should say: it's a little girl, and for all one can tell from reading it, she ends up as the protagonist's dinner. But the reader has no idea whether she actually does or doesn't, or (as with everything else in much of that early fiction) what to make of such horror. Or, indeed, what the author himself wishes us to make of it: we simply *submit to the destructive element*, so to speak.

Curious, though, this particular letter's invitation to my soul. Its author has written before and has been rebuffed by means of my standard letter—but now here she is again, restating her case to me. A single mother, down on her luck, with this terrible reminder every day of what fate inflicts so indifferently upon the innocent. Slightly to my surprise, I find myself trying to imagine her, this woman, trying to make her come to life the way one finds a character in a book come creeping into one's reading mind dressed in borrowed flesh and blood and clothes, in that extraordinary conspiracy of separate human imaginaries that fiction (and *only* fiction, as vividly as this) can bring about. I try to make her come to life for me, I try to make her become *real.*

All the same, and in the same moment, I can feel something else as I imagine her, that pulling-away from what this woman must really be. Fiction, Raymond used to tell me, doesn't take you any nearer to anything that has actually happened. Instead, it makes things up. It doesn't recreate anything that has actually been, he told me, it doesn't bring anything back to life. It replaces it, makes it redundant, confirms its death. An obsession of the Master's, this, particularly as he got older and, to be truthful, a little less reliable: art's incapacity to be real, to allow access to the living, breathing world—to change things. *To be consequential:* his words. To make things happen.

All this was at odds with what I'd learned from him when young. Wasn't that the point of art, to redeem reality, wasn't that one of the things he'd been given the Prize for? But he seemed to change, alas, in the years after he won it, and as his illness bit into him. He took his growing obsessions—paranoia, even—too far towards the end of his life, as you will recall. Would that he had stopped where Phyllis Button stopped, pressing and smearing the paint onto the canvas with her fingers—even, later and extraordinarily, using some of her own bodily excrements in a final, desperate effort to make art *real.* Instead, Raymond tried at the end to reach *through* the canvas, so to speak, to what was behind it—in effect, to this lonely woman and her child, to life itself, although in his own peculiar and driven way.

Strangely, disconcertingly, I find myself asking his latter-day questions: who *is* she, what is this life of hers actually like, what is its value, what will she make of it? What can *any* of them *do*, these beggars whom Art leaves behind on its path to Stockholm?

And I find I just can't manage it. I simply can't imagine her. She doesn't belong to the literary world I've always lived in, the world that's made, and still fills, my imagination. It is a world that feeds on humanity—I, of all people, know this, as you will see—and it seems to give back to it by drawing it and teaching it. *But does it really?* Does it *really* do what the citations for the great prizes assure us that it does? Is it *really* about anything at all apart from itself? And, if not, are the great prizes and awards in fact and therefore—meaningless?

These are the questions my uncle has left behind for me, and which frustrated him most, and led him down the strange, lamentable path that he took, in the end, to his terrible death.

She's gone now, this imaginary woman who has written to me this second time. She fluttered briefly in my mind a few moments ago, but she's gone. I choose the standard form onscreen and begin to print it. Here it comes, here it comes, chugging slowly out to me: *Dear Sir/Madam—*

Long before the beggars started to fade a little in number, Raymond's celebrity entered its second stage. Its historical moment came when I spotted a figure one night from the Chicken Coop, a man skulking around the rear of the Residence below. The police were called, an arrest was made, charges were brought: but instead of the occasional would-be-burglar we've had from time to time, this, it turned out, was (so to speak) the first swallow of summer, a genuine lunatic besotted with the idea of Raymond as much as with what Raymond had written, but besotted most of all with the notion that *he himself* had won the Prize. *Fame is the spur*, was Raymond's response, which got somewhere near the heart of the matter: it was as if his celebrity had become a substance, a thing you could touch and take away with you, something you could steal in order to make your life a little better.

This fellow had even got himself up *as Raymond*, if you please, as if that would somehow make him different from himself!—well, got himself up as best he could, I should say, given that he was taller, younger, and heavier. But the sharp beard was there, and the rimless glasses, and the hair pulled back from the brow, though less sparsely so: and, most telling touch of all, a pair of calf boots exactly like the ones Raymond used to wear in those days. *He's pinched me boots!* Raymond cried when he first saw the man, and, then, *he's pinched me!*

Which flattered the impersonation, to tell the truth, but excited the impersonator himself no end as he stood pinned against the police car with his arm held up his back and a twelve-inch steel torch shining in his face. Like a demented younger brother, someone said when the matter went through the courts. The first of many such, someone else suggested, and *that* certainly turned out to be true.

This Raymond Thomas Lawrence (name changed by deed of poll, of course) turned out to be a summer gadfly, a harmless idiot who was in and out of our lives for some time until he was finally put away. There were worse problems than Raymond II, as we called him—*Raymond III's on duty*, I can remember our secretary Dot Round calling out, or *Raymond IV*, whenever she spotted one of his many successors peering lugubriously in at one or other of the Residence's windows, looking for—what? Not much: there were worse problems than these sad, would-be replicas.

What were any of them looking for, though, these crumbs of dust clinging to the shoes of history—the strange, lonely people we'd see down on the road, looking up, or being chased off the property by the dogs: or the groups of people we began to notice early on, standing by the garage and staring up at the house in twos and threes and sometimes more, and just looking, looking, as if there really was something to see in the woodwork of the Residence and the damp grey slate of its roof, something they might take away with them in order to redeem their shabby, fallen lives?

It's the same with our visitors, our tour parties: I watch them feeling the fabric, touching the walls, and their long, long contemplation of the Master's portrait. What is it, what do they want, what are they trying to find or find out? What is it they think they're taking away with them when they steal the ashtrays, the books, the wax fruit and the toilet rolls?

The Visitor Book yields me little as I go through it looking for clues to the thief of the ashtray. Naturally, I seek a pattern, a name that occurs again and again, a recurrent address to follow up: or, absent that (and, indeed, there was nothing), perhaps a recurrent form of handwriting, a suggestion of the forgery of different names by a single, persistent visitor—and, yes, under that heading there *does* in fact seem to be something. But is it really there? I peer at the signatures and the comments beside them. The latter, of course, are nearly always appallingly banal and commonplace. *Very moving. I had a real sense of being close to something here.* Or (particularly gormless), *I'm stunned.* And, time and again, the ubiquitous and lamentable *awesome*: what *can* it mean, what can it be *supposed* to mean now its *real* meaning has been dislodged?

Some of the comments, regrettably, are worse than this. *Bored shitless not worth money. Get a new fucking fridge.* Or (shades of Daisy Ashford), *Open the shitter to visiters.* And, even below that level—alas, but, it seems, inevitably, even in a higher venture like ours—shameful entries always and unoriginally obsessed with sex, race and excrement. *Ray wrote shit. Nobel Prize for Fucking.* Or (mystifyingly), *Donald Duck is a Jew.* Naturally,

Raymond being Raymond, he liked this last kind of entries best, but I can assure you that, as soon as he left us, I inked them out, every shameful one of them.

The Visitor Book is an enormous thing, by the way, not unlike some ancient elephant folios I once saw in the British Museum library, and it was being kept long before the Residence was opened up to the *polloi* and, for private visitors, even longer than that. Overwhelming the lamentable rubbish I've just quoted, there are, on its earliest pages, the entries I treasure most, the acknowledgements of Raymond's growing status in his late middle years, when the hope of his eventual triumph had started to become a possibility and, then, something slightly more. As far as the Prize was concerned, for ten full years he had been considered *papabile*, nominated annually (I made sure of that, through the local branch of PEN and elsewhere) and with increasing rumours of shortlistings that were never quite more than that, since, of course, the Nobel committee doesn't actually announce shortlists. But the rumours were part of a rising tide, a growing clamour that, as it began to engulf me, was by far and away the most exciting thing I'd ever experienced in my life.

The acknowledgements from local writers were one thing, overdue though meaning nothing to Raymond, who kept few friends among his fellow artists in our tiny literary fishpond and, to tell the truth, seemed to set out to make as many lifelong enemies as he could. Acknowledgements from overseas were something else, though, and here they are in front of me, in the book's earlier pages—from Tom Keneally, who on his visit (I remember) regaled us long into the night with his yarns and his Gough Whitlam impersonations, from Raymond's favourite novelist, Walker Percy, from Robert Creeley, who sat at Raymond's dining table as he went through the verse of the eager young poetasters gathered at his feet, from the great Seamus Heaney—he who some said had been robbed of the Prize the year Raymond was awarded it. And so many more notables, all of them making their pilgrimage to Cannon Rise and leaving their traces in this very Visitor Book. '*Oh! The view!*' '*My first taste of roast lamb and kumura*' (sic). '*I have to leave all this?—horresco referens*'. And so on.

Bliss it was, you might say, in that dawn to be alive. And, then, finally, when it came at last, *the moment itself*, the quickening realisation that the impossible was about to become possible, then probable, that the phone call in the middle of the night was actually the phone call we'd waited for night after night, year after year, the call of calls: and Raymond, standing with the receiver to his ear, his face unreadable, no emotion showing at all as he looked out across the lights of the city and listened to the voice of the secretary of the Swedish Academy.

Finally, the receiver cradled, the pause after he turned to me, and his words—he couldn't resist them:

Well, George, we knocked the bastard off—

You can imagine what happened next, the tumult and the shouting, the tremendous sense of living in the moment, as if time itself had been annihilated or suspended, the sense of being at the very centre of history at last. For us, the entire world had stopped to applaud! Suddenly, Raymond's face seemed to be everywhere we looked, smiling back at us in triumph, the phone seemed never to stop ringing, the mailbox all but burst with cards and letters. We travelled to Sweden with him for the ceremony, the four of us presently on the Trust—I was his private secretary by this stage, so accompanied him, naturally, and Marjorie, I recall, re-mortgaged her house to pay for her ticket. Julian, I know, sold his car, and how Semple got himself there I don't know, but there he was in the end along with the rest of us.

Hurried, hectic, wrenching it was: but, looking back, I can't imagine how Raymond would have managed if we hadn't made the effort to get there. He was a seasoned traveller, of course, but the constant media attention and the repeated interviews wore him out. *They keep asking the same fucking questions and I keep giving the same fucking answers!*—I can remember him saying this to me, and that his performances became increasingly just that, performances, his public accounts full of wilder and wilder inventions.

At one stage he made his claim to have actually taken part in the Algerian wars of independence, and didn't *that* attract the attention of the media world! So cantankerous did he become with all the questioning the day of the ceremony was a nightmare—he threatened, finally, to go home uncrowned, something Marjorie cajoled him out of the way you talk a spoilt child to bed. The dress requirements were the main issue: in the end he agreed to a haircut and beard-trim *or* a tie, but not both. The tie won out, so that he remains embalmed in the imagery of the moment looking like a wild colonial Santa Claus, his head a mass of curling locks and bristles and everything short of actual twigs and birds' nests.

We waited for his acceptance speech just as anxiously as we'd waited for the triumph of the tie. What would he say?—we'd gathered together before the trip and drafted a few ideas for him, which he read out loudly and satirically as we handed them to him one by one. Yes, that's right, he said. *Mankind will prevail. Our fate hunts each of us down. Life itself is whole enough to tell us what we need*—what the hell's that supposed to mean? In the end he wrote the speech himself and we had no idea what he intended to come out with, and, knowing he was capable of doing absolutely anything, feared the worst. And what he produced was simply wonderful, what one member of the committee said was the best Nobel acceptance speech he could remember: so simple, so moving, so direct. These days it'd all be on YouTube, of course, and we could relive and relive again the magic of that moment: now much of it is gone, alas, the way everything belonging to that time seems lost to us now, in that *dark backward and abysm*, that vast *Then* before today's transient, unpleasing, light-headed *Now*.

Such an innocent age, when first we felt our way into what engulfs us in the present day! I can remember the time we bought a golfball typewriter for Dot Round, Raymond's typist, to replace the old Imperial she'd typed the Master's work on for so long, and how we gathered around to marvel at the wonder that had come among us—the tiny lettered ball, punching the paper as she battered the keyboard as if it had a mind of its own. *What now?* we all wondered, *what next?*—unaware as we were of being caught (as Raymond was to explain in his Nobel lecture) in the middle of an *epistemic change*, a once-in-three-centuries rupture in the very way the world thinks and believes, and not realising that our amazing new electric typewriter would soon become as outmoded as the ducking stool.

These words are not mine, by the way, since, as I say, it was Raymond, even from within the event, who first explained what it was that was happening around us—now, *there's* a touch of genius for you. Goodbye print, is what he told us. Hullo cyberspace. We had no idea what he meant at the time, of course. We had no idea how much of what is good and great in our heritage we would have to *defend*—he no less than us, of course, he no less than us.

The Lord giveth, however, and the Lord taketh away. It was in Stockholm that I first thought he had something wrong with him, Raymond, I mean, when I watched him moving from the lectern after making his acceptance speech at the banquet—he was over to one side, a little, and seemed to be putting his right foot down in a different way as he walked. I mentioned it to Semple, and immediately wished I hadn't. By the time we'd got ourselves back home it was no longer a suspicion but a fact: the old man had received his comeuppance at last, he was being punished for his past sins, both public (details all pretty well known) and also, according to Robert, private. There was nothing I could do to stop the whispered public embroidering of the story of Raymond's triumph to the effect that he had been struck down in his pomp, as if the prize itself had brought the illness with it as in some medieval allegory.

The rumours became monstrous—Raymond was dying of meningitis, Raymond was dying of AIDS, he was dying of syphilis contracted during his misspent *Wanderjahr* in North Africa years before: he had weeks to live. In the end it was a relief, almost, when he told us what his doctor had just told him. Parkinson's. Seems I'll be going around interviewing people, he said, which was classy, we all thought, given the circumstances: very stylish indeed. But at least we knew he would be with us for a good while more, though in quite what state, at that stage, we simply didn't know.

I had it out with Semple after that, I really did. *Now* are you satisfied? I demanded. He really *is* sick, he really *is* being punished? *You* told *me*, is what he replied. *You* started it off! Anyway, he said, everyone knows he's a prick, he's got up everyone's nose who's ever met him! He might well be *difficult*, I told him. I've never pretended my father was perfect. *Uncle*, he said. Ray's your *uncle*. Father too, I reminded him. Adoptive father—now, what about this other stuff that's going around? What other stuff, he said, and I thought he looked furtive when I went on the front foot to him like that. You know very well what other stuff, I told him. Oh, *that*, he said. Well, it's true, isn't it? *You* remember the things he used to get up to, don't pretend it didn't happen to you. It happened to everyone, all of us. *I've no idea what you're talking about*, I told him. *And if there's any more of this we'll sue—*

I still find it hard to forgive him, to forgive Robert—to forgive all those who simply had to drag down a man like that in his finest hour. He'd been a public figure for some years, and inevitably there were stories that had been doing the rounds in that time. Some of these had something to them: after all, Raymond had been in and out of enough bedroom windows actually to have been spotted at some of them. And, yes, he was a difficult man, I'm sure *that's* becoming clear to you by now, he was a *very* difficult man indeed. He was an artist, and he was difficult *because* he was an artist: and an artist because difficult. The two things were one.

That's what I try to remind the others on the occasions that something comes up from a past they seem to remember in far greater detail than ever I can—I, who, unlike them, actually shared his house and life, who was actually *present* at the times they talk about. I've had to reprimand each of them more than once: Julian least, perhaps, since he had least to do with the Master as a young man, coming somewhat later to the scene as he did: although, of course, he's as susceptible to suggestion as the next man.

Remember what Raymond brought us! I reminded them all, and still remind them. Remember when we were waiting, remember when it happened—remember Stockholm! Remember when we were *together*, is what I meant, when we had a sense of purpose in our lives, a sense of meaning and magic. Because, dear Lord, there's no doubting he brought us some wonderful times, an excitement we'd never have known ourselves without him. What would we *be* without him? I often ask, and I don't just mean the four of us on the Trust. He was a gift to us all, a gift to everyone.

For myself, I know I made too much of him when he was younger, despite our difficulties—*because* of our difficulties, in truth, *because* of them. Nothing is simple, nothing straightforward. I used to love him more when those things happened that I found so hard, sometimes so *wrong*, but that was when he meant more and more to me. The two went together, the pain and the love. They were the one thing.

By the time I was a young man I thought of him not as a mere human being but almost as an incandescence—and it still doesn't seem a completely extraordinary thing to confess that to you. He could do no wrong—even when he did. He was Raymond, he was the Master. He transformed everything he touched, everyone he touched. I knew to let him do it, because he was who he was. Some people make their own rules, and others are there to obey them. That's just how it is. One simply submits to the greater force. One submits to a force of nature.

And all of this now, it seems, a long lifetime ago. Somehow, he has gone, and the excitement and unpredictability he always brought have gone with him: here I am, somehow, left policing the theft of an *ashtray*. A glance up from my desk here in the Chicken Coop and I see the roof of the Residence beyond and below my office window, its distinctive tiles flecked with yellow-green moss, its guttering slumped along the bargeboard and hanging from its ties like a row of grubby hammocks. This is the sort of thing I think of now, and the question of how to pay Val, the sole remaining full-time gardening lady, and the others I am obliged to think of as well—the Butts, most obviously, both of them pensioners now and thus to some degree self-sufficient, both of them (I have to admit) kept on for sentiment's sake as much as anything else. Each requires a notional salary of sorts, not to mention the Chicken Coop building to go on living in: more expense, more expense and more decisions.

In the Blue Room this evening I put away these thoughts as I watch the sunlight leave it, its glow fading from the walls and from the Medal and from the Citation below it. The sherry glass is crystal, Waterford, of course, and one of the many treasures from Raymond's parents' estate at Hamilton Downs, while the sherry is Amontillado: the music, that Vivaldi castrato piece I've mentioned earlier as the *nonpariel* on the other side of a Geminiani Concerto Grosso disc.

Finally, opened across my thigh, and worn from the habit of use, Raymond's third novel *Flatland*, with its imperishable opening sentences: *July. No green left. The pines, the pistachio trees, the palmettos and the cork-oaks black against the rust of the earth*—I don't need to read the words since I have so much of the Master's work by heart: but I adore the simple *fact* of the book, the feel of the *work* and the *use* in it, the embodied thought in my hand as I raise it and let the words on the page meet yet again the words in my head. Such *economy*, and yet such pungency of expression: almost nothing between the reader and the world that is realised upon the page. *I want the words to disappear*, he used to say, and here he has all but made them do that, in a passage of extraordinary delicacy and originality and authenticity.

His book is here tonight not so much to be read as simply to *be*, to reassure, to *give to the moment* as the extraordinary voice of the boy builds and soars and takes me with it to that other world the old man told me about and promised me and so very nearly took me to, and which so surely exists and is where he dwells now. Here it comes, here it comes at last, as the sun winks, and the evening falls, and the glass tips, and the words reassure, and the music climbs to heaven in the pretty mouth of the butchered, ruined boy.

Extraordinary, extraordinary—the insoluble puzzle at the heart of beauty, the Master used to say, *the killing in the middle of it*. That is what he showed me: that, I think, was his especial, demanding gift, the knowledge in those traditional words the Italians used to say:

Evviva il coltellino!

Long live the little knife!

III

Actually, if you want to know the truth, Patrick, what I usually did first thing in the morning was, I'd wipe the old man's arse for him. That's what I usually did. You told me, just the facts, you'd sort them out yourself, well, there you go, there's the first fact for you to sort out! Make something out of *that*—go on! Every morning I'd check him, and that's what I'd have to do because sometimes the poor old bastard'd cacked himself in the night, not every night but most nights he did. I'd clean up the bedding and I'd clean him up, too, and I'd do everything else you'd expect me to do. If they get Parkinson's they get bunged up, see, so I'd give him a couple of the old senna pods at night, about 7:00, and exactly twelve hours later it's *ba-boom*, stand back, know what I mean? Full or empty he'd go off right on time, you could use him to set the Atomic Clock. So I always had to be there. *Close sport*, that's what we call it in the weight room, it means looking out for someone when they're lifting, in case of a fail? Anyway, sometimes I'd get a bit generous with the senna pod and then it'd be like I say, a lot of work for me when I turned up, I'd put him on the throne for the big moment at 7:00 a.m. Bombing Dresden, he used to call it. You'd hear him through the wall, *bombs away*—

Well, *there's* some facts for you to sort out! Dare you to start it off like *that*, this Raymond Lawrence book you're going to write! Anyway, I've been looking through the other questions you left me and I'll have a go at them, I can't guarantee anything but I'll have a crack at them for you anyway. If you're such a great sorter you can tidy me up the way I used to tidy him up the last five years! There you go—you asked how long I worked at the Raymond Lawrence residence, it was ten years. The first five I wasn't living-in, I'd cycle over twice a day and sort him out when he wasn't too bad, the last five I was his live-in semi-pro nurse and his body-servant as well—since he got worse, poor old bastard, that's when I had to do more and more for him. Know what I mean, body-servant? The story is, see, I messed up my exams at uni and then I went off overseas, usual thing, know what I mean? And when I come back I need something to do, and Barry at the gym, he says to me, try Bailey's, and it turns out a lot of the body and weights guys go there to get work lifting old people. Bailey's Care they're called. You don't just lift and turn, you have to do a course first, you have to learn how to inject on oranges and that, and I tell you what, some of it got me a bit rattled—like, putting in rectal thermometers, you ever tried putting one of those in? *You know what you can do with your rectal thermometer*—just joking, guess you had to be there. Some of the stuff I was meant to learn, though, it just went right over my head first off, medication and that—tell you the truth, I didn't even much like injecting the orange, first time round! But I got on top of it all in the end, no trouble.

Anyway, that's how I met Mr Peter Orr, after I'd done the training course. Bailey's give me his number—you know, *your first potential client, don't stuff it up*—and I ring this Peter Orr, and he says to me, *are you able to lift and turn*? Sounds like a dance move, eh? But I'm like, no problem, bring it on. Then he says, *what're you studying*? And I tell him the truth, I tell him I hadn't really studied anything worth mentioning but the main subject I'd *enrolled* for was Geography. *Geography*? he says, even on the phone you could hear him wrinkling up his nose. You mean colouring-in? he says. Well, I think there's a bit more to it than that, I told him, but really for all I know, that might've been all there actually was to GEOG 114 Environment and Resources, just colouring in different countries and trying not to shade over the border into

Nicaragua, know what I mean? But I hadn't been to any of the classes so there's no way I could tell what GEOG 114 was really about, was there? All I knew was what one of my mates told me who was doing it, and that was *orthographic lifting*. Something to do with the weather, apparently, that's what he reckoned. So there you go. Orthographic lifting.

And I told him that, Mr Orr, I said maybe I'd have done a bit better if I'd shown up even just the once. Oh, I *see*, you didn't *pass*, he says. I didn't realise. And then he says, we were looking for someone with literary interests, preferably a graduate. A *graduate*! I told him, I laughed out loud when he said that—I mean, me a graduate, did I look like a graduate to you the other day? I can lift and turn, I told him, but I'm not a graduate, I haven't passed anything. Oh, and I can inject. I didn't tell him I never even showed up for the exams. Why would you?

Anyway, he said he'd see me, and I can tell you what, he changed his mind about me when I turned up in his doorway, this Mr Peter Orr. He's a funny weird skinny bent-over prick, by the way, quite tall—guess you know that—do you? I thought if the job involved lifting and turning I might as well wear just a singlet for the interview, singlet and jeans, know what I mean? What the hell, if he didn't like it he didn't like it and if he didn't want me he didn't want me. That was my position. I didn't know the house he told me to come to was anything special. There was this woman there bent over working, you know, the way women do over flowers, and it turned out, that was Val Underwood. There was a team of them, all women, they kept an eye on the garden—you could see it'd had a hell of a lot of work put into it, you could see that, it's a great garden—and Val was the youngest but not really young. So I call out, Mr Orr in? and she straightens up. She had pretty good tits. That was good, I like that. I'm Thom, I told her, and I spelled it out for her, T-H-O-M. You like a Bounty Bar? I had a spare one on me. So we stood there and we shared a Bounty Bar and that was how I met this really nice lady, which is what she is. Old Val.

I guess you don't really want to know about this stuff but it's what happened so there you go. The point is, she took me round the back of the house and up to the Chicken Coop, up behind the main house. They reckon they call it the Chicken Coop because there really was a chicken coop there once but they've built that second house on it now, know the one I mean? Looks out over the roof of the one where Mr Lawrence used to live? Curtains and a lav and bedrooms and so on. Up there's where Mr Orr's got his office. So I'm standing in front of this open door and he does this bullshit thing where people know you're there and they go on scribbling just to let you know they're Mr Big Shot and you don't amount to Jack Shit pardon my French? Anyway, he looks up when he's good and ready, and that's when he does this big double take and he forgets he can even write! Mr Ham, he says to me, you could see him looking me over. All the time I hadn't spent colouring-in at GEOG 114 I'd spent in the gym lifting weights, so there was definitely something for him to look at—well, you've seen it all so you know. I don't make out I've got much else.

And so—big laugh—turns out I wasn't wasting my time doing all those cycles after all, because he offers me the job on the spot! Forget the Geography, he says to me in that funny little flirty voice he's got—know what I mean? Like he's always walking away around a corner from you all the time, like he's talking to you over his shoulder? *Come on*, I'd like to tell him sometimes, *spit it out, say what you bloody well mean*. No need to ask if *you* can lift and turn, he's telling me, and I half thought he'd get me to lift *him* up and turn *him* round just to see! So, anyway, then he tells me who it actually is I'm supposed to be lifting and turning, and I just laugh out loud at him. Raymond *Lawrence*? I said to him, you're kidding me! And I was, like, shaking my head—the Nobel Prize-winner, after all the stir when he won! Like I told Mr Orr, I'm not into books that much, but how could you get away from the racket when the news came out, d'you remember it?—can't be anyone who doesn't, you heard about it till you wanted a rest. Bloody Raymond Lawrence! Well, I'm not a reader like I say, but even I sat there and watched a couple of interviews on the box at the time, and I wondered what it'd be like, to become as famous as that, world-famous overnight, even if it was late in your life like it was for him, near the end, before he got really sick, I mean, and then of course I thought of the money side of things as well—I mean, you would, you would think of that, wouldn't you? You would think of the money?

I'll tell you what really made me think, though, it's this, it's how you start from nothing and end up with something, I mean something really big. What I mean is, he sits there for years making stuff up in his head, he just pulls it out his bum for all I know. And it gets printed and so on, it gets published and that, but it's still not *real*—d'you see what I mean? But everyone wants to know him, that's the thing, it's like it's magic dust or something. I'll bet you not everyone who was after him like that'd even read the books, I'll bet not half—less—all the same, everyone wants a bit of the action. I mean, *you* do, Patrick, you're one of them, Christ, you're paying me to spill the beans on him, you said you wanted *every detail however small*—that's what you told me. You're paying me to spill my guts, and what're you going to do when I do?—you're going to make it into another bloody book! A book about his books! Then I suppose someone'll do a book on *your* book! And it'll all have come out of nothing—know what I mean when I say that? What's *inside* the book is still—you know—not real. *That's* what I can't get over. And all the time he's just a poor old cocksucker, Mr Lawrence, I mean, at the bottom of it all he's just what we all are, *ordinary*, I've seen everything when I was training and he was, you know, average like the rest of us—except of course he was in worse shape, poor bastard, the way he'd switch off and on like he did, you'd never knew where you were with him, you never knew whether he was alive or dead sometimes. Switching and twitching, that's what I'd call it, just one poor old bastard slowly winding down and never bloody still, it'd give me the tomtits sometimes watching him when he was asleep, *twitch twitch twitch.* This was later on, of course, right near the end, he wasn't like that at the start—whoops! *Shit—*

*

An extraordinary entry in the Visitor Book this morning: *A mausoleum to Art, a monument to Death.*

Who could write such a terrible thing, who could even think it? I struggle with the signature, but it's scribbled, compressed, crouched over, turned in on itself as are the eight words that precede it: their letters lie curved on the page like dead wasps. *Who could it be?*

The initials to the right show Julian to have been the tour guide, but when I ring him he has no explanation. A Japanese tour bus, he says. I don't think they really knew where they were, they spent most of their time taking photos of each other out in the garden. But this isn't what an Asian would write, I tell him. And I'm sure the signature's deliberately disguised. But why would anyone go to the trouble? he asks. Well, then, how d'you explain it? I ask him back—but of course he can't. Someone having a bad day? he suggests. That's just silly, I tell him.

It stays with me, this message, as I turn to this week's emails and letters. *Someone is playing silly buggers*—one of Raymond's phrases. But who, who is it? And why?

In the envelopes today, just the usual stuff, some addressed to Raymond himself, as usual, and written as if he were still with us. Not everything that arrives here at Cannon Rise is bleak and dispiriting, of course: much of it is from scholars all over the world—almost as soon as the initial excitement about the award died down, the requests from the academics, as I've said, began.

For them, though, the Master had no more time than he had for literary folk in general. *Piss off*, he would actually write on the bottom of the letters that came requesting access to his manuscripts and for interviews, and often he'd post them back before I could intervene. On a request for a meeting *with a view to a possible biography* he wrote a dreadful limerick about a young girl from the Azores. One about a young man from Uppingham replied to an early request to make a documentary of his life. Whenever the phone rang near him he would almost always ignore it, but sometimes he'd lift the receiver and engage with the caller in what he called his cleft-palate voice. At other times he would feign idiocy or an obscure foreign accent. *Hold the line, I'll just get him,* was another ruse, followed by the dangling of the receiver on its cord and, for the unfortunate caller, a long, fruitless silence till the penny dropped—or in fact didn't.

Of course I used to remonstrate with him about this behaviour, but it was no use. These are the folk you write for, I'd tell him, these are the folk you write *about*. This is your *readership*, you'd be nothing without them. Cattle, he'd say back. Fuck'em.

Even when he was alive he was a fortress: that is what I'm trying to say. His concessions at the time of the Prize were reluctant concessions to say the least, nearly all of them coming to some kind of grief. Nothing I've done for his estate since he began his decline has been at odds with what I saw in him before it, but none of it has come anywhere near the rage that close encounters would bring about in him as he was dragged, reluctantly, into celebrity. If it's true that *possessiveness and control* are what motivate me in my management of the Trust—Semple's words—such things are no more than extensions of what I saw the old man driven by when it came to protecting his writing and his heritage—or even to the simple business of putting up with people, having folk come near him when he didn't want them there. *Fuck off!* he'd yell through the hedge at sightseers when they tried to peer through it to the Residence. *I'm not a performing fucking seal!*

There'd been some interest in Raymond and his work before the Prize, naturally, albeit somewhat muted: no one seemed quite to know what to make of him at first, since the early novels were so *outré* and caused so much uproar when they appeared—*Miss Furie's Treasure Hunt*, I mean, and the two Algerian novels that followed it, *Frighten Me* and *Flatland*. Beautifully written, yes, yes, they are: but all the same these are the works I have most trouble with myself, to be candid, with their excesses and the misjudgements of a writer slowly beginning to come to terms with his own genius. They certainly have some extraordinary moments.

The initial response to them, most of it in reviews, is meticulously kept in Raymond's papers. I've winced my way through each of them long ago, and through the comments scrawled in the fading near-sepia of their margins—*Amazing! Can't read English! Stupid shit!*—along with his underlinings and splattered exclamation marks. Some of his comments, alas, are even less publishable than these, far less so. He had a mouth on him, as I'm sure you're beginning to gather.

The worse the review, though, the more delighted he seemed to be: and for the first three novels there was much to delight him, since the critics were nothing but negative, expressing shock, appalment, even outrage. The revulsion was almost unanimous. In those days, only his overseas publication by a heroic, masochistic boutique publisher in London kept him afloat. No recognition from anyone—not even a momentary acknowledgement—that for all his excesses he might have had a mission in those early works, a purpose in taking us with him into the abyss. *What can we possibly gain from this perversion of a great European story, what does a giant child-eating beetle contribute to our understanding of the life we live in these islands?*—novel number one. *Once again children are being eaten, but this time by humans and with the added outrage of recipes as an appendix to the book (one hesitates to call it more than that)*—novel number two. *The torture scene at the centre of this work is outrageous and unforgivable, tinged as it is with a lingering sadism and even more questionable sexual tastes, which, if practised, would see the practitioner answering grave charges in court*—novel number three. By now, we're well in Algeria during its war of liberation (hence the titles of *Frighten Me* and *Flatland*). Or, some would say, we are well in Raymond's strange, haunting, mythical, sado-masochistic version of that country.

Now and then—not often—I would find among these reviews a grudging acknowledgement that the young man could actually write (*he is wasting his frequently evident talents as a writer of English on mere adolescent sensationalism*), and I was always fascinated by the way his words could suborn a reader from the paths of righteousness. (*The writing is seductive in both the best and the worst ways, and it is sometimes shocking to come to one's own senses, so to speak, and realise that one has simply accepted without question what one has just read.*)

Inevitably, at some point in all this, it began to occur to me to check out the reality behind what he wrote. One afternoon, when I knew he was away in Phyllis Button's bed, I rummaged his passport out of his bedroom drawer. This was early on, at a time when I was refusing to believe a word of anything he told me, any word at all—in my rebellious years, such as they were, when I was sure he made up everything he said and did, and, the more he told his stories of North Africa, doubted the more that he'd ever stepped from his native soil in the first place. And, of course, he had: his passport, a British one at that stage, was almost falling apart from constant branding. I could hardly believe some of the countries whose names were stamped into it. *Peru*, for God's sake!—what *could* he've been doing in *Peru*?

Marocq, the customs stamp stated for his most recent trip. That was his usual way into Algeria, through Tangier and then into *Alger*, as the next stamp read beneath the curl of the *abjad:* and then *Marocq* again on the way back out again to Tangier—Tangier, visited incredibly early in his travels, and then Algeria, revisited again and again until (as I remember it) a long spell in the late 1950s, when he was in his mid-twenties and had plenty of occasions to do all the things he claimed to have done, various and changing as they were.

Sometimes I'd ask people what they thought. Was he really caught up in the war of liberation back then? I'd ask them. In Algeria? *Yes, of course*, most of them replied, but when I pressed them the only evidence they had was the books themselves: they seemed plausible, so what was in them must surely be true? Only one or two pointed out the inconsistencies—the early stories written from the viewpoint of the *colons*, for example, where the indigenes are clearly, passionately the enemy, atrocities simply something that must be gone through and the *Paras* pouring into the country unambiguously heroes, and then the later writing from exactly the opposite point of view, set in this rebellious *wilayat* or that. His reminiscences switched sides like this and back again, too, any protest provoking a gaze that froze the heart.

Then, of course, it was rumoured he'd been posted to Sidi Bel Abbès after an unhappy love affair in Britain and had actually fought for the Foreign Legion!—something I tracked down to the man himself, who hauled out a book with a photo in it he insisted was of himself in the distinctive Legion uniform of the time, second from the left and three rows back with a date in 1954. I switched sides, he told me. *But that's nothing like you*, I told him back: though the more I turned the magnifying glass on the image in the following weeks and months the more I became convinced that in fact it might very well be him—and, in the end, that, indeed, it actually was. Wasn't it?

Others were less convinced. How much of the early fiction d'you think is real—how much d'you think is based on what he actually did? I asked Semple at one point. None of it, he replied. Bastard probably stayed pissing up in the hotel bar in Algiers writing down what he heard other people say about the fighting.

As you can see, he too had breakdowns in his belief

in the Master—we all did from time to time. On this occasion, I think I remember, the old man had just chucked Robert's latest poems back in his face and then bought him a colouring book and crayons: that or something like it was what lay between them at that particular moment. *It's just stuffing, what you write,* the old man had told him. *Stuffing, stuffing, stuffing! Find something different! It's meant to be* *__behind__* *what you write, not in front of it!* That was when he'd thrown the poems. *You can fucking talk*, Robert had shot back at him, his face dark with anger. *You can fucking talk.*

Hence his scepticism, Semple's, I mean. A little later, though, I caught him out in a drunken boast to the effect that, in truth, he'd never read *Flatland*, or at least that he'd never read it quite to the end— something like that— and I shamed him (as much as he was capable of being shamed) into reading my copy of the novel.

No one else writes like that, he said, as he handed it back to me when he was done. No one, no one in the world.

You could see he was rattled. He meant no one could write as well as that, but also that no one could write an account like the one Raymond had written in that novel without having *lived it*, without having *been there and done that,* as he used to say. He did it all right, Robert told me. No doubt about that. The old bastard, he did it all right.

I realised that if he was as shocked as this he couldn't possibly have read *Frighten Me* either, the other early Algerian novel, and I bullied him into reading that as well: and he was equally shaken by what he saw there, too, once he had. No wonder people tried to ban them, he said. Jesus, I'd no idea. They're so *realistic*, they're so *shocking*, it all actually *happens*—

Oh, the relief, though, when I finally *caught up* with the Master back then—when I'd read everything he'd already written and could open something of his that was new, something made while I was in his life, in his house and beginning to become a part of him.

One of the most wonderful things about his later success, as far as I'm concerned, is that it pasted a new narrative over the excesses of this early writing, you might say, a narrative of which I thoroughly approve and in which I had no small part myself in the fixing: Raymond as the growing conscience of the nation and then, as he went on, of the world, of the civilised world: Raymond the humanitarian, speaking on behalf of the wretched of the earth, wrenching our mistakes, naked and quivering—Lord, how some here *hated* him for this—into the eyes of the teeming globe.

There is general agreement among the critics that in his middle phase—from *The Outer Circle Transport Service*, say—his work began to acquire that depth and resonance, that *maturity of vision*, which was so much remarked on when he won the Prize and which so fully explained his winning of it. *For his holding before our collective gaze the wretched of the earth*—part of what the Citation states about his achievement. Other-people, he had begun to call them, the wretched and the damned: eventually the title of one of his last novels and certainly his most disturbing.

Slowly, slowly, all this has become mine: the compassion, the humanity, the love of the victim and the fool, of the man who dares to be different—of the man who dares to *be*.

*

I've told you what he was like at the ceremony at Stockholm: the attention he received when he returned home interested him even less, and, except for those occasions when he was feeling unusually generous, he tried to avoid it. The illness got in the way, it has to be said, though of course there are always those naysayers who claimed it made no difference whatever and that he was unbearable and unpredictable long before the first tremor in his arm.

Admittedly, there was a disastrous civic reception at the town hall here quite soon after the award, in which he made what even I have to confess was a most inappropriate speech, a truly embarrassing speech. After this it was agreed that he should begin to pass things more and more to me—to the others who were to be in the Trust, yes, but, primarily (given that by that stage I was formally his secretary and personal assistant), to me. More and more it was Raymond's name that was advertised but mine that was offered in its place, in the introductions to the various public meetings I insisted he continue to agree to: or he who would precede me onto the stage, or before the cameras, but I who would follow him and, after the brief, distracted few words he could be bothered to give at the best of times, I upon whom he would rely increasingly to give substance to these occasions—to flesh him out, so to speak.

And thus, imperceptible to the public gaze, a gentle transition from uncle to nephew, as, increasingly, I began to steal the show with a growing public narration of Raymond's life in the years after the award. At first these public lectures were illustrated by a steady accumulation of slides in a carousel: then, as time went on and with Julian's help, by electronic means. Scenes from the ceremony at Stockholm—Raymond receiving the award in his reluctant tuxedo and tie, his hair awry like Beethoven's, Raymond and the four of us with him, all in our youth (wry self-deprecation always worked well at this point of my presentation), Raymond with King Carl Gustaf, Raymond delivering his acceptance speech at the banquet, Raymond receiving his applause.

From his return home and after, there are scenes from the reception at Government House: Raymond with the Governor-General, Raymond and the Trust members with the Governor-General, the five of us with the prime minister of the day, the five of us with the local mayor and his council, Raymond alone with the mayor and his council. Scenes from the town hall reception, from the garden of the Residence, from Raymond's writing life—and, all the time, my voice, knitting together the anecdotes and the facts for his followers, with Raymond sometimes present, in the early years of all this, immobile yet sharp-eyed, but, later, inert or not present at all, and, after a certain point, almost always silent wherever he was. Sitting there in his *fauteuil roulant*.

Until, eventually, once the dreadful matter of his death had been delicately sorted out, it was me alone at last and at stage centre, *neveu et héritier*. The role finally engulfed me, and I in turn embraced the role: it was as if it had been written for me and for me alone, as if I had been created for it and for nothing else. The triumph of the writer *manqué*, some people said—Marjorie, of all people, was one of them, in the only really serious argument I've ever had with her, shortly after Raymond went and our roles were being settled in court, as, unhappily, became necessary. *You're well in now*, I remember her shouting at me outside the courtroom when it was all over and done. *Raymond the fucking Second. You've become a significant literary figure at last—now all you have to do is write something!* We were in the middle of the bitter row that followed the publication of his will and its clear delineation of our relative positions. *You're not even a fucking writer!* she said to me. *I just don't get it, what did you pay him? You can forge his signature, did you forge the rest of the will as well?*

From time to time they raged and stamped, but less and less frequently over the years and never for very long—Marjorie easily distracted as her personal life lurched from *crise* to *crise*, Robert as much so by his ongoing obsession with juvenile pulchitrude. Julian, always affable, put up little resistance in the first place.

Often, after this, they struggled to keep up with my plans, my feints and manoeuvres. *So Raymond's going into four different international libraries but no one's actually going to be allowed to see anything he ever wrote once it's there, have I got that right?* Marjorie creaked at me, carefully, when I outlined the arrangements I'd slowly been putting together in the final years of the old man's life. He's going bit by bit, I told her. We've still got a lot here in the Residence to catalogue. *Yes, but could you explain the thinking*, she said. *If no one's ever going to be allowed to actually see his manuscripts and so on, you know, actually read them and work on them, shouldn't we just burn them here and now and be done with it?* She didn't understand, alas, she simply didn't understand.

More than this: one night after a Trust meeting I overheard Semple outside, in amongst the slamming car doors down by the garage as they prepared to leave in the usual way. *He can't let the old man go*, he was saying to the others. *Norman. He's got all Ray's droppings saved up in bottles under the Blue Room—he's got Ray down there as well, he gets into the sarcophagus with him every night and shuts the lid!* And then Marjorie's laughter, and Julian saying *now now, Robert.* And all the while my blood running cold: *Lord, if only they knew what it really was they were laughing at—*

On the other hand, I do have to admit I *did* have difficulty separating myself from the Master when the time came. He'd absorbed me so utterly into his life and with so little resistance on my part that, once the fuss about his extraordinary, devastating end had faded, it could hardly be different. I'll even admit to you the existence of a little reliquary I keep in a drawer in his bedroom in the Residence. His upper denture (his lower teeth were his own) and (each in a little pharmaceutical sample-bag) a snip of his beard and another of his hair—the former white and tightly kinked, the latter slightly waved and grey, with a slight hint of russet left in it like the henna in the hair of a dead pharaoh. His spectacles of course, both the little half-glasses he wore around the place to peer over and the full-sized, wire-framed bifocals whose temple-bars Phyllis so deftly caught with that single flutter of paint in her greatest portrait.

Some nail-clippings, too, from both fingers and toes, and the ring he always wore—curious, this, given he never married—on the second finger of his left hand. And then, simply, bits and pieces: a cigarette holder and lighter, a dried-up toothbrush from thirty years ago, an ancient packet of suppositories half used up, a sebsis from his kif-smoking days in North Africa, its bowl tortuously, tinily carved and yet its stem just a plant stalk pulled from somewhere. Other objects, too, less loved and treasured than, simply, *there*, *his*, unavoidably part of the record of his existence.

Here, too, I keep the stick he sometimes used on us,

alas: on Robert, on me: sometimes, even, on Marjorie—on anyone, it seemed, including the Kennedy kids next door when he caught them about his property. Fifteen inches long and tightly covered in stitched brown leather: it still terrifies me whenever I see it, reeking of the exotic as it does, like a distant row of camels, like an endless, billowing, many-peaked Bedouin tent. An unquestionable part of the old man's North African story from the moment he began to spin it to me, early in my time in this house, part of his wondrous *gallimaufry of bullshit*, as he described it once when, yet again, he'd drunk too much. At other times it was quite separate and with a life of its own as a pure object, a thing that could cause terror and pain. There were days when it was about, I remember, and there were days when it was not: but always it was *there*, always it was present, always it was somewhere. It never ceased to exist, always reeking of the Barbary coast and the mysteries of *l'Arabie*.

Yet, somehow, for all the fear in it—the terror—I could never bear to throw it away, or anything else of him: in fact some of these relics I carry about with me secretly, quite often, in order to fortify myself, to reassure myself that he is still with me in some way. How often have I sat in a meeting of the Trust with the half-glasses in my shirt pocket, or his ring sliding around on my little finger, or his gnarled old toothbrush inside my jacket! Raymond, Raymond, synecdochal Raymond, hidden about my person!

Quite apart from anything else, though, and if the truth be told, almost the first thing he did to me was to cut off my writing arm, just like that. At some callow moment, and tremulously, the teenaged me gave him some dreadful juvenile thing I'd written: *There's to be no more of this*, he said when he returned it—when he held it out to me, that is, and then pulled it away and hoisted it up and out of my reach. *Look, look carefully*, he said, *watch*, and turned, and opened the lid of the kitchen incinerator and thrust my work into its flames. *You're. Not. A. Writer,* he said, carefully. *You're something else, not sure what, but take it from me, whatever it is it isn't that. You're something, but I haven't decided what it is yet—*

Dear God, how I hated him for that—I still do, in part of me! You see that I can write, somewhat, a little, and (I like to fancy) sometimes more than a little: a tendency to overwrite sometimes, certainly, to be a little self-consciously 'literary', and too many long sentences over-reliant on parentheses and colons: this is what my friends tell me. All true. I try to improve, to be disciplined. In the most ambitious sense, though, in the fullest sense of the Artistic—off came my writing arm from the shoulder, in a single swipe and with no anaesthetic to dull the pain. I gave up the idea of high artistic achievement there and then: *he* was the writer, and no one else. He'd made that clear. No one need apply.

Sometime later—I mean years later, when I was eighteen, perhaps, or nineteen—he suddenly told me he'd finally decided what it was that I would be. *My bumboy,* he told me. *When I tell you, you drop your daks and touch your toes, that's what you do from now on.*

This was when we'd had the last of our really violent disagreements—the end of my adolescence, really, the end of my innocent years—but it was also a time when the possibility of the Prize was first coming clearly into sight. He'd been nominated several years in a row by then—and I think he had a growing idea of what might happen to him soon, perhaps, and, consequently, of what it was he would need from me. I was bookish, I was obedient, I was efficient, I could add up a row of figures. I would do: as you will see.

More than anything, though, I was *his*. When I was three, my father—Raymond's older brother—much older, ten years older—died in an accident at the family farm near Springfield. My mother remarried almost straight away, to a man I'm sure had been in her life already. Raymond was always the forbidden uncle I overheard my mother and my father's replacement discussing, in due course, through the wall: whenever I appeared at these moments they'd fall silent and turn from each other as if they'd been talking about something else.

Little by little, I became fascinated by him, this forbidden uncle: what was the thing he'd done wrong? *It's not so much that as who he mixed with*, my mother said to me once, cautiously, reluctantly, when I'd pestered her enough on the topic: and that was the point at which the naughty, smoky word *bohemian* entered my life. He was an outlaw!

From somewhere in the house I found one of his books—the only one my mother had forgotten to throw out—and pored over its cod Hansel-and-Gretel cover, as I later learned it was supposed to be. *Miss Furie's Treasure Hunt*, it was, that very first venture: he glowered from the back cover, a sharp-bearded man with a disturbing, iron gaze. He terrified me even then.

So I sought him out. This deliciously forbidden, forbidding man had returned from overseas the year before and bought a property on the hills to the south-east of town—*as if he was trying to get as far away from the farm as he could*, I overheard my mother telling my stepfather through an inefficiently closed door. His address was in the phonebook, delightfully taboo: 23 Cannon Rise. His house, equally proscribed, was but a bike ride across town and a fifteen- or twenty-minute toil up a hill road. Once there, puffing, unfit, I stood before a low iron-red cliff at the foot of his property and then scrambled up it and onto his lawn.

At the far end, up the slopes of the banked grass and beyond the raised flowerbeds, the house was exactly as it is today. I always have the sense, though, when I remember the moment, that the Blue Room was in the process of being added, out to the left: but that can't possibly be true, as you will come to understand—although, equally, you might in fact come to see that it *must* be true, can *only* be true.

Seen like that, the house gave me too little, and so the following weekend I returned to it, and again the weekend after that, and again after that, always hoping for more. Each time, it sat there and looked back at me.

Eventually, though, it yielded what I had come for, Raymond Thomas Lawrence himself, aged—what? Not quite forty, I imagine. The Raymond Lawrence who had returned from the UK the year before and was just starting to conceive of *The Outer Circle Transport Service*, as I was to discover soon: the novel that seemed out of place at the time but which looked, when all was done, like an attempt to break out of what no less an authority than Dr Geneva Trott herself has designated *his somewhat overblown earlier style*.

And indeed, as I was to discover, it did have some funny moments here and there, if rather elephantine ones: written by this man who turned and stared at me that day half a good long lifetime ago, in shabby cardigan and trousers and rubber boots, as I remember him, and amongst autumn leaves and pale smoke, if (again) those details are true. I remember a fine drift of rain and the smell of the smoke in the rain, and from him a smoky pale-blue gaze, even though I know that in the photos and the paintings the eyes are another colour, somewhat darker: and a moment of engagement quite unlike anything I had experienced before in my life, a clinch so intense it was almost paralysing. It seized me, it held me: and, then, a moment after that, a turning away, as if to say, *I've got you*, or, *I've caught you now, you're mine.*

A stirring in the forest—

It was so odd, so disturbing, that I never told anyone about it: even my mother, whom I trusted at the time, although that was beginning to change in the usual way. Somehow, the man had uncovered me just by looking at me, had seemed to bare my eleven-year-old self to itself in some primitive way: and then had turned indifferently back to his autumn leaves and his funeral pyre.

Back home I found *Miss Furie* again and began an attempt to read it properly and the process at whose far-distant end I'd read all of Raymond Lawrence's books for the first time through to (perhaps) *Bisque*. At which point, I had a sense of having lost something about the man that was more important than anything I'd gained by reading him. I never quite got back that crisis of being *known* by him in that first meeting, of being *possessed*. Not quite. The man I first saw through the infernal smoke of his rubbish fire was an image I carried through everything that was to come, as if all his subsequent manifestations to me were just slightly diminished versions of that first, Mosaic apparition. I carried this image in my mind as you'd carry a photo in a wallet: the nearest you might get to the thing you were trying to remember, but never again quite the thing itself. A replica, and the more so each time you refer to it, the more so each time I saw him. But, as I came to know him more, always, always, Mephistopheles.

IV

Hullo? Sorry about that, nearly dropped the recorder on the floor. Thom here again, Patrick—it's not Thomas, by the way, I see you put Thomas on the cheque and I'll have to get you to change that when we meet up Thursday, they're not going to bank it the way it is and I need the dough! You can change it when I hand you this tape back—Thom Ham and that's it, T-H-O-M new word, H-A-M. *Wham-bam-Thom-Ham-thank-you-ma'am*—

Just played some of that back and I want to say, *ordinary*—you know I said that? The old man? He was just *ordinary, average*? Well, he was, he was just a body like everyone else. But if you look at him another way, he wasn't all that ordinary at all. Once met never forgotten, know what I mean? Get a bit confused when I think about him, it's all mixed up and, *Christ*, he did some terrible things, he made people do some terrible things—me, he made *me* do some terrible things, look what he made me do. But he was this little old geezer at the same time, I'd get him up and I'd walk him—d'you want to know this sort of thing, d'you want to know what I'd do with him day to day? It'll probably sort itself out for you, it's not that interesting. Well, some of it is. The walking part is, that's weird. I'll tell you about it. There'd be times when he'd be okay, you just had to rub his legs a bit when you'd got him sitting up in the bed and after a while he'd do the rest by himself, I mean he could get himself up and walk. It took a bit but he could do it. You'd be surprised to see him when he got going. Then, other mornings, sometimes the very next morning, he'd be the opposite, you'd have to, like, take him over from himself because he couldn't do a single thing, know what I mean? I'd have to get him by the armpits and lift him up and it'd be like he was nothing? Mr Orr'd say to me, *are you sure you can manage him*, and I'd tell him, there's nothing to manage! I don't think he believed me, he'd stand there watching and he could see me wearing my lifter's belt, it looked all serious but it wasn't, I'm telling you the truth, it was like lifting nothing, it was like the old man'd already gone and I'm holding nothing up in the air, just the space where he used to be.

And one day I'm standing there holding him up like that from behind, and Mr Orr's there watching me, and I'm right up against the old boy like I'm doing the Heimlich maneuver on him—that's one of the things Baileys teaches you, the Heimlich maneuver, in case your client chokes on his rusk—and Mr Orr, he says to me, what's your secret? And I couldn't help it, I told him, *I've got him propped up on my dick*. I thought it was a hell of a funny, I'm laughing now, you can hear me, excuse me—excuse me—sorry—yeah. Jeez. Anyway, Mr Orr, he *definitely* didn't think it was funny, he just blew his stack at me, I thought he was going to sack me on the spot? *Shit* he was angry? This is Raymond Lawrence you're talking about, he tells me. He is a great man. You're literally holding his life in your hands. You're paid to care for him and that means what it says, you're not paid to disrespect him. He told me stuff like that. I tell him, keep your hair on, and he gives me this funny look. I'd often tell him that, to get under his skin. *Keep your hair on, Mr Orr,* I'd tell him.

Right, what was I saying? That's right, getting the old man walking. You see, there's times when he just couldn't move. I'd hold him up from behind, no problems, like I said. I'd hold him there and hold him there and you can tell he just couldn't get his legs going, he couldn't get his feet moving on the floor. So I'd give his left leg just a nudge from behind with my kneecap, then the right with the right, same thing, and then the left with the left again and so on. And he'd start to move. What it felt like when I was doing that is, it felt like I was putting him on like I was putting on his clothes. Now *that's* a weird feeling, I mean, becoming someone else. It's like he was getting his life out of me, sucking it out of me—can you see what I'm trying to say? Like when you give another car a shunt along the road with yours to get it started? Felt like that. Weird.

After a bit he'd start moving his feet on his own, as long as I was holding him up. Then after a bit more I could feel him pulling away from me and moving himself, and he was separated off, and—well, there he'd be, in front of me, he'd be moving away from me. It was like teaching a kid to ride a bike, you know, you run along behind and hold them steady for a while and then they're off, they don't need you anymore? It's like I'd made him, it's like I'd made him—*happen*. I said this to old Peter once—I'd never call him that to his face, by the way, all the rest of the Residence staff called him Mr Orr, so I was supposed to call him Mr Orr, too, but I tell you what I called him, I called him Either-Or—get it? Peter Orr, Either-Or? Just to myself. He called me Gradus and I called him that. Anyway, I say this to old Either-Or, I tell him, *when I get Mr Lawrence moving again like that it's like I've made him, know what I mean?* And he says to me, *you've been working here too long, you're starting to think like a literary person, Gradus, not a colouring-in person*. He does it in that smart-arsed smirky way that makes you want to hit him—like he's from somewhere special. And I knew he'd got that name from somewhere, Gradus, I knew it wasn't meant to be a compliment, I could tell that just from looking at his face, the way he said it—*d'you* know what he meant, by the way, Patrick? Gradus?

Anyway, doesn't matter, he was the same with everyone, it wasn't just me. No one liked him, not even the other writer people Mr Lawrence knew, Julian and all the others that still hung around him—d'you know Julian Yuile? He's not a bad guy but not exciting, definitely not exciting, none of them's exciting on the Trust. It's because he doesn't like himself, Val said—this is Mr Orr she's talking about, not Mr Yuile. It's because he doesn't like himself, she reckoned, that's why he's the way he is, and I thought about that for a while. It's because he's frightened of liking you, she told me, that's also in the mix. And because he's frightened you might like him back. Not much chance of that, I told her. She's a good woman, Val, sometimes I think it was a shame she was just a little bit outside my target area for taking old Jumbo for a walk.

But anyway, getting a bit off the topic here, aren't I? Telling you about old Either-Or trying to wind my clock, but after I'd thought about it for a while it seemed to me he was actually trying to say something else about me and this Thomas Hamilton, and what he was trying to say was the same thing I've been trying to say to you just now, when it seemed like I was putting Mr Lawrence on like clothes. I wouldn't mind talking to you about it sometime when you're free, because it's niggling at me. It's true, what old Either-Or says is true, you do start thinking different things when you get caught up with people like that, and I don't think it's always for the better. I don't think writers are all-that-happy people, to tell you the truth, not as far as I've seen, anyway. I don't know why they do it, writing I mean, it doesn't seem to make them any happier. Nothing personal, no offence intended. I don't

*

Wednesday afternoon, and here I am, limping my car over judder bars and into a little world of quadrangles and cloisters and tight-ribbed stone staircases. Years ago, when every other college of our local university departed to new accommodation in the north-western suburbs, the College of Arts remained here in the city, in charming mock-Gothic buildings first thrown up nearly a hundred years before. Its desks are still gouged with the names of young scholars long since rooted out of their tabernacles.

The English Department is in the old Physics building here in this second quadrangle, near a large Japanese gingko tree that flowers magnificently in spring and emits a terrible stench in autumn. You can imagine what Raymond made of something like *that*—his fiction is full of gingkos that drop their noisome seed at inopportune moments. The Raymond Lawrence School for the Creative Arts is next to the English department, in a building now almost completely repaired following the events of October 2007. It's scheduled to re-open next month.

Ah, yes, the Raymond Lawrence School of Creative Writing—focus of the greatest arguments Raymond and I ever had. Of course the others in the Trust were involved, too, even though that body had yet to be formally established at the time I'm talking about: we were his friends, in effect his family, even though not all of us especially liked one another—and most like a family in that, you might say.

But we were united in wanting to commemorate the great man tangibly: so that, when the Registrar of the University here contacted us a dozen years ago on behalf of the University's council to sound out the possibility of setting the School up in Raymond's name, we leapt, collectively, at the opportunity. What better thought? Even the suggestion that we might join the other funders of the project, a wealthy local law firm, seemed acceptable: at that stage Raymond's sales were at high tide and there was money elsewhere and of course from the Prize itself, though the family farm at Springfield was—and still is—tied up in a trust.

Money, at that stage at least, was never the problem: *Raymond* was the problem, and what turned out to be his extreme reluctance—nay, outright resistance—to the entire adventure made in his name.

Oh, thank you, thank you, do I get a say?—his opening shot when first I put the proposal to him. *This seems to have got a long way behind my fucking back, do I not count for anything anymore? I'm sick in the head now, so you go around me, is that it?*

Alas, moments like this were becoming familiar as his illness developed, and I'd learned to ignore them since, at this stage at any rate, they tended to disappear moments after they occurred. It was as if he was losing control of his emotions, or as if his self were breaking up into a number of different people, each one a possible and partial version of what he once had been or might have been. We seized one of these mini-Raymonds *en passant* and got its initial agreement, only to be overtaken by another such, a day and a half later. *This fucking creative writing school*, he mumbled at my bedside in the Chicken Coop after waking me in the middle of the night. Put your teeth in, I told him. *They are in*, he said, but he was lying. *I've changed my mind*, he said. Well, it's too late now, I told him.

And so on: in due course, after many more such changes of mind, he gave his final approval but with the quintessentially Raymond condition that the School be set up not in the English department building but in the toilet block next to it. He knew this block was being rebuilt—*repurposed*, as they put it nowadays—and that some other department was supposed to go in there, but as far as he was concerned there was no other place for the Raymond Lawrence School of Creative Writing. It would open in the former men's room or it wouldn't open at all. *Only place for it!* he said. *They should've kept the trough and the stalls.* And so, enclosed by walls bright and slick with paint and radiating hope and purpose, the writing classes began where once (I distantly remember from my student days) the urinal stood, wan beside the cubicles.

As the opening approached, Raymond was as cantankerous and wayward as he'd ever been before the ceremony at Stockholm. What's his problem? I asked Marjorie, the one to whom he seemed closest at the time. There's no *him* so there's no *his*, she replied, as succinctly as I've ever known her to speak. Sometimes he's the Ray I remember, she said, but mainly he just moves in and out of focus—it's like he thinks the Ray who won the Prize is someone else, it's like he wants to leave him behind. Watch out for his speech at the opening, she told me. He could say anything.

Well!—it wasn't what he *said* that was the problem at the opening, because he hardly said a thing. The problem was what he *did*. The audience was appalled—we all were appalled, we were shocked and embarrassed to the core. Even Semple was taken off guard: *he's gone and done it now*, he told me. I'm sure you recall the subsequent uproar in the media and among the public, and talk of the Prize being withdrawn from him: although there was no precedent for that and, as all things do, the hubbub eventually died away—though not quickly, as evident in the proliferation of those little plaster models of the old man as the Manneken-Pis.

Certainly, this shocking and regrettable indelicacy marked the end of the road as far as his public appearances were concerned: that was the point from which, in truth, we began progressively to hide him away. It was for his own sake as much as anything else, since the media were hovering as they do, eager in their usual dispassionate way to bring about any individual's public humiliation and destruction for their own passing advantage.

From this point, and increasingly, the future members of the Trust became his public face—or *I* did, the others would claim, and who am I to say no? As I've told you, I drank it up, the challenge, the responsibility, the importance of the role I'd found at last. I knew nothing like the moment of my first entry to the public eye in his place, and that particular magic has never gone away. *The nephew—the man who cares for him—his spokesman*: I still felt it, undiminished, when I came in here a few moments ago to open the School year as I always do, with some words about the Founder. The thrill of it, the excitement—the joy of simply *being Raymond*, of knowing that as I step into each reading or award ceremony or literary festival people are nudging each other and nodding their brows towards me: *that's Raymond Lawrence's son*—even, sometimes, *that's Raymond Lawrence*. The special, reverent hush as, spotlights dazzling my eyes, I step out onto the stage, the writer himself. The expectant, sacred moment *that now is mine alone—*

Today I'm early, and there's time to wile away in the campus bookshop. What do I find—here, immediately through its doors—but global publishing itself in the form of the world's latest writing sensation: or, in fact, his replica in cardboard, larger (unless he really *is* from another planet) than life. How many years is it since I last saw Raymond himself here in similar form, standing stiff and flat and proud behind piles of his own work, a two-dimensional Ozymandias beaming out at the world?

This young man has just won a big literary prize in Ireland and so is everywhere, his image replicated—so it seems—throughout the known universe. I see him on the news and the talk shows and the sides of buildings and buses, in lifestyle magazines and advertisements for clothes and toiletries and music and wine—or at least I *think* that's who it is each time, although sometimes his skin seems a little lighter and sometimes not, and sometimes he seems smaller and sometimes larger, and at others he seems no longer to be a male at all: instead, faun-like, an epicene girl-woman, frail and vulnerable.

Sometimes, too, he is a touch oriental in appearance—indeed, he seems truly international, even supranational: born in a Middle Eastern refugee camp and shrugged into the West without a word of English in him, but writing now a version of it all his own that everyone, it seems, wants to read, to bear witness to. Here it is in front of me: I gaze at the sprawl of words across its pages in the novel in my hands, their drift towards and away from meaning. I stare at his image on the back cover. He has something for me, I know that, even if what he has will always be four-fifths beyond my understanding. For *he* is what comes next.

I tried to explain something of this to the old man at one point—to explain it *back* to him, since it was he who first talked about the times we're going through. *This* is what writing's become, I tried to explain to him with some new young writer's latest first book in my hand. I knew that in some part of him and however much he raged he *did* understand what is happening around us now and that he himself was always going to be pushed aside and relegated to the dinosaurs. You have to try to understand, I'd urge him: you were the one who told us all this was coming. *Yes, but who'd know it'd be so fucking vapid once it arrived?* he'd ask me back. *It's such shit, all of it.* You're looking for the wrong things, I'd try to tell him. *Yes!* he'd shout back at me. *Content'd be nice! Be nice if they wrote about something now and then!* We just can't *see* the content yet, I'd tell him. It's us, not them. He'd refuse to believe me, though. *Be nice if they had some fucking history in them!* he'd bawl. *Christ, it's hard work being out of date—*

It *is*, I always told him when he said this. That's the point, we have to work to understand what they write. And so on, quite without effect—he still went on saying terrible things. *It's not real anymore,* he'd say. *No one actually reads books anymore—they just review them and give them fucking prizes. Soon they won't even read the reviews. Then we really will have a virtual fucking literary culture—*

I, on the other hand, always insist on buying and reading these youngsters. Why?—to find the new Raymond Thomas Lawrence among them. Not yet, not so far, but I know he's waiting: or she, of course. This young Afghan citizen of the world, looming over me in cardboard? We'll see. I gaze at him, at his darkness, his otherness. In one sense he's Anir, of course, the boy who haunts the Master's writing, coming in and out of focus from novel to novel, dead one day and back on the page the next, insisted upon and insisting. Could he never see this, the old man, could he really never see that he'd made this young man himself and that the young man was writing back?

At the till here's Bevan, the manager, and from the workroom behind him the smell of coffee and the faint sound of classical muzak. He doesn't look up, just nudges another book at me along the counter with his elbow.

Flutter By, it's called, with a sash that says *Riveting First Novel*: its cover blazes with bright bird-colours.

'Read that,' he tells me. 'She does it with another bird. The main character. And here's me thinking all they ever do is bite each other's beaks.'

Since the incident the Raymond Lawrence School of Creative Writing has been temporarily quartered in the English department buildings. I look into its larger tutorial room: two instructors, team-teaching. In the smaller room next door I find Cosmo Dye, the School's director, looking up at me from a class of two dozen: he nods and beckons as he talks. Twenty-four would-be Raymond Lawrences: can there *really* be so many of them here in front of me? I tiptoe in, and find a seat against the rear wall as Cosmo tells the class that if they aren't happy with their first draft, they shouldn't be afraid to write a second.

I look about myself, and wonder what I always wonder in classrooms like this: *which is the One?*

Opposite me, over the students' heads and behind Cosmo, a whiteboard carries one bold statement: *FIND YOURSELF/ WRITE YOURSELF/ FIND YOURSELF AGAIN*. Above and beside this, posters: Salman Rushdie, with the slogan *1989: LEST WE FORGET*. Beside that, a simple, optimistic statement *sans* image, *WRITERS RULE THE WORLD*, and near it another, this time an image *sans* statement, of Edgar Allan Poe: always furtive, always unreliable. There's a poster of Mavis Carpenter peering earnestly at the camera whilst one of her fists supports all of her jowls, and another of Roy Sharp receiving the Commonwealth Poetry Prize.

And make sure you serve up a really *good* sentence every page or two, Cosmo tells the class. Keep the reader's interest up!

The largest poster by far is of the Master himself, a famously candid shot in greys and blues taken during his later middle years when he was slightly drunk, and showing much that was most attractive about him, as, surprised and momentarily disarmed, he turns to the lens. It was before he began regularly to wear glasses, and his eyes seem bared, and warmed and softened by the alcohol, his features loosened, particularly about his mouth: his entire expression is open, vulnerable, trusting: the man himself, and a Raymond I like to think I alone *really* knew. The slogan on this poster is the same as the slogan on the front of his T-shirt: *END POVERTY*. Combined with his demeanour in the photo it has an effect curiously if imprecisely optimistic, and in its time the image was everywhere. I'm delighted, of course, to see it again and being used in the School, although of course there are various framed photographs of him about the place, albeit in slightly less eloquent poses. *END POVERTY*: perhaps I alone remember the rest of the statement, on the back of the same T-shirt: *KILL THE POOR AND EAT THE BASTARDS*.

What does this new generation of children make of him, though, these golden lads and lasses gathered around me now? What, come to that, do they make of *me*? At one level, I know, Raymond's public shenanigans in later life, and particularly his disastrous performance at his final public outing, became part of his myth. These stunts gave him a certain *cachet* amongst the young in particular: Raymond was *cool*. There've long been urban legends involving things he never did at events he never attended, as well as things he certainly *did* do which have been embroidered into wild fantasy, all of this a nonsense that rivals some of his own tall tales about his earlier years. And the more we hid him away, in those days, the more the stories grew, as if breeding out of the fact that he was no longer there—as if his absence from public life had become a blank wall for the graffiti of rumour.

The garden gnomes were one thing, but it was another phenomenon that really disturbed me, something that began just after he'd left us and was quite different from the many cheap attempts there've been to slander him or cash in on his fame. It took me completely by surprise when I first saw it: a little mannequin left behind in the Residence after a tour party had gone through, a tiny, homemade, thumb-sized Raymond, just a few judicious twists and knots of string and—there he was, somehow, with miniature specs and boots and one end of the string making a little white beard—plus (this is what was extraordinary) *tiny wings*, made from a couple of white feathers stuck in his back.

At first we suspected Raymond Thomas Lawrence II, since the development had the hallmarks of his down-at-heels obsessiveness. But apparently he was still locked away somewhere making ugly things for the poor: and, besides, after a while these angelic midget Raymonds started appearing all over the place: thumb-sized feathered replicas you'd see pinned to people's clothing like a brooch or stuck to noticeboards and walls. They seemed to have acquired a particular meaning out there in the culture that didn't have anything to do with what he'd written or who he was. Just the idea of him, no more, passed to another generation and its unreachable lurch away from us, into that frightening void in which *they* are dancing on our graves and *we* lie in them, eyeless, inexistent, forgotten.

Raymond as an angel: as I'm sure you'll understand, *that* was a thought that never occurred to me while he was alive. But at one level it made sense, since there are angels in *Bisque* and there are angels in *Kerr* and there are angels elsewhere in his writing. Want to look like a great artist? he asked, as he was coming to the end of writing one or other of these—*Kerr*, I think it was, the raft-journey novel, his greatest novel, the one that was so memorably filmed with Bob Hoskins. Put a fucking angel in, Raymond said. Everyone'll think you've read Rilke so it *must* be great Art—they haven't read the mad fucker but they know about the angels!

Of course, he knew there was much more to it than that. As I've said, his writing began to mature in this early middle period, as some of the critics have called it, and *Bisque* was his first obviously substantial work—a firm second step, you might say, on the road to the Prize. Its title refers not to the seafood dish but to unglazed pottery, though you'll probably recall that you can read the book from one end to the other and not find the latter mentioned: instead, the word is a figure for the unfinished state of the young woman depicted in it (Julia, her name) as she enters the excitement of Ibiza in the Mediterranean. Bisque, in that sense.

In *Bisque*, you'll remember, this Julia is a would-be writer, and you'll also recall that after a run-in with an American conman she falls in with an older fellow who is a doctor and, it transpires, a Nazi sympathiser and *Franquista* as well: and you will remember, too, that, late in the novel, he takes her for a picnic on what turns out to be the site of an abandoned concentration camp. Anything but an angel, then, this doctor: no, instead, the angels are the young *pilluelo* Julia keeps running into around and about the island: street urchins. There's that extraordinary moment when she comes to believe, late in the novel, that these are the spirits of the children who have died in the deathcamps of Europe, and that they may not in fact exist in the normal sense at all.

Angels and death camps! Raymond said after the book was shortlisted for what was then the Commonwealth Writers' Prize. Can't miss with that combo, must be an important writer if I'm writing about angels and fucking death camps as well!

But I knew not to believe what he said, not least because I'd caught him in tears the day he finished writing the book. *Blue*, he said, brokenly, and shoved the final pages at me as he wrestled a hankie against his snout. Turns out the whole fucking thing is about *that* after all! It just came up out of the writing, he told me—the colour he was to become more and more obsessed with, and which occurs in everything he wrote from that time on: *the colour in which we see the intangible becoming tangible*, he told me years later, *infinity becoming finite*. Not any old blue, he said. *Sky* blue. The colour of liquefaction. Of the Blue Flower.

All these thoughts, provoked by the sight of the string Raymond-brooches on two of the creative writing children sitting in the class. Nowadays, I get a jolt in the chest whenever I see these odd little gewgaws appear. Somehow—don't ask me to explain—they seem to touch on everything I've felt ever since Raymond left us, seven years ago now. On that, and on something more that I just don't understand.

Now, suddenly, I'm back in the teaching room: all eyes are on me. Cosmo, it seems, has just introduced me—*who better to talk to us about this wonderful writer than his nephew and literary executor?*—and there is a silence that is mine alone. Time to perform once more! *Peter will be opening the refurbished writing school building next month,* Cosmo adds eagerly, as I reach the lectern.

A flutter of applause: not much to it, no real enthusiasm. Things are not as once they were, I'm aware of that, I'm well aware. I try to reach for common ground. The words come easily enough, since they've been said so many times before: *When I was seven or eight years younger than the youngest of you now, I first met Raymond Thomas Lawrence, and I've never left him since, and he has never left me. Sometimes I've hated him, really hated him, sometimes he treated me badly, really badly, and sometimes he was the most wonderful uncle a nephew could ever dream of having—*

And so on. Over the years, the Raymond I fashion for people on occasions like this has changed. At first I used to speak in open adulation, giving them the artist as Childe Harold, a self-doubting hero pushing against the boundaries of the tiny culture he'd been born into and breaking every one of its rules: each of his books was a clear step on a predetermined path to greatness. I always concluded with the opening scene from *Kerr*, where the protagonist's long, mad, meandering journey on his home-made raft has brought him to Ibiza, which heaves-to over the horizon and then seems to lift out of the dazzle and glitter of the morning, out of the sea itself, slowly turning and turning in the glittering distance before and above and beyond Kerr's raft: at which point it becomes something else, something mysterious, something out of this world: something even from the heavens—

An extraordinary piece of writing, set in a flash-forward at the start of the novel and one of the many sublime moments in the Master's later work: the magnificence of it makes my voice break with emotion whenever I read that opening page aloud, even after so many years.

In the early days Semple—cruelly—accused me of

speaking, when I addressed public meetings on occasions like this, in *the first person hysterical*. But my emotion was always genuine and often surprised me in the way it seemed to well up and engulf me as I read aloud. Where did it come from, was it real, was this even me who was reading—were the words in fact reading *me*? Was that it? At these times, the power of the written word shocked me, the way the text could take me over as I began to speak it. My audiences were moved by how moved I was, by what they saw as the purity of my soul but was actually the purity of Raymond's or whomsoever's spirit it was—one of his earthbound angels, perhaps—that took us over on these occasions, writer, reader, audience, all. Some of them wept as I read.

And then they didn't. I don't mean they stopped just like that, in the midst of a particular outpouring, but that after a while, over a year or two, I became aware that audiences' responses were changing. I felt it as a change in myself, a tendency (I found) to listen more and more to my own voice as I read. Did I really believe the things that voice was saying, did I really feel the emotion I could hear? At the same time, the status of the public Raymond changed. He left us, in the way with which we're all too familiar—terribly, yes, but—inevitably—in a way that revived much interest in him, albeit interest of this new and unexpected kind. Its grace note was the appearance of the little string dolls I've mentioned, which just seemed to pop up out of nowhere around that time. Out of the culture itself, I suppose, as it tried in its collective way to make sense of what it was that had just happened.

At last someone spat it out: *He died for us*—sprayed anonymously on a wall beneath a shorthand Raymond one sometimes began to find in public places, particularly near the University and the site of the writing school: just a few strokes rendering spectacles and beard above a pair of boots. Then, after a while, a sophistication: a scribble drawn at either side of these, suggesting arms outspread. Now he really *was* dying for us: and now, in my public appearances, I put on an imaginary black armband, so to speak, and introduced a new, plangent *leitmotif* to what I said: I made their transformation of him my own.

As I spoke, he began to change from the questing, larger-than-life figure I knew so well—Don Quixote, Childe Harold, Napoleon himself—to a victim cut down in his moment of triumph. He'd spent his career making enemies, treading on toes, pushing people away—who better to know *that* than I?—and, as I've made plain, there'd been at least as many negative responses to his elevation as there'd been positive, as well as those who openly revelled in the news of his illness when it came. Suddenly, from the nature of his death, all this vanished. Raymond belonged to the ages. How much I made of that!

Today, though—and this is the first time I've felt this—today it feels as if he doesn't quite belong anywhere at all. There's a mood change in the room, something which is new again in turn and which I am slowly picking up as I talk. I'm sure I'm not wrong. The wry self-deprecations get no response at all, the practised little jokes fall flat, the emotion as I read—from *Kerr* again, with as much fullness of feeling as ever—reaches out to dead air and fails. Near the back, a youth even seems to have his eyes closed, with anything but a rapt look about the rest of him. Another, unforgivably, is at work on his wretched phone, pressing away at it throughout, his brows a knot.

Eventually, I come to my peroration. It proceeds. It ends, magnificently as always. I wait.

Nothing happens. Not anger, not outright rejection,

but worse—nothing very much at all. In fact it seems that they *can't be arsed*—

Now Cosmo stands up.

'Questions!' he says brightly, grinding his palms, the one against the other. 'Questions?'

Again, nothing.

We wait. Then, at last, a lass near the front:

'How d'you get stuff published?'

This interests them: there's a stir. The texting youth stops and looks up. Publication!

'Well!' I smile at them. 'First you have to write something!' Not a dog stirs. Did I sound condescending?—unreadable, this group. No, unwritten, that's it. *Unwritten*. I scramble to recover. 'I'm sure Cosmo and the team have discussed this—'

And it's at this point that the door simply *flings* open: Robert Semple—he's standing there in his fedora, looking in, looking at us! The class turns as one and gazes, lost to me in a second.

He gazes, confidently quartering the room. Now he steps in and presses the door shut behind him.

Someone has just asked me a question. 'King Carl Gustaf,' I reply, as I watch Semple stepping awkwardly between legs and feet. 'The King of Sweden. Although the actual Prize was presented by the chairman of the panel.' And: 'Yes?' to another questioner.

Now Semple has paused to bend over a young student: I can hear his robust, sibilant whisper: *yes-yes?* She nods back up at him: *yes, yes*. I try to ignore them. Another child-woman is putting a question to me, flatly and without eye contact.

'Why should we read him today? Lawrence?'

Semple has found a seat now, near the back, between two young women who also seem to know him well.

The questioner is one of the little-string-Raymond-wearers. I point at the tiny thing on her blouse. 'Well, let's start by *me* asking *you* a question. Why do you wear that? What does it mean to you?'

She stares down herself as if she's forgotten the thing is on her, almost as if she's astonished to see she has a body. She looks up and past me.

'Nothing,' she says. 'I just wear it.'

'You just wear it?'

'I found mine.' This is the student next to her. She looks down and gives her mini-Raymond a little flick. 'I didn't realise it was him, then someone told me.'

'Does it mean anything to you?'

'It's sort of like what you were saying.' This is the first young woman again. 'Just now—you know, you were talking about, you know?'

'I found it on the ground, and I'm like, y'know, what the fuck—?'

'You can get them crucified.' This from the back. 'You know, on a cross, an actual cross—'

'Yeah, but have you, like, *seen* one?' This from about midway in the class. 'Like, you know, actually *seen* one?'

Cosmo intervenes. 'What's your favourite Lawrence novel?' he says to the class, encouragingly.

A pause.

'They're fucking *long*.' The first woman again. 'I tried a couple but I was like, you know, fuck it—'

'I haven't even started him!' This blasphemy from a cheery youth to the left brings a dreary titter. 'I got one for *Christmas*, but—y'know?'

Semple stirs and straightens: his brown hat seems to elevate at least six inches as he sits up. '*I* haven't read them all and *I'm* on the fucking Trust!' he says. A great belch of laughter from the class. 'Not sure I've read *any* of them right through!' Another great belch, and the hat settles contentedly back down. There are several seconds before the laughter dies away: I could wring his neck.

'Thank you, Robert!' Cosmo. 'In your usual form! Right! Let's have a show of hands. Who's read *one* Raymond Lawrence?'

A few hands go up.

'*Two* to *four*?'

Fewer.

'More? No'—here he points at me—'*You* don't qualify, Peter, you've got an unfair start—'

Lifeless, soundtrack laughter. I realise that, among the creative writing students at least, no one in the room has read all of Raymond—and, astonishingly, some cheerfully admit to having read none of him whatsoever, none at all!

'Oh, dear,' says Cosmo. 'Some work to do here. He *is* demanding, I have to admit, Raymond Lawrence does take it out of you. A great figure in our pantheon, for sure, but—well!' He claps his hands together meaninglessly, cocks his wrist for his watch, claps some more. 'Thank you, Peter, for your fascinating account!'

Again, a dispiriting sputter of applause. Semple's hat begins to levitate: Cosmo's big, soft, pink, teacherly hands start popping against each other again. 'Time for our second visitor!' he cries.

Semple is up, and stepping his way carefully to the front, leaning, touching, murmuring, as he makes his way familiarly through the class. Everything here is known to him: he is in his medium, the peculiar little snowglobe of university life.

I suddenly realise. He's going to read poetry—no one has warned me: I make my way to a rear seat and shut my eyes. Ah, God.

Robert's performance never varies. One moment he's

joshing amid the motley, the next he's approaching the lectern and the business of riffling through his papers as if suddenly called upon by Hera herself. Always a long, studied pause, once he's at the lectern, as his fingers flutter the pages this way and that and he mimes the crisis of decision: and then, always, the sacramental moment as he smuggles a headband from his hip pocket—the only time his hat ever leaves his body, this, baring thick, implausible, metallic hair: slowly, reverentially, he places the band about his own head, low at the temples, and pauses, before settling down to read—

Oh, how Raymond lacerated him for this vanity when he first heard tell of it! *You pretentious little turd!* he told him. *Who d'you think you are, Napoleon at Notre Dame?*—and so on, and sometimes worse than this, too: but to no effect, since Semple goes on crowning himself in public readings to this day and has even spawned younger imitators amongst his creative writing progeny who do much the same. For he, too, like so many others, attempts to teach that which, according to Raymond, cannot be taught: his coterie call themselves *the Cuffers*, after one of his earlier collections, titled—lamentably—*Cuffing Myself.* The public readings of our small, charming but shabby city are full of solemn boys and girls who announce their translation from this world to another with much the same flim-flam of self-coronation as he does.

I open my eyes: the Napoleonic moment is over. We are in the sanctum.

'Lady Blue,' the poet begins, in the piping, spectral voice he seems always to reserve for these moments. He coughs into his hand, a little, shrill, unmanned cough, suitable for higher things. He begins to read—

And the phone in my pocket starts up!

Dear God, dear *God*, how embarrassing—I hate the

thing at the best of times and use it only for purposes of the Trust: and now here it is, singing out its desolate little grace note. An involuntary shout of laughter from the class and then I'm up and stepping unevenly between legs and feet and fumbling in my pocket—Semple left at the lectern palms to face and his headband forlorn and disempowered, popped up slightly from its usual grip on his brow.

At the door I turn back and mouth *sorry* to him: and step outside, into the corridor and then the bright, leafy, eye-squinting quadrangle, the phone pressed to the side of my head.

This voice in my ear, its strange mixture of sounds—I know it, I know this woman, but it takes a few seconds for my mind to catch up with itself.

'—tried your office but, no,' it's saying into my head. 'Then I found this number and I thought you wouldn't mind—'

Geneva. Geneva Trott is on my phone.

'—important new development I'm sure you'll be interested in,' her voice is telling me. 'And of course the other Trust members as well—'

Geneva Trott is speaking to me—

Geneva Trott. Long the bane of our lives on the Trust, long the cross we've all had to bear, and the one person in the world who can unite the four of us in rage—all I have to do is bring up her name. For many years now she has been a senior lecturer in English at a distinguished university to the north, and, in all those years, the dogged, mulishly relentless devotee of the only writer she seems to know of or care about in the whole wide world—quite possibly the only writer she's ever read: Raymond Thomas Lawrence. How many years is it since she first burst in on our little world with *Raymond Lawrence: Years of Lightning* (1983), a literary-critical biography published in a tired life-and-works series that was a graveyard for third-rate lit-crits and fifth-rate writers? A bolt from the blue, or into it: and riddled with the dozen dozen tiny errors (plus a few real howlers) that came from its attempt to get around our collective gate, so to say, without the common courtesy of a rattle or a knock.

Let me count the ways. For a start, she got Raymond's birthdate wrong—only by a day, but a full twenty-four hours nonetheless, a slip that spoke volumes about the efficiency of long-distance guesswork, her primary scholarly *modus operandum* as far as we were able to judge. Then she dated several of his publications wrongly, and wrote his novels *The Outer Circle Transport Service* as *The Outer Service Transport Circle* and *Nineteen Forty-Eight* as *Nineteen Eighty-Four.* Thomas Hamilton, the protagonist of both those novels, became John Hamilton in a couple of places, and, once—rewardingly—John Thomas: throughout, other names, both those of characters and those of actual people, wrinkled and slid. I was referred to throughout as Peter Or—well, I was mentioned a couple of times in her rotten little book and that is how she had me in each, as if I were nothing more, as far as she was concerned, than that single prepositional conjunction Raymond first identified in me, as you'll see in a page or two. I was livid, of course—I mean, the *cheek* of it. The cheek of the whole thing, come to that.

Her biggest howler of all, though, was to have Raymond brought up in a place in which, to our knowledge, *he had never even set foot!* A wrong turn here and another there as (I presume: if she can make things up, so can I) she drove about North Canterbury in her (again, I'm guessing) Trabant, her ordnance survey map on her lap and the dazzle of the sun in her eyes. And in the end she settled (it seemed) on a dreadful little property up a long driveway off the even longer desolation of Cornwallis Road, too nondescript itself even to have a name—nothing much else to be seen, so this (she presumably presumed in her *lumpen*, oafish way) must be it.

She seems to have got up the drive far enough to catch a look at the farmhouse and its surrounding buildings, because her description is vivid in the way a townie could never make up, with small details beyond her invention that she could have seen only at first-hand: and it is among these that she placed young Raymond in her richly subjunctive account of his early years—*Young Raymond would have wandered the rugged, rolling hills, learning them till they became as familiar as the back of his hand*—putting him out to milk cows never farmed in the area at that time, forcing him to shiver through chilly nights that whistled between parted weatherboards far different from the sturdy brick clad of Hamilton Downs, the two- (and in places three-) storey pile in which (until boarding school smiled at him its beckoning, Sodoma smile) he was actually raised.

Hamilton Downs was—still is—about twenty miles due north of the Tobacco Road nightmare she had him in, on 2500 acres of rolling pastureland. It ran Corriedales for the dry conditions, and when things got wetter in the 1970s it switched to Highlanders, which (Ernie, the farm manager, informs me) are what it runs to this day. Not a cow in sight, there or anywhere else. Raymond, being Raymond, claimed to have lost his innocence amongst the farm animals and would provide details unasked, not least in a notorious interview with a bewildered Swedish journalist at the time of the award ceremony, one of the few relicts of that time you can still find on YouTube

('Raymond Lawrence + gumboots').

This was after the publication of *Raymond Lawrence: Years of Lightning*, so Geneva was not able to fold it into her meticulously improvised long-distance Freudian psychoanalysis, which made so much of the various ties, walking sticks, telephone poles and tall trees in Raymond's *oeuvre*, not to mention the occasional cupboard or cave—the scene in *Flatland* in which protagonist and antagonist shelter together under a ragged outcrop of a hill *while she holds his walking stick* seemed almost to drive her into a frenzy of hermeneutic retrieval.

On the other hand, it has to be admitted that she got some things right, disturbingly so, and there were details in her book she couldn't possibly have known unaided and which made the hair on the back of my neck stand up when I read them. Where had she got them from—which member of the inner circle had let them slip, who in the Trust, which of the gardeners, which of the accountants, who else in the support team, larger as it was in those days? *Which of you took the thirty pieces of silver*, I asked them one by one: and it seemed, at the end of it, that the answer was: none of them.

That, I didn't believe, and I acted accordingly. What other than a betrayal—a series of betrayals, dozens of betrayals—could explain Geneva's extraordinary, dangerous moments of knowledge, never stated but always there, somehow, between certain of her lines? No need to say anything further at this point, or, indeed, anything at all: and, of course, those of you unfortunate enough to know Geneva's sad little book, with its brave, jolly, life-affirming cover, may have some idea of what I'm talking about. We still seek some of the culprits.

And now here am I, standing beneath the gingko tree appalled and shocked and with her voice still in my ear.

Tapes, she told me. *Video*tapes? I demanded. No, no, audiotapes, she said. Sound tapes. Tapes of an interview. Interview? I asked her. Who with?

*

Oops. Tape stopped. Where was I? Yeah, most of the time all I had to do was fish him out of the downstairs garden room when the sun was going and get him onto the elevator, you know, the wheelchair platform that comes up by the front door? He was in good shape then, he wasn't shaking all that much earlier on because I was injecting him same time each day and ditto with the pills, and the massage helped, too—wasn't paid to do that but he asked me, he says give us a rub, go on. Every now and then, though, I'd notice things on him—like, I remember he'd been biting the inside of his bottom lip when he was eating, he told me that and I looked and there was quite a big wet-sore in there. Didn't used to do that, he tells me. He'd got a mouth full of blood.

Anyway, that first day at the Residence Either-Or takes me through the house, see, he makes me do the tour and first up he says I have to sign the visitor's book! Why do I have to sign it, I ask him, and he says*, well, you're a visitor, aren't you, or do you live here?* And that seemed fair enough even though it was a bit sarky. So I signed up, you know, *Wham-Bam Thom Ham Thank you Ma'am*. Turns out there's all sorts of people've signed, he wouldn't let me read all of it but like for example there was this guy who'd done the tour the weekend before and he just signed himself *The Bishop,* you know, like he's dropped in off a chess board? And then there was that painting there, too, on the wall I mean, you must've seen it, Patrick, you know, where you come in?—craziest painting I ever seen, just the back of his head? Why'd they paint it back to front like that? I couldn't see the point, you know, just zits and hickeys and a bald spot?

So I'm just having a look-round and Mr Orr, he says to me, *Don't touch the ornaments, please, we find they're getting stolen.* Just looking, I tell him. Is that Mr Lawrence there?—because there's all these photos and there it was, it was Mr Lawrence, I recognised him from the telly only he was much younger in the photograph, his hair was black and his beard was black and white in patches, he looked like a badger. *That's him,* says Either-Or. Who's that with him? I asked, there was this young man in some of the photos but he wouldn't say who it was. Then he says, *the Master loves humanity but he can't stand people*, and when I look at him, y'know, like, *what*? he says to me, *it's a quote*, and he turns away like I'm the dumbest prick in the class—like I'm in old Tinny's special class, that's how he talks to me. This teacher at my school, took all the mongrel kids?—Mr Tinetti.

Well, next thing I had a look in the bog and I'd never seen a throne that size, you could bath a baby in there, you could just about get in there and have a bath yourself! *It's because of the age of the house,* Either-Or says. *Now here's the second bedroom, he sometimes writes in here at this desk in the evenings*. And we're in the little bedroom it turns out I'd end up sleeping in for a while before we all shifted up to the Chicken Coop—I'd no idea back then it'd come to that but it did! I'd turned into, like, a male nurse at that stage. There was a big rolltop desk in the little bedroom and I'd stack my camp bed in behind it when I packed up for the day, that and the sleeping bag and so on, and I'll tell you what, it was as uncomfortable as anywhere I slept in my life. But I had to be nearby because he'd started not making it through the night by that stage, the way I've been telling you. And I'd give him his lunch, too—big joke, that was like pushing a meat pie through a keyhole, he was that disinterested those days—you'd need a bloody microscope to find a meat pie round the Chicken Coop, by the way, did I tell you that, they were all vegos? First thing in my time off, I'd go out and find myself a good meat pie or a burger, whatever'd got something in it that'd looked over a wall, that's what my old man used to say. I looked in the fridge for a feed when I first got there—up at the Coop, I mean—and what they'd got in there was that healthy it made me sick. And I thought, maybe that's why Mr Lawrence isn't interested in his lunch, maybe I should smuggle him in a T-bone? They were starving him, that was half his trouble, so I used to give him a Bounty Bar now and then and he liked that, he used to say *shit hot a Bounty Bar* and he'd rub his hands together—

Anyway, Mrs Butt—she's the housekeeper, and her old man, he keeps the house and garden together. They're some weird religion but I don't know what it is, I reckon all religions are pretty much the same anyway—like casserole, for years I just thought there was just this stuff called casserole, then someone says to me you can get different kinds, like, for example, they don't always have to have carrot? Anyway, the Butts, I used to call them *Left Butt* and *Right Butt*, y'know, you wouldn't want to come between them? Guess you had to be there. Old Edna, she's Right Butt because there can't be anyone righter than her—old Eric's Left Butt because he always gets left out, even when it's raining? Anyway, Mrs Right Butt, she catches me looking in the fridge and she says to me, *plenty of walnuts in the barrel*—they've got this big walnut tree up the back, full-grown, beautiful thing, and they'd pile the walnuts in this barrel and that's what they seemed to live off, fucking walnuts pardon my French. Walnut loaf, the first time I had a feed up there I thought it was meatloaf and I pigged in and boy was I disappointed, I had to have a couple of Bounty Bars afterwards. And I tell you what, they had this dog up there—Rommel it was called sometimes but then sometimes it was Daisy, I could never work out whether there were two dogs that looked the same or just the one with two names—and anyway, they fed this dog walnuts! I never seen such a miserable-looking dog, eating a bowl of walnuts, and I tell you what, it needed a bloody good wash and I used to do that, I'd give it a dunk from time to time when the old man was snoozing. I'll tell you what happened to *him*, sometime, too. Rommel. Unless it was Daisy.

Mrs Butt, though. You said you wanted to know about the staff back then when I started and she was one of them. I couldn't believe how many people Either-Or had round the place when I turned up, I mean just for one man, you know? It's like it's Raymond Lawrence Incorporated or something. Seven women who did the garden when I first got there—that's what really got to me, they did it all for nothing back then when I started?—not just Val and the six others, but all of them as far as I can see. That's an exaggeration, because there's the Butts, they were paid from the start. When things first got difficult with Mr Lawrence old Eric Butt'd drive him round in the Dodge as well, this big old car he had in the garage—every bastard and his son went for a drive in it as far as I can see, just not me, I was the only one that was kept from inside the car out of all of them, and I still don't get why! Not for months and then suddenly I'm allowed inside it, I'll tell you about that sometime, too.

And there was Mrs Round, too, Mrs A. Round, but I never found out what her first name was because they only ever called her Dot. Dot Round, what a name—she'd been typing up his writing for a hundred years by the time I got there,

Mr Lawrence's, and she turned up every afternoon and she typed his stuff up that he writes out in longhand. She reckoned she was the only one could read it. He'd sit down there in the sunroom with this funny little desk thing across his knees and he'd write, it was years since I'd seen someone doing that, you know, writing with a fountain pen? When I ask him for a look at it he says to me, what did you expect, a quill? It's a Parker 51, he says, it's over fifty years old, that pen. That must be worth a bit, I told him, but he never said anything when I said that. He just made sure he took it back off me! And then he went on writing with it—bright blue ink, I remember that—though Val told me he was just going through the motions more and more those days, they reckoned what he was writing wasn't up to much, they just let him write.

And old Dot, she'd turn up each day and type it out for him at the dining table in the front room, page after page of this bullshit. She'd got this old electric typewriter, it used to go like a bloody machinegun—that's what I called her, Machinegun Round, but she didn't seem to like it much when I did that. Dot, she'd say to me, call me Dot. Didn't do her much good in the end, but I'll tell you about that some other time, too. I've got that much to tell you and most of it you won't believe. Oh, yes, and Mr Semple, he told me they were all Catholics, see, I mean everyone at Raymond Lawrence Incorporated, and I said how d'you know that, and he says well, Thom, they've always got colds, that's how you tell whether people are Catholics or Protestants, the Micks have always got a slightly runny nose. And, you know what, it took me a couple of weeks to realise he was pulling my tit?

Right, where are we now on the guided tour?—the Blue Room. Right. At least forty-five minutes it's taken us to get to this end room and he's still going strong, Either-Or, in this big actory voice. But then, that's what he is anyway, a big act. I told him at the end, *you should sell tickets*, and he looks at me like I'm a fly on a fruitcake and he says to me, but we're open for the public good, Mr Ham, that's the point. He used to say it like he was Noddy talking to his dinner, *Hullo Mr Ham, hullo Mr Salad*. This is before he starts calling me Gradus. Anyway: *The Blue Room*, he says in this special voice, like I'm colour-blind, know what I mean, can't see what the bloody colour is when I'm standing there staring at it? *This was added on to the Residence as the Master's fame was beginning to bring him the material rewards he cared for least. Here we find the most treasured*—and off he goes again.

I can't remember it all—what he said, you know—but I can remember what I thought when he was saying it, I thought, we're all onstage now. It was like a play, all for show, everything too neat, like in a museum, and Mr Orr, he's going through the story of Mr Lawrence's life in pictures and I'm thinking, *for God's sake, open a window!* Because it was that muggy in there I couldn't hardly breathe. And of course the main part of the show was up on the wall in amongst the posters and the pictures of the old boy, it was the medal he got in Stockholm, Mr Lawrence, all framed up on the wall and another frame underneath with the citation thing that goes with the medal. Of course it's not the real thing, I found that out later, the real one's in a bank and this is a fake—you wouldn't put a twenty-four carat gold medal up on the wall and then call the public in, would you? But the citation's the real one, apparently, no tricks there, it's bolted to the wall. And the medal looks like a medal, you could have fooled me it was the real thing, I don't know why he tells people it's not. Fakes always look real to me, anyway, I mean, what's the difference if they both look exactly the same? Which one's which?

Well, I'm taking all this in because it's the best part of the tour, and I'm standing there staring at the medal and I'm thinking, how much'd that be worth? And Mr Orr, he stops talking. He hasn't stopped doing his routine since we come up the steps and in the front door, hardly, and now, all of a sudden—boom! I take a look at him and he's just standing there looking up at the medal, and I can't tell you what his face was like, it was that weird. Well, he almost looked nice, that's how different he was, he almost looked like a nice person for a minute, he looked like he wasn't bullshitting and he wasn't putting anyone down—almost like he liked himself after all, just a little bit? Can't describe it. I haven't seen it on him again. He's just staring and staring at the medal, and then he says, very low, *oh, he's a great man. He is a great man*. And I don't know whether he's saying this to me or to himself, because he's not looking at me and I can't hardly hear him, so I don't say anything. To tell you the truth it's all a bit up-close-and-personal for me and I don't really like that, I like to keep things, you know, floating along, how's-your-day sort of thing, know what I mean? So I turn away very slow, and I make out I'm interested in other things, up on the walls and that, and I creep out a bit and into the little hallway the bedrooms go off and I sort of tiptoe back into the dining room after that, back where we started, and I'm standing there wondering, what do I do next? Do I just fuck off there and then, or do I wait for Mr Orr to finish his prayers?—I didn't even know whether I'd got the job or not at that stage.

And then, just like that, there's this loud click downstairs, and this really deep buzz starts up under my feet, you know, *bzzzzz*, and I can feel it in the floorboards, it's really giving them a shake. It's coming up through my feet and after a few seconds this weird thing starts happening—this ever happened to you, Patrick? It's like it's going through the floorboards and up my left leg, and I'm thinking, oh, no, oh bloody *no!*—it starts giving me a silly! The weirdest thing, me standing there watching the elevator platform starting to go down—it leaves this big square hole in the floor by the door when it does that—and I'm getting a hard-on from the vibration! *It's* going down *bzzzzz* and *I'm* going up! And then it stops—the buzzing, I mean, not the hard-on—and you can hear a bit of shuffling down there in the downstairs room, and then it starts up again, *bzzzzz*—and in a few seconds this head comes up through the trapdoor then his shoulders then his body and it's like Old Nick himself, in front of me and coming up out of Hell—I couldn't move!

Then the noise stops—and there he is. He's sitting there, the old man, in a wheelchair on the elevator platform, this little old geezer with a white beard and hair and no rims on his glasses and a bit red in the face—there he is, large as life in front of me—*small* as, I should say, he was small, he was a little bloke, he wasn't that big but I always remember him bigger than he was. There he is in front of me, Mr Raymond Thomas Lawrence, Nobel Prize winner for writing things. And he sits there staring up at me in his wheelchair—I can hear Either-Or behind me all the time this is happening, he's coming back from the Blue Room—he sits there staring at me and staring at me, the old man, like he can see everything, he can see through the front of my jeans. And he says to Mr Orr, *who the hell's this fucking prick*? And then he looks back at me and he does this strange, strange thing, Patrick, he looks me straight in the eye and he fixes me with a wink. He looks straight at me and he winks, and he *fixes me*—

V

What was I doing in Raymond's world, anyway, why was I living with my uncle in the first place? I know I left him looking very dramatic and forbidding as he turned away from me over that autumn garden fire the time I first glimpsed him, the image of my late father caught in the family album and, hence, his very image in my small young mind. Later, I worked it out: at that point, he was almost the exact age my father would have been when there was that business with the tractor. When he was killed, I mean.

Pater renati: the family resemblance was remarkable, but the *emotional* impact of things unconsciously recalled and discharged into my very limbs was far greater than that. Seeing him again—in effect, seeing my father coming out of a past I could barely remember—turned me to jelly. It took me several weeks to tremble my way up Cannon Rise again. Those were my first moments of adult life, I suppose, the first times I felt emotions pushing and pulling me at the same time, my body doing something while the rest of me was trying to get away. *The great hee-haw*, Raymond used to call it, not especially helpfully, and at other times he'd say *remember Jacob*. I toiled up his hill, full of apprehension, and leaned against my bike again, under the little red cliff that marked his lower boundary, and could hardly move.

And on this second visit to Raymond's house I found a completely different man. That is how it seemed to me. This time he spotted me first: *Back again?* he called out. *Casing the joint?* Just the voice at first and from behind: he'd been following me up the road from Tony Martin's store down the bottom, with a loaf and a carton of eggs held against his jersey. *Or d'you want to buy the place? Might be a bit beyond your pocket.* I could smell his sweat as he caught up to me. *Come on in, though, come in,* he said, as if an interest in real estate really was what had brought me there. All this lost, of course, on my unlick'd eleven-year-old self.

And, for the next half hour or so, he bewildered me even more, as he took me around the place.

As he did so he assumed the role of a real-estate-agent-cum-tour-guide, pointing out the view at the same time as he showed me his work-desk (*of course, I do my best work downstairs, with the doors open to the garden*). He pulled out the sliding wooden tray in the kitchen to slice his loaf, and demonstrated the gas range, the like of which I'd never seen before in my life—I've never turned that range on in the years since without associating its initial, edgy burst of flame with that first day with him in what was to become the Residence, and, for me, quite soon, a completely new life. *Boof!*

There was no elevator in those early days, of course, but he took me down to the garden room under the house via the front steps and the garden itself: *here's* where it happens, he told me. *Here's* where it *really* happens. In that chair there, on that little wooden lap desk thing—it's called *un bureau d'écritoire*—and with paper and a pen! That's how you write books. Forget typewriters, he said. They're the invention of the devil!

And so on: quite a performance for a bookish young lad to take in, I can tell you: it gave me goosebumps.

Isn't it extraordinary, by the way, that I insistently remember the Blue Room as being present when I think back to those times, long before it was actually built more than twenty years later—that I remember it in every detail down to the sofa and the Steinway baby grand, remember him actually taking me through it? A fact that surely casts doubt over every single thing I'm telling you here, I realise that, I really do understand that.

In due course, the tour was done. He stood with me in the kitchen, looking down at me as I stared at the trodden green-and-red linoleum, and at his shoes.

Make me an offer, he said. *Go on.*

I think you might be my uncle, I replied.

I've never known what to make of his reaction to this. *Yes, yes, yes,* he said, and turned back towards the room we'd just left. *Now, guess what's special about that piano?*

Had he already worked our relationship out, and, if so, how? Not from appearance, since I look little like either parent, as it happens. Was he dismissing a potty intruder, a juvenile would-be Raymond Thomas Lawrence IV? Or had my offer in fact taken him by surprise, and was he playing for time?

Whichever the answer, he always behaved as if my appearance in his life was completely to be expected. As far I could tell, the only surprise was my surname, which had changed with my mother's funeral-baked marriage: *Orr!* he said. *How wonderful! I collect parts of speech!* Prepositions (properly, in my case, a *prepositional conjunction*, as he pointed out) joined things up, and thus were the most important parts of any sentence that really was trying to communicate something. *They control relationship!* he said. *Try to imagine writing anything even slightly complex without them. They're the parts of speech most susceptible to sociolinguistic change, and when you're gaga and you start to forget everything, they're the last parts of speech to go, did you know that? Prepositions? The cockroaches of language, they'll survive everything!*

This sort of thing later on, when I was more nearly

up to it and had registered that his secretary was *Mrs A. Round* and his cleaner *Mrs During*, and later, when they came along, three of the gardening ladies *Mrs Upton*, *Mrs Underwood* and *Mrs Overton* and his housekeeper and handyman, hired later, *Mr and Mrs Butt. I'd never employ a verb*, I remember him saying a few years after that, at some drunken *soirée* or other. *They always run off with my objects.* (*What d'you expect*, he demanded when Geneva's unofficial biography came out in due course: *Trott? A bloody verb!*)

A hundred little Raymond moments. The two of us at that piano he tried to deflect me towards on my first time inside his house—the piano I remember, impossibly, as being at the far end of the Blue Room: its propped-up lid, the grave depth of its French-polished finish, the solemnity of its keyboard, the horror of the scales he taught me, the lumbering first rites of the music lesson: eventually I got as far as *Für Elise*: but do so many of us get so very much further? Then the chessboard, with its large, frankly carved wooden pieces, redolent of North Africa and with which, eventually, I became able to play him at the reasonably sophisticated level of Armageddon and lose nevertheless. The art lessons, mainly from books—at this stage Phyllis had yet to paint her series of portraits of him, but he had one or two good local pieces whose depths he tried to explain to my fuddled, uncomprehending schoolboy-brain.

Throughout all this, language—*his* language, his peculiar, made-up version that's always stayed with me in bits and pieces, often with embarrassing results once I took them to school with me. *Acreptic*—for how many years did I use this word to describe something that was *dried up*, before someone asked me what on earth I was talking about? *Slorpent* was another (tired, sleepy), as well as *sloash* (tea), *shrinky* (underfed), *borgent* (overwhelming), *cranidumb* (a small head), *mentulous* (well-hung), *arker* (penis), and *tendacious* (insistently untrue). There were so many more, too, whose meanings I've forgotten—*fleculent*, *fuscative*, *casulous*, *argile*, more. And then his peculiar little phrases: *bombing Dresden* (for serious matters on the lavatory) mystified me until I read some history, but at least *research outlet* was reasonably self-explanatory—he used this phrase only among academics.

Then there was the first time he broke wind in front of me. I'd been coming to his house regularly each weekend until, after about a year, my mother found out. I told him she had done so, and his response was simply to let fly!

I stood there overwhelmed with embarrassment—lost, I can assure you, with no idea at all of what to do in response. Come on! he called out from the kitchen, where he was making a *bestila*. Your turn next! And he wouldn't let me go home until I'd answered with a pathetic, redfaced, humiliated little toot. Hardly worth waiting for, he told me. I wouldn't even put a match to that. The *posterior trumpet*, he said. That's what Pope called it—no, Pope the *writer*, you silly little prick, not John Paul the fucking Second! Popes don't fart—no, hold on—Pope Zephyrius, he *must* have—

And so on. That's how he got me, bit by bit, in the rippling, unfolding *thisness* of him. I've represented the moment he transfixed me in his gaze, and, afterwards, I experienced the work of *that* often enough to know that there, *there* lay his ultimate power over me, his power over everyone. But, for me, to tell the truth, it could almost as easily be added up from the thousand little things that glued me to him after that. He was a man, after all, but then he was also something else that was different from and larger than that, something I still don't fully understand—but which survives him, whatever it is, and as if he has in fact not gone from me at all. It is that in him which stalks his house at night. Yes, I know how mad that sounds. It frightens me, too.

*

Geneva's voice, dying away from me as I stand here in the smaller quadrangle, outside the English Department. How strange it is to think of *him*, after hearing *her*—we've never met, this woman and I, but I've read her details on her university's website, the dreadful biography made much of amid the endless list of articles about Raymond's work—Raymond Lawrence and the gender trap, Raymond Lawrence and Rainer Maria Rilke, Raymond Lawrence and the Holocaust. More is less. I've gazed at the image of the woman who has produced this rot, at the harmless lemon of her face, her large, unloved bosom and the brave flutter of gauze at her neck.

That such a woman should stand in judgement of such a man—

Little enough anyone anywhere has written over the years comes near him, as far as I've read, but there's not a sign in *this* woman's writing that she understands anything of him at all. I mean the essence of him, the thing that made him different. His strangeness, his mystery, his genius, his madness. She makes him sound like Anthony Powell.

Bright today, the weather, but cool: the gingko's yellow-green leaves surge above my head. She's rattled me, Geneva, she's rattled me not just by ringing—she's never rung us before—but by what she's had to say. *Audiotapes.* I'll have to call a meeting, of course, of course I will, but, really, I've simply no idea what to make of this sniper shot she's just fired into our midst. *A number of audiotapes.* Her unexpected voice, raw like broken eggs, telling me this from several hundred miles away. *A person of interest.* Geneva Trott, dragging *there* into *here*, *then* into *now,* where it never belongs.

Ah, God, the present tense, I remember Raymond saying once—more than once: *how I hate it!* He didn't have to explain. *That's why we write things down,* he said. *The present is so fucking unsatisfactory. That's why we write fiction.* I remember him gesturing about himself. *This is never going to mean anything, is it?—not on its own, not without a little help?*

I feel it now, what he meant back then. Here am I, pushing at the letters on my phone, tapping and deleting and starting again, *tap-tap-tap-tap-tap* in a travesty of normal, traditional communication: *mrgncy mtg rsdnce*—I can't type capitals on this thing, I can't even do numbers quickly: it takes so long just to say *7:00pm.* But—*there*: sent at last, to Marjorie and Julian only, at this point, in case Semple is still performing to Cosmo's class a few feet away from me now. Have I sent it, though, or have I saved it?—and how do I find out? How have we got to such a pass as this? Is this how to live in the present?

You can't plot the present, that's the trouble, my uncle used to say. *You're only safe when it gets away from* <u>*now*</u> *and you can start lying, that's when it all starts to add up. That's when it gets real, when the bullshit starts. The bullshit makes it true.*

Back in the car I find I'm trembling slightly, a weakness just above each elbow, nothing much but *a sure sign I need to read something* (Raymond's voice in my ear again) after the deep unsatisfactoriness, the outright *unwrittenness* of the morning.

A curious little episode, by the way, as I drive home from the university, and something that comes about, surely, because of my thinking the various thoughts I've just shared with you. I look in my rear-view mirror—and there, right behind, me is a 1948 Dodge exactly like Raymond's, its bodywork the very same dark damson blue! I'm so shocked I almost swerve off the road. When I look away and look back it's still there—real enough, it seems: and for a few seconds I genuinely do believe it's the old man himself here in the present and after me again, irrational though it might be to think so.

I signal and pull in to the kerb and, as he whizzes past me, get a glimpse, nothing more, of the man at the wheel—clearly a man, perhaps an older man, but in the half-second I have to look into the car there's nothing more I can see of him. The Dodge is exactly like Raymond's and could easily be his, except that, of course, and for the obvious reason, it can't possibly be so. Really, though, it's *exactly* like his old car. It even drives off as he would have driven it, as Raymond used to drive, far too fast and overtaking everything ahead, and with an eager hand on the horn, I can tell you, just as his used to be.

*

So, anyway, Patrick, that's how I got started at the Raymond Lawrence Residence! Part-time at the start and that suited me fine except I had to get the old geezer out of the sack first thing every morning, and, just my luck, he's always up at sparrow-fart! So I'd be up before six just to get there on time, I'd bike across town and up to Cannon Rise and he'd be lying there reading *Auto Trader.* He'd always say, *got a Bounty Bar on you?* I'd tell him no, and he'd say, well, looks like a country breakfast, then. He meant, just a pee and a look-round.

Sometimes I'd ask myself what I was there for, other times I'd be earning my money because I'd have to get him going the way I told you. Never very often back then, and if you ran into him later in the day you'd never pick anything wrong. Then I could do what I liked till the evening, I'd bike to the gym or I'd spend time with Raewyn, this woman I was seeing, and then I'd bike back across town and up to the Residence and he'd be ready for me to help him into bed, ten or earlier. A hard life!—not. Tell you the truth, I couldn't work out why they'd hired me?

He'd work in the downstairs sunroom like I said, but he'd go into it from the garden not the house. I'd look in the drawers in his bedroom upstairs and there'd be his things there, like hankies and ties I mean, but he never went in to get one. It was like he'd left his life in the Residence behind. Old Either-Or caught me doing that, one time, having a look-round, and he gives me hell. I'm just getting him a hankie, I tell him, and he says, *Mr Lawrence has plenty of handkerchiefs up in the Chicken Coop, there's no need for anyone unauthorised to be in the Residence*. But he's the author, I tell him, and he gives me his fly-on-a-fruitcake look. *The Residence is a museum*, he says to me. *No human life occurs in it, it's about the past, that's the point of it.* Something like that is what he says. He says, *like his fiction, it's about the past and the pastness of the past*. And then he says—just turning away, this is his style, you know, fuck-you Noddy just piss off, know what I mean?—he says to me, *as you'd find in his work if you were able to read it*. Well, up yours, is what I thought, and I made up my mind right there to have a go at one of the old man's books sometime, though like I've said, I'm not a reader. So a bit after that, I slip one of his books out of the Residence. It had *treasure hunt* in the title, I thought it might be interesting, I thought it might be a mystery story?

Well, I have to tell you, Patrick—have you read it? I guess you must've. Anyway, I couldn't make that much of it, I'd read a bit and I'd be thinking of something else, and then I'd make myself read some more and I'd be looking out the window. I'd look down and it'd be like, you know, *page five*. Couldn't get anywhere with it. I skip ahead and there's weird things, like when the children get into the forest and this witch turns up, except it's not a witch? Is she really doing what it seems like she's doing to them? How'd he get someone to *print* stuff like that? And give him a prize for it? And what's she meant to *be,* this witch lady, what's she meant to be if she isn't a witch? All this death stuff all the time, on and on about death. Is she a beetle in the end, is that what she turns into? I had a peek at that bit but I couldn't work it out. I gave up on it. I felt bad about that but I thought, how can anyone read stuff like that? They give you the Nobel Prize for *that*? Crikey dick!

Anyway, where was I—yeah, I was telling you about the Chicken Coop. The Butts are in one of the bedrooms and Either-Or's in one of the others, and Mr Lawrence, he was down the end, he was in this bedroom with an *en suite* that opens on another bedroom the other side, and that's the one I went into when I shifted in later on. Four bedrooms. I'd just walk through into his room, and when I'd give him a shower I'd lug him into the *en suite* and I'd get the wet weather gear on and I'd hold him up under the spray with one hand and soap him up with the other, and I'll tell you something, Patrick, the only way you can do that is while you're thinking of something else! Doesn't worry me now, but it sure as hell did when I started off, it shook me up but you don't want to know about that. So I'd think of Raewyn while I was doing it and sometimes I'd think of Val, the way I'd call out to her when she was gardening just so she'd stand up and I'd see the Jersey Bounce.

Where was I? Right—early days, that's what you asked for. When I turned up the place was still crawling with visitors, and that's when they first started talking about shifting Mr Lawrence out—he didn't like it, I can tell you that, he kicked up a hell of a fuss, you should have heard the language. *I* swear a bit—can't help it, just comes out—and I thought I'd heard everything, but Mr Lawrence, some of the things he used to say! And he said it to everyone, he didn't care. I asked him about it once, I say to him, ever have your mouth washed out when you were a kid? And he stares at me that hard I wish I hadn't said it. *What d'you mean?* he says, and I tell him, your language. And he says, *what language*? I was getting a bit rattled by now. The bad language, I told him. *What bad language?* he says. *Enlighten me. Listen, they're all just words and no one tells me which ones I can use and which ones I can't, right?* And he screws up his eyes at me when he says that. I thought he was going to hit me, I really did, that was the first time I thought that, and then later on he did, he did use to hit me towards the end, not hard but he was trying.

Right, where was I?—yeah, back when he got the big prize and everyone wanted to know him. Mrs Butt told me the day the news come out, the place was crawling with people. The Nobel people ring you up, she said—you know, *how's your day, oh, by the way, you've won the Nobel Prize*? Then they announce it and everyone wants to know you. There was reporters and cameramen hanging off the trees, she told me. One minute it was peaceful, she says, and the next, there's the phone going all day and there's twelve dozen bunches of flowers delivered in four days! It was October and we had a garden full of spring flowers, she reckoned, but there's flowers in cellophane out the house and down the path to the garage, we were giving them away? Any Tom, Dick and

Harry'd turn up with stuff, they'd bake the old fellow a sponge or they'd leave a bloody casserole on the front step! There was people standing down by the garage and just staring up at the house, just staring, and she used to wonder what it was they were after, she told me. It's not his books, she says, apparently there's special things in them but it's no good people like us trying to get them out. That's what she told me. Fancy folk like Mr Orr and his friends, literary folk, that's their job, that's what they do, that's the point of them, she says. Down at the university. Well, after I'd had a go at reading him like I said, I reckoned she was right, Either-Or and his arty-fart friends can keep the books for themselves and the rest of us can have what's left over. The people who come to visit the Residence, they're after something else, she says. Mrs Butt, Right Butt, she told me that. They don't care about the books, she said. There's something else they want.

*

OK, from Julian, when he replies to my text, and from Semple, after I contact him later in the day: *Thks fr fkg up my rdg.*

In person, though, when we gather in the Residence dining room, he seems to have got over it.

'Where's Marge?' he demands, and then, inevitably, makes an unpleasant suggestion, one which I won't record here.

'*You'll* have to be Hon. Sec., Jules,' he says. 'Be buggered if it's me.'

Julian, being Julian, reluctantly agrees: he fumbles up a piece of paper and begins to scribble at it. I look at my watch. 7:07pm.

Semple has a paper package, though, which he is sliding onto the table.

‘Guess what I’ve got here,’ he says.

The three of us stare at it. Oh, where is Marjorie, that we might start?

‘Look!’ Semple, tearing the wrapping from the parcel.

Julian stares. ‘Well—what d’you know?’ he says. ‘It’s back!’

The stolen ashtray—the stolen paua shell ashtray, unwrapped and on the table in front of us!

‘Stuffed in my letterbox sometime last night. Just that, no writing.’

I stare at the thing. That’s it, all right, I’d recognise it anywhere—the size, the ancient smear of cigar ash, so much darker than cigarette ash, the oh-so-tiny chip on its finer edge. *His* ash, *Raymond’s* ash—my heartbeat quickens. I can’t stop staring at the thing, as if it’s arrived from outer space. Raymond’s ashtray is back—*Raymond* is back. First Geneva, and now him.

How? Why? From where?

‘Well—well!’ I’m trying to sound calm. ‘You really *have* upstaged events. What an extraordinary thing.’

‘Second thoughts,’ Julian says. ‘Isn’t that what it is? D’you think we’ll get anything else back? One of the wax bananas went last week.’

‘Really? Why didn’t you tell me?’ But I’m gazing at the shell in my hand. ‘I’ll put it back on his desk.’

‘Who d’you think’s behind this?’ I can hear Julian as I tread the gunshot board in the hallway. Semple is saying something back to him, but I can’t make it out.

The Master’s desk is against the sill of his bedroom window. There’s an ancient bowl of potpourri on it, a baccarat paperweight, and a lamp that throws a small, soft light on all these when I turn it on, and onto the ashtray beside it.

A paua shell ashtray, already in place, near the lamp.

I stare at the thing, and at the other shell in my hand.

'Look at this,' I call to the others.

Julian comes in and stands next to me, mouth-breathing audibly. Together, we gaze at it. In the circle of light the shell has a dull, subtle gleam.

Semple is behind me. 'Bugger me dead,' he says. 'Look at that.'

An extraordinary moment. The shell in my hand: and, at the same moment, it seems, on the desk in front of us as well—

I look more closely at the interloper. Exactly the same size, exactly the same shape, and with exactly the same ancient dark grey smear of tobacco within: it could be the shell in my hand, caught at exactly the same moment of its former usage and held there. Except that the shell in my hand is a separate thing. It is a shell in my hand.

The moment seizes me. I take the shell from the desk and, slowly, fit it against the other. The two halves come together as a single thing, complete, entire. For a second, I can imagine what it originally was, and, for that second, doing so seems the most powerful idea in the world, something that urgently needs to be thought through.

We return to the dining table and sit.

A silence. Julian breaks it.

'Robert brought in the one that was returned to him yesterday—and the other one—was already there?'

'Correct. Placed there by persons unknown. They're identical. And—look at this.' I pull them apart and put them together again. 'They turn into the former—animal. Creature. Whatever it was.'

Silence. Then:

'Whoop-de-do. So fucking what?'

'No, no!' Julian is eager. 'I can see what Peter means. It sort of recovers the *status quo ante*—'

'They're just seashells.'

'*Identical* seashells—'

'Yes, but *are* they? Really *identical*?'

And so the two of them sit there turning them about, and squinting at them at the ends of their noses and then again at the lengths of their arms. Julian brings down the spectacles on his brow and Semple brings up the half-glasses that always hang from the cord at his neck. With these he has to tilt back to see, and I find myself looking away from the sudden, wild, preconceptual tangle in his nostrils.

'You know what?' Julian says, after half a minute. 'They really *are* the same—' He flicks me a glance, full of significance. 'It really *is* two parts of the original thing—'

Semple thumps his shell onto the tabletop. 'No, it *isn't*,' he says. 'They don't fit. They never did. They're—what's the opposite of bivalves?' He cups his hands together. He pulls one away. 'There's only one of them. They cling to rocks. Like *that*—' He slaps one hand on the tabletop. 'Just one shell. The whole thing.'

'Really?' Julian is still fiddling with the shells. 'I'm sure these're fitting together, though—'

'They *can't*, they're not *oval*, they're—'

'Yes they are.' I seize them from Julian. 'Look—'

'It's nothing *like* a fit—look, there's an overlap—'

'Not much of an overlap.' I hand them back to Julian.

Semple leans heavily back in his seat. 'The point is, someone's playing tricks with us,' he says. 'That's the point. Whoever sent me the parcel's playing tricks. You're wasting your time.'

'No, we're not, it's a message.'

'Message my arse—'

'I think Julian's right, I think we're being told something.' I didn't really want to say this, but I'm encouraged by Julian's reaction. 'I think it's a clue.'

'A clue about what?'

'Well, we don't *know*, do we, that's what clues are, they're just hints, they're not answers—'

'Clues from who? Raymond? D'you *really* think he's still out there somewhere like Elvis? Living in a fucking cave in the desert, horribly deformed? With JFK and Hitler?'

'No, I *don't* think that,' Julian says. 'But if the shells aren't actually *from* someone, then explain these—' He holds them up like castanets. 'Explain why they're the same.'

'*All* shells are the same—the same as all *bananas* are the same. Except wax ones. Look, I could find you a hundred more fucking shells clinging to rocks and they'd all look the same.' Semple struggles up from his usual slump. 'You know what's happening here, we're back to the last meeting—you know? *Is He present in the wafer?* We're back there, it's just a different way of asking the same question. It's Cavaliers and Roundheads all over again—'

'We *are* back there!' This is Julian, amazingly.

'We're *not*—they don't join up, there's no original fucking bivalve—'

'—and you want to know something?' Julian holds the shells up again, but together this time, closed, as one thing in his hand. 'I'm changing my mind!'

'About what?'

'I'm going back on what I said last time about the furniture. I'm changing my mind because these things *fit*.'

'Because of two paua shells? What are you *talking* about?'

'Order—'

'Oh, fuck off, Norman.'

'I've been thinking things through since the last meeting, and this'—Julian gestures towards the two shells—'this seems like, I don't know, a message. It's more than a coincidence.'

'So we're being told by higher powers we should pay homage to the organic wholeness of the past? As represented by two fucking abalone shells?'

'They're two *halves* of—'

'They're *not*, I *told* you, they're only ever one shell, stuck to a rock.' Semple stares at us wildly. 'That's how they *work*, there's no lost original with two shells waiting to be discovered. You've got one in each hand—that's all you've got, a different animal in each hand—snails, or whatever they were—'

Julian slowly brings the shells together again. 'I don't think we should touch anything in the house,' he says.

Now there really is a pause.

'You mad fucking bastard,' Semple says. His voice has dropped—he's really angry, I can see that. 'I can't believe this. It's a set-up—which one of you planted the shells, which one of you told Marjorie to stay away so she couldn't vote?' He stands up from his chair. 'There's no vote, anyway—we voted last time, the furniture's up for sale and that's *that*—'

'There's no vote on the table now because the meeting hasn't started. We're simply discussing the return of the paua shell. And the fact that somehow there's a second one.'

A pause. We look at the shells. Then:

'Which *is* the second one?'

Julian.

It's an awful moment. I stare at the two shells in front of me. Which the second, which the first? After Julian and Robert have picked them up, and passed them to each other, and passed them back, and returned them to the tabletop—I don't know. I just don't know.

I can feel the panic rise.

'This one.' I point at the one on my right.

'You mean that's the second? Or that's the original?'

'That's the second.' But, really, I'm not sure.

Semple stands and stares across the table. 'No, it's the one on the right. *My* right. Your left.'

'No, that's the first.' I hold up the one on my right. 'This is thc sccond.'

'No, the second one's the first one.'

'No—the second one's the *second* one. I can tell.'

'*How*? If they're the same? You've just said they're exactly the same, haven't you—?'

We sit there, breathing hard at one other.

And Marjorie walks in: unexpectedly, but, given the situation, not at all unwelcome.

'My reiki man stood me up,' she creaks at us. 'Just think, I've got nothing better to do than come here.' She dumps her unhappy clutch of bags on the floor. 'My, there's an atmosphere in here, are you all cross or something?'

'Norman's having a crisis. He's lost his original.' Semple indicates the seashells. 'They're both replicas now.'

'No—no, don't touch them.' I push Marjorie's hand back from the two shells. I'm staring and staring at them.

'Why are there two ashtrays, anyway?' she asks. "How come they're back? How come there's even one? What's happening?'

It's a long evening, as you might imagine. There's an argument whether Marjorie should take over as Hon. Sec., there's an argument about what to do with the paua shells—eventually it's agreed that they should be placed *à deux* in the Trust's safe, up in the Coop. Julian remains

Hon. Sec., with little opposition from Marjorie. By now it's nearly nine and the Trust is showing fatigue. Semple in particular yawns and lolls about, though with him it's never quite clear whether he really means it, and maybe after all these years even he doesn't know whether he's tired or just pretending.

Geneva's name certainly livens them up again, though! Hardly is it out of my mouth at last than Semple is crashing forward in his chair:

'That slut again?' he cries. 'What's she want this time?'

'She is not a *slut*.' Marjorie. 'She may well be a major pain in the arse but she's not a *slut*—'

'Let's put it to the vote, then—those who think Geneva's a slut say aye—'

'You're out of order,' I tell him, and then he makes his out-of-order joke, and Marjorie, as she always does when he does, says *Oh for God's sake, Robert, grow up*. Then I ask: *Well, what d'you* <u>*think*</u> *she wants?* and, of course, Semple has a schoolboy answer to *that*, too—

Marjorie turns away from him. 'What's Geneva got cooked up this time?' she asks me. 'A best-selling sequel?'

I tell them, carefully, paying it out before them, across the two shell ashtrays.

A pause.

'What d'you mean,' Julian asks. 'A tape?'

'A *series* of tapes. She's come across them somehow.'

'What kind of tapes?'

'Audiotapes. From a few years ago.'

'You mean audio cassettes?—who uses *cassettes* now?'

'Do they still work—is there anything to play them on—?'

'You'll have something,' I say to Julian. 'In your studio? Some old tapedecks?'

'Yes, I do. Has she played them through? Geneva?'

'She claims to have heard all of them. She claims to—'

'What's on them—where'd she get them from?'

'Yes, who's the vendor?'

'She wouldn't say.'

'What's all this about—?'

Marjorie looks at me shrewdly. 'Why are you being so mysterious, Peter—?'

'Oh, you know Norman, he likes holding his cards.'

But the thing is, I don't *know* what's on the tapes. I know what I *fear* might be on them, but of course I'm not going to mention *that*, not in any company.

When she told me on the phone my hands went cold: my neck, my face, even my feet went cold as I stood there. Many hours of interviews with one source, she told me: identity unknown, relationship with the Master unknown, and one detail revealed, only one, but enough to convince me of their authenticity.

'She didn't say what was on them,' I tell the others. 'But I have reason to believe they're authentic.'

Then of course there's the other business as well: her price, I mean. *And your purpose in telling me this*—? I asked her, as coolly as I could manage. *Well*, she said, and I thought of her coyly be-scarfed online image. I'm sure you understand, she said, that I'd like to write another book on Raymond? On Mr Lawrence? I asked. Yes, on Mr Lawrence, she replied. I understand the official biographer hasn't been appointed yet.

So there you are. Either (a) she keeps these wretched tapes and pours their unknown contents into another unauthorised life of the Master over which we have not the slightest control, or (b) we authorise her imperishable new work and get the tapes in return and at least some idea of what is really in them, and, of course, some measure of control of what gets put into print. *Possibly*—

Naturally, I'd prefer the latter, she breathed down the line at me when I spelled things out for her like that. I'm keen to pursue my higher promotion, she said, and an authorised biography would give me even greater standing in my career. It'd acknowledge my status in Raymond Lawrence studies. And that's something I feel has been neglected over the years—a full and proper recognition of the work I've done for Raymond?

All this I spell out now to the other members of the Trust.

A moment's pause, and then an explosion:

'*Official biographer!*' Semple slams both hands on the tabletop. '*Christ*, what a cheek—what a fucking *cheek!* Official biographer! Fuck me *dead!*'

'Does she *really* say that?' Julian. 'I can hardly believe she'd come right out and, you know—did she really just *ask* for the job, straight out?'

'She's holding us to ransom. It's a stick-up—'

'*Official biographer*—?'

'That's what she wants, yes. Pretty much.'

Then Julian asks the key question: 'If she's holding us to ransom, what is it she's got on us—?'

Marjorie looks at Semple. Semple shrugs.

'Was it that bad, back then?' he asks. He shrugs again. 'I suppose it was. But how'd anyone know?'

'It's all in my book,' Marjorie says. 'Isn't it? The way Ray treated people?'

'In ravel-me-up—?'

'You *know* the title, Robert, dear, *do* try to get it right. The love-hate thing, I mean. The way he'd make you kiss his arse and then cut you dead. It's all in *Unravel Me*.'

'Nice try, Marge.' Semple shakes his head. 'But it's *not*. There's lots more to it than Ray's charming habit of wiping his backside with his nearest and dearest from time to time. It's usually called sado-masochism, as far as I recall—'

'There was that rumour, wasn't there? Just before the Prize.'

'What? Which one's that, Marjorie?'

'Order—'

'The kid he brought into the country, he was supposed to have—'

'No, that was in *Natural Light.*' This is Julian, bless him. 'And *Other-people.* It was in those two, wasn't it?'

'No, it really happened, I'm sure of that, he—'

'You weren't here, you were overseas at the time—'

'Well, so were you—apparently Ray brought this teenaged kid back from—'

'Order—'

'Teenage? I heard he was—'

'No.' Julian again. 'It's fiction—what you're thinking of is fiction. It's what he *wrote.*'

'The North African boy that thing brings back. The hero. What's his name? The protagonist? He brings back that albino boy from Algeria?'

'*Albino?* I don't remember that.'

'Yes, that's why he bumps him off—'

'I thought he gets bumped off because—'

'Order—order, *please.*' I let my chair drop forward. 'We're drifting away from the agenda—'

'What agenda? All you've got's a piece of paper with today's date on it. We're trying to work out whether Geneva's got a loaded gun or a load of shit. Until we know that, we can't tell whether—'

'Yes, yes, I *do* understand, I *do* understand. My assumption is that she's heard a number of these tapes and—has some information she believes we wouldn't want to make public. That's what I'm assuming.'

We look at one another and away. We all know we're on dangerous ground here. As I've said, we each have a past with Raymond, and each past involves—well, a *different kind of intimacy*, as I heard someone put it once: sardonically, but with a certain amount of knowledge, albeit not at first hand. Each of us in the room knows something of what this might mean, but none of us knows all of it. Even I, who know so much, can't yet put it into words. Least of all the topic that they've raised. Of all things, we need to steer clear of *that*—

'I'll ring her back and see if we can get a sample cassette,' I tell them. 'She wouldn't hand over the lot. I'm not even sure exactly how many—'

'Stewart,' Marjorie says, abruptly. 'In *Understanding the Cardinal*. The hero. His name's Stewart. I've just remembered. The one who murders the albino boy. Youth. The wog person.'

'*Understanding the Cardinal* is short stories. It's a collection of—'

'Oh—is it? Yes, that's right, of course it is. Then which one's the one where he gets, you know—?'

Such an *unsatisfactory* meeting: the business of the paua ashtrays still lingers, for one thing, and Geneva—who seems now to have been conjured up, somehow, out of the very return of them—Geneva needs to be dealt with, too. All this chaos, all this confusion: once again, once again, *the curse of the present tense*—

Afterwards, as so often following one of our meetings, I stand at the top of the front steps and listen to their voices down by the old garage, and then the slamming of car doors and the gravel crunching under tyres, and, after that, the fall of silence upon the house once more. A sort of silence: the sea wind is in the pines outside and in the eucalyptus trees, and, up behind the Residence, it hums and moans richly through the walnut tree.

In the Blue Room I sit in darkness with the two ashtray shells. The possibility that we're in the middle of another of Robert's stunts has already occurred to me. He, after all, is the man who, some years ago, persuaded an elderly professor at the local university to dump his telephone into a bucket of hot soapy water in order to improve reception from overseas. But Robert likes the payoff for his japes to come fairly quickly, and to be revealed—likes to reveal himself, usually—as he most thinks we think of him: the licensed fool. And you've seen his reaction above, which seemed nothing like that. Or is he becoming subtler?

I press the shells together and snuff up the smell of them: salt, the sea. Dear Lord, the thing that has come up tonight! It's always there, of course, that's the difficulty, quivering on the boundary of Art and Life, waiting to be dragged in either direction. I know that in this long, dark room I'm at Ground Zero of the whole strange business, the place where the *yin* and the *yang* of the entire venture of Art always meet: the Medal and the Citation up there on the wall, their vivid fulgence lost at the moment, and, somewhere under my feet, their opposite, the rest of the adventure: equally unknowable, there but not there, both imaginary and real. The thing that can never be mentioned.

I press the shells to my nose again: the smell of salt, the smell of the sea. It is as if I am snuffing up the past itself, the *very* past.

I say the name out loud, terrifyingly, into the old house's knowing void, its sentient emptiness.

I wait.

I wait—

The smell, salty still, musty, gradually insistent,

gradually declaring itself to me: something that hasn't been in the house for years. I lift the shells, cupped together in my hands, and smell them. Yes. No. *Yes, yes—*

Now, slowly, a slight change in air pressure in the house: as if a door has been opened somewhere, as if something has begun to happen. I'm in the Blue Room with not a light on and thinking all the thoughts I've been giving you—where else to think of them?—and they've taken me away from where I am and why.

Something has definitely happened, something is definitely changing—

I've already stood, as if I'm somebody else. *Something is going to happen.* Oh, the *smell* of the place: it suddenly overwhelms me, that *pastness of the past* I know from what he used to tell me, Raymond, the man I know I'm awaiting, madly, long after he has died. Dear Lord, he'd be over eighty now: what am I thinking of, what am I imagining? Yet there's somebody here, somebody is in the Residence with me: I can hear him, out in the dining room, *someone is moving about.* I can hear the creak of the floorboards—*the* creak, *that* creak, from the little hallway just outside the door—

I can't move. He's standing there. I am beginning to see him in the dark, and at the same time I can't see him in himself: he is visible to me only if I look away from him, like a distant star: he is an absence, like a vortex, he is what everything else is not. A default, a lack, a someone, a something, nothing, standing there in the doorway: standing there *surely*, or come up through the floorboards to me:

He's back—he's coming back—he's coming back to me—

*

Anyway, there's that and then there's the car. I'm shining up the Dodge one day like a sort of hint and all of a sudden he says to me, *get in*. The old man. Just like that. It's early evening, round six, I'm squatting down shining one of his hubcaps for him and I see him coming up behind me in the chrome I'm polishing, Mr Lawrence, he's leaning on his stick and bulging at me in the chrome. I stand up and I take a look at him. *Go on, go on, get in,* he tells me, and he jerks his head at the car. *Go on.* And then he says—I'm going round the passenger side, see—he says, *no no no, you prick, the other side.* And when I stop and look at him he says, *what, can't you drive one of these things, what sort of man are you? Go on, it's easy.* So there I am, getting into the Dodge at last, I'm slipping in and I'm sitting there with my hands on the wheel and I'm feeling like a prize tit because I don't know what to do next!

Breathe in, he tells me. I sort of look at him, like, what? *Go on, breathe in,* he says, so I breathe in. *That smell's blue,* he says. *That's what blue smells like, that's what the past smells like. That's where we're going, we're going into the past. When you've learned to drive this thing properly. Know what this is?* And he points to the steering wheel. *It's called a horn ring, he says. What d'you think of that, got one on yours?* Then he says, *now, what's that*? and he points to a lever off the side of the column. *Go on, try it,* he says, so I give it a tweak and there's this sort of double thump up behind us, one on each side, and he starts laughing. *Know what they're called?* he asks me. *They're called semaphores!*—the indicators, they popped out the top of the door posts when I tweaked the lever. *Isn't that great, semaphores?* he says, and then he says, *I'll tell you what, when my semaphore can't do that anymore I'll know the game's up!* Which is really sad, him saying that, because, I told you, I used to shower him every day. Talk about hunt-the-thimble. You don't mind me saying that, do you, Patrick?

Anyway, on with the story. Next thing is, he gets me back in the Dodge for another lesson? Turns out he means double-declutching—and there's me, never double-declutched in my life! But I made out I had, so out on the road he pulls up and swaps sides and he says, *go on, then, show me what you can do*. And I'm in behind the wheel and he says, *where's the gear lever?* He thinks I don't know but it's on the column, anyone knows that, and I know what's going on down on the floor, too—they're the size of dinner plates, the floor pedals on those old cars, you ever seen them? Clutch brake accelerator, I tell him, and he says*, yes, but which one's which, go on?* And wouldn't you know it, it'd been that long since I drove manual I got the wrong one. *No no no,* he says, *on the other side, it's on the other side, you prick.* And then he says *All right, ignition,* and I turn the key in the dash and it's *whoom-whoom-whoom-whoom-whoom* from under the bonnet, great sound to it, always works for me. Straight six under there, thought it was eight but he told me six. Into gear and we're off, *whoom-whoom-whoom-whoomp-whoom—*

Well!—the first time I go to change gear out on the road, you'd think I'd wrecked the gearbox it sounded that bad. I let the car roll onto the gravel berm, and he gets out and swaps back with me. *It'd help if you didn't tell me lies*, he says, and then off we go with him driving. And I tell you, he could drive the Dodge. He took us up the hills and he just let rip, he'd wind it round corners like my mum stirring the Xmas pud. Great fun, but I tell you what, I was shitting myself. Pardon my French. *Watch my feet,* he calls out to me—and you should've seen them going left and right! Because that's what double-declutching's about, see, what you're basically doing is, you're changing gear into neutral and giving the engine a rev, then you're changing into the next gear you want, up or down. See? Like neutral's a gear? *Clutch-and-change-into-neutral, accelerator, clutch-and-change-into-gear*, he says to me. Got it? *Yes-yes-yes*, I'm telling him. Course I got it.

Weirdest feeling, back in the driver's seat. You driven a manual, Patrick? I suppose all you older guys started out on manuals, no offence meant but you know what I'm saying. Tell you the truth, I didn't even know they were still around—well, I hadn't even thought about it, really. Forgotten how different it was, I mean, just sitting in a car like that was different, it's like you're in a tank! But after a minute it smooths itself off and we're crackling away down the road, and when we're doing that it feels almost like an automatic? I told him that when we were out and rolling along in third, I said to him, feels like just another car, and he says to me *just another car, what do you mean? It's not just another car,* he tells me, *it's a time machine*.

Where we going? I ask him, and he laughs and he says, *we're off to the shops!* Not sure he was meant to be going anywhere, to tell the truth. But down to the foot of the hill we go, know where I mean? *Here!* he says, and we pull in and he's out of the car before it'd hardly stopped. I watched him shuffle off down the pavement on his stick—that stage you couldn't tell he had anything that wrong with him except he was old. I got out after him and what-you-know, it's the butcher shop he's after—*look at that,* he says when I come up next to him, he's standing there he's perving the meat! *Look at that roast,* he says. You're not meant to eat meat, I told him. *Who says,* he says, and he really was just about dribbling while he was looking, he couldn't take his eyes off it. *Look at that rump steak,* he says. *Look at the arse on it*.

He's rubbing his hands together. *I haven't got any money,* he says. Either have I, I told him, which was a lie but it was true he wasn't meant to eat meat on account of his heart. Like I said, they only fed him walnuts and this soy stuff you can buy that tasted like this time at school I ate the end off a rubber eraser for a dare? It tasted like that, like nothing and something at the same time. You ever tried eating that, Patrick? Soy substitute, I mean, not rubber erasers.

Well, next he says, *wait in the car. Go on go on*, he says. *Turn the engine on and be ready to go*. He's tapping off down the footpath and he's heading into Tony's, you know, the store down there? *Go on,* he says over his shoulder. *Don't worry, they know me in here.* And I'm telling you, he was in and out of there like a robber's dog, you'd think that's what he was the way he comes out with a packet of something in his mouth. He's scuttling along with all these bits and pieces clutched up against his chest and one in his mouth, and he's looking left and right. Then he tries to get in the car too quick and he gets tangled up in the door. *Move it*, he says like in a gangster movie, and then he's straight into one of the packets. I was concentrating that hard getting the old bus out into the traffic I didn't notice what he was doing, but when we get moving again and we're off up the hill *whoom-whoom-whoom* I look across and he's lacing into a meat sandwich!—that's what he'd got from the store! *He was after me,* he says, *he spotted me. The prick who owns the shop. He knows I pinch stuff off him so he chased me out.* You *stole* that? I ask him. *Well,* he says. *What am I expected to do if I want a feed, sell my body for money?* Then *no no no, you silly shit, not in here*—I was starting to turn off for Cannon Rise—*keep on going, we're not going back home!*

So up the hill we go and the Dodge is just sucking the road up in top, no bullshit, and me really starting to get used to it, though the more I did the more I felt I wasn't completely in control, like it was alive, you know, like an animal? Some hairy moments but we got to the top, I mean the Summit Road—I took that hairpin left by the tearooms and I had to change down for that, and I did all right but there was a bit of a grind in the gearbox, just a little crunch, and I could feel Mr Lawrence jump a bit when I did that. But then we were okay, we were cruising along round the bends and there was the view across the city and you could see the wind in the tussock—I could watch that all day. Well, turns out we did—we drive round for a while and then we come back to the viewing bay near the hairpin and we sit there for hours with the light going, well, two hours definitely, and it's getting harder to see and then harder than that. The sun's gone about an hour by then, more, and the wind's coming in off the sea and it's bustling round the car, it's rocking even a car that size, quite a breeze, I'm telling you. Wasn't the warmest, either, I'm starting to wonder what we're up there for—he's just sitting there looking out his side of the windscreen not saying anything. That's okay, but once the sun's gone it's all getting away on us pretty quick.

Then all of a sudden he says, *there!* like that. *There it is!* he says, and he's pointing through his side of the windscreen. Where, I'm saying, what? I'm looking round and I can't see anything to see! *In front of you,* he says, *right in front of you, what d'you look with, your nose?* Well, I didn't mind that. It's a bit like Mr Tinetti's special class but it's not too bad. Because I *was* being dumb, I'm looking straight at what he's pointing at and I can't get what he meant me to see—the lights, the city lighting up for the evening! One minute there's nothing, just the smudges across the city, mist and smog and that, and you could see houses lit up further down the hill and onto the plain—nothing much—then, couple of seconds and there's something, lights coming on in ribbons, the streetlights, everything at once or almost, streets coming on, *flick flick flick* like that. I never expected it but he was right, it was worth looking at.

Oh, right, I tell him, the lights. But then he says, *what else?* And he's leaning forward next to me and jabbing his finger at the windscreen. This stage I hadn't seen him that lively. Well—just the lights, I tell him. *Yes, the lights*, he says, *but what about the lights? For Christ's sake look and think.* And *that* gave me a jolt, it really did, 'cause it's *exactly* what Mr Tinetti used to say—it was his words, even the *for Christ's sake* bit. I looked round sharp at the old bastard then, I can tell you! That was one of the times I thought there was something going on, I mean it was the first time I thought he might be—into something? Plugged into something maybe even *he* didn't really know what it was? Something big? Up there in the dark on the hills, and the car lifting in the wind every twenty seconds, up on its chassis and no one for miles—*that* wasn't where I wanted to be when I felt *that* about him, either, I can tell you. It was like we were going to take off, and *then* where'd we be heading? Where'd we go?

Anyway, all of a sudden he says, *Oh here he is*!—and I look out the window and, bugger me dead, there's Rommel outside the car, suddenly he's jumping up at the door and barking his nuts off! Remember I told you this dog of his'd gone missing and we were worried he was off attacking sheep? Well, there's Mr Lawrence opening his door, and Rommel's coming in, and he's all over us both, the dog, I haven't been licked that much since I gave Raewyn this Indian sex manual for her birthday? And Mr Lawrence, he says, *I brought him up here last week, he's been up here five days.* You brought him up? I say to him, and he says, *yes, and let him loose. Life's not a bed of roses, I wanted to see if he could make it on his own, feed himself, I'm not going to be here forever by the looks of things, I want to know he can look after himself. Come here, Rommel,* he says. *He's a bit thin but he's definitely been eating something. He has to learn to kill*, he says, *he has to learn that again, we take it out of them and it has to be put back in.* Then he looks across at me. *Ever killed anything?* he asks me. *Ever killed a living thing?*

And *shit*, that was a queer moment, I can tell you that for free. I had us rocking back down the hill half a minute later, I didn't care how I was driving, I just needed to get us back to Cannon Rise, back to *people*—anyone'd do, even if one of them was Either-Or! This was after we'd settled on what to do with the dog, I wanted to take him with us but no, the old man wouldn't have it, he booted him out and shouted at him to get away till the poor old pooch was just sitting there looking at you the way dogs do when you're leaving and making this sound I couldn't listen to—I lurched the car off down the road just to get away from that, too, and I made up my mind to get back up there as soon as I could on my own to get some meat to him, to Rommel, though where was I supposed to find any meat at Walnut City? Where

VI

I'd been visiting Raymond secretly almost every weekend for well over a year when my mother and her second husband were killed instantly in a road accident fifty kilometres up the motorway north of the city. *Kenneth Newstead Orr* and *Catherine Orr*, the newspapers called them, my polite, slightly indifferent adoptive father and his wife who was my late father's widow. *Architectural designer* and *primary school teacher* their occupations, their car a *late model saloon*, the weather conditions at the time of the accident *normal*. An ambulance and two police vehicles *attended the scene of the crash*, and my mother and Ken *died at the scene*. The driver of the other vehicle, a mobile library, was *shaken but unhurt*.

I remember the words, I remember all the words.

In fact I can remember every detail of that afternoon—the principal of my school appearing at the door of the classroom to ask for me, the hush over the class as I stepped carefully between the desks to follow him out, the linoleum of the corridor rolling beneath my feet as I walked, the policeman and policewoman waiting in the principal's office, my clear understanding that something of tectonic significance had occurred. I can remember every detail of that office in the moment the policewoman spoke the simple sentence to me. There was a plastic lunchbox on the principal's desk and I can recall wondering if it was his. Did he have a lunchbox exactly like mine, and had his mother placed inside it sandwiches, biscuits and an apple, as my mother had done for me that morning?

There was a section of his office wall I especially remember at the moment the words were spoken: it was between the end of a bookcase and the dull green curtain on the right side of the window. Its *faux* woodgrain is bonded forever in my mind with the words of the sentence *I have to tell you your parents have died in a car accident on the northern motorway.*

Would you like to sit down, dear? the policewoman asked me.

The northern motorway.

No, thank you, I replied, politely. I'd rather stand, if that's all right.

I have to tell you—

Death, and laminated Pinex.

What were they doing there, on the motorway, my mother and the man she married so soon after my father died? That was one of the things I remember thinking as I stood in front of the principal's desk, waiting to be told what to do next. That, and this: *Uncle Raymond, I'll be able to live with Uncle Raymond—*

I remember him as pushing in past the door of the principal's office at that very moment, as I was thinking that thought, as if he'd come into existence entirely through my thinking about him. He didn't knock. He walked in and stood there and stared at me, holding his hat in both hands by the brim, pushing it around gently in his fingertips in front of his belly: clockwise for him, anticlockwise for me. He didn't say anything, just milled the hat around and around and stood there like a *non sequitur* embodied, a *thing* that had presented itself requiring explanation: my uncle, as if come up through the floorboards and standard-issue public service linoleum the colour of chewed gum.

The hat intrigued me: he rarely wore one. It was a big decision, he told me later, much later. *I wanted something dramatic*, he said. *I was thinking of a cape as well. A cape and a stick and a hat.* But how did you know to come? I asked him. *Oh, I made the whole thing happen*, he said. *The accident. Why d'you think they ran into a mobile library? It'd have been a bus or a truck if it'd been left to anyone else. Nice touch, don't you think?* And, when I wondered where they might have been going, the two of them, my mother and her husband, driving up the motorway: *they were trying to get away from you,* he said. *They were sick of you, they were making their getaway. They'd had enough, they'd had a gutsful of you. That's the explanation. I decided it was time I stepped in and took you over. Took your story over, made sure it was worth telling, made sure you amount to something. Made a man of you.*

All this he said two or three years after the event. By then, following a long war with the authorities, I was well lodged in the way of his life at 23 Cannon Rise and the house that was eventually to become known as the Raymond Lawrence Residence.

War with the authorities was his phrase, but it wasn't entirely melodramatic or an outrage uncalled for: I was twelve and he was a single man in his late thirties, and there were always those early, child-munching novels of his for people to fret about as well. And—worse, worse—he was a *writer*, of all things—a *writer,* for goodness' sake! All but unemployed! An alternative lifestyle! He was *different!*

Eventually, it was decided by the courts and the social workers that Raymond had sufficient proven contact with women in his life to be thought more or less *normal* (Lord! If they'd only known about some of *them!*). It was also concluded that I'd begun to form something of a *positive relationship* with him, which was more or less true, of course: I had conversational French (no other language allowed during my visits, after a while, till I was *au fait*), I could thump out *Für Elise* for the court-appointed advisory panel, I could sit there in front of them playing chess. And—look!—behold!—I was following a reading programme! On the basis of such things it was decided that I should have a trial period in my uncle's care involving monthly invigilation while I settled in. Raymond's anthropophagous early fiction didn't even come up: none of them knew about it.

I remember him at his scrubbed-up hair-slicked-down necktie-strangled best in this time, when the court-appointed advisory panel made their laborious inspections as, alas, they did—*menstrually*, as he described the timing of their visits. I remember the frenzy of each day-before, too, as he worked his *upright*—his name for his old Hoover—across rugs and carpets still in the Residence as I write this, while I ducked around picking up magazines and books and glasses from the floor and emptying ashtrays.

A bloody Anglican vicar! he said after the first of these ordeals, as he thumbed the cap from a bottle of Ward's Pale Ale. A vicar and a professional virgin and what was the middle one, d'you think, a girl or a boy or a potplant? Fucking Protestants, he said, and upended the bottle at his mouth. There was a glugging pause. Been dodging them all my bloody life, he said when he'd done. And here they come through my own front door to spy on me!—see them looking in the crapper? I wish I'd put *un préservatif usagé* in there for them. Talk about *dis pas fuck à la femme du mair*—

Eventually, though, and at last—at long last, it seemed to us—their final visit, and the same front door closing on the three of them, and the sense of a collective exhalation of breath long held. I remember Raymond turning to me with one hand still on the doorknob and his head down slightly as he looked at the floor for ten seconds, as if he was counting. Then he looked up. *Got you, you little bastard,* he said. *Now, d'you know what Ouzo is?* I wasn't quite a teenager then, not even into my teens.

The moment I came into his life, he told me years later, he stopped writing. He'd been in the middle of a short story collection, set variously here and there—*there* being the Mediterranean, of course, the North African coast of his recent past. You walked out of the words, he told me. I knew why you'd come. It felt as if I'd been waiting for you. That's why I had to arrange the car crash, he said. I hated doing it.

I'd *stare* at and *stare* at him when he said things like that. But, from the moment the door closed on the social workers, from the moment he really had *got me*, it seemed he was able to begin writing again.

Point blank, completely unprepared, I was confronted with what that meant—for a start, with the abyss of despair that seized him each morning when he *entered the salt mine*, as he used to describe those times when he was being pulled by his muse and pushed by Quentin Wilson, the new publisher who came into the picture about then: and with the stupefied figure, half-clothed and wandering from his bedroom each morning, butting into doorjambs, dropping cups in the kitchen, spilling tea or coffee or water and all the time *farting like a carthorse*, as he used, alas, to say and do.

When I first saw this horror I thought he must have been drinking again, as he sat there muttering and swearing to himself and even, sometimes, terrifyingly, crying like a little boy—crying into his hands, crying over nothing that I could see or know or understand. I remember endless morning searches for his slippers and in due course his upper teeth, and the time I realised he'd somehow put his trousers on back to front, and pointed it out to him, and watched him standing there looking down himself, stupefied: how could this possibly have happened to him? *Lordosis of the flies*, I heard him mutter to himself. He hardly knew how to dress himself!

Through two doorways I'd watch a half-clothed monster sob its way to the desk and sprawl itself against it, and reach out to roll up, and then down again, the piece of paper he had left the night before in the little Olivetti he sometimes used to try out particular feints and phrases after he'd been scribbling with his pen. After that, the groaning: appalling when first heard, shocking—what, was he dying?—remember, I was a bereaved child at this stage, an immature child—the groaning, and then the muttered words and half-sentences. After *that*, and eventually, silence, and the faint scribble beginning of the nib of his Parker 51, just audible in the utter, unbreathing quiet I kept up for him: that sound, and the occasional chuckle at his own wit. His writing day had begun. Once again, as happened each morning, it seemed that he had given birth to himself.

On other days, though, it just wouldn't happen—that's how he'd describe it, *it won't happen, it's put up its hand to me and said no, it's just not happening, it's giving me the fingers*—without any explanation of what *it* was: the birth process itself, perhaps? Or the life that began immediately after? Sometimes this terrifying blank, as it seemed to be, would follow a day of chirping, whistling activity at his lap desk down in the sunroom, with Mrs A. Round a floor above him hammering away on the old Remington as I brought the freshly written pages up the front steps for her, the ink on them still drying.

On his lay days, though, as he sometimes called

them, he would become more and more panicky, more and more hunted. And days they were, as a rule, plural, sometimes lapsing into a week, then weeks, a prospect that terrified us as they stretched on and on. The mood would begin to grip everyone: his secretary, the gardeners, his housecleaner, me. Unease came up through the floorboards, like a miasma.

It didn't take long to get drawn into all this. The entire business fascinated me, once I got the hang of it—he wasn't mad, he wasn't dying, it was just that *artists* were different from *civilians*, as he used to call those who do not create. Artists, I slowly began to realise, came from a different planet.

As soon as I saw this I began to be drawn towards it: I wanted to live on that orb, to feel the massive gravity of it anchoring me: I wanted to write, or, failing that, to be a handmaiden to the strange, messy, captivating nonsense I saw taking place in front of me. I stared, uncomprehending, at my uncle's books and into them, I crept into his bedroom when he was out and gazed, rapt, at his upstairs desk and the pieces of paper on it, I stood in the downstairs garden room and gazed at his *bureau d'écritoire*. When the stories were published as *Natural Light* I learned to see myself in some of them: not the local stories, to my surprise, but the North African ones, first as one of the Pieds-Noirs, a boy called Gaspard, and later as a Berber boy called Anir, a young *Amazigh*, *djellaba* and all, sly in the background, running secret messages, risking his life, squatting at night to poop in the sand.

Means *angel*, Raymond told me. Anir. Is he supposed to be me? I asked him, excitedly, pointing to the name on the page. No, you're supposed to be *him*, he replied. And how I learned to live my way into the reality of *that* remark!

In due course, too, I accompanied him to the launch of *Natural Light* at Bevan's bookshop down at the university, and there met literary folk for the first time, those strange, broken-winged seagulls who follow writers around, looking for—*what?* I still don't know the answer to that question, I still don't, and yet, in truth, I sometimes fear that, over the years, I have become one of them: another literary camp follower, looking for scraps, seeking immortality, following the shoot in order to *mumble of the game*—and that I am nothing, nothing without it, nothing whatever or at all. A captive of the secondary muses, and less and less than that as my creator fades away.

And, slowly, I was drawn further in. *Wear this*, he said to me one day as he walked in the kitchen door. *Go on, go on, shut up and put it on.* He'd been to a garage sale and *it* was a *frock*, for goodness' sake! *I'm not wearing that*, I told him: but I did, because he kicked me in the bottom with his knee, firmly and twice, and with a fist tight around my upper arm while he was doing it, *really tight*. That held me still, all right. He *dug* his nails into me, I remember that, he dug them in till I bled.

I'd no idea what was going on, though, until he'd finished watching me walking around for a while in this frock. You make a fucking awful teenage girl, he said. But not a bad heroine in a book, d'you know that? I'd rather have been a hero, of course, but despite myself I was tickled pink when I realised what was happening. I just need a *presence* around, he said, I want the feel of a young person in a dress for a few days while I work something through. Your name's Julia, by the way—no, you don't have to wear it outside, you silly prick. Just don't *go* outside for a few days, that's all, outside'll still be there when we're finished—what d'you think, the great outdoors is going to pack up and piss off just because *you're* not out in it? Who d'you think you are?

And thus it was that I became Julia Perdue, protagonist of *The Outer Circle Transport Service* and (I like to think) a recurring figure in a number of the later fictions, where, sometimes, she has a different name and different details but is always, at heart, I feel, the same child-girl-woman. And that child-girl-woman is—*me*. I can still read parts of *The Outer Circle*, the early parts, and find myself living and breathing there. The magic of writing, the magic of reading it! And of *being* that person—because that (I remember) is what slowly took me over as the frock absorbed me into itself.

I can remember, too, the day I first wore it *for me* and not just for him: he was out or away or late, I can't remember which, and there was no one else about the place either. I stripped myself to my underclothes and slipped the thing over my head as I had learned to do, with my heart bumping away naughtily in my breast. It was when he was writing *The Outer Circle* still, and there was a scene in it he told me troubled him, in which Julia sees a particular man on her bus and follows him home when he gets off it. *Why, what happens, why does she do that?* Raymond wanted to know. *She gets off and follows him and I've no idea why she does, no idea what they do together. I haven't got her, I haven't got her today,* he said, *she's not mine. She's so bloody difficult, this girl—*

I sat there listening to the afternoon wind blowing about the house, I remember, and knowing why I'd done it, why I'd followed the man, and knowing as well why it was I wouldn't tell Raymond about it, ever. *He* was the man, that was the thing, and the power he was talking about was the power I felt I was coming to have over him.

I sat in his room, the room of the man in the book, and *felt that power for the first time, the greatest power of all, which is when a man wants you and you both know he desires you and he knows you know and you know you'll never let him have you, ever. It was the first time I felt that, sitting in my pale blue dress in this dull, close room of his as he watched me and watched me and tried to work me out. And all the time I wanted him, too, that was the thing that was hidden from him, the fact of it and my knowing it—*

That was her. That was me. That was when I became a fictional character. I've never felt so utterly whole before, so absolutely complete, I've never felt so utterly *written* as in those days—*written up*, *stitched up*: *stitched together:* the Great Wound closed at last. Annealed into Art, if you'll forgive the mixed metaphor. Healed and made whole—yes, that's it! That's it! *Healed and made whole—*

The Outer Circle is his breakthrough novel, it's generally agreed, the work in which, if you go back, the Raymond Lawrence who was to win the Prize of Prizes may first be seen, stepping out towards Stockholm. It's set in Birmingham, England, of all places—when he was first overseas he'd worked there for a while in minor public schools—but is full of a yearning for his homeland that took everyone by surprise when they read the book. Its Julia is a young colonial who, in the usual way, has to go *there* to appreciate *here*, but realises that if she comes back to her birthplace she will still feel the pull to leave it that is a part of being born in this particular time and this particular place: the bus service of the title takes her around and about the outer limits of Birmingham city as a figure for her plight and, courtesy the obvious reference, for the human condition as well.

All very shopworn, you have to say now and as Raymond did at the time, almost as soon as it was out: an excellent example of his prescience is the fact that he was the first to reject it, as if it'd been a drunken overnight assignation he'd woken up to regret. In fact even now it reads well, if slightly unfashionably, with real poetry in some of it—much of it—and a continuous wash of literary reference that most reviewers mentioned as one of its greatest achievements. Julia's names are only the first of this slub of received writing that can be felt through his text. *Make it sound literary and they'll like it,* he told me. *Drop in Dante and two fucking Shakespeare quotes and suddenly it's great art, suddenly they forget all the buggery and bestiality and cannibalism in the first three books, now I'm fucking shortlisted for a prize!* And so he was, too, and won it, the National Book Award for the year, edging out another Mabel Carpenter trot (quite a fuss about *that*) and a find-yourself-in-nature novel about a man scraping rust. He was on his way.

For all their excitement over the *frissons* of classical literature, though, what the reviewers and readers seemed to like most was Julia herself. *By far his most believable character to date,* one of them said. *Now he's got his first three novels out of his system,* said another, *he's found a subject he makes worth writing about: a young woman, waking up to the world. Who knew he had it in him to make something memorable of a weary theme like that? But he has, no doubting it, in an extraordinary act of empathy.* And a third: *She lives and breathes as few characters do, leaping off the page and into the mind as the pages turn. Given the nature of his early work—his juvenilia, as we ought now to begin to term it—one inevitably wonders where this Julia Perdue comes from, so to speak.* And Raymond's verdict?—*Terrible book, easily my most fuckable character. I kept writing about her because I wanted to get to the bonking scenes—*

I read all this in *deep* confusion, as you might imagine. There was no doubt about it, Julia had become a very real being in his mind. There was also no doubt that, to a large extent, certainly in her origins, she was *me*. Only I would know that, of course, because only I knew what he'd asked me to do while he was writing it.

I ought to explain here what I was in early teenage, which is the time I'm writing about here: not *much* of a young man, it has to be said, since I was still betwixt and between, as you might say. I mean that not everything that usually takes place at that stage of life had in fact necessarily done so, and in the end—I mean when I was fifteen and still flute-voiced—I had to be given a course of tiny, bitter-tasting hormone tablets to *gee me along*, so to speak. Quite soon (almost overnight, it seemed at the time) I grew a foot and more, my voice began and then completed the awkward business of breaking, I started to grow a muscle or two and all the rest of it.

At the time I'm writing about, though, when I was first caught up in Raymond's cross-dressing art-world, I was still the Flying Dutchman of adolescence, as you might say, caught between earth and sky in a state of perpetual androgyny. *You looked like Audrey fucking Hepburn,* Raymond told me much later. *Wished I hadn't got you those bloody pills—ruined everything, look at you now!* And so on: *should've had your knackers off*, he told me on another occasion. *You were at your best when you were a boy soprano. I should've bitten them off there and then and been done with it. I've done that before, y'know—*

And so on. He'd just finished *the fucking Birmingham novel*, as he always called it after that, and he wasn't quite his true self. Or perhaps he was. Whatever he was, he was worn out, he didn't know what he was doing, he was beside himself—and then, suddenly, one night, he was beside *me*. I woke and there he was, next to me in the dark little second bedroom of what was not yet called the Residence. I could smell the aniseed on his breath—he'd been drinking Ouzo, the nearest he could get, here, to the anise he used to drink in North Africa. I didn't know that then, I mean its proper significance to him, and all I could smell was his strangeness, the terror of *difference* tasted for the very first time: for me, it would always taste of aniseed, just as it was always lit by that redolent *boof!* of the gas burner.

Here, hard up beside me, was all the rest of the world, everything that existed that wasn't me, and it was *touching* me: my throat, first, gently stroked, my earlobes, pinched, no more than a touch, and then (*then*) down to my chest—my breast, I suppose, my breasts, since who knows what I was to him in that moment? Julia, I guessed, the imaginary character of his fiction, the young, flat-chested girl-woman of his imagination, made real, in his sodden mind, in the form of an epicene youth with his breath held tight: what would the man do next, where would he go?

And, yes, of course, the thing he was mumbling all through this was (I realised much later, much, much later) the Herrick poem, Herrick's Julia poem, with that wonderful word in it that melts reality into itself and becomes the whole thing, the very thing that it is about: words—language falling into imagination: *words* creating *things:*

The liquefaction of her clothes—

Realising that, being able to think like that, arrived much later, long after I'd begun to try to come to terms with what Raymond had made of me in the time in between. The morning after that first midnight visit to my bed he was comatose: I have no doubt he remembered nothing and, certainly, I told him even less. Of those times I, though, remember everything, but I remember them the way I remember what you read on the page—the way I remember the Birmingham novel itself, in those scenes where Julia is liquefied into reality by his words, and walks across the page for the reader (and, increasingly, runs, for that Outer Circle bus that comes looping past her every day).

That, I remember, is what it was always like—always unrecalled, always scented by the Barbary coast: until the point at which, as I grew older and those times began to fall away from me, and, as I say, they started to have much the same slightly hallucinated reality that *The Outer Circle Transport Service* had, or *Natural Light* before it and *Bisque* which came next, and in which Julia appears again in her early twenties or *Understanding the Cardinal*, where she makes a curtain call in two stories as a slightly older woman. No more reality, and no less, either: all I have to do now is uncap the ancient, seven-eighths-full bottle of Ouzo still in his drinks cabinet for the scent of her to come back, which is the smell of that time, those times, and the reek of him as well—what a mixture, what an elixir! Proust's Mediterranean madeleine!

These evening thoughts, as always, in the Blue Room, as the sun sets and the Medal is touched yet again by this particular day's final, plangent light. Tonight, from the radiogram, the music of Schumann, turning and turning—he to whom I came late and guiltily, suddenly seeing his genius where I had been blind to him and resisted it, thinking him an unsubtle piano-thumper, but then gradually finding my way to him, or he to me, through the earlier works, *Papillon*, *Carnaval* and so on, till I was mature enough to approach at last the *Dichterliebe,* so long withheld from me by my mereness of sensibility: but, now, filling the room with its knowing sad beauty.

Where does reading stop? Who reads us? What does *writing* mean, when you share your life with the writer? Where do we ourselves stop, and where does the character begin? What is *ours* and what is *his*? And what, then, is a novel? Or was writing always like this?

*

Bugger. Tape ran out. Can see why you get pissed off when I run off the rails! Anyway, next thing the old boy decides I'm going to be his *chauffeur*, that's what he calls it—no money in it, no flash uniform or anything, he just fancies having someone big and buff driving him round like he'd got a bodyguard. Either-Or wasn't happy, you should've seen his face first time I showed up at a function behind the old man. This reception at the Town Hall, I was meant to be just dropping the old boy off, idea was they'd come back afterwards together in Either-Or's car—by the way, he drives a Beamer, did you know that?—feeble. But then when we get there, Mr Lawrence, he tells me, *come on, you're my date for the evening*. And I'm thinking, what the hell, why not? He looked really sharp toddling off in front of me in his penguin suit with the white shirt and black bow tie, he even had his teeth in! Little geezer rubbing his hands together, can't wait to get in amongst it—Mr Magoo! He seemed to light up when people started shaking his hand and clapping him on the back, he was talking away and laughing and I was laughing, too—couldn't tell what they were saying but It looked that much fun I was joining in, part of the crowd, know what I mean? And then this young chick comes up in almost like a Bunny outfit and she offers me a thing on a stick off a tray and a paper napkin for afterwards, and I knew I'd arrived, I knew I was in with the toffs.

About then is when Either-Or spots me, just when I was sucking a shrimp off a toothpick. *What are <u>you</u> doing here?* he says to me. He's looking round and trying to keep his voice down. Mr Lawrence invited me in, I tell him. *I told you to wait in the car,* he says back to me. No you didn't, I tell him, you said, drive back to the Residence and wait there. *I'm your employer,* he says, *remember that.* He looks me up and down. *You're improperly attired as well,* he says. Well, he had a point after all, I was the only one there in T-shirt and shorts and flipflops, but then I hadn't expected to be invited in, so what did he expect? I'm not a mind-reader, I told him, I didn't expect to be here. The Bunny girl with the tray was quite near and she had an arse on her like an upside-down heart, know what I mean?—couldn't take my eyes off it. *He's just making trouble,* Mr Orr's saying. *That's his life's work.* I can see he's as angry as hell but he's not really saying it to me. As soon as he's gone someone starts stuffing something into my back pocket—Mr Lawrence. *Keep an eye on that for me,* he tells me. *Whatever you do don't eat it, it's my supper, I'm off for some more,* he says. I had a feel-round—couple of sausage rolls in a paper napkin, and a minute later he comes up again and this time it's cupcakes, not proper cupcakes but little fancy cakes with cream and that, know what I mean?—anyway, in they go, into the other pocket. Then it's four little sandwiches, all wrapped up like the other stuff. *You'd think they'd supply doggy bags,* he tells me. *Bloody sausage rolls at a civic reception, they'll be serving fucking pizza and doughnuts next—*

Is Mr Lawrence putting food in your pockets?—Either-Or again. I've only got two pockets, I told him, and I've got my snot-rag in one and my inhaler in the other. Which was more or less true except for the inhaler. *He's not meant to eat this sort of food,* Either-Or says. *He's on a carefully controlled diet on account of his condition. This is* *__not__* *part of your job description,* he tells me. *He knows it's not appropriate, Mr Lawrence, asking you to come in, you know that, don't you? I'm considering bringing this up with Bailey's Care.* But just then some prick goes *ting-ting-ting* on a wineglass—you know, oh-shit-no *ting-ting-ting, could I have your attention please ladies and gentlemen?*—and the speeches start. The bloody speeches. All those words and I can't remember one of them?—I couldn't remember the front end of the sentences even when the back end was still coming out! But then after a while it was the old man's turn, and I tell you what, Patrick, I won't forget what *he* had to say, I won't forget it for a long, long time, I was laughing that much I thought I was going to have to go outside. *I'm feeling my age,* he starts off, and then he says something about Groucho Marx that not everyone liked—I was a bit surprised myself but I didn't really get it, not all of it, but some people did and you could see they weren't happy with it. Mr Orr was standing across the room from me and I could see his face just clamp up like a Venus flytrap, you know those plants? You'd have thought he had a blowfly in his mouth. *You're only as old as the woman you feel*, that's what Mr Lawrence said, it's just come back. Mainly it was the men that laughed. I laughed, like I said, but there was a real murmur went across the room when he said it.

Old Mr Lawrence, he wasn't put off, though, he went on, and there's a few more laughs and one or two people begin to walk out, which I thought was stupid. I can't remember everything he said, just the good bits, especially how he finished up. I didn't quite follow this last part, either, but it was some weird yarn about a turd and a piece of orange peel floating down the Mississippi together, and after a while the turd turns to the orange peel and it says, *what time do we get to Baton Rouge*? And the orange peel turns to the turd and it says, *what d'you mean, we*? I remembered it because I couldn't quite get it, you see, and I wanted to keep it in my mind so I could work it out later on—can *you* work it out, Patrick? You can tell me what it means next time you pick up the tapes. Funniest thing I'd ever heard when he says it, though. *What d'you mean, we?*—all these toffs in evening dress and he just comes out with it and says *turd*. Big up-you sign, might as well just give 'em the fingers and leave! You could hear the gasps, a lot of people laughed and a lot of people didn't. I clapped as hard as I could. The old bugger just didn't seem to care what any of them thought, he seemed pretty pleased with himself. Out in the foyer afterwards, though, there's this blazing row, him and Either-Or, like an old married couple. The mayor's just given you the freedom of the city, Either-Or's telling him, and *that's* how you say thank you? And Mr Lawrence, he didn't take any notice, he just says to me, *Home, James, and don't spare the whores.* All the way back to the underground carpark he's fumbling in my back pocket. *Where're those fucking cupcakes?* he says. *You didn't sit on them, did you? If you've squashed them you're fired. Like my speech?*

And I told him it was the best speech I'd ever heard, which it was. The thing I had trouble working out, though, he didn't seem to care about people who read his books—all the people who'd turn up when he did a reading? I drove him to some of those over the next couple of years before he got too sick, and they were a lot more boring than those people at that Town Hall function before he came on. Mainly women, as far as I could see, I mean the ones that came to his readings, that's one thing I noticed, women on either side of sixty with whitey-silvery hair cut like a German tin helmet, almost—know what I mean? Hundreds of them. *Brenda,* he says to me, *they're all called Brenda and they'll blow anyone who's written a book, man or woman, doesn't make a difference what the book's about, whitebait or sandflies, doesn't matter, as long as it's a book down they go and start sucking, no questions asked, you can hear the joints crack from out on a Korean fishing boat.* Really? I'm saying to him, is that true, do they really do that? And he laughs at me when I ask that. Then he says, *to hell with these* and he hauls his top teeth out and he puts them in the ashtray, it's a little semi-circle thing sticking out of the dash? He lays his top plate there and he folds his arms. *There you go,* he says. *Look at that. Perfectly fitting dentures.*

It might've been that time but it was definitely sometime around then he got me to drive him back up to the hilltop after one of these functions, back to where we'd been when we'd watched the city lights go on and Rommel'd come bouncing up to the car. We drove up past the tearooms and I dropped a cog and hung a left and after a couple of minutes we pulled in at the same viewing bay off the top road we were in last time, when it was really cold—remember? It must've been spring or early summer this time, though, because I remember there was a breeze, but it wasn't as cold as the first time. You could see the shape of the hills in the dark, these big blank shapes with no lights on them, they were really *there*, like you could feel them, like people, almost? Looking back at you? Well, we sit there in the car together and he tells me about the city lights again. *Look,* he tells me. *Everything's regular from the centre out, the centre of town, see the lights? Like a waffle iron? And then,* he says, *after that, the further you go out, the more disorganised the city is—see?*

Well, I looked hard at the rows of streetlights and I could get what he meant, sort of, but it seemed to me he was making more of it than what was really there. *That point,* he says, *where it stops being organised,* he says—*see? Where the street plan starts going all over the place? That's 1948,* he says. Right, I tell him, but I'd no idea what he was talking about. *Everything inside that square is before that date,* he says. *And everything outside it is after. And that's the date you've got to remember. 1948.* Right, I said. I see. But I didn't, I thought he was raving—I mean, does it make any sense to you, Patrick? And anyway, he could tell I couldn't understand. *That's the date they started to build houses again, you silly prick*, he says. *After the war. It's all about the war,* he says. *Don't you get that? That's what we're looking at.* Right, I told him. He'd really lost me by that stage, though, I was just pretending, and I wasn't feeling all that comfortable with it, either, to tell you the truth.

About then, though, this Commodore station wagon comes up next to us in the viewing bay with this young couple in it. The bloke looks across at us for a second. *Let's move it,* the old boy says. *Don't want to cramp their style, do we?* So I reverse the Dodge and we go back down to where the tearooms are. *Park over there,* he says. *I want a piddle.* So I park in the viewing bay and watch him creak out into the wind and walk across and up to the tearooms. They're closed! I'm calling out to him, but of course he can't hear. Takes me a minute to catch up with what he's doing, standing there looking in the front door of the place. He's peeing on the door. I *laughed*—I mean, you can't help it, like, of *course* he's peeing on the tearoom door, what else would he be doing? Doesn't he ever stop?—that's what I'm thinking. Then here he is, back again. *Come on,* he says. *Should've given them enough time by now.* Who? I'm asking him.

But he's off, and I have to follow him because he doesn't look like he's coming back. Off like a rabbit and onto this track that runs under the top road—I didn't even know it was there. I could see the tip of his walking stick flashing back and forward up ahead of me and his back bent over and bobbing along. Probably five minutes—then he stops. *Shh*, he says, though I'm not saying anything, breathing a bit but I wasn't saying anything. We're standing there and he's got us back under the viewing bay where we left the Commodore!—I can see the grille and the number plate through the wooden railings up above us. Worked out what he was doing, Patrick? That's right, he was up by the car, he crawled up, he's crouched down near the back doors, and he starts flapping his hand at me, *come up, come up*. And I'm shaking my head at him, *no way I'm going up there, no way*. I'm quite clear about that. Because by this stage I know what it is he's doing and I'm not having any part of it.

Except—I *did* go up there with him, that's the bit I can't understand even now. There I am, on my knees next to him at the back of the Commodore and this young couple hard at it inside. How does he *do* that to you, Patrick? How does he make you do exactly the opposite of what you'd do if he wasn't there, how does he make you do what you'd never do in a hundred years if it was just you left to you, and there you are, doing it like you've suddenly become a different person, or just nobody, you don't really exist at all? That was the first time he took me over like that and it scared the shit out of me, I didn't like it, I didn't like the way it made me feel afterwards. I mean, nothing *happened*—well, you know what happened and there we are listening to it, right through to the end, you know, *ooh-aah-ooh*—and I kept thinking, what if a car goes past, what if the cops go past? But mainly I was feeling like a piece of dirt, all the time we were listening and all the time we were crawling down to the track afterwards and back to the Dodge. My heart was going like, y'know, *boom-boom-boom*. The wind blowing round the car and neither of us saying anything.

Sick—it'd turned me on, see, that was one thing, and then it was having him there next to me listening made it feel worse, it felt really mental. I couldn't look at him. *Home, James*, he whispers to me. We drive down to the Residence a bit and he says, all of a sudden, *my mind's not right*. I think for a bit and I think, well, you can say that again. He was sort of telling it to himself, he wasn't really saying it to me I didn't think. But I reckon he was onto something. And all the time, this is the other thing, *no Rommel*. We didn't go looking for the dog that time, and he didn't come looking for us. Good thing, really, I mean, imagine if he'd turned up while the pair of us were crouched down at the back end of the Commodore with these two hard at it inside. But it was a bit disturbing, when I thought about it. Where *was* he, I wanted to know that. That's all I said to the old man when we got back to the Residence. No Rommel, I said to him when we were getting out. *That's right,* he says back to me, quite calm like he wasn't worried about it. *No Rommel*. And I took him inside.

*

Then came the moment, when, suddenly and abruptly, I was replaced.

Piss off, he said to me one morning when I came into the garden room downstairs, as I usually did.

I stared at him: I had the frock over my arm. What on earth could he possibly mean?

P.O, he said. He had his back to me. *Go* <u>*on*</u>. *Buzz off. You're not needed anymore.*

There was a pause, and then he looked across my shoulder.

Meet Julia Perdue, he said. *New version—*

I turned: a girl—a young woman—of (it seemed to me) about the same age I was: attractive enough, with dark auburn hair in ringlets now long gone, her tomboy freckles with them. Her face, I remember, was at that stage completely unlived in: quite simply, *unwritten.* In those days she was docile—we all were, even Robert when he turned up was docile—confronted as we were with a being of a sort of which, to that point, we'd never conceived, a phenomenon we could never possibly have imagined: *Artist Erectus,* the artist rampant. No: worse than that, exceeding those words, exceeding all words.

As far as this young woman was concerned, her unwritten quality—her emptiness, almost, as I came to see it—seemed to be exactly what Raymond wanted of her, of all of us. *There was something missing,* he told me at a much later stage: *not sure what, but it just wasn't there, she had a kind of docility about her, a kind of passiveness.* What was attractive about that? I asked him. *Nothing to get in the way, you silly prick,* he said. *What d'you think, I wanted her to have a bubbly personality? I wanted to* <u>*make*</u> *her, not find out more about her quivering inner being, for Christ's sake.* And, later: *you're the same, I made you—you were nothing when you came to me, you were barely even a boy. I was the Blue Fairy and you were Pinocchio. I made all of you, I can unmake all of you—*

As if I could forget. At the moment of usurpation, this sudden changing of the Julias felt like the utmost cruelty, the most terrible desolation. *You can get your pants on again,* he said to me, and then, to her, *my nephew. He dresses up in girls' clothes—of course* <u>*you'll*</u> *need something a little more mature in style, Miss Perdue.*

And then (back to me) *Go on, piss off, you're not needed anymore.*

I thought I was being banished altogether, of course, from the house, from his life, from life itself, and broke down there and then in childish sobs. Naturally, she remembers it all completely differently these days, or very much of it—herself a good deal younger than she obviously was at that time, for a start: obscenely, impossibly young. I was a child when he first got his hands on me, she said once, when she'd been drinking. He should be in jail. You were sixteen in your book version, Semple reminded her. In your *magnum opiate*. That was my publisher, she said, my publisher made me say I was legal. And it's called *Unravel Me*, Robert, *dear. Do* try to get it right. When I was writing that I couldn't prove how young I was when he got to me. And, besides, the old charlatan was still alive when it came out. Now he's gone, she said, I'm thinking of writing what actually happened—you know, when he came to me in my cot with his cock in the air? What you going to call it, then, Semple asked. *Unravish Me*?

Yes, this young lass was Marjorie, of course, as you'll have seen straight away when she entered the story of the Master: she was the docile girl who replaced me as the fictional Julia halfway through the writing of *The Outer Circle Transport Service* and the source of an undeniable lift in that character's personality from that point—it's true, it's true, I have to admit it, it's there any time I read the wretched book, and, anyway, sufficient reviewers and critics pointed it out when the novel appeared—yes, an undeniable lift in the protagonist's characterisation as she made her way out of that novel and into *Bisque* and onto the island of Ibiza.

He actually took her there, he actually took Marjorie to Ibiza in the Balearics, to the Mediterranean, Raymond did, he took her to the very island he'd reached alone years before on a flimsy raft he'd made himself, and from the Barbary Coast, of all things: the same mad, suicidal feat that became Kerr's in *Kerr*. God alone knows how he'd managed to get there, but then God alone knows how he managed to do it a second time with a fourteen-year-old schoolgirl in tow: but he brought it off all the same, leaving me at home in an absolute *paroxysm* of jealous rage. *I left a girl and returned a woman,* she claimed later on, when she really *had* become a woman, in body at least: *he debauched me in a tiny pine forest near the old cathedral up in Dalt Vila with a donkey watching—I think he debauched the donkey afterwards as well.*

As you'll know, of course, if you've read *Bisque*, that's exactly where Julia loses her innocence in the novel, although the debaucher in the fiction is the charlatan poetaster American whom she meets soon after arrival on the island. The donkey is there, too, and so many of the other things Marjorie claimed to have experienced herself on Ibiza that it's obvious the character has become as much a part of her as she was a part of the character. He made her on that island. He *made* her, and he unmade her as well, as you will see.

The American poetaster whom Julia meets on Ibiza is modelled (it is generally agreed) on the younger Robert, although he of course has always refused to see anything of himself in the American's greasy hair, his troubled complexion and his shocking teeth: replaced long since, in Robert's case at any rate, by plausible, well-fitting dentures Marjorie told everyone about when she found a dental adhesive in his bathroom cabinet whilst exploring during a party.

Instead, he sees himself in Thomas Hamilton, the

cruel, romantic hero who dominates the early fiction and who, at a later stage, has his way with Julia Perdue. Even Raymond's heartless pastiches of Robert's verse in Adam's poems (the American in *Bisque*) seemed to give him no clue to the character's provenance: the old man's pitch-perfect mimicking of the slightly cloth-eared quality of Robert's writing, those opportunities always narrowly missed, those risks never taken, escape his eye and ear. *Who d'you think is Robert's muse?*—a question at a dinner party from someone taking both himself and Robert far too seriously. *L'esprit d'escalier,* Raymond replied.

Robert turned up in our lives, I mean Raymond's and mine, not long after the Julia business began in its first manifestation, in that time soon after I'd become my uncle's charge and my uncle's alone, his *petit jouet,* his *bonbon. Another silly young prick wanting to be a writer*, is how I remember Raymond announcing his entry to our lives when a callow, embarrassing letter arrived in our letterbox unbidden—no envelope, just a fold of paper: barely a letter. Rich and famous, Raymond said. He actually says he wants to be rich and famous. Well, he can mow my lawns for a start, that'll make him rich and fucking famous!

He did, too, once he turned up, Robert, a gawky boy who'd already outgrown himself and who had dreadful snaggled teeth and a shady complexion almost lunar in texture. *You a darkie, is that it?* Raymond demanded when he first saw him. *Touch of the tarbrush somewhere in the family?* To me he said *he's got a face like a truffle*. I cringed from this, of course, and again when I eventually worked out why he'd sometimes call Robert *Heathcliff*. Whenever the boy was toiling back and forth with the push-mower Raymond would take visitors to the front window to look down on him at work: *Come and see the worst young poet in the country mowing my lawn*, he would say, and then read aloud poor Robert's latest piece of *juvenilia* as the boy worked on obliviously below: *Lips like wine, raspberry breasts* is a line I particularly remember from that early vintage, along with shrieks of accompanying laughter from Raymond's visitors, as well (alas) as my own. *Simon*, he sometimes called him, or, more obviously, *Semple Simon—*

What did we see in a man like this—in Raymond, I mean? I know we all asked ourselves that question, and each other, over the years. I also know I'm not going to be able to sell him to you easily: or, quite possibly, at all. Once, when very drunk—very deeply drunk—Robert claimed Raymond had destroyed him as a poet and as a human being as well, an extraordinary admission in someone who usually took his own writing far more seriously than was required. When sober, he claims Raymond did exactly the opposite, and that he would never have got where he has—wherever that is—if the Master hadn't taken him there. Brutally, unforgivingly, my uncle made a writer of him, made him a man and a poet: as far as Robert is concerned, that's the official line. *Tough love on the road to Parnassus, and a few hundred feet up its side as well, but no further*: that line is Raymond's. *A few inches,* he sometimes said. *Six. Six inches up Parnassus and then he runs out of oxygen, same as when he's fucking. Make that five and a half inches. No, four. Three—*

Robert had some other pretty wild claims that drunken night, too, and I put his earlier statements in there with them, as ravings, pretty much, as self-pitying fantasies. I won't dignify them by repeating them here. He has survived, after all, as a sort of B-grade poet who, in this country of the blind, passes for better. Some years ago, he won the Kennerman Prize for a chapbook of harmless, inoffensive poems called *Up Yours*: before that, there was a writing fellowship somewhere or other, and then other, lesser, appointments in between. Of course he teaches part-time in the creative writing school, as Marjorie does, too, and he still lives among the students near the university. Half his old house he rents to a rollover population of the young, with whom he socialises and to whom he stands as an odd combination of soothsayer and (in a scrambling, increasingly intermittent way) lover: *a poor man's Raymond*, someone once observed. Raymond without the talent: which of course comes to mean nothing very much at all.

Between and among his present and discarded women—each marking an ancient glacial movement in his life, each resigned to her Jurassic or Cretaceous fate—he lives a life I sometimes feel I do not quite understand. At other times I find myself gazing at him across a room, afraid he might, after all, be *mon semblable, mon frère*. We are all Raymond's children, whether we know that or not. Each of us, all of us.

Does Marjorie know what we all see in him, in Raymond, I mean?

She certainly spread him across the headlines with the loose, wildly confessional *Unravel Me*, in which the Master appears almost undisguised, as Begg, a great painter who casts his spell over the (equally undisguised) *ingenue* who is her protagonist, named (in a bold theft from Raymond himself), *Julia:* the writer representing herself as a fictional character based on a fictional character played by her actual self when young. Or was she just Julia after all by this time, as she claimed, had she actually become the fictional thing, Julia through and through? There's no me, she said once, when in her cups. What chance did I have to become a person? He took me when I was a child and I'm just that character in those books of his and now he's gone there's no book to be in. We're all like that, she said. All four of us, even Jules, even though he came in late he's a part of it, too. We're all looking for our book. Even him.

Ah, yes, Julian. He's been much on my mind lately, after that episode the other night at the Residence. Such an extraordinary moment, that, with its frightening sense of imminent transition—the change in air pressure throughout the house was genuinely disturbing, and that strange, salty-seaweed smell. I felt as if I were trapped in a sunken ship.

The whole business was made all the more extraordinary for me because it was so much alien to my usual ways: I'm *not*, I can assure you, in the habit of visiting the paranormal—until all this business began, I didn't even believe it might exist! Thus, for me, that moment of apparition in the Blue Room was an extraordinary experience, the shock of it still in me even now, a couple of days later, in my body and, more, in my mind. For, as far as I was concerned, it really *was* the old man, at that moment, appearing in front of me in the darkness at last.

And, then, a click as the light went on—and there was *Julian*, staring at me popeyed, just as I (I'm sure) was staring back at him. *Peter*, he said, and I said his name, or maybe it was the other way about: and then we simply laughed and laughed and laughed. We were both so relieved—we'd given each other such a shock! And after all it was just Julian, and after all it was just Peter!

What was interesting, though, was the way each of us had been quite sure the other was the Master, come back to haunt. How, why? I asked: *the two paua shells,* he said. *It felt like the past coming back, I could smell it, I could almost smell the Mediterranean—you know, as if the old boy had taken us back there?*

So, there you are: I wasn't imagining things!—in the moment, I, too, had thought of *Kerr*, that strangest of Raymond's many strange novels, with its solitary raft journey across the Mediterranean. And it was a strange conversation, too, I have to admit, as we sat together in the Blue Room we'd painted together years before. I remembered again that moment I've mentioned, when we stood there, the four of us, paintbrushes in hand, our work done and ourselves worn out but transfixed none the less by that sense I've tried to convey to you already of being *returned to the start of things*, when our collective story was about to begin—all brought about, it seemed, through the perfect achievement of a particular colour, a particular hue and tone.

So? Raymond said after we told him, I remember, when he'd turned up to inspect our newly painted Blue Room. Why the surprise? And it was true: there should have been none in it for us, because, after all, he'd gone on and on for years about the colour blue. The colour of transition, he told us. Not just any old blue, but (he pointed to our still-drying walls) *that* blue, *that* one *there*. Sky blue! The colour in which the abstract is able to become real, the colour that allows the static to start moving—the colour that lets things turn into words and words into things! That is what he said, and that is how he said it, in that occasionally operatic manner of his. I remember what he said next, too. *Now you've done it. Now you've set the cat among the pigeons. Anything can happen in this room now you've got the colour right—*

Quite something to remember at a time like this!—and we *were* like two young boys, Julian and I, I suppose, sitting there a few midnights ago in the perfectly preserved time capsule that is the Blue Room. We could feel him all around us, the old man: even the *smell* of him, since we celebrated the trick he seemed to have played on us by getting out his Ouzo—*his* Ouzo, literally his, that very last bottle he'd owned and with little more than the neck drunk out of it. We unscrewed the top, the two of us, and had a drink to him in his very own *aqua vita*, to acknowledge what he had done to us. Very unusual for him, for Julian, and even more so for me.

The old man had fooled us both, all right, properly put the wind up the pair of us the way he'd used to do in the good old days. The past rattled around and about in the sound of the wind outside and the familiar slight tremble of the French doors that was always incurably present on nights like this, the death-watch-beetle sound of time itself passing by. At such moments *then* always became present, in the creak of the floorboards, the dark at the windows, the cones of soft light from the corner lamps: Raymond himself could have walked into the room in his slippers and dressing gown and sat down with us for a shot, no water and nothing else, either, just the Ouzo. *Sissies!* he'd bawl at us if we put anything into it. And his perennial toast: *here's follicles on your bollockles*—

So it seemed almost inevitable that, after a reflective silence as we sat there in the darkened Blue Room, Julian should reach deep into the past, after we had calmed down a little, and speak the unspoken words. *Does she know about it—Geneva? Is that how you can tell the tapes are for real?*

I sat there for a moment: after so many years it had been extraordinary, shocking, to hear Geneva bringing back something of what happened, to hear her give voice to the past, in effect, and it was just as disturbing to hear it aloud in Julian's words.

Geneva? I asked. Another long wait, as I thought about it. Yes, I said. She seems to know something. Another pause. Jeepers, he said. How much? Just the fact that there's something to know, I told him. Remember, we agreed never to discuss it, we agreed to keep it between the two of us. Yes, he said. We did. But someone's obviously got to her. No, I mean we agreed never even to discuss it *ourselves*, I told him. Remember?

Julian's name fascinated Raymond, when he turned up not long before the award of the Prize to catalogue his papers for the local university's research library. At some point he let slip that he published poetry in his spare time, on an enormous old American printing press in the studio behind his house. Like many other local poetasters, Robert fell around his neck as soon as he heard this, and in due course Julian brought out his fifth volume, *Cuffing Myself*. A limited edition of fifty *or some crap like that*, as Raymond disgustedly put it.

He accosted Julian, I remember, at the launch. *Chapbook?* he demanded, feigning ignorance. His smile, as he approached this evidently harmless and decent man, chilled the heart. *Is that a book written by a chap?* And so on: it got worse, much, much worse, and was not at all pleasant to watch. Some reeled away, shocked at Raymond's mounting brutality.

The thing was, though, that Julian seemed not to notice. Patiently, he explained to Raymond what a chapbook is, and Robert's appalling title as well. *He's got no idea what it really means,* Raymond said in the car on the way home: *I can't believe it. He actually thinks it's about Robert's shirt.* At length, too, Julian explained his mission to publish, eventually, as much local writing as possible. Raymond was appalled: *he actually wants to encourage all these fucking lady writers*, he said. *All this shit people write about their hip operations—art as therapy, tomorrow will be another day, all that weak shit. How're we going to stop him, what are we going to do about it?*

It took so long, so *long* for Raymond to realise the truth of Julian's name, and of his existence beyond it: that, like the fictional Julia, he is another *ingenue*, but this time one that lives and breathes and walks around, somehow, without the need to be written: a medium-sized man with hair the colour of hair, someone who *resisted conscription* (Raymond's despairing phrase). *I don't get it, I don't get him,* he said after another party and another meeting with Julian. *I don't know why he's here.* At this party? I asked. *No*, Raymond said. *On the planet. What's he got to do with literature, what's he got to do with writing? He doesn't write, he's not sick enough in the head, he just wants to help people, what's wrong with the man? How am I going to get to him, how am I going to break him down, how can I subject him?*

Ah, yes: that was the thing, you see. Julian *resisted arrest*, as Raymond's Marjorie-Julia-Marjorie and the rest of us so signally failed to do. In a sense, *Julian* was the anti-*Julia*—the antidote, as the old man once said, to the poison of art. By that stage he had more or less accepted Julian's role as a sort of literary functionary, someone who got things done: published other people's unpublishable books, recorded the visits of the famous, arranged readings and made sure the microphone always worked at them, spoke up regularly for this or that promising youngster on air till the monthly arts programme he ran on local radio was—of course—defunded.

In the middle of all this, Raymond tried to capture him in one of his stories—he was writing *The Long Run* collection at the time, I think, or maybe it was later—and that was when he came up with *hair-coloured hair. I can't do it,* he said. *He just won't sit still and be a subject. He's unwritable. It's never happened to me before—I've just spent half the fucking afternoon trying to find a word for his hair, and there isn't one!*

Marjorie, on the other hand, seemed to slip into his language without resistance. Did he really take her to Ibiza underaged and debauch her there, as she claims—as Raymond claims, too?

This is what she has happening, in turn, to the Julia in her novel, in such a layering of art and life that it is impossible now to know what is real and what invented. Reading *Unravel Me* I felt it was actually her, Marjorie herself, Marjorie in truth, walking the pages in her *bonne vie* as a fictional character: full, rounded, complex, complete, and believable as none of us can possibly be in the living world, full of purpose and the glow of inner life: caught in a narrative curve that has a beginning, a middle, and an end. She is real at last, carrying the novel throughout, its heart, its soul, the young woman of today making her way in a man's world, finally standing triumphant as the embodiment of a fine and palpable womanhood. Life itself, growing on the page, the epitome of the grand humanist tradition. *The fullest possible validation of the imaginative act,* as one critic described this Julia who was Marjorie who was Julia who was Marjorie. The author as she possibly might have been: but as she could actually never be.

Fallen below this, lapsed back into the quotidian, she goes on being just Robert Semple's condescended *Marge:* perpetually dabbing at her nose, forever lugging her many bags and grips about with her, always improvising in the classroom, always in the toils of *this* unsatisfactory relationship or *that*. It is as if her novel is the life and she's been forgotten from her fiction: the protagonist's best friend's sister, perhaps, whose name you can never quite remember once you've finished the book, someone you think you might actually have known once, distantly seen now sitting in the bus shelter, much of her face covered by her hat as the bus goes flying by. Rusticated from the world of Art, always a little late to things, condemned forever to shop.

Look, Marjorie said to me once, and showed me a photograph. We were in her house, a little way up the most fashionable hillside in town—a little higher than the Residence, on the next spur to the east. Her parents most certainly did *not* approve of her daughter's association with Raymond, and, although an only child, Marjorie was astonished when, in due course and after all, she inherited the house from her widowed mother. This, ten years ago and more, but to her as if yesterday, as if this morning, even: as if *now*, and of this minute.

I know, I *know*, she told me once. I'm worse than Ruskin—I should paint everything white and wander around calling their names out, the way he did when his Dumb and Mad died. I know I was meant to sell up and be sensible and buy a townhouse, she said, but I can't touch anything. Their clothes are still in the cupboards, I just can't bring myself to do anything about them. Talk about daughters-of-the-late-carnal.

And this is where she showed me that photograph: her boyfriend, I realised straight away, a businessman called Fahti—yes, yes, I know—who has been in and out of her life for a decade at least. The image in the photograph shows him wearing a dark cap and standing very straight as he looks off to the left with a walking pole held in his hand as if he is about to do great things, like Roald Amundsen.

Fahti, I told her.

No, you silly prick!—and she pushed the photo closer. It took me several seconds more. Then: Raymond! I said. For goodness' sake! Can't get away from him, she said. I stared at the image: I'd forgotten how striking he was in his prime. Is that really him? I asked her. I can't really even remember him like this. So handsome! Well, how d'you think he got me? she said. Striking, yes, particularly when you're aged ten. She took the photo from me. Why d'you think I took Fahti so seriously? she asked me. Well, I've never met Fahti, I told her. I've no idea what he looks like. Oh, the usual thing, she told me. Small, dark and handsome. Pointed beard, rimless specs. All the other stuff as well.

The other stuff. Fahti is but one of a stream of unsuccessful lovers who have replicated one another in Marjorie's life, all of whom replicate this Original in the photograph. Like him, like them, he issued her with instructions, gave her ultimatums and threats, went in and out of her life as he pleased, had other women, returned without explanation and offhandedly resumed his commerce with her. That it turned out he was married through all this hardly needs to be mentioned. Of *course* he was married.

I asked Marjorie during one of his absences whether he'd ever beaten her. Oh, *you* know *me*, she replied. Doesn't work without it. Doesn't work with it, either. Choose one. Well—he's gone now, I comforted her. They're *always* gone, she said. Every time. They're gone before they arrive. I spend half my salary on counsellors and we talk and talk and talk and then we agree what the problem is—*Ray*'s the problem, *I love him I hate him I love him I hate him*—and then we agree, next time I'm going to make more sensible choices and have a really adult relationship. Then out I go and find someone I think's not like Raymond at all—and guess what happens next?

At one stage she was in a relationship with a tall, frightening Dutchman because she thought that that was what *not-Raymond* meant: taller (or fatter, or thinner, as others turned out to be one by one, or with different-coloured hair or none at all). She used to say that her *time with Raymond*, as she called it, was the longest she'd ever been with a man: I'm *always* with him, she said, that's the trouble, he's never gone away. Everyone else is Raymond-lite, she said, looking around herself for her box of tissues. They come in one door pretending to be him and they go out the other and abandon me—

On one of these occasions I reminded her that Raymond really *was* my father, legally so, and that it was curious to hear her talk of him as her own. The difference is a piece of paper, she said back to me, dabbing at her nose. They ask me, *what about your biological father?* These counsellors. Then they don't believe me when I tell them my biological father was a long drink of warm gin and I had no relationship with him at all—why do they think it was I fell into Ray's clutches so soon? I wasn't ten, but I wasn't much more. You were fourteen, I reminded her. Yes, she said: but *fourteen*?—aren't you shocked by that? *I* am. I can't believe it was me. But he had me the minute he met me, he turned up to do a reading at my school—I was like those women in the Cavafy poem, d'you know the one? They can't wait for the barbarians to come? *I* seduced *him* as much as *he* seduced *me*. Yes, with the donkey watching, I reminded her. You told us all about it. No, she said, *long* before the donkey!

I've heard these things several times, of course: she used to say she was drawn to me as a confidante by my lack of compassion, my ruthlessness, by my (her phrase) *neuter quality*. Sometimes, at these moments, when she talks about her early days with Raymond, I tell her she's fantasising: and she always stares past me when I do. I can't tell, I remember her saying on one of these occasions. It's all fantasy, isn't it? One shrink told me I was fantasising about what I wanted my father to do to me. He was a Freudian, he said it's *all* transference and projection—relationships, he said that's all they are, that's how they start, he said, and they end when the transference and the projection have served their purpose, whatever that might be. I *cried* and *cried* when he told me that.

She wiped her nose with a tissue and flicked a naughty glance at me. He had *you* at ten, she said.

She'd made this sort of claim before. I *met* him at eleven, I reminded her. And he did *not* have me. Yes he did! she said. Every time he hit you with that bat-thing of his he was having you! It's about pain and power and humiliation, doesn't that sound like sex to you?

At this point I stopped her short. He hardly touched me, I said. Anyway, he was trying to make a man of me. She stared back at me, boldly, I remember. He broke your back, she said. That's what *he* did. He did *not*, I told her—I wanted to get this straight there and then, to get it straight and put it away for good and all. That was the hormones, I told her. They did the trick but that's the price, spinal scoliosis in later years. She was still staring at me. Hormones my *bottom*, she said, coolly. He beat you to death. Then he tried to bury it, he tried to cover it up.

Oh, I *stared* at her when she said that, I *stared* and

stared at her. At what level of fantasy was she speaking when she was saying something like *that*? What did she *know?*

*

There's a terrible scene in *Flatland* where the protagonist, Hamilton, takes a young Amazigh deep into the Algerian desert, beyond the Aurès—a youth, really, barely that—and eventually, lingeringly, kills him. It's appalling for all the obvious reasons, and for the details of the business itself, which seems to go on and on: but it is appalling most of all (I can barely let myself write this) *because of the love in it*, and the way that love suffuses and elevates the writing, and draws the reader into what is being described, however much we try to resist its pull. The scene is unreadable, and so extraordinarily, obscenely beautiful that it *has* to be read, it *must* be read. It pulls you down into itself, it makes you into itself and of itself.

When I first read it as a youth—half a boy still, really, more than half a boy—I was numbed by its obscenity. I wanted to stop and I couldn't, I wanted it to end and it wouldn't. And so I was sucked under, appalled and by degrees, till I'd become a part of what I read—an agent, a protagonist, in effect Thomas Hamilton himself: I was a torturer and a murderer, I'd done these things myself and felt the love and the desire in both of them. Oh, God, to admit that! He'd reached into me as his reader, Raymond, and made me realise how much I was complicit in every single thing I'd made him describe for me in such painful, lingering detail. I've never quite forgiven him for it. Remember, I was the Amazigh's very age at the time: well, more or less, whatever it was. I mean I was *him* as well, the boy as well, the youth. You have to understand that, you have to understand that to know what I'm trying to tell you. *He was me. I was him.*

At its end (I remember) I burst into tears, and when Raymond came into the room I flung the book in his face. *I wish I'd never read it!* I screamed at him. *I wish you'd never written it!* But you *did* read it! he said to me. *You* made it happen! *You* read it to the end! It didn't exist till *you* made it exist! *You're* as guilty as anyone!

He was delighted, in other words. Turn you on, did it? he asked. And he seized me by the wrists when I tried to hit him, or hit out at him: nothing very much, of course, and easily enough handled. I'd never done this before—I'd never so much as raised my voice to him—and here I was, pushing and pulling at his shirtfront. I think I even tried to knee him in the crotch!

He shoved me back and pinned me down. We were on the Louis Quatorze couch in the Blue Room: there was the weight of him on me and the cheesy smell of his breath. *This is how it started with the little Amazigh shit in the desert,* he said. *Up close and personal, like this. Dumb prick tried to pull a knife on me. Remember, you haven't got a knife.* And he held me there for several seconds more as our bellies breathed against each other. His eyes were pale, grey, almost no colour at all, that fine dark ring around each iris like nothing I've seen in anyone else before or since.

Of course as far as I was concerned at the time it was all a part of the act, this insistence that he'd actually done the things he wrote about himself, sometime in his overseas years. There was no doubt he'd been about the globe in this part of his life—there were photos and memorabilia, after all: that Shoji screen in the Blue Room, for one—and

North Africa was obviously one of the places he'd been, and stayed.

But his claim (for example) to have lived with the Berbers for years took me some time to understand, as you might imagine. *How did you get there, though, how did you get to actually be, you know, with them,* I remember asking him when he first brought it up. Oh, I landed up amongst 'em, was all he'd say. I'd been smoking *kif*, not too much before and after when you're smoking *kif*. There I was, and there they were, looking after me, he said, that was all. It was like the beginning of time.

You have to understand that, *sidi*, he told me on another occasion. We all have to remember being born, we can't just rely on being told about it. We have to know our beginning or we can't understand what comes next, we can't understand what we mean, what our lives mean. We can't understand the end of things. I remember they killed a camel and wrapped me in the hide to keep me warm, I can remember the stink of the camel fat to this day, it smelt the same as rancid butter but peppery as well. They looked after me, they'd rub me with argan oil and wrap me up and they'd keep me in their tents. They took me everywhere they went, they were looking after me till I got better. *Yes, but what was wrong with you?* I asked him. *It doesn't make sense, what you're saying doesn't make any sense.* I'd say this to him over and over again—*what was wrong with you, why were you sick?*—and he'd answer like that, by not really answering at all.

And then one day I asked him one time too many, and, suddenly and abruptly, he turned on me. *Fuck* it, man, he said, *I was being born*—don't you *understand* that, what's wrong with you, why is it I always have to spell everything out to you? It's in the book, if you can't understand it, read it again, if you still can't understand it, fuck off and do a creative writing course. Go to teachers' college. What d'you think writing's *for* if it doesn't make things *real*—?

Well! I was fifteen by the time he told me this, you understand, or maybe sixteen, definitely not more, and, as I've said before, fighting my own rather curious battle with my hormones: or in fact *not*, since there was nothing much, at that point, to fight. I could've been taken for twelve or less, to judge from the photos of the day, or quite simply for no age at all, like Peter Pan: I was still paying half-price at the cinema and on the bus! Given all this, it was rather a lot to expect of any young lad—particularly one as literal-minded as he sometimes accused me of being—to make the leap into the mythic world I came to realise, over the years, he was talking about. The physical world had such a claim on me at the time, after all.

Did *he* believe it, did *he* believe in it, was it real? Sometimes in the next few years I would think *yes*, sometimes in the next few years I would think *no*. Now, of course, now—*yes*, yes absolutely, of *course* it was real. Especially given that it seems he's started coming back to tell me about it. Because surely that's what's been happening, isn't it—? He's coming back to tell me something? Of course it was real, that world he was talking about. Of *course* his story was real—

What Marjorie said about the old man beating me and burying me is absolutely true, and completely untrue at the same time. *I'm going to teach you about pain*: I remember him telling me that, one day early in my time with him. *I'm going to take you through pain and out the other side*. I remember him staring and staring down at me when he said that: those blue-grey eyes, that thin dark bezel around each iris. I remember my *terror*. If you're going to come to anything in life, he told me, you have to know pain. Otherwise you're just going to spend your life pursuing happiness like every other stupid prick on the planet. *Christ*, he said, *happiness*—and he spat the word out as if it revolted him.

Take your shirt off, he told me. Come on, come *on*, do as you're told. Haul it up at the back. *What d'you want?* I asked, but I was pulling it over my head all the same and my singlet, too. There's nerve in a man's back, he said, and he ran his thumb up and down my spine. If you find it you can paralyse him. *Paralyse him?* I said—Shut *up*, he told me. Sit still—

I couldn't move, I couldn't let myself breathe.

We used to do this out on a haraka, he said. Saved a bullet. *There*—his hand stopped: everything stopped. I sat there, smelling him: sweat and aniseed and dark cigarette tobacco. I press *there*, he said, and you'll never move again.

I sat there. I could feel his thumb against my spine.

I sat there.

Don't press—I couldn't believe the voice that came out of me. No no, don't *say* anything, he told me. Hold your tongue. Just try to *think* what it is that's happening to you. Just think what you're close to now—will I press or won't I—*please don't press,* I snivelled up him. I'm going to count to ten and then I'm going to press, he said. Or maybe not—you don't know. Count with me—

And then he pulled away from me: his hand dropped. For God's *sake*, he said. Go and clean yourself up—go on. *I couldn't help it,* I whined. Just clean yourself *up*, he said. *It just happened,* I told him—I was crying now. *I couldn't stop it*. He turned from me as if I was nothing, nothing at all, nothing to do with him.

Trust, he told me later on. And *courage*—for Christ's

sake, I've never met a kid who *cries* so fucking much—*it's what you do to me*, I told him, and started crying again, poor child that I was. *This is what I went through over there, fuck you!* he yelled at me in some later episode, when I failed some other test of his. *This is how they do it over there and they know what kind of universe it is we're all fucking living in!*

That is why, *au fond*, there was always a certain level of contempt in his treatment of me: I couldn't quite enter the world as he saw it, the world in his head and on his page: not fully. You might say he couldn't *write* me—and he tried to do that once, literally, at a time rather later than my miserable little performance above and when I'd learned to fight back a little. We were struggling together over something or other and suddenly there was a knife. No, he said, I'm not attacking you, you dumb little fuck, not yet—stay *still*, stay *still*—no, don't *move*, fuck you—

He was trying to trace the tip of the knife, the very tip, into the skin on my neck—*no*, I told him, and pushed him away.

If I do this you'll never forget me, he said. Wherever you go. I'll be written on you.

No, I said, and he came at me again—

I failed his trials and his tests, as he called them: I broke down and gave up long before the end and I learned nothing better from them than to fend him off as I've shown you here. I let him down, and he treated me accordingly and turned elsewhere. But as it happened his contempt served a purpose, it turned out that it had a role to play in me after all. It became a part of me, and—I know this, I told you that I know something of myself—it became my defence against other people. Turned end for end, so to speak, and applied to other people, it became what I know I'm known for now. It became part of the thing that I am, the thing that is me, the thing that protects me.

The price lies somewhere else. In these years there slowly evolved between us what I came to think of as a *lash of love*. I don't think I've ever been so *close* to anyone in those moments when, somehow, I got something right—except in those moments when I got something wrong. Almost, I began to yearn for these failures: not quite, not exactly, but very nearly so. I became less and less able to know what I felt, who I was: whatever had happened, that moment of feeling close to him—of being forgiven and feeling loved, even—put it all right again. I yearned for them. When he *punished* me, and then *forgave* me, and I was shriven and made whole once more.

And, slowly, as I grew older and came to terms with my youthful passage through his strange, strange imaginary life, it became for me the price of greatness, the price of knowing it, of living with it. I came to understand that if I hadn't accepted the things he made me do and the things he did to me when I first came into his life, I would never have walked with gods. We all did, the four of us, I know that, the four who have become the Trust: and I know that in their different, limited, fumbling ways, they know it, too. I tell them so, from time to time. *Look where he took us*, I tell them. *He took us to Stockholm—*

VII

Back then, I was just starting out, see, I hadn't got to the stage when I shifted into the Chicken Coop to look after him full-time, it was early days and I was in and out like I told you. It was just a job—except the bullshit-*chauffeur* business, that wasn't in the original contract, and I was starting to do more and more of that. And I really fell for it, I almost wished I had a uniform so people could see I was official, so they could see I was with him. I've got to admit, it was a big buzz. I remember I drove him to some interview on the riverbank, all these people hanging round watching, and he says, *stand behind me and look staunch.* On the news that night it was up close and you couldn't see I had shorts on. He says to me, *you know you've made it when they stop asking you about books and they start asking you about the Middle East—what do I know about the Middle bloody East, I'm just a writer?* You sounded good, I told him, and I meant it, he just rattled stuff off. *That's because I was talking bullshit,* he said. And then he says to me, *you look pretty good yourself, standing there. But, d'you know what, you've got a weak mouth?* I didn't mind that, I know my head's a bit on the small side for my body, or maybe my body's a bit big for my head. It's more a facial expression sort of thing, though. Now and then I've caught myself in a shop window and I've always got this stupid grin like I'm waiting for something to happen. That's what he said to me. *It's like you've got no thoughts of your own,* he tells me. *I'm going to shape you up, you're my private bodyguard, remember that—what's that programme with the bodyguard?*

It really helped when he told me that because I just started to be like the actor who was the bodyguard in this series except

I wasn't losing my hair like he was. The old boy told to me to chew gum to help with my mouth, too, *make it look less weak,* he told me, *make it do something, maybe even tighten your lips up a bit after a while.* So I drove him round and I chewed gum, and I sort of fell into his way of life, I sort of fell into this part I had in his life, and soon that was all I had. That was the start of the problem. To tell the truth, I didn't notice till Raewyn started to moan about it. We're not seeing each other enough, she starts telling me, you're always up at Cannon Rise, isn't it meant to be a part-time job? And that suit, she says. It's too big on you, it's too loose, you look like David Byrne. Mr Lawrence'd bought me a couple of suits, see, and a whole lot of other stuff, shirts and even undies? Socks, too, and hankies because he said I should be ashamed of my old snotrags—*what, you only own the one or something,* he says to me. *Look at it, what did you do, deep-fry it or something?* Him and Mr Orr had a row about buying me clothes, I listened through the wall of his office and Mr Lawrence, he give him as good as he got. *I'll do what I want,* he kept saying. *I'm not dead yet, and you're nothing till I am, if you're not careful I'll change things.* That shut him up, Either-Or, he's saying *oh, oh, well then, well,* and *that* made me laugh. But it put another edge on things between me and him, me and Either-Or, specially if I turned up in the new clothes. I'd be loading the old man into the Dodge and I'd be dressed up in my new duds, and he'd be watching from up in the Residence, and I'd feel his eyes boring into my back.

I'll tell you some of the things we did in town, the old man and me. I'd leave the car in that personal parking spot he's got at the uni—he'd remember where everything was that'd used to be there. *There was a bike shop over there,* he'd tell me, *and this was Warner's.* A pub, I guessed, because in a minute we'd be in some walk-in bar and he's ordering *Ouzo,* would you believe that? And there's this guy there and he says *Roger, how are you?* And he shakes hands and then he says, *this is Thomas Hamilton, my bodyguard,* and he points to me. Pleased to meet you, Thomas, this Roger says to me, and he shakes my hand. And I didn't say back to him, *no, it's Thom Ham*, and I'm not quite sure why. I didn't stop him. Thomas Hamilton. After that it's back to the uni, he's striding along ahead like we weren't togther, me with this big white David Byrne suit flapping each time I took a step—Raewyn was right, it *was* too big, even for me, but that was the size Mr Lawrence reckoned he wanted. Over the road we go and into this bookshop, and he's looking round and then he spots something and he says *ah* and he goes over to this stand that's full of his books! Big cardboard cutout next to it of him much younger, and this sign saying *Nobel Prize-Winning Author* and so on, and all these books, and quotations written up in capitals.

This crap, he mutters to me, and he's pulling books out and looking at them. *This fucking new edition my publisher's brought out,* he says, *meant to be a standard edition, will you look at it?* He shows me one of the books, and it's real leather-looking with this gold lettering. Why's it in its own little box? I ask him, and he says, *oh, that's called a slipcase, how fucking pretentious can you get?* Then he looks round and he says, *here*, and he shoves it inside my jacket! He shoves a couple more in, and looks round, and shoves in some more—hold on, hold on, I'm saying to him, but of course you've got to keep your voice down, this guy's stuffing books into the jacket of your David Byrne outfit as fast as he can go and you don't want to start telling people he's doing *that*—

Then, *come on*, he says, *let's get out of here*!—and we're scrambling out with six or eight books in my jacket! I was shitting ball bearings, I can tell you. But the same time, I was excited. I thought, *that's why he made me buy the David Byrne suit, for shoplifting!* That's all we stole first off, and just *his* books, books he'd written himself. Once we're away from the bookshop we find a dumpster and he makes me shove the books in. *Go on, go on!* he's telling me. *Hurry up!*—and he's looking round the place. But they're good books, I told him, they're brand new books—*throw 'em in*, he says to me. *You stupid prick—that's the point, that's why we're getting rid of them, can't you understand that? I sold my soul to the fucking devil,* he says. *Getting involved in all of this, it's the only way to put it right. I sold myself for thirty pieces of fucking silver*, I remember him saying that to me but not then. *The Judas of world literature,* he tells me, *I should fucking change my name and put it up in lights, Judas Lawrence.*

Course, I'd no idea what the hell he was talking about at that stage, I was just caught up in all the excitement, and I tell you what, he was *bloody exciting*. We shoplifted that much stuff, I feel really bad about it now, we never had a drink in a bar he didn't slip the empty glasses into one of my pockets when we were done. We pinched *that much*—sometimes I'd just about cack my David Byrne outfit. What if we get caught? I ask him, back in the car, what do we do then? *What d'you mean, we?* he says, and he's laughing up at my face with his teeth out. *Remember the turd and the orange peel!* he tells me. *Remember them, on the way to Baton Rouge! The glasses are in <u>your</u> pockets,* he says, *it's <u>you</u> that's wearing the suit—why d'you think I bought it for you in the first place?* But later on he gets all serious with me. *You're breaking through something,* he says to me. *That's the first thing we're doing here. You've never done anything real in your life,* he tells me, *hardly anyone has, that's the trouble. Prostitutes of the* *unconscious, that's what you all are.* I'm saying *what? Who?* And he tells me, *never mind.*

Death, are you afraid of death? he says to me one time. We're sitting outside a McDonald's with each of us a double meat burger with cheese and fries and a Coke, and he asks me that! *I'm* not, he says, *are you?* Well, I didn't like to say anything, like, you know—what's the point? *I'm not,* he says. I am, I said, and I don't know why, it just sort of blurted out either side of my double meat burger and cheese. And he's staring up at me and chewing away. *And you a meat-eater,* he says. *You accept death every time you eat meat,* he says. *You know that? That's why they fill me up with that shite up the hill,* he says. *Fucking walnuts. They're afraid of death and they give me walnut loaf.* Isn't that because of your cholesterol and your heart? I ask him. He stares and stares at me and all the time he's getting rid of the last bit of the burger. *Ever kill anything?* he says. Just like that, out of nowhere—he's wiping his hands together and he's still chewing away and looking up at me. *Ever kill anyone?*

He's asked me this before but I just about choke on my bun all the same. *Kill* anyone? I ask him. What *d'you* think? He stands up and gets his hankie out. *I think you need to kill something,* he says. *That's how I overcame my fear of death. I killed someone.* What? I'm asking him. What are you talking about? And it turns out he reckons he's killed this boy while he was in North Africa. *A youth,* he says. *Walad, they call them, just the scrapings off the streets. I caught the little shit stealing off me. Life's cheap over there, he knew that.* And then he says to me, *I knew he'd knife me if I let him, so I shot him. I took him out the wasi and I shot him, I played around with him for a while, I shot him in the gut and I waited a while, then I shot him in the balls. Right up close, bang, like that. I took my time,* he says. *I wanted to watch someone die, so I took my time with it. I shot him again a couple of times and he died of blood loss, that's how he went in the end.* And then he says to me, *the death agony's quite something, it's like listening to Bruckner—*

I'm just sitting there staring at him while all this is coming out. There's people around and I guarantee they can hear everything, and I'm thinking, *this place'll be crawling with cops in a minute*—so I get him up and walking, and after a minute he takes the lead, like, *come this way* sort of thing, and all the time he's telling me over his shoulder about the guy he reckons he murdered. Keep your voice down, I'm saying to him, and I'm looking around the place. It's partly because I don't want to hear him myself, see—like, he's telling me where the blood came out of this guy when he shot him, and you just don't want to know, Patrick. In the end I put my hand across his mouth and he got that angry I remember thinking, maybe it's not all bullshit, maybe he *did* kill that kid? Because he did look like he could do it, not so much when he was really angry but the minute he closed all that down, he switched it off like it'd never been there—he goes from one thing to another and he's looking up at me and it was just the eyes, I can't explain it. Of course it might've been his condition, I've never known him before he got Parkinson's so I don't know, do I? But his eyes were flat, not dead but flat, blue like I've said. They used to give me the shits, those pale eyes. They could go *dead*, like *that*. Just staring up at me like a cod on a block. He'd stare right at you, he'd stare right through you and then just go on staring. Right through you.

Anyway, all this time, he's taken us back to the varsity again, you know, where the college is, where we left the car. You going to kill someone here, then, I ask him—you know, he's been talking about murdering someone all this time, I thought, maybe he's got someone in mind? *Not yet*, he tells me, and you can see why I'd remember to tell you *that! Not yet*, is what he said. He's walking on ahead of me, past the bookshop and on a bit, and through under the archway again—you know where he's taking me, Patrick, you know what's going to happen. Yup, the writing school building. That's the first time I had a good look at it, we'd parked the car up against it the first few times we'd been there and we'd walked away. It was the first time he really talked about the place. The Raymond Lawrence School of Creative Writing—that's what it said, there was this sign on the building. You know where I mean. What's this? I ask him. He's standing there with his hands in his pockets and he's looking up at the place. *My biggest bloody mistake,* he says, but it's like he's not saying it to me. *Lending my name to this fucking abortion,* he says.

And that was the first time I knew he had a problem with it. At that stage, I didn't even know what creative writing was—I'm still not sure! And I still don't know why he was the way he was about it, either, the way he was talking it was the worst thing in the whole wide world. As far as I could see when he told me what it was, it was just these people trying to be writers. Just writing stuff out of their heads? I ask him. *Well, it's what I've spent my life doing*, he says. *Difference is, I didn't need some stupid prick to tell me how to do it, and d'you know why?—because you can't, you can't teach some fucker inspiration, you can't teach technique, you can't give them something to write about. You can't let them think they're going to be fucking famous when they'll be off selling cars in five years' time or insurance door to door or crockery.* This is right outside his own school he's saying this, yelling it out, this angry little old geezer with crumbs all round his mouth, and there's me next to him in my big white suit, leaning over him going *shh, shh—*

And you want to know something else? he says. *No one should be allowed to start to write until they've killed something or killed someone and watched them die!* These two women walking along across the other side of this quadrangle and you could see them turn their heads our way when he's yelling that! Shh, I tell him, and he says, *don't shh me. You've got to kill something if you want to create,* he says, and he's gone all wild in the eyes by this stage. *Death and killing's at the heart of the creative act!* All the time I'm trying to edge him away from the place because it's obviously not doing him that much good being there. *I* don't want to kill something, I tell him, and *I* don't want to be a writer. *You don't want to be a writer?* he says, and he starts pointing at the writing school building. *You should join up with them,* he says, *they'll help you with that!—when they finish with you, you won't want to pick a book or a pen up ever again!* And he's so pleased with *that* line he slaps his hands together like he's clapping himself. I didn't have the heart to tell him I hardly ever pick a book or a pen up anyway. And of course at that stage I had no bloody idea what

*

On the following Monday a single audiotape arrives by post, as promised. It's in a bubble bag that's been reinforced within, unnecessarily, fussily: I get a little whiff of a *someone* when I see the cotton wool that has been pressed in around the tape. Bitten fingernails anxiously picking at things: on the finger a nicotine stain, perhaps. Geneva Trott.

In bright blue ink that obviously imitates the Master's,

its label states *Interview # 7, 24 August.*

Of which year? Where? Who is interviewing whom, and why did I not know it was happening?

I park the car in the rampant couch grass of Julian's berm and walk up his drive. On the tangle of his twitchy lawn his old black dog casts a knowing, world-weary eye at me and away. Here is the fallen, unachieved rural property of the visionary utopian: every view a vista of unfinishment, crazy paths half done and overgrown, a vast vegetable garden all blowsy cabbages and seed-heads, a pergola so long unpainted that incompletion has become its completion. Chickens, stepping and pecking among fruit trees whose branches trail long on the ground: a stooping wooden bungalow with a propped verandah, behind it a studio in which that massive printing press takes up half the space.

Blue and white plastic strips stir in the breeze at his studio door: I press through them.

Inside, Julian has rummaged up for me from his extraordinary reliquary of antique electronic devices a 1980s tapedeck, a Panasonic with six flat black buttons along the bottom and a slightly toasted plastic finish, as if it has been placed under a grill. Its upper half has begun to lift from the lower where they join, as if the whole thing is about to snap open like a playground lunchbox. When he presses the first of the buttons, the dulled plastic lid of the portal slowly lifts, like a portent: *here is the news.*

He stares at the audiotape. 'So,' he says. 'She sent it after all.' He brings his glasses down from his brow. '24 August which year?'

'I was going to ask you.'

'Well, it's an old tape, but she could've recorded on it last week for all we know.' Julian puts the cassette carefully into the portal and presses the lid shut with his big, soft, reddened hands. 'Isn't it funny none of us've ever met her?'

'Geneva? Not really.'

'You never know, she might turn out to be a smasher.'

Now, abruptly, entering stage left, Robert Semple, pushing his way through the plastic strips: they trouble his hat and the long cigarillo centred between his lips. He has his overcoat hunched dramatically over his shoulders like a cape, its arms dangling, emptied.

'Ooh,' says Julian. 'Put out that light.'

'I'm nearly through it. Who might turn out to be a smasher?'

'Geneva. Julian's got her audiotape in the deck here.'

'Come on, Robert, you know the rules around here.'

'Three more puffs and it's history. So the tape's arrived, has it? What's on it?'

'Haven't started yet, we were waiting for you and Marjorie.'

'No, she's not going to be here, Fahti the farter rang and snapped his fingers. She told me to tell you. Play the thing, go on.'

'Point of order, no smoking, there's a sign on the wall.'

'Point of order be buggered, this isn't a Trust meeting. Press the tit.'

Julian presses, and there's a soft, fat, synchronised *cluck* and then the furred sound of the tape starting up.

Semple leans dramatically against the jamb of the studio door, blowing smoke into the garden. 'What are we listening to?' he asks, over his shoulder.

'That's what we're trying to find out.'

'Shh—*shh*—'

Julian and I bend over the Panasonic. The faint, rhythmic *swish*, *swish* of the tape.

'Is that something—there?'

I bend to the deck. The spools turn dimly under the scratched plastic of the lid. It really is impossible to tell. There might be a voice, buried somewhere in the sound of the work of the tape or deep beneath it: or there might not. It might be an effect of the machine, a mechanical voice, an accident, a phantasm. The ghost in the machine, as they say. Or it might be nothing much at all.

'Plenty of time,' Julian says. 'Don't forget they're two-sided, these things.'

Semple is still at the door, looking out at the chaos of Julian's yard. '*Si monumentum requiris, circumspice,*' I hear him say, but not to us. He flicks the cigarillo butt and turns back inside. 'Heard anything yet?'

'Shh—'

'Is that it? Is that someone speaking—?'

We all bend forward to listen. I'd expected something unequivocal, a voice—voices, somewhere we could begin. A narrative of some sort. Most of all I expected Raymond's voice, speaking to us, to me, out of the past, and with a tale to tell, even a message from the great *beyond.* I hadn't expected what we're getting instead: irresolution, indeterminacy, plain old waste. It seems somehow at odds with the space-age promise of the tape and the deck—not their promise now but the promise they had back then, twenty years ago, thirty years ago, fifty, when they lay smart and bright on desktops around the world and, along with Dot's golfball typewriter and a hundred other marvels, implied the coming command of the stars.

Instead—here, now—there's something almost vegetal about this performance, in the slight buckle and curl of the plastic of the deck, the fungal blur of the portal lid, this damp, mossy miming of recollection that is performing itself right in front of us. Who knew, back then, that the future would prove to be creeping and confused like this, random, dendritic, not forward-looking at all but forever peering back over its shoulder, as if asking for further instructions?

Now, though, Julian is ducking down, his head on one side. 'There,' he says. '*There*—'

The three of us lean again, towards the swish of the turning tape.

'She's pulling our tit,' Semple says. 'Geneva is.'

'Shh—*shh*—there's something *on* it—'

'*There*—'

Is it? The machine definitely has a voice, by now I'm clear about that: whatever it plays, this reedy mechanical sound will come out of it—the voice of an age: time's voice, the spectral, Apollonian voice of the late twentieth century, speaking to us with a mouthful of dust. But there's something else as well—is there? *It's so hard to tell.* I'm *sure* I can hear something: someone's voice, something human that is speaking to us—

'No.' Semple, pulling up and away. 'I told you, she's pulling our tit. What a fucking waste of time—'

'Shh—*shh—there*—'

Julian's right, there *is* something. It sounds lost, distant, as if from the bottom of a well, as if time really is a long, dark tunnel we draw things from and toward ourselves. But a voice, faint, down there in the distant waters, a reedy, metallic voice, half of it just the machine speaking but half of it something else, a human being as well, *we're going to eat it raw*—

'Turn it back. Reverse it. Just a bit.'

Julian whizzes the tape back a few seconds, and stops it and starts it again.

You didn't tell me to bring anything, I tell him—so we're going to eat it raw, he says back. I thought, Christ, he's going to shoot a sheep—

'That's Raymond.' I tell them. Dear Christ—that's Raymond!

'Well. So. That's Raymond.' Semple. 'So what if it is?'

'No, it's not,' Julian says. 'Peter? It's not Ray, I don't think it's Ray.'

'Well, if it's not Ray, why are we supposed to be listening to it? It's an interview, isn't it? Isn't that what she says it is? This fucking Geneva woman? So, who's being interviewed if it's not him?'

'She didn't really say what it was, she said we'd know what it meant when we heard it.'

I bend down again: Julian has the volume raised now but what's coming up to us is more static than anything else. A voice, all the same, forming out of it, Raymond's voice—*What we're really waiting for, we're waiting for the peas*—

A little tickle of memory, something unwanted: I pull back and away. 'Raymond,' I tell them. 'It's him. The Master.'

'It's no one, it isn't anybody.' Semple again. 'I'll tell you what she's gone and done, Geneva, she's given us the wrong tape, the bitch, to throw us off the scent. That's what she's done—'

'She's just given us the wrong tape, plain and simple.' Julian. 'It's a cock-up, that's all. She cocked the book up and now she's cocked this up.'

Now, though—suddenly, unexpectedly, splendidly, in hat and dark glasses—Marjorie, bursting through the doorway behind us: plastic strips fly about.

'Why is there a dead dog on your lawn, Jules, dear?' she asks.

'It's Nebuchadnezzar. He's always like that.'

'There's stuff coming out of its mouth and it's not breathing.'

'Oh, hell.' Julian's off, through the plastic strips.

'Listen to this,' I tell her. 'Who's that?'

She leans to the tape recorder and listens. 'Oh—it's him,' she says. She straightens up. 'So this is whatsit's tape, one of her tapes?'

'Geneva. It came this morning. It's Raymond, isn't it? Raymond's voice?'

'No, it's not.'

'See,' says Semple. 'Told you it wasn't.'

'It's whatsit,' Marjorie says. 'Whatsisname—'

'Who—?'

'How can you be so sure? That it's not—?'

'Because it just *isn't*, Peter. Plain and simple *not*. No, it's thingie—'

Julian bustles in again. 'I think he's eaten another plastic bag,' he says. 'Nebuchadnezzar. Damn.'

'Is he dead?'

'Thomas,' says Marjorie, as if she's trying to get rid of a hair in her mouth. 'It's Thomas.'

'No, he isn't dead. But then he brings them up again, that's the problem. The plastic bags. He vomits them back up.'

'Once he's got the goodness out of them?'

'Tom. That's who it is. On the tape.'

'The bags the meat comes in, he gets into those—he had to be cut open at the vet last time and he had *four* of them in his gut, can you believe that?' Julian stares at the tape, which is still mewing away on his worktable, unattended. 'Tom?' he says. 'Do we have a Tom?'

'*You* remember. Listen.'

We all lean in to the tape, all four of us now. It's what I've been trying not to think these last ten minutes, the knowledge I've been trying to deny since the disembodied voice began to form. Slowly, the Master's voice I've confidently heard coming up through the static dust of time turns into something else, higher, looser, sloppier, a tenor which takes the beginnings and endings off words and elides the consonants between into a rolling sludge of language, lifting lifting lifting to the end of each sentence and *collapsing* into the next so that, soon, soon, there *are* no sentences, instead just one long diarrhetic flow punctuated by pellets of giggling, sprays of tittering, loud flatulisms of inanity that pass as laughter—

Gradus.

'Oh, *him*.' Julian pulls away, nodding. 'For goodness' sake.'

'"Thom with an H—*my name's / Thom Ham*—"'

'"*Wham-Bam / Thank you Mam*—"'

Laughter.

'Remember the trial? It wasn't funny. Poor bastard.'

'Yes—he got off, though,' I remind them. 'Remember that.'

'Well, so he should have—he obviously had nothing to do with it.'

Not this again. 'But he was *there*, for goodness' sake—when it *happened*. He was *right there!*'

'Oh, come on, Norman, he just happened to be there. Apart from anything else he was too fucking stupid to do what they accused him of—wasn't that the defence, he was too thick to follow a plot?'

'And the jury bought it!'

'They didn't *buy* it, Marge—'

'Don't call me Marge—'

'—they could *see* it was *true* and they let him *off*, *that's* what the jury did—'

'Now, now.' Julian the peacemaker. 'It's all in the past—'

'No it's not, not as long as Norman Bates here still

thinks Thom was a secret agent from—what did you say it was? The BLT?'

More laughter. I despise them, I despise them.

'The French foreign intelligence service,' I tell them, as coolly as I can manage. 'The DGSE.'

This to Semple, in fact, since he's the one who has most to say on the topic. I'm appalled that they should treat it so lightly, given what it involves. *Gradus.* I'm resolved to say nothing more on it, though—I regret my outburst a moment ago, but the miscarriage of justice involved has always been too much for me. *I can't believe I'm having to think about this man again—*

The full meaning of what's happening is still coming to me as I stand here watching the other three fiddling with the tape. I'm beginning to understand something of what Geneva has done and what this new irruption into our lives really means: she's made contact with this dreadful man, with whom I associate such chaos, such utter destruction—she knows him and *that is who is being interviewed—*

'Are you all right, Peter?' Marjorie has caught sight of me. 'Just eaten a plastic bag or something?'

I stare at her. Of course, I can't say a thing. She really *is* blackmailing us, Geneva, of that I'm certain now. Towards the end Raymond would blurt out anything—who knows what he told this idiot who was looking after him then, and who knows who's been paying him to find that out? Who knows what he says on these tapes? Who knows what Geneva knows?

Again, in my rear-view mirror as I drive home from all this, the damson-coloured Dodge. It's as jolting a moment as the first time I saw the car looming up behind me where there was nothing a second or two before, far too close and very determined to overtake me—again, I signal and pull over to let him by. This time, as he blares past me, I'm *certain* that it's him, Raymond, crouched over with that grubby little trilby hat on as he holds the wheel—yes, *surely* it's him: he even flicks me a glance as he goes past. You, is it you? He gives me a couple of long blasts on the horn as if to tell me *yes, yes, I'm still here—*

*

Quite apart from anything else, *Thom Ham* is, by a slightly disconcerting coincidence, two fragments of *Thomas Hamilton*, the name of the protagonist of the Master's early and middle-period novels. I remember telling the old man, back then, that I was about to interview one of his characters for a job at the Residence: he seemed unsurprised.

Naturally, I'd been keen to have some kind of literary applicant to a position the Trust had felt was well overdue for creation once the old fellow began his long, lamentable slide towards his end. All this was happening more than fifteen years ago now, not long after the apotheosis at Stockholm and at a point when it was becoming clear what the final stages of Raymond's illness were actually going to bring us.

For a long time, the occasional unfortunate lapse in his social behaviour could be seen as a hiccup within a normality that was often better than that: whatever went wrong, within hours it seemed he was Raymond Thomas Lawrence once again: familiar, reliable enough around the house at least and well worth the occasional risk outside it—capable of walking Daisy the dog, for example, even up to the Summit Road and down again, in those days, or down to Tony's and back again with a small order of groceries, arriving at the door pleased with himself and puffing, apple-cheeked and white of beard like a miniature Santa Claus. It was charming, there was no doubting that, often it was charming to see, and, given his condition, not a little touching as well.

The thought that he might in fact be in the process of crossing some sort of psychological Rubicon was prompted when he went missing for two days—you can imagine what we thought had happened and the relief when we heard his car had been found on a riverbed outside town and then Raymond himself a little later on, at the foot of the nearby motorway bridge—it was when this episode occurred and once we'd brought him back home that we made our decision. He was raving on about industrial fertiliser, of all things, and it took us a while to work out what he might have meant by *that*, of course. As far as he was concerned he'd been back in North Africa in the late fifties, no question about it, and fighting the *Pieds-Noirs* once more, blowing up bridges and railway tracks—at one point, he claimed, an entire Esso fuel dump. *Boof!*

And then, shortly afterwards, there was that unfortunate—most unfortunate—event that I've mentioned before, at the opening of the very writing school the local university had gone to the trouble of setting up in his name. By this stage we were in no doubt that, for him, things had begun to turn about, and that his lucid episodes were becoming the hiatuses in an emerging pattern of misjudgements and misfortunes and, sometimes, just plain old disasters. It was his condition, we thought: it was the illness taking him over.

Bailey's, Marjorie said. She meant a geriatric-care firm: she'd used them for her parents when their time came. They were very good, she said: first-rate. Polished my father off in six months and my mother in twelve.

Bailey's. No one could blame them, of course. The initial phone call told me little: yes, in point of fact, they said, there *was* someone they'd just trained who had a university background, though they couldn't guarantee the degree was actually in English literature. Ah, but can he lift and turn, I asked, shrewdly foreseeing impending requirements. Oh, yes, they said, he can lift and turn all right. We'll send him round, you can take a look at him.

Take a look at him!—there was no alternative. He appeared the following day at my office: he simply walked in. I looked up from my desk and couldn't believe what I saw. The most extraordinary build, first of all, massive, looming, filling the doorway to the top and sides, his height even requiring him to duck a little to get his head quite under the lintel. Six foot six or seven, in the old measurement, or a couple of metres in the new?—whichever way, the effect was overwhelming. Yes, weights, he said when I asked him: weights footie boxing and that. He bowed the legs of the office chair I'd indicated he should sit in.

It didn't take very many questions for me to decide, privately, that this was not the man for the job. For a start, the way he spoke began to irritate me, the way each of his sentences sounded like a question, lifting up at the end as if it were asking something when there was nothing in any of them that actually required to be answered, and, in fact, nothing particularly much in them at all. Then there was the laugh, itself like a form of punctuation that occurred every few seconds, a cachinnation completely without purpose or wit and which, at the moment, I'm completely at a loss to find words for. A silly, irritating neighing sound, or sometimes (it used to occur to me, when I heard it coming through the wall of the Residence or up in the Coop) like the honk of a goose. It appalled me, it obsessed me. It was the desolating, contentless quack-quack of the universe, the very sound of vacancy itself.

Oh, there was more to my response than just these things, I assure you of that, and I'm willing to admit that in himself he didn't entirely deserve all the reaction that he received from me in the time he was with us. I'm not as utterly shut off to myself as some have assured me I am, not at all.

As the interview went on, though, it began to dawn on me that this fellow—this Thom Ham person, I mean, this enormous, inconsequential hunk of muscle and meat that had come through my office doorway—had no idea whatsoever of where it was he'd come to. I mean that he'd walked right up to the Residence—had even banged at the front door down there, he told me, and looked in at the windows and tapped at them and called out before he'd turned away and tried the Coop next door—all this without the slightest inkling of where it was that fate had brought him. He'd even walked past, and ignored, the sign that read *Raymond Thomas Lawrence Residence/ Home of the Nobel Laureate/Tours by Arrangement*—!

Raymond Lawrence, I said to him. Nope, he said. Raymond Thomas Lawrence? I asked. Never heard of him, he said, and gave that extraordinary laugh again as if he had not a single thought in his head. Not heard of Raymond Thomas Lawrence? I asked him. Do the words *Nobel Prize* mean anything to you? Nobel Prize, he said, to himself, as if it were a question off *Mastermind*. Then: Nope, sorry.

When I spelled it out for him, though, he couldn't believe what I told him. The *Nobel Prize*? he asked, and he kept saying it to himself over and over again. He lives right here and he won the Nobel Prize? Far out, he said.

You wouldn't credit it. Then he said, tell me again what he won it for?

So I took him on a tour of the Residence. And that is where he met Raymond, and the whole terrible business, as it would prove to be, began.

They hardly met, no more than a minute at the top of the elevator once the old fellow had come up on it, rather unexpectedly, to find out who it was he could hear me taking around the Residence. After that—and rather impressively, I have to admit—this weightlifter person carried the old man up to the Coop for me, wheelchair and all, and then he left us there and off he went on his racing bike, which seemed tiny beneath him, I remember, ridiculously slight, like a wafer between his massive legs. Cheers, he called back to us, over his shoulder, and of course I hated that, too. What can it mean: what's so very wrong with *goodbye* or *thank you*?

That's the man, the old fellow told me as soon as the weightlifter had gone. *What's the bugger's name?* I stared at him, I remember: I couldn't believe my ears. What d'you mean, I demanded. What d'you mean, *that's the man*?

This is the moment that really took me by surprise. To my knowledge, none of the Trust members had said anything to Raymond yet about getting a little help for him—as far as we were concerned, we thought we'd find out what was available first, and then, if we found somebody suitable (and I'd already crossed this feckless iron-pumper off the list in my mind), we'd set about the business of gently breaking the news: *Raymond, we've come to the conclusion that maybe it's time to look for a little help*—and so on. A companion, we were going to call this person: someone who, if not quite in their eighth decade as he was, would certainly be closer to it than this inane failed geographer with his enormous body and (it has to be said) his tiny, disproportionate *cranidumb*. Someone to *hang out with*, we would have said. A mate.

Well, what Raymond meant by *that's the man*, it seemed, was that our search was at an end. I presumed it was Semple who told him that it had begun in the first place, though of course he loudly denied having done so when I confronted him later that day. Raymond had worked it out for himself, he insisted: we all of us knew he had a second sense about this sort of thing, we all knew he was nobody's fool. He'd obviously worked it out, he said, and he'd gone and made his choice. After all (he reminded me), he was the one whomever we hired would have to work with, and he'd obviously decided this was someone who could work with him.

Love at first sight, he said. Go with it.

But he's an idiot! I said to Raymond, after I'd finished with Semple. He doesn't know one end of a book from another! *That's* why he's the man! the old fellow said—I couldn't believe it, I simply couldn't believe he'd say something like that. But surely you want someone you can talk with, I suggested, someone you—but at this point he really exploded at me, Raymond, he simply blew up in my face. *Fuck* it, man!—and he brought his little fists up like a boxer and bared his grimy bottom teeth at me. I don't need someone to sit with knitting under a fucking *travel* rug, he hissed. I want a fucking *follower*!

It was a disturbing moment. I gazed at him, I remember, trying to assess the status of what he'd just said to me. It was easy to see these explosions as part of the illness as it was taking him over—and perhaps as part of his frustration, too, at a world that was becoming more and more in-and-out-of-focus for him, presenting alarming *non sequiturs* out of the blue, moments of sheer, inexplicable terror at the presenting world. On the other hand I could remember these gallus performances from when I was a lad, that boxer's stance of his and the bared lower teeth: seeing these once again always brought back memories, made me tighten up a little down below, revived some of that old primal fear and panic. Around Raymond at any age, it was easy enough to become twelve years old again in half a second: less.

Here, at this particular moment, though, I put his behaviour down to the illness, and the slight tinge of paranoia and grandiosity of the sort you can see in what I've just told you I attributed to the same thing: just an episode, a momentary flare-up. Oh, what a misjudgement that would prove to be, I can tell you, the decision to discount an open statement of intent like this. I had no idea then—how could I?—that Raymond was already planning his final chapter, his *dénouement*, his *Götterdämmerung*. And that (if you like) the Sorcerer had found his Apprentice.

*

First thing I did when I turned up, I sorted out his pills for him. He had to take them at different times each day and I'd mark it off on a chart every time I'd give him a dose. Then someone said, get those bubble packs, the chemist sorts the pills for you, you can see straight away when there's been a miss. One of his pills, though, if you miss it you have to phone the specialist straight off and tell him you've cocked it up. But I never cocked it up, ever, not once. The big change for me was when I moved into the Chicken Coop, and that'd be—I don't know, 1999? When he started falling out of bed and having nightmares? Jeez, the nightmares. What happened was, I was more or less living with Raewyn back then and me and her were in the sack and it's past midnight and the phone goes—Mrs Butt's ringing me, old Edna, Right Butt, and she's saying, *Mr Lawrence isn't well at all, he's talking to a chair, Mr Orr's not here and we don't know what to do—*

So next thing, I'm up at the Residence again, and there's the old boy sitting on his bed having a good old yack to someone who's not there! Part of me knows what's happening and part of me's got the tomtits big time because it was *that* weird—I mean, you could see he really thought there was someone sitting in front of him. Get an ambulance, I tell the Butts, they're just standing there, turns out they didn't want to because they didn't believe in ambulances!—ever heard anything like that before? They wanted me to get down and pray with them instead! So I go up to the old fellow and I say excuse me, and he says, *excuse me, I'm talking to this young lady here,* and he points to the chair in front of him. There's no one on it, I say to him—and he reaches across and smacks me across the side of the head! *Don't you be so bloody cheeky,* he says to me. *You black bastard.* So I thought, bugger you, and I wrestled him down on the bed. I can hear the Butts in the next room praying, and after a while the old bloke stops struggling and then he mutters *I've pissed myself*, and that was that. I tell Either-Or when he turns up later on, and he says, *Julia? He was talking to Julia?*

Anyway, that was split city for poor old Raewyn, she told me it was like I was running another woman except it was an old man, and if an old man turned me on more than what she did, then it was time I got a hold of myself. And next thing the trust people decided to shift the old boy out and up to the Coop and me with him. And he *did* change around then, there was the shakes and the nightmares but they were just seeing things from one of the pills he was on, it might've been the Clonazepam. The doctor told us that, he put Mr

Lawrence on some new stuff and maybe that was why he seemed to become sort of—less human? I don't know. Just now and then, you'd look at him and it was like he'd switched off, *boom*—tell you what it was like, it was like he'd changed gear? There you go—he'd double-declutched himself! He'd driven off somewhere else and we didn't know where it was!

But I'll tell you when I first started to think, *there's something really weird going on here.* It was one time he took me up the hill with him to look for the dog. It was me that drove, I'd started to get on top of the double-declutch thing, sort of, anyway, but he'd yell at me if I tried to sneak a change without doing it. He was brought up on old jalopies out on the farm, he learned on an old Essex out at Springfield, he told me, and he could double-declutch a car in his sleep. Once we're up at the top he says, *we're back there.* What d'you mean, I ask him, and he says, *now, I mean now, we're back in 1948.* He waves out at the city. *See?* he says. *You wait, when the streetlights come on later you'll see, the city'll be that much smaller, it's a smaller city now it's 1948, it's only a few thousand people.* Then he turns on the radio in the dash—and it starts playing music from back then! *What'd I tell you!* he says, *we're back in 1948!* I got a hell of a shock, I can tell you, I'd had a go at it earlier on and it wouldn't even turn on when I tried, and now here it was, all these Yank stations and a woman singing *inju-u-ure yerself, it's later than you think*—what's that she's singing? I ask the old man—*injure* yourself? He's laughing and laughing at me and I don't know why. *Doris Day?* he's saying to me. *She couldn't injure a baby!*

Then he says to me, *it's my new novel. This,* he says. *What we're doing now. It's my new novel. Living like this. It's what I'm writing now.* Like, you know, he was making it all happen himself?—him, me, the car, the wind off the sea—even, you know, the hill the car's standing on? *It's what I'm writing now,* he says. I'm writing all this. So I ask him, what's it called, then, this new book of yours? *What d'you think it's called,* he says. *I've told you, and it's not new, it's the book I've been writing all my life, it's called 1948.* Right, I tell him. *I'm going to stick it up Orwell's arse,* he says. *It's backwards that matters, not forwards, it's 1948 that matters, not 1984.* Then he's out the door and round the back and he's opening the boot, and here he is with a bloody shotgun!

Well, talk about fill my pants—I thought I was going to fill the car. But then he says, *come on, wheel your arse, we're going to get our dinner! Where's the stuff I told you to bring?* You didn't tell me to bring anything, I tell him—*so we're going to eat it raw?* he says back. I thought, Christ, he's going to shoot a sheep. I'll go back down and get the stuff, I told him, but what I really meant was, I'd go back down and ring the cops. And I went back down to the Residence and I sat there in the car under the bluegums and the pines, and what I found was, it felt different compared to the way it felt back up the hill. He seemed so happy, Mr Lawrence. It was fun, I've never spent that much time with an old bugger like that, my parents died fairly young and my grandparents, too. So I just helped myself to a few things around the house, you know, couple of mugs, couple of plates, couple of knives, couple of forks and a few other things, a skillet and so on, and I grabbed some fruit out of the fruit bowl to piss Right Butt off—apples, hand of bananas and that—I load all this in the Dodge and I dodge back up the hill with them.

Early evening by then, still light but not that warm, and there he is above the road, he's up on a bluff and he's waving to me with the gun! *Up!* he's saying—hardly hear him in the breeze.

Up! So up I go with the stuff I'd got from the Residence, and he just can't wait to tell me. *Shot the bastard,* he calls out before I'm twenty foot away. *Wasn't easy but I shot him and dressed him and he's cooking.* Christ, I thought—he's shot a ram, that's going to be tough eating. He drags me down the other side of the hill and there's gorse and this little sheltered area there and he's got a fire going and the meat's on it, right in the fire. *Give us that skillet,* he says, and he grabs it off me. *It's burning the way it is, good thing it's so fatty.* I could see a tin of peas in the fire, too, and he had a bullet-hole through the side of it as well—you wouldn't believe it, he'd shot the tin of peas? Turns out he's got a lot of things stashed away up there. *This is where I'm going when it starts to happen,* he says to me. *You never know what it's going to be like when things really start to happen.*

When *what* happens, I ask him, but he doesn't say, he's got his head in the gorse and he's pulling out stuff he's hidden away all wrapped up in an old piece of waterproof jacket, I could see the pocket on it when he brought it out. There's a few tins of peas wrapped up and some dried stuff, and he pulls out a bottle as well. *Good thing no bastard's found that,* he says. *Catch!* And then he pulls a pouch out of the waterproof pocket! *And this,* he says, and he starts to roll one like he's done it a few times before. You're not meant to smoke, I tell him, and he gets really pissed off when I say that to him. *Might as well be back down there if you're going to talk to me like that,* he says. *Eating fucking walnuts with the rest of them.* All the time he's rolling the paper and licking it like he wanted to eat it up. He puts it in his mouth and ducks down into the fire for a second and then he comes back up and it's lit. *When I was fighting with Rabah Bitat,* he says, *we'd light up with a pistol shot.* Oh yeah, I said. *One silly fucker tried it with a rifle, took the end off his own bloody nose, the silly prick.* I never really listened when he was slinging me that sort of stuff. He's sitting back and he's sucking the smoke in like it's the best thing he's ever done in his life. *This is my world up here,* he says to me. *Now. 1948. Before it all started to go wrong.*

What d'you think he meant when he was talking like that, Patrick? Maybe he just meant, *this would all be in his book, this was what he had to do to get it going.* And all the time he's poking the fire and stirring the meat and turning it over, and it's starting to smell pretty good—and I have to tell you, Patrick, it wasn't that bad up there on the south-east side. It's out of the wind, we're wrapped up and there's the fire, plus you get the view across the harbour. I'd had a couple of shots out of his bottle, it looked like water and it tasted like liquorice and the good thing was, it did the trick. He's talking all the time I'm drinking and admiring the view, he's telling me about when he was a kid back on the family farm. Hamilton Downs it was called, and he reckoned he used to have a hideaway there like this one, and he'd shoot rabbits and possums there and dress them and cook them for his supper on an open fire the way he was doing in front of me while he was talking. He was always going on about the farm but he never went there except the once at the end, that I'll tell you about when I get there—Christ, I'll never forget *that*.

And now and then he'd poke at the meat in the skillet and then he'd lean back and smoke some more—he rolled three while I was counting. I can't remember what he said but I remember it was funny, Christ, he could be funny, he made me laugh all right and he made himself laugh a bit as well. I stopped taking notice of the weird things he'd said earlier on—like I told you, we had really good times together and that was one of them. I'll never forget the times we had like that. And all the time there was the meat, it was starting to smell good. *What we're really waiting for, we're waiting for the peas,* he said. *That can's going to be a bugger to open hot.* It was too when he got round to it, he swore a lot and he kept dropping it and flapping his hand and blowing on it but in the end he got the opener going and worked a hole could shake the peas out, half on each plate. *There you go!* he says. You could have done that at the start, I told him, when it was cold. Opened it with the opener. *Yes, I could,* he says, *but I wanted to put a bullet through it, then everything we're eating's been shot by me, see?*

What about the bananas? I ask him, and he says, *bananas?* Stole some bananas for you, I said, and I showed him. *You silly prick,* he says, *they're wax bananas,* can't you tell the difference? And he marches off with them and puts them on a rock. *Target practice after supper,* he says. Then he's back and shoving a piece of meat into his mouth and gobbling at it. *Here,* he says, he's holding out a plate. *Wolf that down, the meat's falling off the bone. It's better than it looks, get that in you.* And I was that hungry I wolfed it down like he told me to. It was pinky-red like rabbit meat but fattier, quite greasy, first off I thought I was eating an old sheep, some full-mouth ewe he'd got from somewhere. But it wasn't fatty enough—to tell the truth though I was that bloody hungry I didn't really care what it tasted like. Him, too. There's the two of us kneeling on either side of the fire tearing at the meat even when the rest of it's still cooking!

It was a good five minutes before I got to where I could ask him what it was. He looks at me. *You'll have to guess,* he says. *Can't*, I tell him. He'd got grease all over his face and his beard and his hands and down his front. Mutton, I told him. *Mutton!* he says. *Where'd I get a fucking sheep from?*

I'd have to climb an electric fence. And so I went through the list. I said possum for a joke because I had a mate'd eaten possum once and he said it was better than you'd think. And then just for another joke I said, *cat. Close to home,* he says, *but it's not quite fatty enough for cat meat, try again.* And when he said that my mind went, *click*. I just froze there with my mouth full of hot meat for five seconds and then I spat it out and it's just sitting there sputtering in the fire. *What a fucking waste!* he says, and he's happy as hell, you'd think it was the best joke ever. I could have *hit* him, he was that pleased with himself.

I kept asking myself *how could he do it, how could he do it?* I'm lying there that night back down in the Coop and he's asleep the other side of the *en suite*, burping and farting—I keep asking myself, *how could he do it*? And of course I asked him, I asked him as soon as I'd spat the meat out, with him cackling away at me—Christ, he can be frightening when he's like that and his top plate's out and there's just his eyeteeth sticking down like Dracula. But then I got *real* pissed off with him and he toned it down. *All right, all right,* he says. *It wasn't easy. You couldn't do it, remember? That was a test for both of us, well, I've passed the test. So have you*, he says, *now you've eaten her.* Her? I ask him. *Yes, her,* he says. *Daisy.* You mean Rommel, I told him, we've eaten Rommel. *I mean Daisy,* he says, *you've eaten Daisy the dog, Rommel's still around. We're both of us in a different place now we've done that, we've passed through something together. Pity you couldn't keep it all down.* And he holds me out another bone. *There!* he says. *Have a drumstick,* and he laughs and he says, *looks like a dog's hind leg!* But I had another good spew instead, right into the fire, I had a bloody good reach, and him laughing himself silly behind me all the time I'm bringing my guts up. *Now you've undone the spell!*

he's telling me. *You're back to square one,* you silly arse—

I'm lying there in bed like I said, and I'm thinking it through, and I start thinking, hold on a minute. This is bullshit. How does a man his age in his state kill a dog? Forget the fact it's Rommel, you know, his four-legged soulmate or whatever he's supposed to be. It's just a dog but how does he do it? No well don't forget it's Rommel, it's all one thing, he's meant to have killed his best friend and cooked it and eaten it, even though he reckons now he's done it the dog's called Daisy and Rommel's still around somewhere. *How did he do it*? He can hardly hold his knife and fork. It was me that had to keep the fire going. On the other hand, he was Dead-Eye Dick when it come to shooting the wax bananas after dinner, you could tell he knew what he was doing, he put a shot through the middle of each one, *bang-bang-bang* like that, and then he shot what was left to buggery. So he could shoot a gun all right.

*

Julian is standing against the carved dresser in the Residence dining room, his trousers drawn a little too tight at the crotch: he keeps adjusting himself.

'So,' he says. 'Geneva's sent us a tape that proves she means business. And we can't hear what's on it—right?'

'Right,' I tell him.

Semple leans back in his dining chair as he usually does, and, as usual, the chair gives out a sharp crack at the moment of apogee. As always when it makes this noise, he eases it forward, carefully, till it's four-square on the floor again.

He flattens his palms against the tabletop, as if he's trying to press it down.

'Where does that leave us?' he asks.

'Yes'—Marjorie now, dabbing at her nose—'I still don't understand what she's got over us.'

Parp, into a tissue.

'Well.' Julian again. 'We heard enough to know it's Thom speaking on the tape. Maybe that's the name she wants us to hear. Thom.'

'So. What did Thom know that we don't want to get out? We all know how Ray went, so—it can't be that—'

'There's not just that, there's what happened before.'

'Everyone knows about that. We talked about it last time.'

'Everyone knows he was a shit.'

'Yes, but that doesn't mean we want them looking into the pot, does it?'

'Thom Ham wouldn't have known about that sort of thing, though—would he? What the old man used to get up to? Ray was past it by the time Thom turned up—that's *why* he turned up, isn't it?'

'He had that stick thing,' Semple says suddenly. 'Ray did.' He looks across at me. 'Is that it? Is *that* the clue? *Pandy*? Did she say that? Geneva? On the phone? *Pandy?*'

What *does* he mean? '*Pandy*?'

'*You* remember. He used to call it the pandybat. When he brought it out. That Arab stick-thing of his.'

'Did he?' For the life of me I can't remember this detail. '*Pandy?*' How could I have forgotten it had a name?

'I remember the stick,' Marjorie says. 'Why'd he call it Pandy, though?'

'Think Joyce.'

'Joyce who?'

'Oh, come on!' Semple, thumping forward over the tabletop. 'Joyce *who*—'

'Oh—*him*.'

'The pandybat at Clongowes. *Stately, plump Buck Mulligan*—'

'No, that's in the other one—'

'What other one?'

'I don't know that I know about this,' Julian says. 'What sort of a stick?'

'I'll get it,' I tell them. 'It's in his bedroom.'

I slip out. Julian's voice behind me, reminding Semple about *Ulysses. What d'you mean, never read it?* I hear him say. Raymond's room smells unaired, with a slight back-story of mould. I remember coming in here and finding the second paua shell on the desk. *Quite a lot I haven't read,* Semple is saying, truculently, back in the dining room.

I don't need the light this time: I know where the drawer is. I reach in and rummage for the thing. *Haven't read Shakespeare?* from the other room. A pulse trills in my neck.

Julian's eyebrows lift to me as I come back with the stick in my hand.

Semple stares. 'For Christ's sake,' he says. 'He's actually kept the fucking thing—'

'Is it a sort of wog-hitting stick?'

'No.' Julian takes it from me. 'I'll tell you what it is, it's a British army swagger stick.'

He explains: a short, leather-bound stick used by British Army officers to help point up otherwise pointless parade-ground choreography. Nothing more to it than that, and definitely (when I ask him) nothing to do with North African peoples—or with anything very much at all, it seems.

So *that's* what it is! And it must be so: peaceable Baby-boomer that he is, Julian knows his military memorabilia, even though it's at odds with every other part of his life.

Now, after all these years, Raymond's story has changed a little. The old man must have found this thing in a North African market: possibly it reminded him in some unhappy way of the school that swallowed up much of his second decade. I wonder at myself for bringing it out: but it seems to be having its moment, it seems to be attracting attention.

Is *this* what Geneva meant me to find, and, if so, what might that mean?

The others are passing it from hand to hand. Semple *thwacks* it reminiscently across his palm. 'He got me with it a few times,' he's telling Marjorie. 'Caught me stealing copper off him, that was the first time.'

'On the bottom? The bare bottom?'

'Me? No! On the back, the old bugger, when I was trying to get away from him.'

'But schoolboys, when they—'

'The Dark Ages are over,' Julian says. He's holding the stick up and looking at it.

'—they used to bleed,' Marjorie says. 'They were flogged naked, apparently. Schoolboys. They used to be flogged naked till they bled.'

'Schools haven't flogged for fifty years.' Julian doesn't look up: he's gazing and gazing at the pandybat. 'Not even the religious schools.'

Robert and Marjorie, though, are still back in the locker room together. 'Really?' he's just asked her. 'You? With the pandybat?

'No, with his hand. On the bare bum, sometimes. I still can't decide whether I liked it or not.'

'But isn't that the point? You love it and hate it at the same time? The borderline of kink?—the kink *is* the borderline, that's where it's at?'

Now Julian is becoming interested, too. They're fizzing!

The pandybat has excited them—the swagger stick, as Julian has renamed it. I wait till the spanking talk around me exhausts itself. It takes a minute or two, and there's definitely more energy in the room once they're done.

Now Marjorie wants to know why I've brought the bat out, what my point is.

'Well—we're assuming there might be something about it on Geneva's tapes, aren't we?'

We're all staring at the stick now, as it sits in the middle of the dining table's surface commanding attention but resisting explication.

'So—he had a stick, and he called it—'

'The pandybat. Apparently he did, I never—'

'—and she's told you it's mentioned on these tapes.'

'*No*—she said she had a name, and that the name was on the tape. The one she gave us.'

'Which we couldn't hear.'

'I think we're going round in circles again.' Julian, of course: he adjusts his trousers once more. 'We're not getting anywhere. We're trying to find a name, and—'

'We want the thing first.'

'No,' I tell them. 'The name first.'

'We need to get hold of those other tapes.' This is Semple, suddenly, urgently. 'We don't know what else is on them—'

I stare at him. Does he know something? He was there at the start, after all, or very nearly. This could be trickier than I thought.

Julian leans forward, elbows on the table. 'Isn't that the challenge?' he says. He picks the stick up. 'To make some kind of intervention?'

'What d'you mean, intervention?'

'To get off our bums and—make something actually *happen* for once?' He looks around, leaning forward, his forearms on the table, the stick up stiff in his fist. 'Here we are, representing one of the most active writers there's ever been, his fiction's full of people *doing* things—people blowing things up, getting killed—*decisiveness*, that's what he preached, isn't it? Isn't that one of the things he preached?'

'The consequential writer,' I remind them. 'The consequential writer and the consequential life.'

'His words. Raymond's words.' Julian rolls the pandybat away from himself, across the table. He sits back. Semple gazes at the stick. He picks it up.

'You're suggesting killing Geneva Trott?' he says. 'I'm up for that.'

'But is bumping off biographers *really* the sort of thing literary trusts do?' Marjorie creaks. 'Don't we just handle copyright?'

'Geneva's an exception. There's no rules for people like Geneva fucking Trott.' Semple *whacks* the pandybat into his left palm. 'Anything goes, that's what I say.'

'What I'm suggesting *is*, we do something about these tapes. We don't know what's on them but we know it might be damaging—and anyway, it's not her story. Geneva's. Isn't that what we moaned about when *Years of Lightning* came out? That book of hers? Didn't we say, it wasn't her story and she'd just helped herself without asking?'

'Oh, Julian! You're getting quite excited, I've never seen you like this before!'

'Yes, but he's *onto* something, Marge, for Christ's sake.' Semple is leaning forward now, his arms on the tabletop, his hands opening and closing as he speaks. The bat lies in front of him: he stares at it. 'Are we just going to sit here and let things happen—or, are we going to, you know—?'

'Lay a plot?' Marjorie. 'D'you realise that's what we're talking about? Isn't that the term? Laying?'

'*Laying*—?'

'Shh, Robert. Grubby mind. That's what they used to say, though, didn't they? Writers? Back in the day? *Laying a plot*? Like laying the foundations for a house?'

He stares at her. 'So—?'

'Well, that's what we're doing, aren't we? Laying a plot? Without Ray to help us? We're all on our own now and we're trying to lay a plot.'

Semple looks irritated. 'I don't mean talking,' he says. 'I mean *doing*.' He stares at me. '*I'm* up for it.' Across at Julian. 'What d'you think, Jules? A commando raid?'

'A *commando* raid? On what, where's she staying? Geneva?'

'Where *is* she staying?'

'Don't know yet. She's down sometime next week, that's all she told me.'

'If we could just distract her—'

'What? And nick the tapes?'

'Get *hold* of the tapes,' Julian says. 'Play them, put them back. Find out what's on them, find out if she's really got something on us.'

'No!' Semple is on fire: the bat is back in his hands. 'We don't have to *play* them, we have to *piss* on them. Then it doesn't matter *what's* on them.' He turns to me. 'Where'd you say she's going to stay? Geneva? In a brothel somewhere? How're we meant to distract her?'

'Take her out somewhere. Take her to dinner.'

'We'll need longer than that. If we're going to listen to these things—how many are there? Fifty-minute tapes—we'd need to keep her busy for—twenty-four hours at least.'

'Well!' Marjorie's moment. 'There's only one man I

know who'd keep a woman busy for *twenty-four hours*!'

Semple stares at her. He pushes back from the table, his hat rising slightly as he straightens. 'Steady on!' he says.

'Come on, Robert.' Julian seems to be serious about this mad scheme that's somehow evolving under our noses to the *thwack* of the pandybat. 'Take one for the team. We have to *do* something.'

Robert stares around himself, wildly. 'I could take her for a drive, I suppose,' he says. 'Someone could take her for a drive.' He looks at Marjorie. '*You* could. You could take her to see the pancake rocks.'

'And meanwhile—?'

'Meanwhile.' Julian has his fists around the stick now. 'The rest of us can take care of the tapes.'

Marjorie stares at him. 'You mean, steal them?'

'Borrow them.'

'But how are you going to get them?'

Julian taps the stick on the tabletop. 'We'll find a way in,' he says.

'Breaking and entering's against the law, Jules, dear. Even a motel room.'

'I don't think we should do this.' I stand. 'I think this is a very silly idea.'

Semple *whacks* his hands down on the tabletop—we all jump a little. He stands there looking as if he's about to do it again. 'We need to *do* something,' he says.

'But we're *literary* folk—'

'We're trying to protect his reputation.' Julian this time. 'Raymond's. That's all we're doing.'

'You're protecting his secret.' Marjorie stands, too, and starts picking up her bags. 'There's a lie at the bottom of this place, that's why I don't like being here in the evenings.'

I stare at her.

'Same thing. We're protecting that. Anyway, he has to have a secret.'

'Why does he have to have a secret?'

'Because all writing is about secrets. He said it himself.'

'He said all writing is about killing.'

'No, he said all writing was a *crime*, each work of art was a *crime*—'

'*About* a crime—each one is *about* a crime—'

I let them rattle on. They're all wrong about this business, although each of them is almost right. Each version is *very nearly* the thing that Raymond used to say. It would appal me whenever he did—as if he were deliberately tempting fate, deliberately flying too close to the wind to see what he could get away with. Here it is, flaring up in front of me, as if he's breathing on the very flames himself: and here it is, come back again: *concealment, secrets.*

From the front door I watch them leave for their cars, down by the garage. Semple is holding Raymond's swagger stick like a club. It's clear something is going to happen, but I've no idea what it is.

Nothing that has occurred this evening has been at all what I expected. Instead, again, the present: inert, insentient, unsatisfactory, rolling away from us in different directions like mercury on a plate. Waiting to become past, in order to find a meaning. Seeking the forest—

*

Wear this, he said to me, abruptly, as I came into the Residence one day in my later teens—exactly the same words that started off that strange cross-dressing business all those years earlier when he handed me the pale blue frock and, till usurped, I became Julia Perdue and, for the first time, entered a work of fiction as a character.

This on *this* occasion, though, was not a dress but a piece of fabric, one I remember enraging Raymond with in my early days by unknowingly using it as a dish-cloth: it was in fact (as he explained to me at the time), a *keffiyeh*, headwear completed by (*look*, *watch*: he assembled these on his head as he explained) the *agal* (*always camel-hair*, he said), the circlet of rope that held it in its place. And with several days' growth on his face he suddenly looked as if he had indeed been in North Africa, had in fact taken part in one of its foundational struggles at a time when he was not all that much older than I was as I stood there in front of him and watched his transformation. He looked newly arrived, and with the sun and the heat still upon him.

Along with his French he'd picked up more than a little Arabic during his rather more than a *Wanderjahr* in North Africa all those years before, and from the start a few Arabic words and phrases were coughed and hawked around casually between us. Most of them I half-understood at best. You'll have noticed he called me *sidi* from time to time—ironically: it means master—and he'd also call me *tefel* and *farid* and *walid*, which always gave me the curious, fleeting sensation of being somebody else. Sometimes, in the early days, I called him *Qaid*, which I knew also had some respect in it.

By the time I'm talking about here I'd got sick of all this, though, not least when he spoke Arabic in front of me in shops. I was well past that course of bitter little Anastrozole tablets I've mentioned earlier, which I'd taken for four months and which had suddenly made me more than a little taller, and I was past the aching joints, the slight exhaustion and the dizzy spells that came with it: hidden, my scoliosis was already beginning its secret, slow, reactive twist. My voice had broken at last (as much,

Raymond said, as it sounded likely to do), and I was ready, in my piffling way, for a fight. I was trying out a *bolshie attitude*, as he used to call it.

Don't tell me, I asked him as he handed me the *keffiyeh* once more: the muse has struck again? And: *no*, as he tried to put the thing on me—that, and a sort of loose shirt arrangement. I backed away from him. This is ridiculous, I told him. You can't go on *doing* this sort of thing to people—*no!*

I really meant it, I remember. I remember really fighting him off as we swept and lurched and slammed around the kitchen—he backed me into cupboard doors at one point and I remember a pot knocked off the gas stove just after that and its contents burped over our feet and the lino, and all the time the push-and-pull on the *keffiyeh* that was between us taut and loose and taut again—

Twenty seconds of this, maybe, and then he stopped, abruptly, and pulled away from me. The cloth dropped to the floor. He stooped and picked it out of the mess of macaroni cheese down there. He looked up at me: there was the horror of his gaze. *I'll cut 'em off,* he said, quietly. *You know that, don't you?*

He straightened up. He meant it, I knew that, I knew this was going to be different. That *thing* in him was back, I could see, I could see: so *cold*, so *hard*. Behind him his hand was in the drawer, I could hear him rummaging blindly amongst the knives, I could hear the clatter of his fingers in the steel. I suddenly realised: *he was going to do it at last, he was going to do it at last*—I knew that and that he *had* to: behind this moment so much history, and no way now to stop it—

I crouched there in front of him, seeing everything happening very clearly, move by move, and his hand coming back up to me from out of the drawer with the glitter of steel in it:

Evviva il coltellino!

Except that, when the moment actually came, what he brought out of the drawer, what he absolutely *whipped* out from behind him, was—

We stood there, the two of us, neither moving, both of us staring at the thing in his fist. To this day I've no idea whether all this was a stunt or a blunder—but no way of telling, either, since he carried it off so well:

An *eggbeater*, for God's sake—

He held it there between us for a terrifying second or two and (it seemed) at the height of his rage: until one or other of us (I can't remember which) started to laugh, and then that was that. Raymond, I think. Yes, it was Raymond. He'd wind the handle in my face for a few seconds and the beaters would mix through each other at the end of my nose, and it really did seem the funniest thing either of us had ever seen in our lives. Then he'd pull it away and bring it back and wind the handle at me again and off we'd go once more. I laughed, I remember, till I cried. The relief! It was over at last!

For *now,* it was over for *now*—

After we'd worked out of ourselves the ten or fifteen minutes of fear and anger we'd been building up between us—worse than that for me: for me, sheer terror—a knife, after all—when that was done he flung the eggbeater back into the drawer behind him and the headcloth onto the sinkbench, and butted the drawer shut with his bottom, and subsided. One over the other he folded his arms, as if tucking them into bed. He seemed to have let something go, or maybe it had let go of him.

You're a strange little prick, he said, quietly, not looking at me: just leaning against the sinkbench as he talked, and looking here, looking there, looking at the floor and up and away as he spoke, and then down at the floor again and all the time getting his breath back while the words came out, and never once looking me, least of all in the eye.

It's been hard, all this, he said. For me. What d'you think it's been like? I took you in, I *wanted* you—I wanted to *make* something *of* you, I wanted you to understand all this shit I'm into. I wanted you to start thinking differently, I wanted you to become a different person. Another person. I didn't want you turning out some fat-arsed nonentity like your fucking awful parents. But it's no use, it's no use.

He stared past me. He looked away.

I mean, it *seems* it's no use, he said. Doesn't it?

Well—you can imagine the effect this had on me. The effect *all* this had on me, the anger and then the sudden calm, so gentle, so regretful, so genuine as it seemed to be at these moments: and always was, I'm sure, I'd like to think that's true. Always so *loving*, after the anger and the violence. Always so *intimate*. I didn't know what to do, I didn't know what to say. I was still on the edge of tears, as usual whenever he brought me to this complicated pass. It felt like love, that was the thing, it felt as if *someone loved me after all.*

You told me not to write, I said. There was a silly tremor still in my voice, I remember. *You're* the one who told me not to go on writing—

It was all I had, it was all I could think of saying back to him. He ignored it competely, of course. He picked up the *keffiyeh* again and looked at it.

What d'you think it's been *like*, he said—murmured—I could barely hear him: it was almost as if he wasn't really talking to me. How d'you think it's been, watching you grow up and away from me like this? What d'you think you've been to me? D'you think I *wanted* all this?—he flung his arms apart, dramatically: the soiled *keffiyeh* flapped and dangled from one hand. I had no idea what he meant, no idea at all. It was almost as if I wasn't there.

Then he simply turned away from me.

That's it, he said. That's it.

He was walking away. He was walking out on me—he was walking out of my life!

I tried to follow him: *Uncle—*

No—he stopped and turned towards me—no, no, don't worry, he said. Oh, *Jesus*, there's no need to start crying in front of me again, the fucking hormones were meant to stop that shit—*stop crying, for God's sake—*

And off again, into the creaking little corridor: I hurried after him. He was at his most opaque, his most baffling, his most utterly seductive. I wanted to call out to him but I didn't know what to say—I didn't even know what to call him: *uncle* didn't seem right anymore, as if he'd just abdicated that role and there was nothing else for him to be to me, and nothing for me to be back to him. *Qaid? Father—?*

C'était notre rupture, I slowly realised, but only later, much later, looking back at all this: I mean the point at which he decided to start letting go of me, or of a certain part of me.

You want to know my biggest regret? he asked later that day, or sometime soon after, and pleasantly, conversationally: we were in the front room, by the fluttering light of the fire in the Residence's stone fireplace. That prick Pepper, he said—Hugh Pepper was our doctor: he was the one who'd written the prescription that had *made a man of me*. Letting him give you those hormone tablets, my uncle said. D'you know that? I wanted you to be my boy, always my marvellous boy. And look what he's done to you!

He was drinking, I remember—we both were, not Ouzo but something else, something neither here nor there in comparison, beer or gin or something like that, a drink with no particular redolence: Ouzo, the poor man's anise, the elixir of transition, drunk as you moved from *now* to *then* and from *here* to *there*.

No more of that for me, I knew: he was giving me up to time, and, whatever it was he'd hoped for me till then (and who knows what that was, who *really* knows what fantasy he had centred on me up till that point), I'd been abruptly returned to ranks. No longer the marvellous boy—if ever I'd been quite so in fact—but about to become the lesser, safer thing I've actually been in the long years since: his steward, his private secretary, his majordomo, someone to be taken for granted. That all-purpose *bumboy*—dreadful phrase, shameful concept: I hate to reproduce it but those were his words: the *factotum* whose role and tasks he announced to me a few months after he said it. His Pooh-Bah. But, also, in due course and (as it's proven) for the best, his successor.

He'd made me clean up the macaroni cheese from the kitchen floor and, the following day, or some day soon after this strange episode, he made me clean the toilet bowl as well. At this time we had a *cleaning lady*, as such people are known, her name (of course) Mrs During: but what about Mrs During, I remember protesting to him. She cleaned it today, she was in this morning? Old Mother During be fucked, he said while he bustled me into the *water closet*, as she always called it. She just scrubs the fucker. You've got to find its inner meaning. Go on—*go on*—

And go on I did, miserably and at length, gazing bleakly at that extraordinarily crackled interior with its lime-green weep that no work of the brush seemed able to revoke. What was it he wanted me to see in the worn *craquelure* of this bowl? My new status, I suppose, reflected back to me in the turbid waters beneath my face. As soon as I was done he was in there, of course, to *bomb Dresden*, and undo thus my hour of work—well, fifteen minutes of it, let's say. *Bombs away!* he called out, as he usually did at these moments—he had a lavatory pun on *Eau de Cologne*, too, I remember that. I was back in the quotidian, and (it seemed at the time) I would never enter hand-in-hand with him again, a marvellous boy, the world from which he had just expelled me.

*

Whenever I'd go through the *en suite* and into his bedroom and he'd be sitting there with his *Auto Trader* I'd know we were in for a good time. He'd put it away fast when I came in, he'd put it under the sheets like I'd caught him with a porno, but I'd just think, *shit hot, it's an Auto Trader Day!* I'd wheel him down to the Residence and round the front and into the downstairs sunroom from the garden and leave him there with his writing. He'd have half a dozen pages by his afternoon nap and I'd take what he'd written to Dot Round to type, and she'd always make out she was pissed off, like, *oh, you're not bringing more work for me* sort of thing, but I could see it was all a big show and she loved it really, you know, *I-work-for-this-famous-writer-he-couldn't do-without-me* sort of thing. Anyway, I'll tell you what happened to her. The old man bumped her off. That's what he reckoned, anyway. I still haven't worked the whole business out, I worry away at it.

It starts like this. We're up at the top of the hill in the Dodge again, him and me, you know, his afternoon drive and all that, we're sitting there watching the wind on the tussock, and suddenly he says to me, *y'know Dot Round? That does my typing?* Yes, of course I know Dot, I tell him, what about her? *Well,* he says, *I'm going to turn her blue.* That's what he says to me! I just sit there and I'm, like, *what*? He says, *you heard me, blue*. Just sitting there next to me. Like, you mean her *skin*? I ask him. *That's right,* he says. *I'm going to turn her skin blue. Same colour as the Blue Room. Did you know I can do that?* So I sit there for a minute, and I've got the list of medications running back through my brain *Sinemet-Ropinole-Mirapex-Eldepryl* and I'm trying to remember if I've dosed him up twice on something or left one of them out and that's why he's hit the jackpot like this? Then he says, *after that I'm going to kill her—she'll die soon. I can do that, I can kill people*—and I'm telling you, Patrick, I didn't know what to do. It might sound funny when you're playing this back to yourself but I was filling my pants sitting there next to him. I needed my bike clips on I was that scared.

So, anyway, I wait there a bit and he seems to go inside himself the way he does every now and then, and after a minute or two I start the car up and take him home. I settle him in for a nap and then I check his medication and I'd been on time with everything, it was all ticked off. I thought, he'll have a blue fit if I go and tell Either-Or and he finds out, but that's what you're meant to do, it's in the Bailey's Care manual, *any variation in your patient's behaviour should be reported immediately to your client.* So there's me tapping on the door of Either-Or's office, and he's doing that trick I told you about where he knows you're there but he doesn't look up because he's such an important prick, and he says, *yes*? with his head still down reading something. <u>What</u>? he says to me, when I tell it to him. *Blue*? he says, like he's never heard the word before. *Turn her <u>blue</u>*?

I've just played that bit back, Patrick—see what I said back there? About the old boy having a blue fit? Well, *I* just about had a blue fit when I heard that—like he was really starting to get into my mind, Mr Lawrence, I mean, he's even in your *words*? But the thing is, get this, *Dot turned blue*. After a while she *started turning blue*. I was with her one day and I saw this mark on her arm and it was *blue*. I don't mean she'd turned bright blue like a Smurf but there was definitely this one patch on her left arm, below the elbow. *She was turning blue*. It gave me such a *hell* of a shock I got out there and then, I just dropped what I was doing and I said *excuse me* and I left. She must've thought I had the runs and I more or less did, it was that scary, I was standing outside swallowing and swallowing and looking around, like, you know, *dear God please find me something normal to look at!*—and there was old Val down the bottom of the garden so I settled myself down to watch her. After a bit I made myself go back into the house and get back to whatever it was I'd stopped doing, but really I was looking at old Dot and her arm and the blue spot, and, you know what, I couldn't find it again?

I hung around her so long she thought I was up to something with her, I think, she was typing away *bang-bang-bang* the way she usually did, and all of a sudden she stops and she looks up at me and she says, *what?* like I was hanging around for something. And I didn't know what to say, I felt bloody stupid—like, am I going to say to her, *sorry, I was just checking to see if your arm's turning blue*?—so I tell her, I'm admiring your style, and she says *awwww* like that and turns back and starts up typing again but you could see she was pleased. I could see there was a sort of a *brown* spot on the back of her right hand that stuck up off her skin, quite big, thumbnail-sized, more, and where I'd seen the patch of blue—where I remembered seeing the blue—there was definitely something, but it wasn't what I'd seen a few minutes before, not quite. So I put it out of my mind again and got busy with other things, had a Bounty Bar and so on.

But I didn't forget it and after few days I checked her out again, and this time her *entire left arm* was blue—I saw it, through a window, just for a second. I slipped away and then I came back for another look, and of course it'd changed, but it hadn't gone away. It was like a kind of iron-colour, her arm, I could definitely see a sort of iron-blue tinge almost under the skin like a bruise. It turned me up, I can tell you, and then when I looked at her face—she's looking round at me again, she must have thought I was stalking her or something—I could see it under her eyes, too, it was a dark bluey-bruised looking. It was *in* her. I was hanging around staring, I was that caught up I forgot what I was doing, and then she stops typing like she did the time before and she says, *Thom, if you've got something to say to me would you mind spitting it out and not standing there like Mr Orr's dog*? And I say, *I didn't know he had a dog*. And she looks at me like Mr Tinetti and then she says, really carefully, *The one that's gone missing*, and that threw me. *Rommel?* I ask her, and she says, *Rommel?* Well anyway, turns out we'd eaten Either-Or's dog for him! *Didn't even know he had a dog*, I told her, and when I said that she sat up straight and stared in front of her like she was posing for a photo, and then she says, *how many dogs have we got around here that you've seen*? Well, of course, there's just the one, and I told her that and she says, *Well, then*, and she turns back and starts typing again.

So—there you go, there's another mystery for you. I'm really feeling caught up in something and I didn't like it one bit. So I decided to fix my mind on other things, I was off to the gym next morning as soon as I'd sorted Mr Lawrence out back at the Residence, and I benched 165 kegs, squatted 200, and deadlifted 200. And *that* took my mind off my problems, I can tell you – 200 kegs! Pity there wasn't more people there to watch me, but, tell you what, I let everyone know about it for a couple of days! But the blue thing never went away once the old man'd put it there. I'd be going about my business and then suddenly I'd be thinking about it, and I'd be off to see if Dot was about, and she'd get all pissed off, you could see she was getting sick of me. Then I got this brainwave, I decided I'd clean the Residence windows so I could look in and check her out while she was typing? So I'm up this long ladder wiping the old chamois across the glass, and there she is inside at the dining room table, tapping away at the typewriter—all of a sudden Left Butt's down at the foot of the ladder and he's like, *what d'you think you're doing, that's my job, you think you can do it better than me or something?* And I'm like, *just giving a hand, Eric, don't worry*, and then I see Mr Semple wandering round the garden in that hat of his he was born in and I think, *maybe he knows what's going on—*

And that's what I did, I was that full of this business by this stage I got down the ladder and I told him about it, even though Bailey's manual tells you *Never break the confidential relationship between carer and client/patient*. But I did, I told Mr Semple, and the main thing I got out of it was, his breath stunk of onions. I kept backing off and he kept coming close like he couldn't hear me. Course, it might've been on purpose, him eating onions and then going up to people and breathing on them, with him you can never tell. Anyway: blue? he says to me. The old boy? Did he say that? What else did he say? So I told him some of the other queer things Mr Lawrence used to tell me and he just laughs! He's no use to me at all, Mr Semple, he's never serious, not with me, anyway, I wished I hadn't told him anything in the first place. Blue! he says. He's going to turn her blue! Then I go and tell him that other thing I told you about, remember, that time Mr Lawrence looks up at me out of nothing and he tells me, *lipstick and wine are made out of fish scales*, just like that? I told him that, Mr Semple, I told him about the old man telling me that and I thought he was going to fall over he laughed that much. Did he *really*? he keeps saying to me. Did he *really* say that? Just out of the blue?

There you go again, see—*out of the blue*. It's like it gets into everything! He must've thought it was *me* that was the problem, Mr Semple must've, because I shot off when he said that. *Excuse me*, I'm saying to him, and I'm off. Next time I see him though he calls out to me, you were right!—he'd taken a look at Dot and he said yes, definitely blue. Sort of blue-grey? I asked him, and he said, no, definitely blue, she'll be the same as the Blue Room next—which is exactly what Mr Lawrence'd told me! So next time she was typing I made an excuse and I managed to get a good look at her. From one angle I'd think *yes*, and then I'd wander round the other side and I'd think *no*. I couldn't decide. So I began to think, maybe he was making it up, Mr Semple, because like I say you could never tell with him. I started to wonder, was he pretending to think Dot Round had turned blue, was he just pulling my tit and I couldn't tell? After a while I didn't know if I was making stuff up, too. But he told me one thing, Mr Semple, he said, did you know Dot isn't all that well? And I said no, I didn't know that and I was very sorry, and then he told me what it was she had but I can't remember the details except she was meant to have regular blood transfusions and that clashed with her beliefs. It felt a bit like he was starting to pull my leg again, like when he told me about Catholics having colds all the time. So I just left it. I tried to concentrate on what I was meant to be doing, but the more time I spent with Mr Lawrence the more I thought about Dot and what he said he was going to do to her.

And after a while she did start to go downhill, and that's when I really began to get the wind up. There was a week when she didn't turn up and then another, and then all of sudden there's this new woman doing the typing. She seemed really nice, pretty young, and I thought, *I wouldn't mind*. This wasn't all that long after Raewyn and me had, you know. So when I see this new chick with Either-Or in the dining room—he was showing her the typewriter and he was telling her what he wanted—I slip back down the ladder and come in like I had to do the insides. Oh, hullo, I say, like I didn't know she was there. Either-Or doesn't look across at me but he says, Aileen's covering for Mrs Round. And then he says to her, this is Gradus. She says to me, pleased to meet you, Mr Gradus, and when she says that he laughs, the prick, it was the only time I ever heard him laugh. It's Thom Ham, I said to her—pleased to meet you, Thom, she says to me.

Really nice girl, I really liked her, though for a while she thought my name was Tom Gradus, she used to put that on notes for me. *Thom Ham*, I'd tell her. *T-H-O-M, new word, H-A-M.* Anyway, Mrs Round, she didn't come back, and a couple of months after Aileen turned up, she died—that's her name, Aileen Cross, this girl that took her place. No, it wasn't much more than two months. Mr Yuile told me that at the funeral. Her liver packed up, he told me. You don't get long with the liver. And it wasn't your usual sort of funeral, I haven't been to that many but it was in someone's house and people took turns to say something and Dot wasn't there, I mean you couldn't see her. I was hoping for an open coffin, I thought I'd be able to check on her colour if she was sitting up in a coffin looking like one of the wax bananas—but the lid was down. I asked Mr Semple, and he said yes, he'd seen Dot just before she passed on and she was definitely blue, but he had this silly look on his face when he told me and I wondered why I'd bothered in the first place.

Right Butt said an interesting thing, though—when I asked her, was Dot blue at all, she didn't laugh at me, she said, no, more a sort of silvery-grey colour. So what d'you make of *that*? I don't know what I think when I look back. But when I go back to when things really started to happen, I reckon there might have been something to what the old man said. I mean, he told me he was going to do it, then her skin definitely changed, then she died. You can't deny that. Every time I try to remember back then, though, I have trouble with the colour. Sometimes I remember what I told you just now, you know, not quite sure, then a couple of times I dream about her, and each time she's bright blue—shit, I feel stupid talking like this! And the dreams started to get mixed up with how I think of it when I look back so I'm not sure what exactly happened.

But the old man was clear about it. *Bright blue,* he says to me. *I told you.* We were down in the garden room, after the funeral, he didn't go to it because of his bladder. *Poor old Dot,* he says. *I sure hated doing it to her.* Doing what, I asked him. *You remember,* he said. *I told you I'd turn her blue and then she'd die.* You mean you killed her? I asked him. *I mean she'd come to the end of her sentence,* he said. *I chose her because of her nickname. Dot. Full stop. Period. She was there to end the sentence. There to end the sentence?* I'm asking myself, and I asked him about that because it seemed such a cold hard thing to say. *She switched typewriters and I didn't like that,* he says to me. *That was the other thing. That plug-in golfball thing,* he says, *why'd she ask for one of those, what's wrong with the old Imperial we used to have? I told you her time was up, and it's up.*

But then when he's said this he looks up at me and he gives me a smile. He's got his teeth in for a change and he gives me this—I don't know—he gives me this really, really nice—smile. No, it was better than that, it was—tell you what, it was like when—d'you remember, Patrick?—when I first come across him back at the Residence? You know, he comes up the wheelchair elevator like Old Nick coming up out of Hell, and he winks at me when he gets to the top? It was like that. I can't explain it to you but it was like something happened between us? It was like he looked right *into* me? These pale blue eyes, I couldn't look away?—I didn't want to. It was like he really *knew* me, and it was like, that was all right, he liked what he was seeing, everything was okay, I could do anything I wanted and it'd be okay. And *he* could do anything *he* wanted, too, that was part of it, and I wanted him to. I wanted to reach out and hug him and say *sorry.* Sorry what for, I don't know, I just don't—Christ, this doesn't make much sense, does it? But you said you wanted to know everything and here it is. I wanted him to do anything, I don't know what it was I wanted him to do, but whatever it was I'd've let him do it, I knew that. I'd've done anything he wanted when he was looking at me like that. I'd've followed him into Hell if he'd asked. It was only five seconds I was thinking all this, but shit, it was big. Making any sense to you, Patrick? You ever had anything like that happen to you? *Shit*, it was powerful. *You are mine*, it was like he said that to me. That's what I thought to myself afterwards, it really got to me. *I am yours, and whatever you ask me I'll do, just ask me and I'll do it.* How d'you like *that*? How d'you like

VIII

Slowly, reluctantly, I settled into my new role—well, that's what I'd like to be able to write, but it's not true, it's not true at all. In fact I settled into my new, responsible, everyday life eagerly, easily, happily, and it became a part of me straight away. I was dismayed—I was appalled! This was the period when we began to make the transition that turned the house, step by step, into the Residence and the centre of the Raymond Lawrence empire. To say I made this business mine simply doesn't say enough.

To start with, we got rid of Raymond's terrible old chicken coop from up behind No. 23: out it went, chickens and all, and in its place came the prefabricated second house that took its name. We'd waited for Raymond to turn his back—by *we* I mean me and the others, Marjorie and Robert, all three of us by now very much wedded into the life of the Master. Then we made our move: and, when he came back from one of his many nostalgic jaunts to North Africa, as they seemed to us then—why, there it was, the Chicken Coop, newly named and a sudden, bland structure looming up behind his own.

He pretended to be much annoyed that we'd *done it behind his back*, but he really *was* annoyed at the colour we proposed to paint it. *Not <u>that</u> blue!* he shouted at us when we showed him the colour-chart: *that's blue-rinse blue!*

Anything but blue, he said, when calmed: the Coop was a civilian buidling after all. In the end we settled on an insipid, creamy-yellow-tallowy sort of colour instead: *might as well be a school building*, he grumbled when we were done.

I managed all this myself, pretty much, young as I was at the time: not yet twenty, not quite—extraordinary, isn't it? Phone calls, lawyers, boundary negotiations, permits, meetings with the builder and his men: above all, the financial jiggery-pokery involved. It seemed I could make decisions, it seemed, above all, that I was *good with money!*

Realising *that* took me aback, I can tell you—what had happened to the sensitive child of the arts, son of the muses? I was shocked to see how easily it all came to me, the *business of business*, and taken aback at how much I enjoyed it and at the banal satisfaction I felt at the end of each busy, phone-shot day. Was this all there was to me after all, had the old man been right all along: was I really made for nothing better than the butyric whiff of the getting-and-spending world? Well, yes, it seems he was right, disconcertingly so, and that a rather large part of me *was*.

Not all, though. The more I spent the day getting and spending, the more I reached, each Friday at six o'clock (and, some weeks, more frequently than that), for the compensations of Art. How quickly I turned to the Amontillado and the Bristol Cream, how eagerly I pressed the black shellac discs onto the soft dark felt of the turntable one after the other and awaited the redemptive, cleansing hiss of the diamond needle. Bach, Schubert, Schumann, Mozart, the incomparable choral works of Johannes Brahms—oh, 'Longing Laid to Rest', with Jessye Norman: this allowed to myself but once a year, so wrenching is it to hear. And Elgar, anything by Elgar. Richard Strauss as well.

From time to time, too (I hesitate to admit this), I would listen to *Hansel and Gretel*, an opera that reduces me to helpless tears from its very first note: ridiculous, I know, but every time I hear it I am pulled, blubbering, back into a world more real than anything else I know: into *that* world—the enchanted forest in which everything is so very much more than just itself, and which has no end. Whose captive children are set free at its conclusion and are yet *are children still*: and *that* is the nature of their freedom.

As you can see, I'd never fully left behind, after all, that magical world from which I'd been banished. It was there as I pressed out phone numbers and totted up lists of figures, found the cost of things, tut-tutted with builders and research librarians alike: it was around me in every daily moment like the smell of an animal. It was in my mind as I explored the beginnings of a trust with the Master and first realised that he intended, to my dismay, that any such venture should involve Marjorie and Robert as well. It was present as I slowly persuaded him, later, that Julian should be part of the venture as a sort of a balance.

It was present again a little later, too, when, out of a clear blue sky, Geneva's crass little critical biography appeared. It was I who dealt with the fallout of *that* venture, or much of it—managing the media and also, when things had settled a little, interviewing our staff to see from whence the leaks had come: our gardening ladies dwindled in number after *that* unpleasant little episode, I can tell you. I still have suspicions about others of the Master's followers—about Semple, most obviously.

There you are! Raymond said to me after a while of this deediness, when I was twenty-one or two or three. You really are a moron! A worldly man, he meant, I suppose: but, oh, how the words hurt me, how like a knife they cut at my soul, at the very bowels of my being. I'd like to say he meant no harm, except, of course, that he did.

A civilian, he meant: *no, no, I'm still an* <u>*artist*</u>, I used to insist to myself each time he made my lesser status clear to me like this. But in my heart of hearts I knew it wasn't true. *An artist?* he would demand, if ever I dared assert myself with a brave little occasional squeak, and then he'd hold up his pen to me, or a page of manuscript, or, indeed, one of his novels entire: *where's yours?* he'd ask. *Mm—?*

Instead, for him, I must have seemed no more than those lesser beings who gather at the foot of Parnassus. At worst, those broken-winged gulls I mentioned many pages ago, people like Marjorie and Robert but also creatures even less than that, far less, the desperate and the disturbed and the inconsolable, squawking and squabbling at the crumbs of fame. At best, no more than Julian or I—useful idiots of the art world, organisers of readings and conferences and even (sometimes) publication, experts at finding funding, handling correspondence and getting writers in and out of taxis and onto planes. *Artholes*, Raymond sometimes called us.

And behind his shoulders all the time, as we his followers scurried about hewing his wood and drawing his water, the rustling of that wondrous, magical, now-forbidden forest. The feared and beloved weald of the European imagination, in which all our childhood minds are formed and from which all our stories come. Gone.

Not so far so, though, that I couldn't hear the rustle of its leaves from time to time. For one thing, I still knew whenever he began to write again. Those sounds, those familiar scents, the change in the mood about the place—they started up straight away, as soon as I'd been banished, as if getting rid of me had set him free in some way.

Such signs were as unmistakable as ever in this time I describe. First, the familiar jaunt to my uncle's spirits that always came with inspiration, the sudden warbling and whistling and flirting, the reckless teasing of Mesdames Round and Butt and even the redoubtable Mrs During as she bent to scrub his loo. *Raymond's in love again*, I remember someone saying when *the moment* of one of the earlier novels arrived upon us like this—*Bisque,* it was, possibly, and maybe it was Basil Bush who said it to me. I remember my uncle bursting out of the garden room one day early in the creation of one or other of his novels back then: *By God, 'tis good!* he cried: *and if you like it you may!*

And, now, as I say, all this was unmistakably with us once again. There was I, his bumboy newly hatched, struggling (I think I remember this right) to get a cache of his documents out of the old wooden garage down below the house and into a van and off to the local university research library for cataloguing. One of the librarians helped me and a miserable, limp-wristed pair we were, too, grunting and sweating each filing cabinet and laden cardboard box out and into the van and off and away. And there was Raymond, up above us in the garden room of No. 23, doors flung wide apart as he sat scribbling at his *écritoire*, and there he was again, bounding up the outdoor steps with fistfuls of manuscript, and hugging Dot Round with delight (as she told me later) above her typewriter in the room above, and there he was yet once more, singing at the top of his voice and urging the others to join in. Ah, yes, a *nest of singing birds* they certainly were at this early stage of things. Such elation!

And then, after that but not soon, the next phase. *Christ on the road to Emmaus*, he used to call it, my uncle: meaning the sense that, suddenly, someone else was with us. *Who is the turd who walks always beside you?* he'd ask when he knew the house had begun to fill with these new presences. *It's almost as if there's someone there*, I remember no less than Mrs Butt saying once when the house had begun to fill with the sense of his creations, or possibly it was no less than Mrs During who said it to me. *It's almost as if you can feel the things he's writing about.*

Whichever woman said it I knew what she meant, and I knew it was uncomfortable for her not least because the apprehension was so plausible—I mean the overwhelming sense that some kind of created presence-of-the-moment really was about the place, *in* this world with everything else—the dog, Mrs During, Mrs Round, the gardening ladies, the milkman each morning at the gate, the paper-boy in the afternoon: present, and up to its unknowable business. These presences were the other side of the process which had started, for me, when he held up that second-hand frock all those years earlier and asked me to be his momentary Julia. We'd stepped into the universe of his imagination: now, back it came, stepping into our safe, predictable little orrery universe, with its house and its garage and its garden and the people who lived in and around them.

No apparitions, not yet: instead, just the creak of a floorboard, perhaps, or the closing of a door that, when checked, might still be open after all: even, sometimes, the sense of the murmur of a voice: something, someone, about the place. Smells, too, of apples or cigarette smoke—or, once, for a moment, petrol—all these when the house was otherwise empty: and, always, always, the smell of the sea. That *Mediterranean smell* as we came to think of it, the smell of his writing. By this stage the ecstasy and the agony were past and the rest of it was just work, the usual toil and pain. Raymond was himself again, become more nearly a human being once more or as much so as he might ever be: a little *buffled*, as he used to say—another of his nonce words—but busy, sometimes tormented in the old way, sometimes less so, and always very much preoccupied, pushing his work along, worrying at it, worrying it along.

What *was* this work, though, what was he writing about this time? *Mind your fucking business*, he told me when I tried to find out. *You'll know in due course. Just wait your patience*, he said to me another time, when I tried to ask the question circuitously. *Like everyone else.* And then: *how's the cataloguing going?*

That was how he kept me away from where I most wanted to be—where I *yearned* to be again, now he'd so utterly cut me from it. He always answered questions about art with answers about life: *my* life, that is, my new life as his *trainee personal assistant* (the term we settled on in due course). He always reminded me, in other words, of what I'd given up and of what I'd turned into. Where've you got to? I'd asked him, hopefully, idling at his door: *Out of ink*, he'd say, briskly, sometimes, holding up an empty inkbottle. *That's where I've got to. Off you go—Stephens Radiant Blue, go on, go on, you know where to get it.*

Then: *ta*, nothing more, whenever I scurried back from the store in the laundry with a fresh bottle for him, as eager to please as Daisy the dog. I'd stand in the doorway of the garden room, the pliers still in my hand with which I always tweaked off each new cap for him, ink on my fingers from filling the Parker 51, and hoping—*hoping*—that he might let something slip about what it was he was writing at the moment. He'd look up: *that's all*, he'd say, knowing full well, I'm sure, what it was I'd been waiting for. Oh, love locked out, locked out!

Thus it was that *Nineteen Forty-Eight*, when it

appeared, was as much a surprise to me as it was to anyone else. A satire of the Orwell novel, of all things!—set somewhat closer to home, of course, in the actual Oceania from which his protagonists—a couple of youngsters not much older than the children of the *Miss Furie* novel—come and go via a dilapidated suburban kitchen remarkably like the one we show visitors to the Residence: a portal to the past, to the year of the title, a period he became increasingly obsessed with as he went on. *It all began then,* I remember him saying to me. *That's when we started to fuck it all up.* As his readers will know, it doesn't become all that much clearer in the novel.

He spent more and more time in the Dodge when he was writing it, I remember, driving around or just sitting there—and, it must be said, he enjoyed the same prepositional relationship to Marjorie, too, at the time: she who, by this stage, had long been his lover well and truly. By this time she was more or less living at the house—much tut-tutting from Mesdames Round and During and from Mrs Butt as well. Marjorie had to be there, of course, if for no better reason than that Raymond's favourite creation was back in this new novel, adding a further dimension to Orwell's famous line *do it to Julia.* It was that kind of novel.

So *that* was what all the fuss was about, this time around: I mean the sense of possession about the house that I've mentioned, the subtle paranoia with which the Master allowed his dwelling to be gripped. I have to confess to a slight disappointment at the end of the process—the novel was pleasant enough to read but scarcely warranted the upheaval its genesis seemed to cause, in my mind at any rate. Nice to see you setting your work *here* and not *there*, one of his sixtyish Brendas said at the launch, no doubt fortified by the free wine. But, Madam, *everything*

I write is set here, he replied. *Your* problem is, you've only just fucking noticed.

Then, though, he started to write *Kerr*. It took a while to gestate and, painfully and a few years later, to emerge, by which time I was well into my third decade and on my way to setting up what came to be known as the Raymond Thomas Lawrence Memorial Trust. *In his ear all the time*, was Marjorie's description of my behaviour in those days. *Why can't you leave him alone, can't you see he's pregnant again?* And indeed I hadn't: which goes to show, alas, just how far I'd drifted from the world of words at that stage, and how firmly Mammon now held me in his grip.

I'm thinking of the future, I told her. I'm setting up a trust, I'm thinking of his legacy.

As soon as she spoke, though, it started to come back to me again, all of it: that forest sound, the smell of it, and of the sea beyond. I began to think once more about writing, I began to think again about *him*. What was going on? Something big, something important this time: the jab at Orwell had been just a prelude, it seemed, a passing moment before he turned to what—evidently—he'd been meaning to write all his life. Of this, when I began to look about me again, I became more and more certain—*at last, this was it*. For one thing, there was his sudden remoteness, the way he seemed to have been swallowed up into himself. There was that, and then there was the return of *fear* in my life—

I remember a moment, not long after Marjorie told me he was expecting again, when I suddenly realised he was gazing at me, across a room that had others in it, that he'd been staring at me and staring at me for some time while the others talked: and I looked back at him at that moment and my bowels turned to water. Lord, dear Lord, some part of me had been caught—*I was in what he was writing—*

I knew what was happening. I was a condemned man.

It was a curious time, I remember, in these heady days and weeks when chaos came again. There was a *brouhaha* involving Raymond and Marjorie in that period as well: she who, not long after our conversation above, *buggered off at last*, as she put it, having *had a gutsful of playing musical beds with bloody Phyllis Button.* As well as Marjorie and Phyllis in their customary push-and-pull there were other women coming and going about the place at this time as Raymond practised his *droit de seigneur* among the wives of the local *literati*—a grace note of any new project of his, along with those moments when I'd catch him poring over what looked to be one of Eric Butt's *Auto Trader* magazines but which I knew was *Mein Kampf*, concealed behind it and always a sign that the humour was upon him and anything could be about to happen.

So Marjorie left for the UK at this time to have another taste of Europe and a life unmediated by Raymond Thomas Lawrence. *Could feel him here*, she wrote on a postcard of Ludwig II's Neuschwanstein: *tomorrow, Dachau.* Robert was gone from us as well, to a six-month writing residency at a provincial polytechnical college in the far north, something that had astonished us all when it was announced. As for Julian, at this stage he'd come into our lives as I've mentioned but was yet to find his full role amongst the followers of the Master. In fact I met him at the other end of one of those filing cabinets full of the old man's papers we were lugging off to the research library it turned out he worked at: *would you like to meet my uncle?* he remembers me asking him.

In that time, in other words, that very uncle and I were much alone in the house together. Each late afternoon the gardening ladies and the household staff would leave the two of us to our extraordinary nights together at No. 23, as my uncle wrote and wrote and I found myelf more and more engulfed by the new world he was creating.

It had happened before, as I've indicated, but not quite like this. That salty, Mediterranean smell, for a start, washing over me when I woke in the night. The first time it happened I sat up in my bed, propped on my elbows, and drew the smell of it into myself. I opened the bedroom window: but, no, it didn't come from outside. It was somewhere inside the house. I drew it in, and when I did it disappeared as if it had become part of me. On other nights the smell came back, though: I'd breathe it in again and think of the vast cedar forests in *Frighten Me* and *Flatland*. I was in them once more, and through to their far side, and down to the sea.

Sometimes I heard him, too. The first was when he was at the desk in his bedroom, which he used now and then: voices, behind its door, and, when I crept out into the little hallway, a soft light from under it. Phyllis Button, I thought, in there for the usual show-and-tell—but no, neither the familiar bassoon of her voice nor the timpani of her smoker's cough. This was something smaller, lighter, less: a flute, perhaps. The old man was trying out voices, that was it, he was speaking in character like an actor—he used to do that, sometimes, when he didn't have a human around to suck into his vortex. A child's voice. That's what it sounded like, I remember. A child.

A night or two more spent hovering outside his door like this, before another thought came up, abruptly, unpleasantly, unasked for. *He actually had someone in there with him, another Julia.*

Another muse, another favourite.

Marjorie was gone, I'd been dismissed from him twice over—we'd been too old anyway, the pair of us, and we'd been replaced, that was the truth or part of it. Was it not? He'd got someone else—*what was he doing to her in there? Who was she?* I found myself remembering the worst of it, the knife at the throat, the finger in the spine: and then, overwhelmingly, from a completely different direction, jealousy, that moment from all those years ago coming back, when he'd introduced me to the adolescent Marjorie and the feast of her bronze sausage curls, the spritz of her freckles, her toothy, sad grin.

It overwhelmed me, the nostalgia for all that was lost, to him, to her, to me. Until relatively recently I'd still been his, after all: Marjorie, too, till the moment she boarded the plane and left the country—he'd drunk himself senseless that night, I remember that. And now—inevitably, I knew that—now, it seemed he had someone else. *Another darling*—

Except that, apparently, he didn't. A new woman? Val asked when I brought the possibility up with her, out in the garden. I used *woman* and not *girl* for obvious reasons, and edged into the topic cautiously, from something quite different. Mr Lawrence? she asked. I don't think so. Nora Butt would've told me, she never misses anything like that. Or Dot, she's in the house almost every day. Then she looked across at me. Isn't he a bit old for that sort of thing now? she asked.

No new woman, then, and, presumably, no new girl-Julia, either—I asked Dot myself and even, awkwardly, Mrs Butt, and they knew nothing of it, either of them, not a thing at all. Surely he's too busy writing to bother with company, Dot told me. I can't keep up with what he's producing, he's on a tear. That phrase surprised me, especially from her, but it gave me a sense of how he was at the time. I keep hearing things, I said. Around the house. Oh, but it's always been like that when he's writing, she said. The place gets haunted!

Yes, the plot seemed to be unfolding, all right: except that the more he wrote the more hidden he seemed to become, and the more hidden he became the more I found myself shirking my supposed duties and listening outside doors and into phone conversations, questioning Val and Dot again and even (sometimes) Edna Butt, and loitering past windows in order to peer into them: at nothing, always, but increasingly with the sense of being on the very edge of a discovery of the utmost importance. He did this to people, he turned people into stalkers.

I can't remember at what stage of all this I decided who this new presence might be, but I do remember that at some point I read *Flatland* once again, and once again was jolted hard by that extraordinary experience, at the shock of that brutal ending and the surprise of finding that reading it yet again hadn't diminished its impact. Again, the wonder at what kind of a man could *write* that.

It was soon after this—I know this is true—it was soon after this that I woke from a dream about the boy, the youth in that novel. I was being beaten with the leather stick, on the back and on the neck, but the noise came from somewhere else. I was awake and it was coming from another part of the house. I was awake, and it was gone. I sat there in the bed, twelve years old again, thirteen, my legs tucked up under me, pyjamas clinging to sweat, heart thudding in ears and neck. I listened to myself slowly thumping my way back down to something more nearly normal, and that was the only sound I could hear as I sat there, that *bump-bump-bump* in my chest and in my ears. The crying had gone. Had it been there at all? Who was it? What was happening?

Kerr, the novel that did most to edge him towards the prize, that was the general consensus. He'd never had universal admiration before, but this time, and at last, he got it. Even he was pleased, and how could he not be? *Perfect*, a couple of reviewers said, and *as near to perfection as it gets*, said another. *A grand work*, said someone else, and *A great and true novel*, somebody after that—*God, true!* Raymond gasped, when I told him this. Another reviewer was of the opinion that *the act of reviewing diminishes this work. It is beyond criticism.* This was the time the muttering about the Nobel began in earnest. Definitely a contender, it was said, definitely a contender.

More euphoria, too, once *Kerr* arrived in the United States—to our astonishment since, as I've said, it writes that entire country out of history but for its debris, some of which goes into the making of Kerr's raft. The latter business was all based on his own experience, he told us, when he was trying to get away from Algeria after the ceasefire and before the election, and hit on the mad conceit of escaping north alone and by sea. *There was all this Yank garbage still bobbing around after the war*, he told me. *I used 75-gallon drop-tanks from Mustang fighters, I floated the raft on those.*

D-model aircraft of the U.S. Fifteenth Air Force, Julian told me, used late in the Mediterranean theatre: the parachute Raymond turned into a sail would've come from a similar source, apparently, and the food he survived on throughout his journey was sure to have been U.S. war surplus, all of it—Hershey bars, Spam, canned corned beef, tins of Nescafé which he lost overboard almost as soon as he set out. There was a pocket can-opener he picked up in a bazaar in Algiers before he left and which looked like a spoon: used in the middle of the ocean, Raymond told me, to dig out a purulent tooth.

In other words, exactly like Kerr in the novel: Kerr and the youth he takes with him in this fictional version and whose early loss overboard in a Mediterranean squall is the central, wrenching event of the novel: Kerr is alone after that.

But for the Yanks I couldn't have made the raft, my uncle told me. And look how I repaid them, I booted them off the planet!

He was a Kabyle, this boy, he said after *Kerr* came out. With blue eyes!—the Vandals came through North Africa fifteen hundred years ago on the way to Carthage, he told me: did you know that? Left all these blue-eyed babies behind them, he said—anyway, the Arabs treat them like dirt. Who? I asked him. The Kabyles? Everyone, he said. The metros kicked the Pieds-Noirs and the Pieds-Noirs kicked the Arabs, the coastal Arabs. Then the coastal Arabs kicked the shit out of the Kabyles. They'd hang round the military camps, the Kabyle kids, the poilu'd give 'em food and fags and let 'em play with guns—crazy, just fucking crazy. Not the adults. They wouldn't let the adults near the military camps. Anyway, this little bastard, he helped build the raft.

In the book? I asked. Yes, I know he did.

No—he looked away, out of the window, I remember, when he said this. No, he said. I mean he helped *me* build the raft. *My* raft. He found the drop-tanks for me. And the parachute. He helped me build the raft and then he came out on the fucking thing. With me. Out to sea. Same as in the book.

I sat there, thinking the obvious thought. And did you

lose him overboard, too? I asked, after half a minute. Like Kerr?

A long silence, as he sat there in a slice of sunlight and looking out above the trees.

I lost him, he said.

We sat there, uncle and nephew. I didn't dare ask what the young Amazigh had meant to him. I thought of the Amazigh youth in *Flatland*, and the terrible end he came to. The same boy, of course, the same boy. Wasn't he? Was that right? And if so, then what did that mean? How did this work?

After the success of *Kerr* I thought he was done with, this Anir, done with and out of our lives, I thought he was drowned at last and at one with the sublime. Certainly Raymond himself seemed finished, as if ready for something else or perhaps for nothing very much at all. He wrote a collection of stories next—this was *The Long Run*—which I thought (in truth) a little uneven: two of the stories were brilliant, but the others were—well—less so. The collection received respectful responses from reviewers who obviously had no idea what to make of them and so were furtively polite and deferential in the way of critics confronted with a writer thought to have *made it*. One of these was Geneva herself, I recall: 'beautifully crafted', 'challenging subject matter', and so on—Geneva, at full trot.

The early twilight of a controversial career, perhaps: his, I mean. *I've done my dash,* he told me one early evening back then, when I came upon him down in the garden room: he had a rug across his knees and suddenly seemed a touch elderly, a little more studied than I was used to in him. He'd been writing in the usual way on his *bureau*, but when I came in I found him caught stock-still above it with the tips of his fingers to his lips as he gazed through the double doorway, at the fall of the lawn and the curve of the larger trees: and, through their leaves, at the smudge of smoke and mist that lay across the city.

It's all changing, he said to me, so quietly I could hardly hear him. *Buggered my pen, too, look*. And somehow he had, he'd done something to splay the nib. *I think it's all starting to go*, he said. *The writing. It's starting to leave me. Feels like someone else is doing it now—some weak bastard. Dunno what's happened, I seem to have gone walkabout*. And, on another occasion, *I'm starting to be ignored, I'm being forgotten, I've become an adjective. Must be in line for something big if <u>that's</u> happening.*

Well—of course he was right. All this less than a year before the moment in which, suddenly and overnight, he became truly the Master, and stood at last before the world redeemed, confirmed, triumphant. I remember what it did to him, too, this wonder, how it seemed to fill him with new blood, new energy, new life, how it restored the sparkle to his eyes. He seemed six foot tall as I watched him in the crowded rooms where people pressed around him, seeking to touch him, trying to grasp the magic of his moment. His head was up, his shoulders back, his face almost incandescent with the wonder of what he had brought upon himself and upon us all. Once more his eyes flickered with their former, unearthly light.

I've done it, he muttered to me on one of these occasions. *I've made it. Now watch what I do. I'm going to fuck it all up—*

*

All right. Okay. Now—not enough detail last time, you reckon, you want to know a bit more about what went on in the shower? Jeez, you're a hard man, Patrick, it's not easy to talk about, that's why I didn't tell you that much! Anyway, I'll give it another try. I'm doing all this for you like you said, out it all comes and it sort of starts to make sense after a while, it's like one weird step after another, on the way to where we ended up, the two of us. Anyway. You know I'd always give the old boy a shower every morning?—pain in the arse. I'd get my wet weather gear on and I'd get right in the shower with him, you ought to see me—like this giant frenchie rustling across the room and into the shower box! Bailey's Care, they tell you straight in the manual: *Showering the patient is an area of interaction requiring the utmost tact. Ensure that you always wear your waterproofs over your clothing and that all aspects of the showering procedure are unambiguous.* So in I go every morning dressed up like I'm checking out that reactor that went up in China a few years ago, d'you remember? No, Japan. Anyway. I take his clothes off, he's usually lying on the bed for that, and then I put my plastic on, and I carry him in under the armpits. He shuffles and he drags his feet and I take his weight for him at the same time, I hold him from behind like I've said, and I lift him and in he goes. Then the water hits him and he starts cursing, it's too hot or it's too cold, that'll be the day it's just right.

Anyway, turned out it took longer for me to get into the wet weather gear each morning than it took to strip him off, so I thought, bugger it, two for the price of one, no one else round and he's out to it, pretty much, there's times when it was like I was holding up nothing under the shower anyway—you know, he's that little and limp? And I thought back to those two guys in the shower in the gym I told you about last time, two guys soaping each other and everyone was looking? And I thought, *end of story*—because all I had to do was forget the plastic gear, slip my duds off and get myself cleaned up while I'm showering him! No problems! And it wouldn't matter if he *did* notice what was going on, because the way he is, a minute later it's all gone again. And talk about cutting down the time I'd been spending, it came down to less than half when I tried it out. Fifteen minutes from go to whoa, that's about what it came down to.

So that's what I did, *all in together this fine weather*, you know the story. Only, when I did it—I mean, when I got the both of us stripped off and picked him up the usual way and we were under the shower together, it didn't feel quite right. I began to wish I'd never thought of it. I'm not saying he wasn't happy, he was just the opposite, some days I was buggered if I knew what he was thinking or whether he was even thinking at all, he was just grinning off into space as far as I could see and his head rolling round. The other thing was, it was harder to hold him with both of us in the nick, he was like a bloody fish he was that slippery and so was I—I nearly lost him a couple of times but we got it done and out of the shower in the end. Then I toweled him down and put a gown on him and sat him on a chair, and I dried myself off and slipped back into my shorts and back to normal. Except it wasn't, because I was all shook up, know what I mean?—Jeez, it's strange talking into this thing with no one else round, Patrick, it really is? Anyway, it was his bare skin up against me, I thought it wouldn't matter but it turned out it did, I thought what with no one watching it'd be all right, but the thing is—*I* was watching, and I didn't like it. This man in the shower with another man, soaping him up and then slipping the soap over himself for a second and the lather sliding down and onto the floor of the showerbox and out the hole. It wasn't right, it didn't feel right, and of course the people at Bailey's would've wrung my bloody *neck* if they'd known.

What d'you know, though—this is the bit I don't get, this is the bit I need to tell you about, but it's so bloody hard—next morning I'm stripped off and into the shower with him again? There. Explain *that* to me. Tell me next time you see me why I did that—and then again the next morning, and then again after that? On and on? It wasn't about sex, I know what you'll be thinking but it wasn't like that—like, I never got a boner, not once. I'd have got out quick smart if *that*'d started happening, I can tell you! What I mean is, showering with him wasn't doing anything for me, how could it, but there was something else going on and I don't know what it was. It was something else that got me going back and doing this thing again and then again, I knew it wasn't right but there I was, holding this bare-arsed whacked-out old man up against bare-arsed me, and soaping the two of us up, the both of us stark bollocky and holding on to each other—

Christ, it doesn't sound right, saying it out loud like that. No way. Like, Raewyn and me, we were in the shower all the time, you know, the way you do, and it felt right with her? But it didn't feel right with him. It doesn't even feel right telling you now! Christ, Raewyn, she'd've *shat* if she'd known what I was up to with the old boy, she'd be thinking that was why we split up, you know, she'd be thinking what she said was right? I kept on doing it, you see, that's the point. I could have thought, *bugger it, that didn't work, get yourself back under the plastic and put the whole bloody business out of your mind*. But I didn't. Instead I'd be stripping myself off again each morning and then stripping him off again, and then—you know, under the shower together, him up against me, the feel of his skin and all that? It *was* quicker, I'll say that, but it was something else as well and whatever it was I didn't like it. I knew it was there but I didn't know what it was even though it was in me, and the thing I didn't like was that, not knowing what it was. I didn't like the idea of having this part of me that's starting to feel like it wasn't part of me anymore. Like it was part of someone else. That ever happened to you?

But then this really weird thing happened, and I don't know what to make of it. I still don't know. We're in the shower, Mr Lawrence and me, and I'm hanging on to him with one arm, and I've got the spray off the clip and in my spare hand, see—and then, all of a sudden, he reaches round and grabs my tackle and he starts giving me an appreciation session down there! *Hold on hold on!* I'm yelling at him, and we're slithering round in the wet—you see, the point is, I could do all this when he was out to it, I could do it easy enough when he was that far gone he wasn't there. But the minute he wakes up on me like that I'm thinking, *shit, he's been awake all the time, he knows what's going on*, and then I just lost it, it was all different all of a sudden. I just lost it—inside my head, I mean. Like, I'm still holding him up, I'm still scrubbing away, and all the time he's feeling me up! And I'm trying to get it all over and done with and the both of us out of there and dried and dressed as quick as I could, and his *hands off me*, that was the thing, I wanted to him to *get his hands off me*. I mean, I was *that* surprised, I was *that* shocked—

And then, guess what happens next?—he's got his bloody fist round my, you know, the old ferret! And he says to me, *you're not much*!—he's giving it a quick stretch, like, *how long is this thing*, and he's saying to me, *you haven't got much*! And I'm like, well, okay, they don't crowd round in the showers down at the gym to take a look, I'm not a cockstar but then no one really is, half of them've stuck that much juice into themselves they look like Donald Duck. I'm not a cockstar but then I'm not on juice either, I felt like telling him that, I felt like saying to him, what about you and your horrible little bathplug penis, what about that, then? But I didn't, you know—*appropriate professional practice* and all that. I just hurried him out and sat him down and started to dry him, and truly, if you'd seen him when I was doing that you'd've thought I'd been imagining it all—I started to wonder about it, like, *was* it me, was *I* imagining it all—same as that turning-blue business I told you about? With Dot Round?

Well, that was the end of the naked showers as far as I was concerned. Couple of days I didn't shower him at all, and he started to smell that bad I couldn't go near him. But then it got so I couldn't go near myself, either. So I had a quick shower on my own and got dressed and back under the plastic again and I started crackling round the bathroom like the brown paper cowboy—know that joke, Patrick? About the brown paper cowboy? He's made out of brown paper and his name's Russell. There you go. Guess you had to be there. Anyway, I couldn't put enough plastic between me and the old boy at that stage, I even put rubber gloves on for a while when I was handling him! After that it'd be into-the-shower-and-out, into-the-shower-and-out, and after a week or two it got to the stage I could kid myself it hadn't really happened, it got so I didn't really need to think about it anymore.

But then it comes back again. Because of *me*. See why I told you it wasn't easy for me to tell you about this stuff? I still don't know what was going on. I spend a lot of time looking back at it and I still don't know. It's like I was a different person then, it was like I was becoming two different people. That's how I felt when I did it again, anyway. There was one morning when I just went in and pulled back his sheets, he was lying there staring at the ceiling and I pulled back his sheets and I stripped him off, and I had the shower going, you could hear it hissing away in there, and then I stripped myself off like that was what I'd always been going to do, and I picked him up and I took him in and under the water. It's pretty hot, and he's yelling *fuck fuck fuck* the way he always did and then I'm soaping him all over and he's right up against me all soft and bony and wet and warm—and I'm thinking, *what the hell am I doing?* And now it's *me* thinking *my mind's not right*—

I got it done and out and I was drying him, and my heart was going like a hammer but I didn't know why. That time, and then again next morning—you're turning on the shower on the way through the *en suite* to him and you're saying to yourself, no, no, you're not going to do it, you're not going to do it, are you?—and you do. It's like when you first start clawing the maggot. Each morning it was just one more time in the shower for me, except it wasn't me coming through the *en suite* to get him, I know that, now I'm looking back from here, it was someone else. I've never had that before, being split off from myself like that, the way I was getting to be back then, and I look back and I think to myself, *that's the point it all started, that's the point when he started to do it to me, you know, playing with my mind.* But then, you know, *excuse me*? *He* started to do it to *me*? This little old guy who's knocked out most of the time I'm with him, he's the one to blame? What's going on here?

I'm trying to be really, really honest here, Patrick. I've told you I liked it, I told you I was starting to do really weird things, more than what I've told you, and it was like someone else was doing them? Like, I started wandering round in the nick, just between his room and mine, through the *en sulte*, and sometimes he'd be gaga and sometimes he wouldn't and he'd be watching me. *And, I have to admit it, I liked it when he did.* Just him, no one else. I liked it when he'd sit there watching me wandering round in the nick. It was like *I* was watching, too, I was watching *him* watching *me* with no clothes on. And I started to leave the doors unlocked, so Either-Or could've just walked in when I was like that. I left the door open! It's like I wanted Either-Or to come in and catch me, too—*Either-Or! Can you imagine that?*

Heavy, eh? Anyway, Patrick, you'll never guess what I did next. I got a whole-body wax. You finished laughing? I'll give you a minute. Cost an arm and a leg but that's only part of what they were waxing anyway so I can't really growl about it, can I, got it cheap if you think about it like that. Even had a Brazilian down there, know what I mean? Bloody *mad* idea, can't believe I did it now! But I'd got to the stage where I'd been doing poses in the mirror in Mr Lawrence's bathroom—I mean, I'd be wandering around raw and I'd catch sight of myself like that and I'd do some of the poses the body-building boys did in the gym. So there's me, spreading my wings in the mirror like that, and I'm thinking, *I'm not bad, I ought to give this body-building thing a serious go*—next day I'm in a waxing boutique having every bloody hair taken off my body! And I'll tell you something for free, when they take the wax off, when it's set hard and three-two-one it comes off—well, you don't want to be doing that every day of your life, that's all I can say. I got myself home and slapped on the baby oil—you need a bucket of baby oil when you've been waxed, I can tell you—and then I took a look at myself in the mirror. I did a fair sort of spread, and I thought, Christ, look at that, I'm turning into another person! I took a look down my back and it was like I was looking at someone else, I was rippling my back muscles and I was shredded like a skinned rabbit. I looked that good I was near crying.

I remember thinking *he's got me now, now I'd do anything, if he asked me to kill someone I'd do it, that's what I'd do next.* I knew that. And I thought, *maybe that's what's next, maybe that's what he wants me to do?* I'm not kidding you. I don't mind telling you this, Patrick, because the point is, it wasn't me anymore. I was looking at myself like I was someone else—and I *was*, I *was* someone else. I wasn't the me that's talking to you now. I took some photos in the mirror, and I showed them to Mr Lawrence. I guess a part of me was testing the old man—you know, how'd he take it, what'd he do, how far'd he go? Well, work this out. He blew up. Explain that to me. He just flipped his lid, I was really scared for a minute and he's half my size, less than that. This little geezer yelling away at me and trying to get up out of the chair—*you fucking keep your nose out of it!* he's saying. *You think you can be him, you think you can go back there? What d'you think* you *are, part of that world? You belong to* this *one,* he tells me. *Believe me, you belong to* this *one, you fucking stupid piece of meat, that's all you're good for.* Then he looks up at me and he says, *what you are is, you're what's left over. Got that?*

All the time he's raving on like this I'm trying to calm him down, *shush shush it's just a joke, didn't mean any harm* kind of thing, and he did calm down after a bit, he settled back in his chair and I tucked his blanket round his legs and I slipped out, I can tell you. He was sitting there looking at the photos, I remember that, he'd hung on to my phone and he was still looking at them. Jesus, I was all shook up when I got outside, though. I'm telling you this because I'm trying to say, that's where he took me, and now I know how it is people do those things you see on the news, there's something happens inside their heads and they just turn into different people. That's what I'm trying to say to you. You get yourself stolen away from you and I don't know how that works and I don't know how he does it, except, that's what he could do to me then. I'd wake in the middle of doing something and I'd think, *am I really doing this, is this really me,* and I'd say, *yes. No. Yes—*

*

Other-people, my uncle meant, the novel he wrote after the business of the Prize had begun to die down a little—*Flatland* all over again, in effect, that *ur*-story of his, that *thing* it seemed he could never let go, that wound he was always scratching. *Flatland* reworked, but with its last layer of skin flayed off it—who knew there was still one left to flay?

Here was what he meant when he murmured that sentence to me at the civic reception. He'd had fame at last with *Kerr* and praise he must have dreamed of, and after that, the greatest Prize of all—and then it seemed he wanted to *push* all this away from himself, to bring about his own destruction with this frightening new book, to bring everything down at the height of his greatest success. This was the time he began to talk openly about having betrayed himself, this was when he said he'd taken the wrong path all those years ago, after *Flatland*, and cursed himself for starting to write for the critics, as he put it. But look at the Prizes! I told him. Look what you've achieved! *Fuck* the prizes, he shouted back at me. *The prizes are the problem!* He seemed all but mad at this stage, to tell the truth, and frightened, it seemed, almost, at what he had brought about—as if he was trying to disqualify himself after the fact, once and for all, with one last unforgivable gesture, one final, unimaginable indecency.

There's an order of fiction in the world that is just

that, unforgivable, almost criminal: unreadable, but nevertheless read and reread. That Jerzy Kosiński novel—I can't even remember its title but I can remember every moment of the scene where a boy watches a man's eyes being gouged out with a spoon. The scene in which Major Marvy is castrated in *Gravity's Rainbow*. *The White Hotel*—magnificent, oh, yes: I can remember devouring it in a single sitting but also that final moment with the bayonet, when I threw the book across the room, appalled and never wanting to go near it again—just as I reacted to the last pages of *Flatland*. Unreadable, and every word of it read and read again. Thomas Bernhard, everything of his that I know in English—*The Lime Works*, with its terrible opening scene, all those people covered in excrement. There's a short story—I can't remember the title—in which a man eats part of his own prolapsed innards, slowly, and in detail. And then there's always *Naked Lunch*. So many more as well—and in all of them, genius and evil crouched together in the dung, conspiring, the one thing, inseparable. Hell itself.

Other-people is one of these works. *Early senility*, someone wondered whom I met in the street shortly after it came out. *A sign of his illness?* said somebody else. *Immensely powerful, crudely written, badly judged:* the closest to the truth of it, in my own opinion, and whispered in my ear, and to my amazement, by Cosmo Dye. For me, it marked the point where Raymond really *had* got there at last. Everything that the Berber youth had meant to him, he whom he called Anir, was finally shown in this book. The conclusion was the conclusion of *Flatland* again but *Flatland* flensed of its last tiny layer of discretion. It is ugly, it is disgusting, it is unreadable. Who knows what might have happened had it appeared before the Prize?

None of this should have surprised me as it did. There had been a moment, as the Nobel celebrations began to die away a little, when I caught him, across a room from me and amidst the babble of others as so often before: gazing, gazing at me, unmoving like a killer that has marked its prey: his level, bezelled gaze never left me.

Anir was back.

I knew straight away. I felt helpless, I remember. He'd mined me for his most successful novel, I knew that, I knew how things worked now, he'd colonised my emotional life more deeply than ever before. Oh, God, what was happening this time? How did it work? He was doing it all over again, I could feel it beginning to happen again. It was the moment of *Other-people*, I realised later, it was the start of the writing of it.

Immediately, in the days following, the voices starting up yet again in my head, the sudden wakenings in the night from dreams that really weren't dreams at all—*were* they?—and that old sense of possession about the house. Was it me, was it him? As he hammered this new work together and I hung around bedroom doors and woke in the night he seemed, bit by bit, to take me over, to own me. My day-work really began to fall away, I started to make silly mistakes, I forgot meetings and deadlines. He needled me about it, and I forgot more.

Then I saw the Amazigh at last.

Just a glimpse, a movement in the garden seen down the lawn from the window of the front room. I knew immediately who he was, I knew as soon as I saw him. He was real, he really was about the place. *I hadn't been wrong—*

The sight of him—what he was, how he looked to me, the fact of him—shook me, it shook me. I dashed out and into the garden: and there was Val Underwood, bent over amongst roses beneath a couple of our huge, leggy old rhododendrons.

Did you see him? I demanded. She was out there, she *must* have—

I remember her look as she straightened up for me. Who? she wanted to know, and I'd no idea what to say back to her. The albino boy, I said, before I had a chance to think it through. And it was true, and that is how I've always remembered him in that first moment: first and before anything: extraordinarily etiolated, bleached almost white. That is what I'd made of him in that glimpse.

Albino? she said, and stood there gripping her *secateurs* and staring at me, hard. *You* know, I said. Pale. Pale hair—which was feeble, I knew that, because I remembered him on this first sighting not as pale but as almost transparent. *Transparent?* she said, when I let that slip a second later, and I was immediately sorry I had. What d'you mean—like a ghost? No no no, I said, but I realised that *yes yes yes,* that was probably what I *did* mean. It'll be one of the Kennedy kids next door, she told me, and bent back to her snipping. They're always over, looking for tennis balls. Kevin's blond. No, older than Kevin, I said. And younger than Blaise. I *think* it was a boy.

She gazed back at me over her shoulder, screwing her eyes up slightly as she looked. I'm quite sure she thought me more than a little mad. I can't blame her, I can't blame her at all, at that point.

But then, not much later, I saw him again. This moment was less fleeting. He really was outside my window this time, *that voice* promising to be fully incarnated for me at last: the moment I heard it I flung myself across the room to see him. There—*there*—down on the part of the lawn now lost beneath the Blue Room, and far more plausible than I remembered from my first shot of him—more detailed, more fully present. All this in fading light, I have to say, at about half past six on an autumn evening: a movement, a hand or an arm, perhaps, and loose clothing, swirling in the wind.

A jolt for me, seeing that last detail for the first time: a story beginning, a start, a past. Where had he come from, who was he, what was he doing here, this imaginary youth, this fictional boy who was real? Dissolving now into other things as I looked again and the light continued to fade, into those flecks and smuts and flying wisps of which the evening is made as they faint into darkness: the blowing scrap of paper, the cat's eye glimpsed in the shrubs, the work of small twigs low down, near the ground, as the wind *push-push-pushes* at them. The brief, jagged passage of a moth.

I've *seen* him, I told the old man, when he came back from wherever he'd been that particular day. But he simply walked past me. I've *seen* him, I called out to his back. Who? His voice, from the bedroom now.

The boy, I told him. Your Amazigh. Your Kabyle.

I stood in his bedroom door, looking in. He seemed preoccupied: books and papers flapped from his arms and bounced on the bedspread. Amazigh? he said, as if he'd never heard the word before in his life. He looked puzzled, foul-tempered—again, buffled. What d'you mean, you've seen him?

Out there, I told him. In the garden.

He stared at me briefly: hard, blue, cold. Oh, rot, he said. You've been reading too many of my books.

I couldn't believe it. His tone was hard to judge—impossible. He'd done this sort of thing before: *so many people in the same body*, somebody once said of him.

But he's your *muse*, isn't he, I asked him. The boy?

My muse? he said, and then: *muse!—Jesus*. I've pretty much beaten the shit out of my *him*, if you want to know the truth. You know how these things go. You don't need muses for long once you're up and running.

I remember him turning away from me when he said that. Then he turned back: he's *dead*, he said, as if *that* was *that*. He's dead and he's buried! I *stared* at him when he said that to me, and was to recall it again and again.

He went on speaking as he bustled around the bedroom, talking of other things, speaking of the world. Then he looked up at me: I'm not ready for this fucking speech, he said. What speech? I asked him.

Again, that halt and stare. *What speech*? he said. The keynote speech I'm giving at the conference tomorrow, for Christ's sake!

Conference? I didn't know what he was talking about. Then I remembered—oh, the *conference*.

He was still staring at me. *You* arranged the bloody thing, he said. He shook his head. I'm going to have to finish it on the plane—in the fucking taxi at the other end, probably, the rate I'm going.

The next day he said to me, *you've been behaving very strangely lately*. I was driving him to the terminal. *I'm* behaving strangely? I asked. Yes, he said. Very odd. The others have been talking about it, Dot and so on. And you're not keeping up with your job. Not to put too fine a point on it. You're forgetting things.

What, lavatory not clean enough for you?—me, getting hot under the collar: but he was quite right, of course, I *had* set up the conference for him, months ago, I remembered that now. I'd agreed to their terms, I'd arranged the plane tickets, I'd done everything—and then, it seemed, forgotten the lot. Other things as well, too, apparently, which he itemised as we drove on. I couldn't wait to get him to the airport and myself away from him, he had so much to say.

Later, I sat in the Residence again with not a soul about and the darkness closing in. To this day I don't know what was going on back then, how much of it was mine and how much of it his. He seemed so suddenly *solid*, so real in himself, as if everything that had bewitched and bedevilled him these last several months of writing had been shrugged off him and onto me. Now he was gone, all that faded away. The wind was the wind again, the birds in the trees just birds in the trees. The surge of the bushes was sound and movement, no more than that: the world began to resume again the business of simply being the world. I felt released from something—from the need to *read* everything around me, from the persistent *nag-nag-nag* of meaning.

The old man had just told me to go to Austin, Texas. At the terminal we'd checked his luggage in and then he'd said it, just like that, as if it made complete sense, as if it was the logical next step for us both. You're getting into bad habits working from the house, he told me. It's getting oppressive. If you're going to be my executor you might as well actually *do* the job. All of it. There's going to be more and more of this. Just a couple of the libraries over there, the Ransom Center, that's one of them, they tell me they're keen.

Off you go, he told me. I'm too busy writing. Get it done.

I was utterly surprised—astonished. For one thing, he'd never mentioned the literary executor position before. Suddenly I was listening to him again. It was my first overseas trip alone, and my first venture as something more than just his *bumboy*. So this is what he'd been planning for me, amidst all this chaos! I sat in the darkness of my bedroom, staring out of the window, aware that everything around me was becoming stable again, steady, known, ordinary: and caught quite, quite off my guard.

The critical reaction to this new novel, I remember, was extraordinary. He was a recent Nobel laureate, after all—and local reviewers in particular, by and large, simply pretended that *Other-people* hadn't happened. They looked the other way, embarrassed and confused—even Geneva's reliable supply of anodyne clichés dried up. There were whisperings, but no more: he often wrote like an angel, it was murmured about—something never in dispute—but he'd got to the stage where, sadly, he'd begun to recycle himself. Happens to so many successful writers: even Hemingway. Raymond was repeating himself as farce.

My, though, didn't the critics overseas know what to make of it when their turn came! *That was then, this is now*, was the kindest thing that was said. *Back to His Old Habits* was a headline to a review in one of the British papers, *Forgotten War?—Forget It* a headline in another. Inevitably there was worse: *an unsavoury theme of his earliest fiction, now forty years old, suddenly returns, like an obsession long suppressed*, according to a reviewer in the *NYRB*: *More young people are being made to suffer*. Another critic was more precise. *What are we supposed to think of what has been done to this boy Anir before the exceptionally disturbing scene in which he is buried, still quite possibly alive? How is this literature?* A disgrace to the Nobel tradition, seemed to be the general consensus. This was about the time of his Manneken-Pis moment, you have to remember, and *Other-people* was—as you might say—of a piece with it.

All this was taken further in long articles on either side of the Atlantic. Then it developed into something rather more significant, after an angry piece by a young Indian intellectual in London who gathered Raymond's work in with that of a number of Western writers. 'Stealing Out of Africa: The New Neo-Colonialism' was the title of her piece, her argument simply that these writers had taken for their own ends the experiences of the colonised. *Having none they're aware of themselves,* she states at one point of her essay, *all they want is the feel of 'the authentic' on their very own page. Every moment they purport to demonstrate their compassion for the non-white underdog, they are in fact taking something from him or from her. They reach out from their own privilege and into Africa, the Pacific, the slums of South America and of South Asia, and, with every word they write, the reality of immiserated poverty and suffering disappears under their ink while the writer walks off with the prizes and awards. <u>That</u> is the real atrocity here, and a new form of an old, pernicious evil.* I could feel her anger burning across Raymond and his generation like a hot wind, that withered every word they had written.

*

Evening, now, at the Residence: I'm doing my chores—the dining table is simply covered in papers.

Geneva is in town at last, evidently, and Marjorie has met her—this news via a text from Semple, written in his customary good taste: MARJ FKG GVA! Something's up, something's up, I know that. Julian has asked me to be here tonight but has refused to say why: *just be there*, he told me. They're up to something, the two of them, but why haven't they told me, if so? Where is Geneva staying? What's going on, what's happening?

Following our last and quite extraordinarily unsatisfactory meeting at the Residence I watched the three of them talking together in the light of Marjorie's headlamps down in front of the garage. Nothing blew back up to me in the surge of the trees. It was obvious, though, that they were plotting something and that it didn't involve me: I could sense the urgency in them. Inevitably, as I sit here now in front of this sprawl of documents, I think of my callow youth and the Master's banishment of me back then. *They* are out there *plotting*, and *I* am in here, no more than a mere factotum—still, in effect, Raymond's abject *bumboy*, all these years after his death.

Instead, the objects of the house press in at me. The carved dresser, for example, to my left as I sit here, the honey-coloured buffet I once liked to think an Henri II original. The voluptuous sculpture of its panels still stops me—that *trompe l'oeil* effect by which something is both true and untrue at the same time, the mind holding both sides of the proposition and so living in two worlds at once, and neither. Clouds, cherubs, leaves, the usual things, but carved, by some lost minor master, into a magical life that's always bewitched me and drawn me into itself. That moment of *liquefaction:* I could always become as much lost in the sideboard's buttery folds and turns as in a book or a symphony.

But not tonight, it seems. Tonight, it's just the work in it I'm aware of, the skill and the labour that made the illusion. Ash, the wood of the panels, according to Eric Butt, and therefore very difficult to carve because of the length of its grain. Ever since he told me this I've been aware of the *thisness* of the thing, its materiality, the way it's put together, the way it sits sturdily on the floor and contains objects. Tonight, I've been trying to trick it back to its magic, closing my eyes and then suddenly opening them again, as if I might catch it returned to its Platonic state—there: I try again, and fail again, and again it goes on being simply a handsome, carved work of some considerable age. Early nineteenth-century, most probably, when (apparently) there was a vogue for northern Italian and southern French work in the style of the first half of sixteenth-century Paris, all of it of the very highest quality.

Things are changing in my world. I've been aware of this for a while now. Oh, how my uncle would have hated the very thought of it, since (he said) it was the sort of thing that only ever happened in books. *Who d'you think you are, Jane Austen's Emma?*—I can hear his voice now, in my mind. *People don't fucking change, there's no narrative curve in life—what, d'you think we're all sitting here on a narrative arc, whizzing along in space? Beginning middle and end? People don't get self-knowledge, they just get worse*—and so on. The usual misanthropic business: except that, for me, for some time now, the world really has begun to seem in different ways, taking me along with it.

That voice of his, for example. It's in my mind, it's imagined and not *out there* anymore. This house. It's around me now, and the sea wind is blowing and whistling in the usual way and making its customary draughts around my ankles: the panes are all darkness and reflection. The usual *mise-en-scène*, in other words—but nothing else, no *frisson*, no lurch of fear: nor, as I say, has there been such for a while. The house no longer looms around and about me when I come in at night, there's no longer that sense I've always had that I'm being enclosed, and entering a mystery—that I'm *entering the forest*. Instead, it feels little more than the Chicken Coop, say, on the rare occasions the Butts are out for the evening and I open its unmemorious door to the vegetal smell of the cooked.

In other words, the Residence seems to have lost its animal capacity to scare the daylights out of me as soon as I'm inside it. A couple of nights ago I turned off every switch in the house and sat alone here in the darkness: I went into the Blue Room and stood still, waiting for the fear to come, waiting to be deliciously engulfed once more. I called my father's name, once, twice, and felt again the small terror of doing so, a little, but I knew he wasn't really there: and that was new, knowing that, and the first time I felt he might really and truly have gone away at last. I stood by the northern wall, close to it, right above the place where the boy is buried, and I thought about that business, too. There've been times when I've almost seen him, lying down there in his rough, hurried grave: almost. This time, though, hardly anything. No: nothing, nothing at all.

On the way out, I try for that precious, sublime *squawk* in the hallway floor once more—and it's just a sound, a woody little creak, just itself.

The painting, then?—here it is, above the stone fireplace, across the table from me now. What an extraordinary thing it still manages to be! *As silly as a wet hen*, Raymond used to call Phylllis behind her back in later years, when the fire had gone out between them and they suddenly found themselves foolish, fond old friends instead. Turning him around to paint his soul was evidence of that silliness—or, alternatively, of an adjacent genius: of some special thing in her, that she could get the effect I've described to you whereby a man begins to steal away from the viewer out of a storm of dots and splashes and improbable tones of grass and earth and sky, to melt away and yet always be just about to turn back to you in every moment, just about to tell you over his shoulder *absolutely everything that he means*. Organic man in person, there and not there, there *because* he's not there, another trick-of-the-eye—*how did she do it?* so many visitors to the Residence have asked me as I've taken them around the place: *it's nothing and something at the same time, nothing and everything*—

Ah, yes, true, true, and I can see all of this as I sit here looking at Phyllis's painting yet again. All of this, and yet none of it. I can't tell you what the difference is—and this isn't the first moment I've been aware of the change, to tell the truth: I've been stealing back to the dining room for weeks now, and staring at the picture, and turning away, and coming back to it once more—but I know something has melted away from me, not just here but in the house, in my life, in everything. *The magical portal has been closed*—a dramatic phrase, I know, over-dramatic. Silly, even, even self-indulgent: but that is what it has felt like.

It feels (yes, yes—this is it) as if I have come to the end, at last, of a long entanglement that began when Raymond turned his back on me all those years ago with eggbeater in hand, and I am simply a civilian once more. No, no, before that: back to the time when I first glimpsed him, Satan over the rubbish fire, back to that moment, back to the very first of him. Yes, that's what's been happening to me, I'm sure of that now. Once again I am that ordinary boy of my mother bred, before the fact of my delicious, illicit uncle was first poured into my ears. Raymond, and all he stood for. My Mephistophelean uncle.

Later, at least an hour later, I'm woken in my dining chair by a *slam* down on the driveway. I stand and move to the front door, but Julian's through it and upon me before I'm there, with Semple head-down behind him: the Stetson seems almost to bounce its way up the concrete steps unaided as he climbs.

Julian thumps the door shut. They stand there, the pair of them, breathing hard at me.

'Fuck me dead.' Semple, his back against the door.

Julian has a plastic bag with him: he tips it out on the dining table. Audiotapes clatter and slide onto my documents. Five of them—six.

'Mission accomplished.'

'You stole them?'

'Borrowed them.' He's still breathing hard. 'From Marjorie's.'

'She's staying with *Marjorie*? You broke in?'

'No. Robert has a key.'

I look across at Semple. A key?

He shrugs. 'Years ago.' He lifts a cloth supermarket bag to the table and eases out two of Julian's ancient, mossy Panasonics: they clump onto the tabletop. 'How long've we got?'

'A few hours.' Julian. 'She's taken her to the Hungry Wok.'

'Geneva? Marjorie has? Does she know you've—?'

Julian shakes his head. 'We didn't let her in on the plot.'

'She's made one of her own.' Semple. He's staring at the tapes up close, one by one, as if that's the way to get into them. 'A plot. With Geneva.'

'Oh, for goodness' sake, Robert.' Julian plugs one of the Panasonics into a wall socket. 'He thinks it's romantic.'

'They'll be at it till dawn. Practising Sapphic alternatives.'

'That's just ridiculous. Look, we've got two or three hours to listen to these and get 'em back—'

I catch Julian's eye.

'Can I talk to you offstage for a moment?'

He follows me into the kitchen and its smell of the domestic past: I close the door behind us.

'They're not as old as the one we used back at my place,' he says. 'The tape decks. We should—'

'He shouldn't be here.'

'Who?'

'Robert. What if he finds the thing we're looking for? On the tapes? What if he—'

Julian, mouthbreathing up at me. 'I never thought of that. When we were putting it all together. Him and me. I just thought he'd—'

'Why's he—?'

'Well. He had the key. She gave it to him years ago, apparently. He insisted on coming, I could've done it alone. He seemed to think it was a commando raid or something—he kept going back into her house, I had to wait for him—'

'Well, how can we get rid of him now? Without hurting his feelings?'

He gazes at the door. 'I never thought—you know, when we were—planning it, him and me. I just assumed—' He looks away. 'All that talk. I didn't feel so brave when I was there. In Marjorie's house. Behind her back.' He looks at me again. 'This is falling apart.'

'We need to listen to the tapes, we need to know what it is she's got over us. Geneva—'

'The secret. Right.' He puts his hand on the doorknob. A pause. 'Tell me again what we're looking for?'

I find I'm staring down, at our feet splayed on the ancient, trodden green and red of the kitchen linoleum.

'The boy. We're trying to find whether the boy is mentioned.'

'The boy under the Blue Room?'

A pause.

'I thought we were looking for the other thing,' he says.

'What other thing?'

'The violence. Or what we burnt—remember?'

'*Shh*—we don't want *that* to get out.'

He's looking down, too, as if the answer is somewhere at our feet.

'No,' Julian says. 'No, quite.'

'I mean, Robert would—'

'—oh, of *course* he would—'

'If he heard it, I mean.'

'You're right.' He opens the door. 'Quite right.'

'If that's what it turns out to be—'

'On the tape. Right.'

'I mean, there seem to be all sorts of things that might—'

'Shh—*shh*—'

Back in the dining room, though, Semple is gone: the Panasonics sit side by side on the tabletop.

'Where is he—where're the tapes?'

Robert's voice, distant: 'I'm having a slash—'

A clatter, from the toilet.

'Shit.' His voice, through half-open doors. 'Shit shit shit—'

'What've you done?' Julian is in the hallway now.

I can hear Semple saying something from the other side of the door, and then the flat, wooden thump of the seat against the cistern.

Now Julian's voice again: 'Oh, you silly prick—'

I follow him into the hallway: he's peering into the little lavatory. 'What's happened?'

Here's Semple, on his hands and knees beyond Julian's legs: he's bent over and fishing around in the loo. 'Bugger,' he's saying. 'Bugger and shit—'

'What were you doing with them in here, anyway?'

'I had them in my hands, I was going to put one in the deck and then I thought I'd duck in for a quick slash first—'

It slowly settles itself into a sentence: Semple, unbelievably, has *dropped the tapes in the toilet bowl*—

'How many?'

He's peering in. 'Five. No, six—'

'You brought them *all* in? You've dropped them *all* down the loo?'

He's standing now: his sleeves are wet. Two of the tapes sit in a puddle on his palm.

'Well, where are the others—?'

Julian is down now, on his knees and fumbling a hand in the bowl. 'They're round the bend a bit.' His voice squeezes up to us. 'The other three, I can feel them.' A slight grunt. 'Here we go—'

'You mean after all the trouble you've gone to—'

'Oh, fuck up, Norman. Just forget it—d'you think I came in here just to drop the fucking things in?'

He presses between us roughly and away. I follow him into the dining room.

'Peter's right.' Julian, calling from the toilet. 'We *have* gone to a lot of trouble—'

'Well, that's bad luck, then, isn't it?' Semple dumps the two wet cassettes onto the dining table. 'It's done now.'

'Any chance of drying them off, Julian?'

'I don't think so. I'll get some toilet paper. There's still at least two more tapes stuck down here.'

'What *is* this secret, anyway,' Semple asks. 'This thing we're looking for—?'

I look out, at the pretty glitter of the city lights. 'There's no secret,' I tell him.

'You said there's *always* a secret. A writer always has to have a secret otherwise he can't write, that's what—'

Julian appears. 'For goodness' sake!' he says. '*Another* toilet roll's gone!'

'*Another* toilet roll?'

And at this exact moment, like an actor who's fumbled her cue, Marjorie sails in through the front door: wrong player, wrong scene, wrong lines—even, conceivably, the wrong play:

She stops short and stares at us.

'Toilet roll?' she demands. 'Has someone pooed themselves?'

We stare at her. She can't possibly be here—but, on the other hand, and undeniably, she is.

'Where's Geneva?'

'I left her at my place. Ringing the police.'

'The *police*?'

'Well, why not? She wants her tapes back.'

'Robert's just dropped them down the loo.'

'I should've known. What a *stupid* bloody idea—she's got a dozen more of them, anyway—'

'What did you have to ring the *police* for?'

'*Really*? A dozen more ? Tapes? Geneva has?'

'Of course she has—she wasn't born yesterday, she only brought half of them down with her—less, there's about twenty all told, she says. She's heard them all, she knows everything.'

Of *course* she does. And of *course* she hasn't shown her hand, not all of it, anyway. We've got nowhere, we've got nothing—

'What does she know?'

'D'*you* know?'

'What?'

'Has she told you? What she knows?'

Now Marjorie's phone, though, starting up in one of her bags: which, which?—the third, she fumbles it out of the third.

'D'you think *she* knows now?' I whisper to Julian.

'Where?' says Marjorie, with the phone flat on her ear.

'D'you think they both know? Julian whispers back. 'The women?' Behind him, Semple slips out into the little hallway.

'What?' Marjorie.

'They've *both* got power over us now,' Julian whispers back.

'Where?' Marjorie, to the phone.

Two doors away, the toilet flushes.

'Has he just had a pee?' Julian turns away. 'There's still two tapes down there—'

Marjorie snaps her phone off. I've never seen her look so grim.

She stares at us. 'Which one of you was it?'

We stare back, Julian and I, two men frozen in front of an angry woman.

'Not me,' I tell her. 'I wasn't—'

'Which one of us what?'

'Which one of you shat on my living room carpet?'

'*What?*'

'Geneva says someone's shat on my living-room carpet—'

'Not me.'

'Robert, where's Robert gone—?'

'He's in the loo again—'

I watch them rattle off into the hallway, Julian first. It's becoming clearer, the thing that Robert's up to.

Marjorie, shrieking at him in the lavatory.

Julian tumbles back into the room. 'I wondered why he went back in,' he tells me. 'At Marjorie's. I can't believe it—he says he wanted it look to like kids had done it—breaking in—'

Marjorie, furiously in behind him. 'She's *not* a dreadful woman at all,' she's shouting back at Robert. 'As it happens I rather like her.' She stops and stares at me as if I've just come in. 'No, not quite *like*,' she tells me. 'It's too soon for that. I'm not sure what I feel.' A curious little smile as she's saying this: to herself, and almost fondly, as if she's only just begun to understand something. She opens her mouth, to say more:

And here, exactly at this point, and suddenly, loudly, shockingly, a sharp *rap-rap* on the front door.

We all come to a stop.

'Christ, what's *this* now?' Julian.

'And harassing an old man into his grave—' Robert, following in from the hall. He stops short. 'What?' he says.

'Just remember,' Marjorie says, firmly. 'No one was as bad as Raymond. Let's be quite clear about that. But I'll tell you one thing he could do better than anyone else, he could organise a decent plot.'

Rap-rap, on the other side of the door.

'That's true,' Julian says. 'We've been hopeless.' He looks across at me. 'What do we do now? Who's this going to be? Does anyone know?'

Rap-rap-rap—

A presence, on the other side: voices, a mutter, not clear. A stirring of shoes: boots, maybe.

Again, a sharp double rap.

I look at Julian. He looks at Marjorie. Marjorie looks at Semple.

Semple looks at me.

I look at Julian again, and then at Marjorie.

Now Marjorie looks at me.

Rap-rap-rap-rap—

The sound of fate.

'Well, go on, open it. Someone open it.'

I start across the room.

'It's only Ray,' one of them calls out, and we all pretend to laugh at that.

IX

The Blue Room, when it came, took me completely by surprise, I remember that—it shocked me, it jolted me to the core. I'd been overseas a month, astonishing myself by how well I performed at the Harry Ransom Center in Austin—so much so that I tried a couple of other libraries elsewhere in the States before I slipped over to England and the Continent for a week. There, I found the Master well known in unexpected places—at Aarhus and Liège, for example, where he was thought exotic, and in France, where (for obvious reasons) feelings about him were rather more ambivalent.

So *that* stage in our shared life had well and truly begun, in those last years before Stockholm—and there was I, back home and barely out of the taxi from the airport and swinging my suitcase onto my bed when I saw something through the window, in the bright, breezy afternoon light of the summer garden. I'd expected Raymond to meet me at the gate, or at the door at least, and to be eager to find out more of what I'd done for him. Instead, a fresh puzzle, from this man of puzzles.

What's happening outside? I called to Edna Butt, whom I'd passed in the front room, where she was busy with vases.

She came in, cut flowers in her arms. Haven't you heard? she asked. We're getting an extension to the house, a big new living room—this bedroom of yours'll have to be smaller, they told me that. And the window's going to be moved!—I think that's what Mr Lawrence told me, she said.

He'd decided all this sometime before, apparently. She sounded pleased as she mentioned it, and sly.

I was flabbergasted. *Decided sometime before, and didn't tell me?* Money wasn't the issue, certainly not in those days: nor was the proposed diminution of the Residence's second bedroom. What worried me was the unexpectedness of this plot development, as it might be described. It couldn't have made me feel more excluded, more pushed to the margins—utterly irrelevant, once again. I was fairly rattled. What had been going on while I was away?

Later, I stood in the garden beyond and below that suddenly doomed window of mine with the sun on my neck and the breeze in my hair, and looked at what had been done while I was gone. Not much, to tell the truth: some of the lawn had been dug up and some hadn't, all this inside an oblong area marked out with stakes, a shape perhaps fifteen foot wide and projecting a good twenty from my side of the house—taking in the mature *robinia frisia* that had long been the bright lemon-yellow spring-and-summer glory of that part of the garden. Some of its upper branches were already sawn and on the ground.

It was with this particular detail that I first confronted my uncle, when confront him I did. Oh, you're back, he said—as offhandedly as that. Yes, it's coming down. Unless you want it growing up through the floor of the Blue Room? The *what* room? I asked. The crowning touch to the house, he said, and rolled out a large piece of paper on the dining room table. Look! He rapped the thing with his knuckles. The Blue Room!

It took me a second to see that they were his own plans, not an architect's but dashed off in pencil on the back of a torn-off square of wallpaper and with barely a ruler used on it—not the slightest sign an architect or a draughtsman had been near them. The drawing had some detail, all the same, and was covered with scribbles, some in my uncle's writing and some in someone else's. Across the top, in heroic fist: *THE BLUE ROOM*.

Hold on, I told him. Where are the proper plans, what about a permit? *These* are the proper plans, he said. And fuck the permit. But you can't expect a builder to work from *these*, I told him. A builder already is, he said. They put those sight lines in, they take the tree down tomorrow. Then—he flapped the paper in my face—*this* bastard gets built. It'll be up in a month. Now the other two've pissed off you'll have to paint it for me, you and what's-his-name. The librarian.

Me? I said—I was aghast. I couldn't believe all this was happening!

It was, though, and it did: the Blue Room was built, and in almost exactly the time he'd told me—by Eric Butt and his unexpected brother Alan, who, it transpired, had been builders in prior incarnations. Together, they woke us each early morning with their hammering and sawing—by this time I'd decamped to a room in the recently built Chicken Coop, where I've stayed—and the spare, distant implication of their talk. The *robinia* came down, heartbreakingly, and its stump disappeared under the boards of the new floor along with perhaps two hundred square feet of lawn and that mound of soil I saw on my first afternoon back from overseas.

And, thus, the Blue Room.

I stood in it once it was done, on its echoing bare boards and between the unpainted wooden panels of its walls—none of it new, as it happens, something the old man insisted on throughout: used kauri floorboards, the walls in recycled pine and the massive French doors salvaged from a local nunnery recently lost to the wrecker's ball

(Raymond delighted in *that* detail, of course). Why nothing new, why so much rubbish? I shouted, as we stood watching Alan Butt banging brown old nails out of used wood and straightening them one by one. Because *men dispossess one another*, Raymond shouted back over the noise: and I knew where *that* quotation came from, without a doubt I knew.

They'd done a splendid job, though, the Butt Boys, as Raymond insisted on calling them, and I have to say that when it was done the new addition completely transformed the house for the better. Against the nostalgic bloom of our freshly painted walls was contrived, bit by bit, an extraordinary, distinctive elegance: the Steinway in the corner, the long *canapé* settee, the *fauteuil*, the carefully placed lamps—not a single thing absolutely matching anything else yet everything unified in a series of happy accidents that took the form of cushions whose colours caught one another in a certain way and in turn picked up a fleck or pattern in carpet or curtains, perhaps, or a tint in one of the paintings—extraordinarily satisfying, once one picked up the rhythm of it, and looking, all of it, as if it had always been there. Satisfying, and, even, at times, sublime.

I couldn't believe so much magic could be found in so little, and I always thought of the house as the Residence from that point on, even though it wasn't officially so till later. Looking back, though, it seems as if he was anticipating what was to come next: the call to Stockholm, I mean. Seen now, it seems inevitable.

It's too long ago now, though, for me to remember exactly when, in all this racket of shouting and hammering and sawing, I began to think there might be something more to the Blue Room than first I'd thought. That mound of earth I saw in my first minutes back from overseas—those upturned grassy clods within the larger oblong of boards and strings that was the Blue Room *in ovo*—that was the thing I began to think about as the actuality of it disappeared under the timber, bit by bit. The glimpse I gave you a page or two back was all *I* saw of it, too, but, perhaps because of that, the thing began to change into something else in my mind as soon as it went from sight. I was well aware of what was happening, but the thought seemed to have its own life in me. It grew.

For one thing, the mound so obviously echoed the last of *Flatland* and then of *Other-people*. In those books, Hamilton digs the youth a grave in the shadow of a curiously flat-topped mountain of the Ouled Naïl range. There's much nonsense in the former novel to the effect that he's come across the body ten days gone and as if it's just happened to be there as part of the roadkill of war, but the latter makes very plain who it is who's really finished the youth off and how: the details are shocking. In both books, the last vision of the lad's face, before it's closed up forever beneath the red, inorganic soil of the Hodna, is agonising, wrenching, and—oh, God—the part that most undid me when I first read it as a boy. Those blue, unexpected Vandal eyes, not quite closed, still looking, and the cicatrice, drawn livid at his neck: the final, final statement. Even as a man, knowing what the scene intends—the art in it, its higher purpose—I find the words unbearable to read, unbearable to think of.

I read *Other-people* yet again. Much that he'd written was demanding—I've made *that* clear enough—but I kept coming back to this novel and its ending. Where I'd used to finish each week with the sherry and the radiogram, now, each night, locked in my bedroom up in the Chicken Coop, I'd turn my back on the daily this-and-that and return to the single, same text. At one stage, late at night, I even went down into the garden and stood outside the nearly completed Blue Room, amongst the scaffolding and the planks, as near as I could get to that secret mound of earth, and read aloud to myself in the sea wind, with a torch on the page, that penultimate scene. It was as if I was trying to bend the words towards a final reality, to a fusion that might unlock—everything, might unlock it all, all of it, at last. Whatever *it* was, *whatever* it was. The *something* that was down there. And yet a part of me has always known.

After too much of this, I confided in Julian. We sat there in his studio, with a fan heater labouring on the floor and moths beating the night against his panes.

His face was unreadable as I began. Lord, but it sounded rubbish when I gave it a voice like that!—I was embarrassed at myself, but I kept going. By now I trusted him enough to do that.

Cicatrice? he asked, when I got to that point, and when I explained it I saw his hand go up to his neck. *Really?*—he *did* that to you? *Raymond?* Well, I think he'd have *liked* to, I told him. On your neck? he asked. With a knife? Really? *Yes,* I told him—something I'd never admitted to anyone. But he didn't mean it, I said. Raymond. I don't think he meant it—it was as if he was writing on me, that's how he made it sound. With the tip of the knife. He did it to the boy instead. I mean Anir. At the end of *Flatland.* And *Other-people.* You remember the burial scene—?

Oh, is it *him* who gets buried then? Julian looked a little puzzled. I'd always thought it was that other chap, he said. The older one—doesn't he get buried at the end? Oh, I don't think so, I told him, and he shifted on his stool a little. No?—I'm going to have to read it again, he said. I was sure it was the older boy. Isn't that him who gets buried at the end? I think you're thinking of a minor character, I told him—reminded him.

We were drinking his homemade elderberry wine, I remember, and that must have loosened our tongues a little—his, certainly, because he was more direct with me than I can remember him being before. And mine, too, since I found myself at one point of the evening confessing my midnight trip to the foundations of Raymond's new room with book and torch in hand. I remember him gazing at me as I told him about this, gazing at me and saying nothing. He was a good listener, as I've mentioned. I found myself telling him more, and more and more—in the end, everything, until it was late in the evening and the moths were gone from the window and small rain was just beginning to splatter on the glass.

So that when I was done, and he sat there for half a minute with his eyes closed and his hands clasped in front of him like a vicar, I was fairly apprehensive. What was it he was going to say?

You need to get away from him. I couldn't believe it. He rubbed his face with his palms, massaged his face. Uncle Raymond, he said. You need to get away from him.

Amazing how clear he was—shocking, shocking. I sat there, on that reclaimed barstool of his.

Right away, it turned out he meant. You've never got away from him, he said. Last month was your first trip overseas and you're *thirty*. Not quite, I told him—I rest my case, he said. *Nearly* thirty, and your first time overseas. I was hoping you'd come back with a better take on him, on Ray, but it's like he's sucked you back in again.

I stared at him. But he's pushing me away, I said, I can't get near him since I got back. From before that, he's pushing me away—

Julian *slapped* his hands together when I said that. *That's* how he holds on to you! he said. Push and pull! Oh, he's a great man, and a great writer, I believe all that—but I've told you before, he's a fucking monster! He manipulates everyone like that!

I was astonished—Julian, saying *that* word? There was more, though: I'd never heard him say so much about Raymond. A *monster*? I demanded, when he was done. *There* you go again, he said, shifting about, across from me on the other recycled barstool. Rushing in to defend him!—you can't wait, can you?

And so on: all of it quite right, too. I'd had more than a glimpse of myself from North America and Europe a month before, a whiff of a different scenario, and I knew in large part, as I sat there, that what he said was true.

Quite right, but (I'd realised this while I was away, too) there was always that magical world. I knew I couldn't stop believing in it. That was the thing. I tried to explain it to him, to Julian, I mean, and he listened as carefully as ever. And, as ever, how very silly it all sounded when I said it aloud to somebody else like that! *D'you understand, d'you understand?* I kept asking him along the way, I remember, and *I'm trying, I'm trying,* he'd reply. Then: *say that bit again, would you? Under the house? What's going on under there?*

That was the detail that got to him in the end, and marked what lay between us. He went silent when I tried to explain it, went silent and looked away. Then: *you've caught his madness.* It was a shock, but I trusted him. *He's a great man*, he said, *but not a little potty. It's part of the greatness but it rubs off on people. And it's rubbed off on you. You just have to remember—sometimes a mound of earth is just a mound of earth—*

It's taken me a long time to understand the full meaning of the things I've been telling you about here. It's taken me so much of my life to begin to understand how this strange, mad business works: writing, I mean. The pen on the page, the type on the paper, the cursor on the screen. *Anything can happen in the house of fiction*, Raymond used to tell us, over and over again, and because he was drunk many of the times he said that I took little notice of him when he did.

But Anir happened in that house, the boy he kept writing about, and the truth is that *he's still there*, and that he *needs still to be there* for all the other things to have taken place that were to come about. They make no sense without him. Of all the critics and reviewers only one seemed to understand that, and to help me understand it in turn: *always in the house of fiction,* this man wrote in some grave English literary magazine or other, *the sacrificial body.* And it's true. Nothing can happen without it. The Blue Room was built for him, I realised, for the boy and for the Medal. They belong together. He *must* be there—

*

There was more to come from Julian. Sometime after this episode, he rang and asked me to come to his studio again. Something rather disturbing, he said. Raymond himself was out of town at the time, and it occurred to me later that Julian had chosen his moment.

Take a look at this, he said as soon as I got through the plastic fly-strips. *This* was a small clipping he was holding out to me: just a torn rag of brown-edged newsprint from some unknown newspaper and showing a headline and a brief telegraph from Singapore, dated in August 1952:

TIMOR SEA CROSSED ON RAFT
SCOTTISH ARTIST'S FEAT

Mr I. Fairweather, the 60-year-old Scottish artist who recently crossed the Timor Sea on a small craft, today said that he set out from Darwin at the end of April to call on an old friend in Indonesian Timor. He built a triangular raft with three old aircraft fuel tanks which he found in a dump, and the minute sail was fashioned from three panels of an old parachute canopy.

There wasn't much more than these few words, and all of them quite straightforward: a report of an extraordinary journey this expatriate Scot had made in the early 1950s from Darwin north to one of the islands across the Timor Sea—several hundred miles through shark-filled waters, and the entire mad, terrifying journey done alone on a home-made raft. His name was completely unfamiliar to me—if he was an artist, he can't have been a particularly successful one. The connection, though, was obvious.

Kerr, I said. That's what Kerr does in *Kerr.*

Yes, Julian said. Worrying, isn't it?

It jolted me, seeing this. Julian had found it while working through Raymond's papers at his library. It was obvious why it was among them. *To call on an old friend:* exactly the fictional Kerr's laconic explanation of the fictional trip he makes in the novel, nearly two hundred miles, albeit through slightly friendlier waters, from Algiers to the Spanish island of Ibiza to the north. *Exactly* the same words.

And on exactly the same raft, too, it seems. After all, as I've said, Kerr's self-imposed task in the novel is to make his vessel from the relicts of the Mediterranean theatre of the Second World War—the 75-gallon drop tanks from Mustang fighter aircraft, the USAAF parachute, found tangled nearby, high in *the paradise of the Kabylia*, and picked by him, bit by bit, from a thorn bush, its three intact panels converted into his sail: those other, smaller details as well. All faithfully drawn from life: but whose?—for here they were, these things, owned in every detail by someone who, by the time Raymond began to write, had already made the journey.

What to say? I really didn't know how to think of this unexpected little scrap from an unknown, possibly Australian, newspaper. *Plagiarism*, I expect you'll all be thinking. Well, yes, plagiarism indeed, except that, legally speaking, we can't plagiarise something that's actually happened out there in the world. Whomever it's happened to, it seems that no one owns an experience: help yourself.

And help himself he had, my uncle. You can see his haughty possession of the things of the world, the imaginary Kerr bundled under one arm and the Scottish artist under the other—about whom he'd said not a word, nor of his home-made raft, nor of his wild trip on it across the Timor Sea. Instead, he'd told the story as his own, first to me and then to everyone in the world, told it as the fact that validated his fiction of it. I saw it straight away: he'd stolen his raft, he'd made his trip without touching the water. Ian Fairweather the eccentric Queensland-based Scottish artist no longer existed, because the fiction now lived in his place.

Raymond had devoured the historical man: he'd eaten him up, and the fact of the novel validated instead the authenticity of the man who had written it, and of his made-up home-made raft trip as well. Now it was real, now it had actually happened—it *must* have happened: he'd written a novel about it and there was the film of the book as well. *How real can something get to be?*

What I felt about all this was made even more complicated when Julian appeared again—looking back, it seems like days later, as if he were on a mission, but I know that in fact it was not long after Raymond died, perhaps six months after the horror of that, and, thus, a few years after the episode above. We were tidying up his affairs, and Julian was about halfway through the business of cataloguing his papers.

He came into my office with a book in his hand and sat across the office from me watching me turning its pages, each of them with its many pencilled underlinings.

A tiny thing, this unexpected book, its spine long gone and its fewer-than-a-hundred-pages long pressed from years crammed on a shelf at the back of Raymond's garage: one of literature's many little freaks, a memoir in French which brought back—vividly, at times, at times astonishingly, in the verbal dabs and dashes of the amateur—the life of a particular time in French North Africa: its author one of the thousand and more curiosities of the late nineteenth century who tried to shrive themselves of Europe's colonial sins on a camel and in a burnous.

An astonishing piece of naïve writing, as I recall it, and I'm genuinely embarrassed not to be able to remember for you the name of this lost adventurer and writer, a young woman who had travelled as a man and soon died in North Africa, alas, and—of all things—in a flash flood. I truly regret I can't bring her back for you, that (in effect) the flood has washed her away.

Or, maybe the truth is that I don't want to.

For Raymond had silently stolen from *every one* of her ninety-or-so pages—a word here, a phrase there, a hundred tiny borrowings. All these moments were patiently identified by Julian with Post-it notes stuck into the text, so many of them that the book looked as if it had grown many-coloured feathers and was about to flap into the air and squawk out its uncomfortable truths to the world. A hundred little sins: more, a small, brave, many-coloured celebration of deceit.

And, it seemed as I pressed on with it, more than that. I read with my heart beating faster. There were whole paragraphs marked out by Julian's pencil, the first of them beginning like this:

> It was the month of July. Not even a strip of green remained on the land's exasperated palette. The pines, the pistachio trees and the palmettos were like blackish rust against the red earth. The dried-up river beds with their banks that seemed to have been drawn with sanguine made long gaping wounds in the landscape, revealing the gray bones of rock inside, among the slowly dying oleanders. The harvested fields gave a lion-coloured tint to the hillsides. Little by little the colourless sky was killing everything.

I'm sure you recognise it, or a form of it—do you? The opening sentences of *Flatland*, before their transformation by the Master. A great improvement, his version, I think you'll agree, better than hers in all the obvious ways: the original text works so hard to present something—it works to please: Raymond's version simply *is*, like the world itself. The words just hang there, creating out of nothing. His mastery is undeniable.

Yet, just as undeniably, the original text is simply not his to improve on—none of it, none of the many bits and pieces, many of the same length as the above, to which (it seemed) he had helped himself in writing his Algerian fiction. As I compared passages from book to book I could see how crucial they were to what he wrote, how he both pared away the original and built around it, expanded it, reimagined it. I could see that: and, also, the exact opposite—the possibility that, without this source, these stolen words, he might not have been able to write anything at all.

My blood, as they say in novels, ran cold. What to make of all this?

At first, starting with the one above, I copied out a number of the passages he'd used, almost as if to begin a case against the old man. After a couple of hours of this, I stopped. *What* case? Wasn't I just trying to make myself feel better, less embarrassed, less ashamed? Wasn't I simply trying to take control of this disturbing new news? What would we do with it, anyway? The horror of Raymond's sudden death was still with us, remember, still raw—the manner of it, the number of young people killed in the blast along with him, the sense that his past had finally caught up and also that, at enormous cost, the truth of it had finally been confirmed. *Boof!*

Terrorist Attack—Revenge For Early Years In North Africa—Middle Eastern Terror Strikes Home At Last: I'm sure you'll remember the headlines, and who can forget the uproar at the time? It went on for a year, more, with diplomats conferring overseas and the trial, and then an enquiry lingering on after that. The media was at its worst—or its most typical—and I was struck by how many new works of fiction were made out of the death of this maker of fictions.

I was shocked—numbed: we all were—in the weeks that followed this obscenity, and barely able to function. All those children, gone—well, little more than children: the youngest student was seventeen. And Raymond, erased in a moment, like a word pencilled on a page, while Gradus survived as if he were ink: the wrongness of *that* disturbed me for weeks, I remember, months, until I began to see the whole thing in perspective. Death, after all, gives you a beginning, a middle and an end, like a character in a book. Gradus was too stupid, too meaningless, to be graced with that. He was an intruder in the house of fiction who didn't deserve a literary death.

Raymond had been proven right, that was the thing. For me, as I slowly began to understand what it was that had happened, there was no doubt of that. As was stated at the time in some editorial or other, if saboteurs could blow up another nation's trawler as an act of vengeance, why could they not do the same to someone who'd talked too much about what really happened at the heart of the north African darkness? And didn't that prove that that particular someone really *had* known all along the truth of which he'd written? Yes, I knew the enquiry was noncommittal in the end and (in effect) the trial, too, and I knew there'd been all sorts of rumours going around—ridiculous inventions which Robert Semple was party to, amongst others, and I'm still not completely certain Marjorie wasn't whispering them about as well.

For me, Gradus's defence at the trial was an obscenity, despite all the supposed evidence brought forward on his behalf. I never wavered in thinking that, and I've always spoken up for the old man since. *The French foreign intelligence service*, I told people when they asked, even when the enquiry had come to its final, puzzled shrug. *Of course, of course,* they'd reply, and turn away. But nothing could take from my pride in him, in Raymond Thomas Lawrence. Nothing could take away my belief.

What a man! I often thought—what a *life*, drunk to the lees as it had been, and with several extra swigs at the end just to make sure he was done. I looked back and saw him plain, in the bright, fierce flare of one man's long existence, bursting out, intensifying, blazing: and then fading, going, almost gone—and extinguished. A life that was whole, ultimately, and complete, integrated, a life lived in a kind of truth. That was the way it seemed to me as I came to my slow terms with him in the months after he died. He really had been where he claimed he'd been, he really had done what he said he'd done, he really did have the courage to tell the truth about it and had paid the price for doing so. *He had written himself through, he had lived himself out—*

And, now, here was Julian again, bringing me yet more Post-it strips sticking out of yet more books. *More*, he said, crisply. I sank my face into my palms. *I don't want more*, I told him.

But I read what he gave me, all the same. Who, this time?—someone hitherto unknown to me, it turned out, an American called John Hopkins whose greatest distinction, it seemed, was to have written a novel called, remarkably, *Tangier Buzzless Flies*. No, the eponymous insects are barely mentioned in it—just once, early on, and perhaps twice more after that. Instead, the novel is full of marvellously precise descriptions of *things*, of the uncreated world and the hovering, implicit, unrealised sexual tension that comes with it.

Just like Raymond's world: in *Kerr*, most obviously—and so it should be, I realised as I began to read the other man. For Raymond's novel is full of him, in sentences flecked with his words but more often in entire scenes, perhaps six or eight throughout, that he works into something that comes to seem his own. That passage early on, for example, one of my favourites, where Kerr is prowling around the enormous lamp in the old Peñón lighthouse, following and following Anir until it's unclear who stalks whom: but there, nearly twenty years earlier than that, are Cabell and the boy Omar, circling each other high in the lighthouse of *Tangier Buzzless Flies*, inspecting the mechanism that turns on a pool of mercury and the beam that reaches out for boats and up for planes and is the most powerful in all of Africa.

I sat open-mouthed at the audacity of this. The detail about the mercury had entranced me—delighted me—when I first read Raymond's version in *Kerr.* The light has *a rhythm of four flashes in each twenty-second revolution*, the boy tells the man in each work, the American's and Raymond's: in each, the man asks the boy how far the beam can be seen and the boy tells him, *On a clear night, sixty-two kilometres.* I'd marvelled at the precision of all this at the time: what *was* there my uncle didn't know? Now, he seemed to be falling apart in my hands like a dry, stale cake.

Or in fact in Julian's hands, for here he came again a few days after, this time with an entire box of books and papers: he *thumped* it onto my desk. You won't believe this! he said. Mark Twain! Mark *Twain?* I asked him. *Innocents Abroad*, he told me, and held it up. Not much, he said—just the description near the start, remember? They land and they get swarmed by the locals? Don't *tell* me, I groaned. He's used it for near the start of *Bisque*? Yes!—Julian, surprisingly cheery for all that was happening—page four, he said. When they land at Ibiza Town. Ray's borrowed just a few phrases, and he uses the word order in some of the sentences as well, you can see that. He sort of writes over the top of them, he takes over their writing voice. It's there if you listen.

Listen I did, and there indeed it was: and back Julian

came, over the next few days and weeks, with more of this sort of thing and then more of it after that. Gradually, as I read and reread, I began to see a pattern in what had been done: to see how, in effect, my uncle built his fiction. Not all of it, certainly. The majority of what he wrote was his own: but the more I reread him, the more I began to wonder what that might actually mean, not just to him but to anyone and everyone who wrote and read literature. Those opening pages of *Flatland*—were they his or were they hers, that long-lost unknown dead woman's? If so, who owned them, and, if not hers, at what point did they become his?—since (of this, I became more and more clear as I thought it through) there was no doubt that what he used *did* become his, wherever he took it from. Or were they none of the above: were they just—*writing?*

Gradually, an answer of sorts: the beginnings of an answer. As you can see, it's something that still occupies my mind. There was a moment when, reading something from Paul Bowles—for, yes, of course, he was in the mix, too, of course he was, along with obvious others, how could he not be?—reading one of his essays, in fact, not the fiction—I heard the Master. I'd become familiar with the experience of reading passages side by side and seeing where the rhythm of the earlier writer—not words, not sentences, but the rhythm—the voice, if you like—seeing where this melted into the later writer's and became his own. Here was the next step, the next stage: of *course* it was, of *course*—

I forget exactly the words and sentences involved. Instead, I suddenly heard Raymond's voice in the other man's writing, almost as if he was in the room with me. I jerked up straight and looked around. Lord, what was this, what *was* this? I looked down and read more, and the old man fell silent: but not for long, because before the bottom of the page or the top of the next he started up again.

I stared at the words on the page, I remember. How did this happen, how did it work?

I asked myself this again a few days later when I found him writing someone else's fiction, a woman's, I think: work that, on the face of it, was nothing like his in any way—but there he was all the same, barking away on her page. And I asked the question once more when I read someone yet different again and heard Paul Bowles in him—or was it back to Hopkins and his first novel, the one set in Peru, with its almost selfless, pared, almost helpless prose, the nearest I've ever seen to somebody giving up and not writing at all? *The Attempt*, its title—writing as *trying*, in effect, writing as a long shot, writing as almost nothing at all: a feint, a gesture. And isn't that how Raymond wrote at his best, with no ego or as little as was possible, just the words on the page, taking care of themselves, living in their own magnificent, independent word-world? Isn't it?

Just how much of other people's writing had he written during his life, and how much had they written of his? Is this how it worked, had I found the trick of it at last? Was this the only world there was, and was *that* why he'd called his novel *Flatland*?—not for the desert world of Algeria, but for the flat, flat word-world of the page, the only world that really is real?

That's how it is. I'm sure. The words come first. It doesn't matter where they come from, they're the first thing that happens. *In the beginning*—

Then, slowly, facts forming from words, the truth coming from the language and—not soon, not soon—

becoming the hard reality we all know and agree on, the sure-footed fiction of our lives. *Yes, yes, of course that happened, of course that's how things were done: what could be more natural?*

It's there in writing!

Julian has told me it's nothing new, this understanding that slowly came to me, that it's been thought before and also that he doesn't believe a word of it. Maybe so: but you've seen how much I loathe the present-moment sequences in this very book—this one, the one in your hands—those sequences which try to account for the bewildering events happening in the ever-moving *now*, the chaos of the living moment, the tyranny of the present, its disconnections and discontinuities, its yearning for the missing hand of the author and its all-too-manifest lack of it. What, oh what, is going to happen next? Where are we being taken?

Then, on the other hand, how much have I enjoyed sections like this, coalescing as they have, forming themselves, becoming truer and truer as the past presents its increasingly confident language to me. Oh, how the Master must have fallen on the young woman's account of her hundred-year-old Algeria when he did, how utterly crystalline must it have seemed to him in its prose, how much hardened by time, how *old* and *lived*, how irrevocably *true* and *real*, how ripe and ready for him to find a way of gathering up all the emotion and grief and confusion he'd brought with him out of Africa. No wonder he seized it as he did, full of yearning as he was to begin to tell the truth of his time there, and the truth, untrue as it might be, of his time with the youth called Anir: if Anir was indeed a youth or something else, and if that was his name and if in fact he had a name, and if, indeed, he'd ever existed in the first place, which he quite possibly did: though, on the other hand, of course, he might not have done so and it might be the case that there was no one back there, no personal angel of his in existence at all—

It's plagiarism all the same, Julian said, when he'd heard me out. Oh, I know he's a genius, I know Ray was a—*yes yes of course*, I said back to him. *A genius. No doubt about that:* and I meant it, I meant it as I hope you can see.

An uncomfortable pause. Well, then, if he's a genius what do we do with all this stuff? Julian, poking a foot at the boxes, as they'd become by now, on the floor of his studio. It's radioactive, isn't it? I presume we don't mention it to the others? Oh, Lord *God*, no, I told him. Imagine if Robert Semple got hold of this—it'd be in the papers in—yes, Julian said, yes, yes it would, it'd be all over the media, we'd be sunk, Ray'd be sunk if Robert got wind of this stuff, I mean, Nobel Prize-winner and all—

Another pause.

We could put an embargo on it, I said. The library, I mean. Ten years, I think that's the maximum—no one allowed access to these things for ten years? No, he said, I think it's as long as we want, isn't it? A library embargo? However long the trustees want? I'll have to look into it. Then there's the legal statute of limitations, I said. Does that apply? Only to published material, Julian said. It covers publication.

The thing is, he said, however long we embargo this stuff, the embargo'll end sometime, and then—

Another pause. We knew, I'm sure, both of us, what was coming next. I can't believe this, Julian murmured.

I can't believe we're thinking this. Another long silence, and then he said, they're pretty much untraceable, I suppose. I haven't made a record of any of this, he said.

Unforgivable, I know, I know—indefensible, even: but understandable enough, surely, given the circumstances. And for the better—well, that's what we told each other as—I'll admit it, I'll admit it—we *burned* these things. Julian and I burned the books and the notes and the incriminating little scraps of paper, everything the Master's borrowings had come from over thirty or forty years. We gave him back his authenticity. The two of us there in Julian's overwhelmed backyard one chilly midwinter afternoon, guiltily popping the poor little rag of a book into his incinerator—the dead woman's dead little book, the first of our sacrifices—and unable, each of us, to meet the other's eye as we did so. A *book*, for goodness' sake, dropped into the face-burning, mote-dancing exhalation of the incinerator. I'll declare it lost, Julian said, not happily. When I get back on Monday morning I'll declare it lost.

And then he said, I wonder how many others there are? Authors *mute inglorious*—you remember the line? Writers who didn't get the Nobel Prize? All those forgotten books, millions and millions of them? Billions? All that writing, d'you ever think of that? All those words, just lying there, no one's reading them anymore, they might as well not've been written? All that thought, all that imagining, all that writing, just—gone?

Yes, I told him. I do think of that, I do. *I can't believe I'm burning books*, I remember thinking. I'm sure this is a oncer, I said to him, the dry heat on my face. I mean, what we're burning now. I'm sure there's nothing else—

I almost said *I'm sure there's nothing else he plagiarised*, but I didn't, and I'm glad I didn't because I've thought a lot about this since and it's become clearer to me that a great artist doesn't do that, it's become clearer that what a great artist does is something subtler and more nearly inevitable and necessary—a duty, almost, to the greater oceanic processes of literature. This is what I've come, over the years since, to think, and I believe it's what Raymond believed, too. I am convinced of that.

I didn't say *plagiarism* back then by Julian's incinerator, and stopped short and held my counsel. I smelled instead the curious, distinctive smell from when I first met my uncle that autumn morning forty years ago and more, the smell of smoke outdoors as it mingles with mist on the presenting edge of rain. And, all the while, the flames, the flames crackling at our unworthy, sinful, book-burners' feet.

One more contribution from Julian, however.

I've cracked the tape, he told me one evening. The one with the secret. I've listened to it. I think you ought to hear it. When he said this to me I was astonished—I thought he'd given up trying. It's on the reverse side, he said, the thing I want you to listen to.

He'd rummaged up a much newer tapedeck, apparently, and had played Geneva's tape on it. Not perfect, he said, but good enough. *Marvellous*, I told him, and I remember he looked across at me when I said that. I watched him push the plug of the deck into the wall socket and slip the tape into its portal.

He shut the lid and looked across at me. He had a remote control in his hand.

Now, you're sure you want to hear this? he asked.

*

All right, time to get down to it. First I know about any of the stuff coming down the track's when the old boy says, *we're off for a drive*. So I pack him into the Dodge and off we go down to the gate. I hang a left and he says, *no no no, we're off to Springfield today, go right*. Springfield? I ask him. What's there? That's the first time I heard him talk about it. *You stupid arse*, he says. *You've been there a hundred times.* No I haven't, I tell him. *Anyway,* he says, *we're going to play a trick on him.* And when I ask who, he says *you know who I mean*. This is what he's like by this stage, he's that much away with the fairies he's like a pack of cards someone shuffles every night, next morning you don't know what you're going to get, five of clubs or the ace of spades. Turned out he meant Left Butt—you know, Eric the gardener, with his bloody organic garden and his walnut tree—turned out we were off to get some nitrogen fertiliser to put on his garden to piss him off. What d'you want to do that for, I say, and the old boy says he had it coming to him, Eric, apparently he'd told on him, he'd told his missus about this packet of savs the old man'd got in his bedroom after one of his raids down at Tony's. So he was going to fuck his garden up for him, that was the story, pardon my French.

An hour's drive, bit more, and then we're bowling past this notice that says *Hamilton Downs Homestead / Working Farm* and there's this house coming up ahead. That's when I start to think what the old boy must be worth. It was stone and if you counted in the dormer windows it'd be three storeys. Been there years and years, by the look of it, turns out no one lives in it anyway because it's condemned—the real farm's behind it, this big newish farmstead building like an ordinary bung out in the burbs but bigger, know what I mean? And *that* must've been worth a bit, too. These dogs come yapping out tails going like it's tucker time, and we keep crunching past on the gravel and the old Dodge she's bucking round like a boat and we fetch up in front of this big corrugated iron shed. *Here we are*, the old boy says. *Told you it's a time machine*, he says. *Here's Ernie.*

Ernie's a big guy, all arse and pockets. He's the cousin that runs the farm for the family since Mr Lawrence's brother kicked the bucket. Did you know about that, Patrick? I didn't. Old Mr Lawrence, he just yarns a bit and then Ernie opens up the shed for us. Don't look over in the corner, he says, and of course we do and there's this big drum of 2,4,5-T just sitting there! Meant to cover that up, Ernie says, and he tugs a tarp off a pile of bags and pulls it over the 2,4,5-T. There, he says and then he points to the pile of bags, they're all stacked up neat and tidy, and he says, there you go, help yourself. All these white sacks with the same thing on them, *Ammonium Nitrate 50kg.* That's it!! The old man says. He's fussing the dogs and he's got their names all wrong, he must've been thinking of dogs from fifty years back because Ernie keeps saying to him *that's not Girlie that's Fly, that's not Stride that's Beauty* and so on. Then he says *what d'you want the fertiliser for*? And the old man says, *we're going to blow up a building*!

Well, me and old Ernie, we just cracked up when he said that, the both of us. I know it doesn't sound funny now but it's the way the old bloke looked, he's got his hat all cockeyed one way and his glasses all cockeyed the other, and he'd have weighed less than one of the sacks of fertiliser at that stage. He's standing there all five foot two of him bent forward with his neck rattling round in his collar—and he reckons he's going to blow up a building! Laugh? I was feeding off Ernie and he starts feeding off me, and then Ernie, he starts farting and he can't stop, and he's going, *oops, pardon*, and then he'd let rip with another run, and he says to Mr Lawrence, he says, *you don't need fertiliser, mate, I'll blow the building up for you myself!* And, I'm telling you, they just about had to throw a bucket of water on me I was that hysterical when he said that. Good luck with that, Ray, Ernie says when he's finished laughing. Good luck with blowing up your building. He tosses me the keys and he says, help yourself, drop the keys back at the house. He's walking off and he calls out over his shoulder, *good luck with the sabotage work!* And he's laughing away, you can hear him, and he's popping away, too, you could hear that as well. *Oops, pardon,* he's saying. Talk about laugh. Guess you had to be there.

So there you are, Patrick, what d'you make of that? Can you blame me? What would *you* have done? What I did was play along with him, Mr Lawrence, I mean. He was taking himself that seriously I played along with him the way I always did when he was serious. I loaded fertiliser into the boot and then on the back seat, you could hardly see over it, and then he says, *diesel, we need some diesel*, and we end up trying to take it out of the old stuffed tractor in there. I didn't even know whether it ran on diesel, I just joined in the game. It was the same way it always was with the old boy, you know, all a big plot, he says *I'll keep cavey and you milk it*, meaning the tractor, though in the end what he did was, we found a jerry-can a quarter full of diesel and he nicked that. *Keep cavey*, that's what he always says when we were up to something around town, stealing or whatever. So we're packing this stuff into the car and I ask him, you going to use Tampax, are you? And he straightens up and he says *Am I going to use what*? On this building you reckon you're going to blow up, I tell him. *You stupid arse,* he says, *you mean Semtex. Listen, I'd like to use dynamite in honour of Mr Nobel, but we live in an agricultural economy, so we're using fertiliser, this fertiliser here.* Fertiliser? I ask him. *Fertiliser,* he says. *The Oklahoma City bombing*, he said. *That was fertiliser. And the King David Hotel, too.* The King David Hotel, I ask him. Is that the one we went past in Darfield?

Can you see what I'm trying to say, Patrick? If you don't know, you just don't know. I'd had that much bullshit from him by that stage I couldn't tell what was real anymore and what wasn't. Anyway, back at the Residence he sort of left me to it. When I look back, there was, like, about a month when I'd notice him round the place and he seemed really busy but he was keeping himself to himself? Except morning and night, you know, when I'd give him his pills and check him out? One or two times he even went off in the Dodge on his own when he wasn't meant to, but he always did it when Either-Or wasn't around. I came across him in Left Butt's greenhouse one time and he looks up at me and he says, *the human body has secret hidden bones, did you know that?* Oh, is that right? I say back to him. But that's where he was doing the business, Mr Lawrence, I realised that later on when I was sitting there putting it all together, he was in this sort of little potting shed area that's at one end. You could smell the diesel but did I take any notice of it? I thought it was Left Butt's lawnmower.

And then *boom*! One evening we're all sitting there up in the Coop, we'd had dinner if you can call eating walnuts having dinner, and we're all sitting there watching the six o'clock news, Right Butt Left Butt Mr Lawrence and me. And d'you remember that time some prick blew up part of the old railway bridge by the North Road? Years ago now, a bit more. Remember that? They reckoned it was farm kids fooling round with gelignite. It lifted this concrete pad clean out the riverbed. You could see it there on an angle, down in the river. Remember that? Well, it comes up on the news and I look across at the old man and he's just sitting there, and I say to him, that you, is it, you do that with your grass seed, did you? Well, his face set, I told you he could be scary even though he was half my size and a hundred years old. *Keep your fucking mouth shut*, he says to me afterwards when I was putting him to bed. *Or I'll get someone to shut it for you. D'you understand?* All *right*, all *right*, I tell him, calm *down*, I was just joking. This is when I'm tidying him up for bed, and he's glaring up at me in his shitty little underpants. *That's how we did it in Médéa*, he says. Right, right, I'm telling him. Show us your toenails. *If I can do it there I can do it here,* he says. Right, I tell him. Tomorrow morning I'm cutting your nails for you.

So next day I'm clipping his nails up in his bedroom and he says to me, *I don't need all that fertiliser*. Right, I tell him. Hold still. *I've got more than half the sacks left,* he says. *And I don't need more than a Coke bottle of the diesel to do what I want to do with it, I realise that now*. Right, I tell him, and I'm clipping away. *It took just a few bags to do that bridge pile*, he says, *and you see what they did*. Right, I'm saying. *Can you get rid of the rest of it for me*, he says. Yeah, sure, I tell him. *The fertiliser,* he says. *I'm going to have to go down to Tony's and nick a bottle of Coke.* All this is going in one ear and out the other, Patrick, that's what you got to understand, as far as I was concerned he was just raving? If he wanted to make out he blew up the bridge support down the North Road that was fine by me, the only part of it I believed was him wanting to nick a bottle of Coke from the store down the foot of the hill, and I nipped out as soon as I'd got him set up in the garden room with his writing board and I went down and bought him a bottle just in case. There you go, I tell him when I get him up to the Chicken Coop for his lunch. Things go better with Coke. He stares at it and he stares at it and then he says to me, *what the hell do I want a bottle of Coke for*?

See what I mean? Why'd you take him seriously? And as far as the ammonium nitrate was concerned, I was glad to be rid of it. A couple of days later I took what was left of it and I emptied it over the lawn in front of the house, every square inch of it, and I flung some of it onto the shrubs and the flowerbeds and then I forgot about it. I forgot about it that much the first time I remembered what I'd done was when the lawn starts growing a foot high, you should have seen it a couple of weeks later, a foot high and thick and it was that green it was blue, know what I mean? *Will you look at that*, the old boy says when I take him into the garden room one morning. It was like we had magic glasses on, the lawn was blue, the flowers were bursting out of their beds, the leaves on the shrubs were like they had a hardon. Left Butt, he was hopping mad. Who's been putting chemicals on my lawn, he says. This is an organic garden, why d'you think I spend all that time making compost? But the old man couldn't take his eyes off it. *Will you look at that!* he says. *A blue lawn! It's a sign!* No idea what he meant by that then, but now I suppose what he meant was, he was on the right track. There's all sorts of bits and pieces he said and did back then that I never took any notice of, and now I look back and it all falls into place.

The thing is, Patrick, I tell all this to the pigs when they first get hold of me—you know, after I wake up in A&E—and they keep saying, *run through that again, you sure that's all there was to it?* And one of the pigs, the less shitty one, he says to me, *now mate, if the bomb's like what you've just told us it wouldn't go off, d'you understand that?* And I'm, like, right, if you say so. And the other one says, *run it past us again, what'd you make it out of?* And we go round and round in circles like that and then the less shitty one, he leans back in his chair and he says, *you want to know something, you're a very clever boy? Y'know that? You make a bomb, it wipes out a car and a toilet block, you have to know what you're doing?* The Dodge? I said. It blew up the Dodge? First time I knew about that, you see. They never told me anything, they just said, property'd been destroyed. I guess they were trying to get me to trip myself up. *You wiped out the Dodge, they told me. And you blew up a shithouse.* It wasn't a shithouse, I tell him. It was a couple of classrooms. *Well it's a shithouse now,* the pig says, and, *boy*, did the other pig laugh when he said that.

Anyway, they keep on telling me how clever I was, you know, and they're like, *where'd you get the detonator from?* And I'd keep saying, ask the old boy, it's his bomb, and they'd keep telling me, *well, Mr Lawrence, he reckons it was you that made the bomb. Does* he? I tell them back, and I'm wondering, why'd he say that? They were just trying to trip me up again, I could see that later on. And they wanted to know where we got the fertiliser from, the pigs did, and I wouldn't say, I thought, why get old Ernie in the shit, he seems like a good enough guy? It's just fertiliser, I told them. You can pick it up anywhere. *Yes, and it was just a Coke bottle, sunshine,* one of the pigs says, *and you can pick* <u>*them*</u> *up anywhere, too, and we've got you on Tony's security camera doing just that, buying the bottle of Coke.* They were bullshitting there, my lawyer told me that. But I tell you what, you have to hand it to old Mr Lawrence—he'd crapped on about what he did in North Africa when he was younger than me, and I'd be going, *yeah, yeah, right*, but it looks like it wasn't crap after all!

Right. So, anyway, you want to know what actually happened when the bloody thing went off. Like, you've got to remember, as far as I'm concerned, all that's happening is, the old boy's getting me to take him down to the uni and park there and how many times did we do that? He never said anything special to me except the one thing and it was this. We got to his parking spot outside his bloody writing school and I put the nose of the Dodge in first and he went apeshit at me. *Turn it round, you stupid arse,* is what he says to me, pardon my French but really it's his French, isn't it, I can't help what he says and you told me, tell me everything. That's what he says. Then he says, *I want the rear bumper in against the wall*, and so I turn the car round and I back it into the park. He's standing by the car and he's calling out *closer, closer*, and then he holds his hand up and he says *stop!* And the bumper's right up against the wall of the building.

Don't have to tell you why, Patrick—he'd got the bloody stuff in the boot! Like I say, I'd no idea. That's all I can remember, it was all a bloody accident anyway. I'm over by the gingko tree putting a Bounty Bar wrapper in the waste bin over there, and I turn round and he's standing next to the Dodge and he's patting his pockets, and just then he catches my eye and he gives me that special smile, remember I told you about it? He gives me that special smile of his and he winks, and I just felt *great*, the way I always did when that happened. He'd give me all this shit and then there'd be this, and it'd make you feel so special, like there wasn't anything he wouldn't do for you because you were the most important thing in his life. Just looking at you and then the smile, that's all it was, and the look, the way he looked at you, like he knew you like he owned you—like he'd taken you over and he was going to look after you for the rest of your life. That's how it felt. Just the two of us looking at each other like that, it made me want to hug him, I don't know why but it did, it made me want to hold on to him and hold on to him.

So that was what was going on when it happened, one second things are like that and the next

X

At the Residence I find a surprising number of visitors, most of them climbing down from a tour bus while the rest walk up the drive from cars parked below on Cannon Rise. Spring air, and weather but one remove from perfection—sunshine, a sea breeze, and, very high, a slight haze that is beginning to wash out the deeper blue of the middle of the day. On the trees, the blush of new growth and a froth of blossom: in the air, the flap and chatter of birds.

It is the start of a new season for the Raymond Lawrence Memorial Residence, and, as always at this time of year, there is the sweet scent of a new beginning, of new life, of rebirth and hope and renewal. As the visitors come gabbling up the front steps I fancy the Master still with me, in the air about us, an invisible presence, keeping an eye on things. Is he, is he here?

I count the arrivals: twenty-two, twenty-three, twenty-four—and, now, another woman jogging after them, up the front steps to the door: twenty-five. Quite a number to get through the signing of the Visitor Book—quite a number needing to be asked not to stand on the elevator platform as we wait. *We'll all take the plunge together when everyone's signed the Book!* Others I ask to wait their patience with their questions about Phyllis's magisterial painting. *All will be revealed in a few minutes!* This time, only one of them wants to know why visitors must sign in: *security, security,* is always my response to this question.

I raise my voice to the group: *Now, we've had some security issues over the years, unfortunately. Over the years some important items have gone missing on tours of the Residence. In order to preserve the authenticity of your experience, the members of the Raymond Lawrence Memorial Trust have always declined to use roped-off areas, and the only items secured to their place are the Painting here, the Citation, which we'll see quite soon in the Blue Room, and of course the Medal itself, next to the Citation. We'd appreciate it if you'd respect the freedom of movement we've chosen to give visitors to the Residence by making sure that you look, but don't touch—*

The Tour begins. They look, but don't touch.

First for them to look at, of course, is the Painting. The questions are the usual ones—why the back of his head? *Because that is where she was trying to reach in the painting, to his deepest, most hidden self.* Why so much paint flung about? *At this late stage of her career, the artist was attempting to reach through the medium to the man himself.* How come it seems so detailed when you really look at it? *Some would say that that is the power of art, to trick the eye and the mind into seeing something beyond mere representation. This is a theme which Raymond Lawrence himself returned to constantly in his writing, and which was especially mentioned by the Nobel Committee: the power of Art to deceive the eye.* What would a painting like this be worth? *The Trust has insured the Painting for a very substantial sum—that's why they insist that it's bolted to the wall!*

Duteous, unspontaneous laughter.

Now, the Tour takes its first collective step—or steps: we need six trips to ferry them down to the garden room on the elevator, four at a time and five at the end. *In his later years the Master, as many of us called him, made increasing use of this elevator each day to take himself and his wheelchair down here to write and then, as evening came on and his day's work was finished, to take him back up to the Residence proper.*

Here, I point out Raymond's *fauteuil roulant,* abandoned in the corner of the garden room: and it is at that moment that I notice another out in the garden, beyond the sliding doors of the garden room, a wheelchair locked into place on the lawn, about forty feet away. It has a high back turned to the house and from this distance anything of the figure inside is too small to see clearly: just a tiny, pale stick of an arm, visible for a moment.

I return to the business at hand: now everyone is crowded into the garden room it's time to give them the video of the Master in those golden years immediately after the award. Of this I never tire, of course. The video player is getting on in years: the tape, too, which catches and slurs at various moments. But it is always the same familiar, irretrievable world that it retrieves for us nevertheless, that most distant of all lost pasts, the recent past, the one we still know and remember and most nakedly mourn, the past that leaves behind every trace of itself to remind us of the finality of our death. It was full summer, I remember, by the time Bruno Prock and his crew arrived from Austria to make the art programme documentary from which this is excerpted, and one can still see on the screen the blowsiness of the trees and the shrubs, can still hear in the background the mad tinnitus of the crickets. It is a summer that never ends.

At the stage caught by the tape Raymond remained plausible, his illness at its earlier stages: his performance for the Austrians varied from episodes of the usual nonsense (here, on the screen, eliciting the burst of laughter this moment always brings from visitors viewing the video, he has his dental plate in upside down, a stunt that was quite beyond the Austrian visitors' collective comprehension) to longer episodes in which, persuaded by Bruno's intensity and concentration, he gave more serious and detailed answers than I'd ever heard him give to anyone else before. Most of all, Bruno was interested in those disowned early novels.

Because violence returns dignity to the violent, Raymond tells him towards the end of the documentary, in answer to the obvious question. *It returns dignity to those whose own dignity has been taken from them.* That part isn't included in this introductory video, naturally, but I remember it because it was something he'd never addressed before, never spoken about directly. And, then: *each successful work of art conceals a crime, an act of violence.*

Now, alas, comes the only moment in the video that I detest. A long shot of the Trust members on the lawn begins, and pauses—all of us younger, Marjorie surprisingly *gamin* and unsurprisingly skittish—pauses, and then pans left to take in the gardening ladies, hard at their work as they always were in those days, bent forward, their hoes moving almost in unison. Eric Butt, hoeing, too, and Daisy the dog, over-excited, her bobbing tail up in a curve—and, now, here he comes as he always does at this moment, his large, broad-shouldered frame visible for a few seconds, that ridiculous head, the loose-lipped, weak-mouthed grin, perpetual, democratic, unquestioning, invariably inane—

Gradus again. For years I tried not to think of him, I tried to exclude him from my mind and concentrate on the story of the Master. He doesn't belong in the life I'm talking about, he has no place in my story—he had no place in our lives back then, he didn't fit in from the start. He wasn't the beginning of anything and he wasn't the end of anything, he didn't explain anything or represent it. He simply *was*, he simply existed. I was horrified he'd been included in the first place, in this sequence that Julian selected from the Austrians' documentary. It's a historical record, Julian protested when I tried to get him to edit the buffoon out. But editing it was too difficult: so there he remains, my *bête noir*, providing the only moment in each viewing of this videotape at which I need to look away. In a second or two, I know, the camera itself will rub him out—I turn back, and *there:* he's gone. He never was. Never existed. *There—*

And, as Gradus leaves the screen, the old man comes back onto it, almost as fully present as in the flesh. The first glimpse of him always shocks me, however many times I've seen the video before: in white summer clothing and a broad-brimmed white hat he comes with a couple of the others through the shrubbery and towards the camera, holding his palms together in front of him like a monk. He is listening, now he is laughing, his head thrown back, and now he looks down at the camera with the smile held: he removes his hat and the lost wind plays with the lost hair. It always feels as if he is looking at me, just at me: as if there's no one else in this garden room now and no one else behind him on the screen. Just Raymond, just me. Always it is that.

We watch, the visitors and I, through selections of the interview with Bruno and to the final shot of the clip, as he walks down the drive and away, as if he's leaving us forever. And now there comes another moment, here it is again, *the* moment of the viewing: he stops, turns, and faces the Austrians' camera as it approaches. His image grows. For this final shot the cameraman, I remember, sank slowly to his knees like a supplicant, and as a consequence, Raymond seems to loom and fill the screen. *Do not move, Ray!*—Bruno, shouting throughout this sequence. *Do not move!*

And there he is—*here* he is, looming, massive, like the

Colossus of Rhodes: he looks down at us as the cameraman moves in. Raymond at last: eternal, magnificent, refulgent and supreme, my uncle as I will always remember him, the Master, forever in the superlative—before, now—*turn away now, Ray, turn away slowly, please!*—he turns from us and his back fills the screen as the camera follows. The cameraman stops: the Master begins to recede, he's moving away, here is the moment when he ducks slightly under a branch, where he moves into flecks and smuts and flying wisps and the *push-push-push* of the wind in the shrubs and the trees, moves off and away and is gone.

Dissolve to black.

I squeeze the remote. Murmurs from the visitors as they come back to life.

I look around.

And that is the man whose house we're going to look at together today—

In the Blue Room I begin, of course, with a few words on Raymond's theory of colour, how blue was thought in medieval times to be the colour of evil, the colour of the devil, and how the Master came to feel instead that blue—*this* blue, the blue before their very eyes, sky-blue at its deepest—was something else, the colour in which the abstract could become transformed into the material world. As always I mention Novalis, I mention Rilke, I mention Klein and all the rest.

Then, as always and of course, I wind the touring party around the room and to the Medal and the Citation, starting with the enormous settee—always, gasps of wonderment at its size—and moving them to the *fauteuil* and the complex, fascinating story of its troubled reupholstering. Thence, through the amusing story of the Shoji screen, to an anecdote or two about the posters on the wall and the display of his books in the bookcases and the others he collected. Not too long on these, for here comes the moment when I draw their attention to the Holy Grail itself.

I never need do more than fling my arm towards it: this, after all, is what they have come to see. There's always a moment as they take it in: and then, always, they crowd forward. I always enjoy reciting the Citation aloud to them from memory as they gaze at it: I never get a word wrong. But when they look at the Medal, there is no need for me to say a thing. It speaks for itself, of course. The Nobel Prize for Literature.

Today, the moment is as sacramental as ever. There are several seconds—twenty, thirty—before the spell is broken and they begin to murmur again, and turn away, and ask their questions. How much would the Medal be worth? Is the Citation a fake, too? Why not just put the real Medal there and tell everyone it's a fake? How much would the fake Medal be worth?

Replica, I tell them. It's a replica.

The precipitating incident occurs a few minutes later, in Raymond's bedroom, just after I've shown our visitors the desk under the window that looks north down the garden and out across the city. I'm turning towards the three-quarter bed on which the Master died when I notice a movement, to one side of my vision.

A woman has just put something on the old man's desk.

I am in the midst of things, naturally, and keep on till the end. *And now, the saddest part of this journey through the Master's life, his last place of rest if not his last resting place.* I look at them: nods from one or two: yes, yes, this is definitely where he died. Questions, as always, but, as always, I tell them I'm reluctant to discuss this part of his life and that I'm sure they will understand, given my closeness to him. Instead, we turn to *the magnificent view that gave him both inspiration and consolation throughout his writing career*—and, as we all turn to the window, here's the woman I have just spotted, pressed up against it as she peers out and down to the lawn.

Has she really just put something on the desk?

She has: the paua shell ashtray is back.

I stare at it, as the visitors begin to gaggle out of the room. *Seventy-four years of age*, I reply to someone's question.

She's returned the missing ashtray—the woman at the window has returned the paua shell to the desk—

His nephew and adopted son, I reply to someone else. *And now his literary executor, yes.*

It's obviously his: an ash-smeared paua shell, not new. I've forgotten how worn it was, how long he'd had it. Now I see the thing, the reality of what it has been returns to me, replacing memory: it becomes a thing once more, a part of the mere, uncreated world, still awaiting the lick of art.

I stare at it. I gaze at the woman.

'Excuse me,' I say to her as she turns. 'May I speak to you before you go?'

She stares up at me: dark-skinned, and a heart-shaped face: not at all unattractive: lived in, but not insensitively or unintelligently.

'Sure,' she says. 'I just have to check my boy on the lawn.'

I complete the tour quickly: the small bedroom—*my own bedroom for a number of years, when I first came under my uncle's wing*—and then the kitchen and a quick reprise of the Master's idiosyncratic views on time-travel and culinary spaces. Laughter: a few words about

Nineteen-Forty-Eight—and we're back in the Dining Room and with the opportunity for them to add a few comments besides their names in the Visitor Book before they go, and for me to take from them the admission fee we charge now, in this new season.

A quick check at the window shows the woman down at the wheelchair, tilting it back towards herself and turning it as she speaks silently down to the small child it half-encloses. The wind bounces in her dark, springy hair. Sunshine, bleaching the sky, creating a democracy of little white clouds that puff across it.

I come down to her from the house, behind the tourists returning to the tour bus, whose driver still slumps resignedly against his wheel. I watch them yack and scramble their way aboard. Down on the road, cars start up. I wave at the bus as the engine fires. Some wave back.

The woman is pushing her child up the lawn towards me in his wheelchair, a large plastic cocoon that contains him in a web of straps. The boy crouches like a little spider in its web.

'This is Anaru,' his mother tells me.

He stares up at my face, querulously, like a little old man.

Now he holds up to me the thing he's been moving through the air while left to himself down here. A model plane, a finger-span long, a jet fighter—

'I brought him to meet you,' his mother says. 'I wanted you to see him.'

'I'm going to be a fighter pilot,' the boy tells me.

I look at her. 'You're Jennifer.'

'Yes. I've been here two or three times. But it's always been someone else taking the tour. I kept coming back till it was you.'

'Why me?

'You wrote the letter. You sent me the same letter twice.' No rancour, just a simple observation. She has one hand on the chair, and looks out across the city, and the wind moves her hair. 'I wanted to see how he lived. How a famous writer lived.' Now she looks up at the house. 'It's not great but it seemed pretty good inside. All that furniture.'

'It's not all what it seems to be. We had a valuation recently and sold some.'

'You can tell when people let things go. They don't have to prove anything. Old money. I got angry when I saw it. The money.'

'There's not that much there, really.'

She stares at me. 'Yes, there is. You don't understand. Of *course* there is. When I saw it the first time, I thought—I can't say it in front of the boy. I thought, *stuff you*, and I took the ashtray. I didn't want it to be something big so I took the ashtray. After I got the first letter. To get even.'

Down below, the little boy is whizzing his plane through the air and providing the sound effects.

'And then I thought, this is silly, it doesn't mean anything, I'll bring it back—anyway, I don't want anything of his.'

'We really don't have money to give away, Jennifer. What we raise we spend on the Residence.'

'That's what I mean,' she says. She's unlocking the straps, she's releasing the boy. 'I want you to see him,' she says.

'Can he stand on his own?'

'Sort of. He's pretty good, actually. Aren't you, boy?'

The child comes out of his cradle.

'I don't care about the money.' She bends down to him: he teeters between her palms. 'But you need to see him.'

Ah. To *see* him. My stomach knots up. I swallow hard. 'Right.'

She holds him with one hand and pulls at his T-shirt with the other. 'No, Mum,' he says.

'Mr Lawrence is going to be a friend of ours, boy.'

'Please, Mum.'

'Just for a second.' She lifts up the back of his little shirt. 'There—'

'Ah.' And I peer down at him, at last. 'Yes. Yes—'

It takes a few seconds, and then she begins to put him together again. When she's done, she leans forward and presses her face into the top of his head and holds him close. Soon his hand brings the plane up again.

'Good boy,' she says. 'Good boy.'

I watch as she holds him up, across the lawn: his tiny, strutting body, his strange, man-in-the-moon profile. It occurs to me that he may be eight or nine years old, possibly more.

She walks him, and he flies the plane. I watch.

After a minute I suggest we take him for a ride on the old elevator. She puts him back in his chair, and we bring him into the garden room.

Now the chair is on the platform, with the two of us on either side. I flick the switch and the elevator begins to rise, with its familiar, low, urgent hum.

The boy holds the plane up, to rise into the air with the elevator.

I turn to the woman, across and above the boy's head and the weaving, ducking fighter. As we rise into the Residence, I feel as if I'm beginning to understand what's happening.

The boy looks up at me. 'I'm going to be a fighter pilot,' he tells me.

I *think* I'm beginning to understand.

Far out on the plain, in a slight depression in the ground, Hamilton found ruined walls and a crumbling mausoleum that had a narrow, high dome. Bou Saada. He could see an old Ottoman bordj farther up behind it on a stony mound of earth. Its split walls were patched with ancient, furred whitewash. Nearby, figtrees, stunted, around a fountain whose sanguine water trickled into a canal lined with red and white piles of saltpetre and salt.

In the bordj he was given a small room that had a reed mat, a chest of drawers and a skin of water hanging from a nail. There were Fez cushions in embroidered leather and the walls were painted white. Lying on the mat he sensed the old building hulked around him in silence, though sometimes a fettered horse whinnied outside, or there was the passing thud of hooves and, regularly, the squeaking of a bucket being let down into a well and pulled out again. Less frequently and from farther away, the low, savage growl of the camels when they arrived to kneel at the gate. All this as evening set in.

That was when he remembered the tangerine in his pocket and took it out and peeled it, and pushed the sweet pulp of it hard against his teeth and palate till it broke and dissolved into juice. He began to think of the boy again.

Back at the military camp he'd been told he came from here, from Bou Saada, though everyone knew the coastal Arabs despised the Amazigh youths and that the boys stayed away from the encampments because of that. This one had come into the military camp all the same and Hamilton had let him into his billet. His first mistake. Before he took the wallet the little prick stole Capitanes from Gost and one of the other Frenchmen, and the week before that something else went as well, guns or ammunition, the soldiers thought, because there'd been such an uproar around the place. Hamilton was sure that was the Kabyle boy, too. A small dried monkey head belonging to one of the Frenchmen, it turned out to be, that such a fuss was made of.

When he went out to it the next morning the little settlement of Bou Saada seemed to have changed overnight around the bordj. Now he could see a service station and a café under the eucalyptus trees, and, further on, what turned out to be a dry-goods store. Houses beyond that, shacks, and, behind them, little more than a cemetery with its bluish domes and white gravestones.

He moved through the streets, aware of children staring at him and of the dark-robed women looking down and stepping away as they passed him by, this Nazarene. But the men stared as he walked by them, stared hard at him, the desert-faced men squatting against buildings and gazing up at him as he walked past. He tried to look back, but found he could not. Berbers, some of them, their smooth faces heavy with dark blood and, when their rust-coloured buzzard eyes were not turned upon you like this, their sense of complete preoccupation. He would walk to the edge of the cemetery and back, and then he would try again to confront them.

For they were the gateway, he knew that, these Berbers, and would bring him to this boy with the name that meant *angel*, in this land where angels live among you and can be seen as light, where sometimes everything is light, all and only light and seeing. And where, at the same time, there was this, the world he had entered now, where you smelled the perfume of wisteria on one side of the street and on the other side the stink of a dead dog. And where, later, he knew, you could smell the night smell of the desert that lay further to the south, which was always the smell of shit and dust and nothing else. The world that looks back at you without pity, when you try to see it. What could change that, how could that be transformed, redeemed? *This is what I have come to find out, behind the gaze of these desert men and in this Amazigh boy who has taken my mahfaza and yet has led me here to find everything that is not money—*

On the third day of looking, miles from the bordj and towards the bottom of a salty incline whose ridge the mule had brought him to, and suddenly, the man found the boy. He was squatting with his back to him, his cloak over his head and his chalwar pulled down. He was doing his daily business. The glisten of it at his heels, coiling on the dry, lifeless soil of the Hodna.

Hamilton pulled the mule's head away from the brink. He knew it could be anyone, this figure down there, but he also knew that he'd found him at last. How could it have been so easy? He'd just taken possession of him again, of Anir, the angel. What do you do with another being, when you own him like this? What is there to stop you? What is there to be stopped? What is the thing you intend to do, and is it really the thing you are beginning to think of?

He remembered the old saying. *A ripe pomegranate on the ground. Whoever picks you up can have you.*

Lawrence, Raymond Thomas

1933–2007
Author, Nobel Prize winner
By G. S. Trott

Biography

Raymond Thomas Lawrence was born on 11 October 1933 at Springfield, North Canterbury, to Adam Raymond Lawrence, a farmer, and Beryl née Adams, who taught at the local primary school. A twin brother died at birth; there were no other siblings. He was home-schooled by his mother and at the local primary school till early teenage, after which he experienced five unhappy years at an exclusive boys' school in Christchurch. From 1952 a further, similar and academically fruitless time was spent at the local university college, followed by a period in southern and south-east Asia, Europe, the Middle East and, at greatest length, North Africa, where he took part in the Algerian War of Independence (1954–62) in the wilayat of Rabah Bitat and, later, that of Larbi Ben M'Hidi, both of these men important resistance leaders. Claims that he was in fact in the French Foreign Legion at this time and a part of the brutal repression of the uprising, and claims that he overstated and even entirely invented this period of his life, have been convincingly dismissed.

His first novel *Miss Furie's Treasure Hunt* (1960) was begun in these years and completed in London; it has been described as a perversion of the Hansel and Gretel story cast in domestic terms, and received strong responses, both positive and negative, from readers and literary critics. His second novel, *Frighten Me* (1965), although more nearly conventional, had a similar, if slightly more negative, reception; together with *Flatland* (1966) it follows the growth and maturation of its protagonist, Thomas Hamilton, a recurring and autobiographical figure in Lawrence's *oeuvre*, as he moves to North Africa and becomes involved in a local war of independence there.

After ten years spent travelling and teaching in North Africa and Europe, Lawrence returned to his home country in 1971. *Natural Light* (1973), his first short story collection, alternates stories set locally with others set in North Africa, exploring similarities and contrasts, not without ironic emphasis. *The Outer Circle Transport Service* (1976) is generally agreed to be the work in which he marks his break with Europe and his first commitment to what, in the title of a later novel, he would refer to as the 'other-people' of the world. It follows the fortunes of Julia Perdue, an *ingenue* and possibly the most attractive character in Lawrence's writing, in her journey away from Western values and towards an understanding of the lives of the dispossessed. This protagonist returns in *Bisque* (1980), where she moves through a series of adventures on the Mediterranean island of Ibiza that slowly darken as she becomes involved with a former Nazi sympathiser and Franco supporter. *The Long Run* (1982), his second volume of stories, was well received, as was the satire *Nineteen Forty-Eight* (1984), which renders Orwell's dystopia in everyday and localised terms while still using and developing his characters; this novel is widely acknowledged to be an outlier, however, in what seems now to be the inevitable progression of his *oeuvre*.

Starting with *Bisque*, Lawrence's next three novels are now widely acknowledged as the core of his achievement and the basis of his Nobel award. *Kerr* (1988), acknowledged as his masterwork, takes its eponymous protagonist on a raft journey inspired by the author's own solo raft trip from North Africa to Ibiza in 1962. Its visionary conclusion and the question whether its protagonist has indeed survived the voyage are still debated by scholars. *The Long Run* (1992) reintroduces the figure of the youth Anir from *Flatland*, in what has been seen as an unexpected return to the Algeria of Lawrence's earlier fiction, a country now transformed into a universal theatre of conflict and suffering without a necessarily specific geography. These themes were continued in *Other-people* (1996), whose Christian connotations and the links made in it between its protagonist and the historical figure of Christ have been widely noted; its extremely provocative final scenes continue to prove contentious and the novel continues to be Lawrence's most-debated work of fiction.

Following the announcement of his Parkinson's disease, in 1996, some argued for a slight decline in the quality of Lawrence's work. *Mastering* (1994) and *Mistresses* (1999) are short story collections mingling earlier and later interests; the slight unevenness of these was remarked on by some critics, though others saw both volumes as demonstrating the stylistic and thematic development of his *oeuvre* over many years. *Constanze* (2001), the last of his work published in his lifetime, revives the character of Julia Perdue as an older woman reminiscing about her life and has been seen as having strong autobiographical undertones; critics have remarked on the sexual ambiguity of his protagonist and the re-emergence of cross-dressing themes from the earlier 'Julia novels' as well as some of his other earlier and middle-period fiction.

In 1976 *The Outer Circle Transport Service* was awarded the John Llewellyn Rhys Prize and the National Book Award. In 1981 *Bisque* won the National Book Award and was regionally shortlisted for the Commonwealth Writer's Prize. In 1989 *Kerr*, too, won the National Book Award and was regionally shortlisted for the Commonwealth Writers' Prize, and for the Booker McConnell Prize in that year. *Constanze* was longlisted for the International IMPAC Dublin Literary Award in 2002. In 1995 Raymond Lawrence was awarded the Nobel Prize for Literature, for (in the words of his Citation) 'the spontaneity and integrity with which [he] has shown what happens to the European mind far from home, and for his holding before our collective gaze the wretched of the earth'. His development and popularisation of anti-realist modes were also mentioned. In 1996 Raymond Lawrence was awarded the Order of Merit.

The Raymond Lawrence Trust has published two of the writer's posthumous works. *Understanding the Cardinal* (2009) collected further stories from earlier in Lawrence's life, including what is now seen as his juvenilia, while *The Back of His Head* (2015) is noted for a distinctive change in the tone of Lawrence's writing and for raising questions as to its authorship. Questions about the quality of these works and the appropriateness of their publication have been convincingly dismissed. Further posthumous publication is planned.

Raymond Lawrence died in controversial circumstances on 14 June 2007, in an explosion on the city campus of the University of Canterbury which destroyed a number of buildings, including the creative writing school that had been named for him; seven young people also died in this disaster. This event was thought for some time to have been the work of agents from his Algerian period or elsewhere in the Middle East bent on assassination or by agents of the *Direction générale de la sécurité extérieure* (DGSE). A subsequent coronial enquiry identified its cause, however, as a fault in a gas supply. Cultic reports of Lawrence's reappearance after this date have been convincingly dismissed.

Raymond Lawrence remained unmarried throughout his life and had no issue, though he adopted his nephew and literary executor Peter Or as his son in 1992. He was involved in a number of significant relationships, with the painter Phyllis Button, the novelist Marjorie Swindells and others. The nature of his long relationship, revealed in *Constanze* and elsewhere, with the artist and poet Driss Dris Batuta (1940–1990), whom he first met in 1953 and to whom he returned regularly in Tangier, Morocco, is not known. His home on the Kashmir Hills in Christchurch was for forty years the focus of a group of writers, artists and intellectuals known for their exclusiveness. Maintained by the Raymond Lawrence Trust, the Raymond Lawrence Residence is open to the public daily from 10:00 a.m. in summer and 1:00 p.m. in winter. An admission fee is charged.

Suggestions and sources:

Trott, G. *Raymond Lawrence: Years of Lightning.* Bumpkin Press, 1983

Trott, G. *The Raymond Lawrence Story.* Hazard Press, 2015.

ACKNOWLEDGEMENTS

This novel's first epigraph was accessed from the *Paris Review: The Art of Fiction* No. 91, on 2 November 2014; and the second from the *Paris Review*: *The Art of Fiction* No. 164, on 27 March 2015. Both interviews are by Sasha Guppy. Enquiry into possible plagiarisms of these writers by Raymond Lawrence is ongoing.

More about the Scottish artist Ian Stevenson's solo raft journey from Darwin to Timor in the summer of 1952 is in Michael Stevenson, 'The gift' (from 'Argonauts of the Timor Sea', 2004–06, accessed on YouTube, 7 December 2014). It is likely that Lawrence came across the newspaper item reporting Fairweather's journey in a Brisbane newspaper while on the way back to North Africa in early 1953. Peter Orr's evident ignorance of Stevenson's remarkable work is regretted.

Lawrence's unacknowledged borrowings from Isabelle Eberhardt may be seen in *The Oblivion Seekers and other writings*, translated by Paul Bowles (London: Peter Owen, 1988), a collection of eleven of her stories and some diary entries. The volume incinerated by Orr and Yuile was probably an edition of *Dans l'Ombre Chaude d'Islam* (1920), an earlier version of *The Oblivion Seekers* mentioned in the introduction to that book. Peter Orr's failure to remember the name of this tragic figure is regretted.

Some of Raymond Lawrence's taste in literary models is evident in his admiration of John Hopkins's early fiction, *The Attempt* (1967) and *Tangier Buzzless Flies* (1972), which he first read in Tangier, where he knew Hopkins slightly. Interestingly, the ambiguously gendered character Hamid in the latter novel seems to be modelled on Eberhardt. Lawrence also recommended Hopkins's *The Tangier Diaries 1962–1979* (1995, 1998), which he greatly admired. Unacknowledged use of these and other Hopkins texts has been found in *Kerr* and other novels by Raymond Lawrence.

Of Paul Bowles as a stylist Lawrence thought slightly more than he did of Hopkins, and as a humanist and diarist slightly less. He acknowledged Bowles's influence in conveying something of North Africa to the page, and also in establishing, for the Westerner seeking ways to write about the Maghreb, a tactful respect for its invincible otherness. At the other end of the spectrum of style, Lawrence's ongoing admiration for C.M. Doughty's *Travels in Arabia Deserta* (1888) is evident in the unacknowledged quotations from that work in his earlier writing.

Lawrence's attitude to violence and the dignity of the subaltern, expressed late in Orr's account, suggests he knew Frantz Fanon's *The Wretched of the Earth* (1963). His belief that a work of art conceals a crime suggests familiarity with Alain Robbe-Grillet's theories of writing, while his account of his 'birth' at the hands of Berbers suggests a familiarity with the purported early life of the great German *Bullshit Künstler* Joseph Beuys, as well as with the film *The Empire Strikes Back* (1980). Lawrence's claims about his Dodge suggest he might have seen *Back to the Future* (1985), too.

Various artists have been obsessed with the colour blue over the years, and Orr names three of them late in this novel. Yves Klein's obsession with devising a particular, ultramarine-based hue for his work led to the development of the colour International Klein Blue (Tanal Dukh, *Klein: Internationaler coloriste*, Cologne, 2001). Prior to Klein, the blue flower was a crucial symbol of the unattainable ideal in the German Romantic movement; it also appears in Rainer Maria Rilke's poem 'Blue Hydrangea,' in D.H. Lawrence's novella *The Fox* (1922) and elsewhere. Raymond Lawrence was a great admirer of Penelope Fitzgerald's extraordinary novel about Novalis and the German Romantics, *The Blue Flower* (1995), and deeply regretted that it appeared too late in his career to be fully appropriated by him. There are glimpses of it in his late novel *Constanze*, however, in the early description of washing drying on balconies and the theme of marrying into the 'wrong' class, as well as in occasional phrases.

The cautionary tale of the turd and the orange peel was first heard by Raymond Lawrence in an academic paper delivered some years ago by Vincent O'Sullivan, who referred at the time to its origins in Robert Graves's response, following a presentation at Oxford University, to a student who over-reached in the use of the word 'we' at question time. Elsewhere in the sentences of this novel about the provenance of writing in the written are the ghosts of many other writers, their themes, scenes, sentences and phrases dotted liberally throughout in a recurent *hommage* that awaits the reader's delighted recognition. The vegetarian plight of the geriatric Lawrence and his meat-porn visits to the local butcher-shop, for example, echo Maurice Gee. The first reader to identify and report all such references will receive an autographed gift copy of Geneva Trott's official biography *The Raymond Lawrence Story* (Hazard Press, 2015).

The author has had much support in the writing of this book, including detailed feedback on drafts, and warmly thanks the following for their gifts to him: John Newton, Nicholas Wright, Mandala White, Andrew Dean, Simon Garrett, Jim Acheson, James Smithies, Nick Frost, Julia Allen, Robyn Toomath, Paul Millar, Nathan Evans, Reg Berry, and, for their early encouragement, Mark Williams, Carl Shuker and Carl Nixon. The author thanks Peter Steel for his advice on how to blow things up and Nicholas Wright for his advice on how to lift things up.

There are special thanks due to Bruce Harding for introducing the author to the Ngaio Marsh Residence on the lower slopes of Christchurch's Cashmere Hill. Anyone who has visited this beautifully preserved museum will realise that many of its details are appropriated in this novel, including the Japanese geisha screen that represents a brothel scene and the video-viewing session in the downstairs sunroom that begins the tour of each of the Residences, Marsh's and Lawrence's.

Parts of *The Back of His Head* have been published, in *SPORT* 41 (2013) and *Moving Worlds: A Journal of Transcultural Writings*, 'Crime Across Cultures,' vol. 13 No. 1 (2013), and acknowledgement is made to these publications. The author is grateful to Fergus Barrowman for getting the entire novel out of him through skilled use of the powers of suggestion, and to Ashleigh Young for her empathetic editing of the work. Once more, the process of publication has been a swift and pleasant experience for the author.

Despite all this borrowing, *The Back of His Head* is not a

roman à clef and all its characters are fully imagined and continue to lead private lives in cyberspace and the cultural imaginary alone. Had the author intended to refer to actual people past or present he would have made it evident that he was doing so. Those who think they see themselves in the novel's pages can be assured they are taking themselves too seriously.